Richard's
Litter

Richard's Litter

"He wanted what she refused"

by

Michael Harper

Atlanta, GA

Richard's Litter.

Address inquiries to the publisher:
Allwrite Publishing
P.O. Box 1071
Atlanta, Georgia 30301 USA
www.allwritepublishing.com

ISBN: 978-0-9887332-7-5 (print)
ISBN: 978-1-941716-02-1 (ebook)

LCCN: 2014910512

Editors: Candice Ellis, Annette Johnson
Cover design by Melissa Phillips, Innov8ight
Printed in the USA

Table of Contents

Chapter 1

An avid golfer, Richard had finally scored tickets to the Masters. Even his best friend Kevin Randal, a far less enthusiastic golfer, couldn't pass on a chance to attend. A cool breeze blew through the 18-hole, immaculately-designed course on that Sunday, carrying the scent of pine and dogwood. The looming trees provided the perfect amount of shade as Richard followed Phil Mickelson, his favorite competitor and a lefty like himself. Although listed as the forerunner, Mickelson had to face number-one-ranked Tiger Woods.

Augusta National Golf Club allowed no electronic devices on the course but had telephones available for patron use. Feeling uncomfortable without his phone or police radio, Kevin went to the clubhouse to check his messages. He returned 20 minutes later to tell Richard he had to leave due to a work-related matter.

Richard felt somewhat relieved because he had a higher level of appreciation and understanding of the game than his friend. Kevin had been looking forward to seeing Tiger Woods, who was slated to tee-off later, but he'd grown impatient watching golfers he held little interest in seeing.

From dating to sports, the pair practically had opposite philosophies. As a Fulton County Fugitive Task Force sergeant,

Kevin had grown accustomed to fast-paced action. As a senior associate at a real estate law firm, some of Richard's most rewarding victories had come after months of drawn out litigation.

Despite their differences, Richard missed his wingman. Without Kevin, his introverted nature took over. He wondered if seasoned attendees could tell he'd never seen a live Masters tournament, or any tournament of this magnitude.

Richard bought a barbeque pork sandwich, a bottle of water, and an apple from a concession stand. He reviewed the pairing sheet while eating lunch. Then he checked out the souvenirs. Figuring this might be a once-in-a-lifetime opportunity, he splurged on a polo shirt and cap. Although Richard had a higher than average income, earning slightly more than $85,000 per year, he was notoriously frugal. His lower middle-class upbringing taught him to save rather than splurge on momentary pleasures.

After reviewing a map and gathering his bearings on the 7,435-yard course, he moved toward the initial hole. Richard's level of excitement grew but started to wane because behind a greenside bunker, he had difficulty seeing the fairway. At 5'10" he felt dwarfish among the sea of patrons consisting mostly of men much taller than him. Seeking a better vantage point, he navigated through the crowd.

Further ahead, he saw something, or rather someone, who startled his senses. He inched toward a mulatto woman with Native American features chatting and laughing with a shorter, fair-skinned Caucasian woman. He smiled in their direction, hoping to make eye contact, mainly with the petite blonde beauty. To his surprise and pleasure, his target noticed him first. She smiled broadly, revealing perfectly arranged, pearly white teeth and indefinite dimples.

With what he felt was a nonverbal okay to approach, Richard moved toward his target's left side, so her friend would be on the opposite side. "Hello, ladies," he began. "So who do you think is going to win?"

"Singh," the taller one answered decisively. With heels, she towered over him a bit. She donned an outfit similar to his: mesh cap, polo shirt, and pair of khakis. He pegged her as more so the golf enthusiast.

The other wore flat sandals that showed off her shiny, pink toenails and a bright yellow sundress. He noted the unwise clothing choice considering the hilly terrain.

"No way," the blonde added. "His drive can't compare to Tiger's."

So she knows the game, Richard thought. "You're both wrong," he told them.

The women stared at him as if he'd broken a pattern in which beguiled men simply agreed with them even if they didn't agree with men.

"Oh really," the blonde said. Her blue eyes gleamed.

"This is Mickelson's match to lose," he continued.

"You sound awfully sure of yourself, mister…" She paused for his name.

"Knight. Richard Knight." He extended his hand to her.

She reciprocated and announced both their names. "I'm Nicole, and this is my friend Hilary. We'll see about that, Mr. Knight."

The trio spent the afternoon together. They made small talk and debated why their favorites would outlast the competition. Richard mentioned that he'd rented a hotel room nearby. He learned that Nicole also lived in Atlanta, and Hilary lived in Macon with her boyfriend.

He wondered if Nicole had a significant other. Certainly, other men had noticed her simple but elegant beauty and charm.

Nicole readily offered her binoculars so Richard could see a crucial shot clearly. When their hands touched slightly, they both knew that an undeniable magnetism existed between them. Richard blushed, but his brown skin hid it.

Once the round ended, he realized their time together would too. He'd planned on leaving Augusta that night.

"Care to join me for dinner?" Richard asked the pair.

"I've got to meet Steven," Hilary said, "but you go ahead."

Something told Richard that Nicole didn't need anyone's permission. He hoped she'd accept the invitation.

"The Public House on Highland Avenue, 8:30," Nicole instructed him. "Don't keep me waiting."

He arrived at the steak house before her and sat in the waiting area perusing the menu. When dining alone, Richard rarely indulged in such extravagance. As a single professional, he typically kept his meals quick and inexpensive, unless he was meeting with a client. One look at Nicole in her tight, red miniskirt made him forget the prospect of a pricey tab. "Petite but definitely not dainty," he thought, as he continued to ogle her. With her hair pulled back in a ponytail, he noticed a tiny, caramel-colored circle, a beauty mark, near her left earlobe.

"Tell me," she said right after the hostess led them to a corner table. "What does a guy like you do when he's not watching Mickelson get his butt kicked?"

"And Tiger missed how many putts?"

She chuckled.

"To answer your question, I'm a real estate lawyer."

"Where?"

"Goldstein, Levy & Finch. It's on West Peachtree."

"Midtown?"

He nodded.

"That's close to my loft off Taylor Street."

"That's not far at all," Richard said, growing more intrigued by the minute.

The conversation paused when the waitress approached. "Wine?" she asked.

"I'll have a glass," Nicole said. She chose salmon and asparagus. He chose the filet special and grilled mixed vegetables.

"No steak? Why'd you choose this place?"

"I figured a strapping fellow like you needed a hearty meal." He beamed on the inside.

"Besides, they have awesome seafood."

"Tell me about you." Richard found speaking to Nicole easier than he'd expected, especially since his last date had been eons ago. Perhaps, he thought, their time together earlier had put him at ease.

"Well, I'm a nurse at a clinic for HIV-positive women. Although it's challenging, I love it." She sipped her wine.

Her luscious, red lips captivated him, as did the conversation.

While waiting for their entrees, Nicole revealed that she'd moved from California to attend Emory University. There she met Hilary, who was a pre-med student. Both completed residencies at a local hospital. Nicole focused on emergency room care at the start of her five-year career but wanted to serve in an environment that promoted helping underserved women without dealing with bureaucracy daily.

"Sounds like you have a real calling. The reverend at my church says everyone does. It just takes some people longer to discover theirs. Do you go to church?"

She hesitated a moment. "Actually, I don't subscribe to any religion. I'm agnostic."

Now Richard wished he had a glass of wine. He pondered this revelation. Even the Masters' final round couldn't entice him to miss worship service. She, however, wouldn't acknowledge God's existence. Richard career was driven by facts and reasoning, but his religious belief was ardently based on faith.

"I consider myself spiritual," she added, "just not religious." She explained that her shift in thinking happened during college. She grew up as a practicing Catholic, but after taking a few philosophy and religion courses, she felt religion in general was simply a social construct necessary to tame and manipulate the masses. She wanted no part of what she felt was government-sanctioned brainwashing. Still, she felt that a greater, divine power existed, but she didn't know what to call it.

"Maybe I can work with that," Richard told himself. "After all, it's not like she's a heathen."

Nicole and Richard discussed lighter subjects for the remainder of dinner. He found her company more refreshing than the meal. At its conclusion, he asked for her phone number.

Flirtatiously, Nicole asked, "Can I hold your hand?" Richard, suspicious but pleased, slowly reached out his left hand across the table. Nicole steadied it with her hand and then wrote her number in his palm along with the word "golf." As she did so, Richard felt that same jolt he had on the golf course.

"So you'll remember me," she explained.

"That wasn't necessary," Richard thought. "Not at all."

While driving back the long stretch of I-20, Richard reflected. Not only had he witnessed a golf legend in action, satisfying a longtime desire, but also he had met a truly desirable woman.

He put on his Bluetooth and called Kevin, who answered on the third ring.

"Kev, glad I caught you, man."

"I was just about to jump in the shower. Make it quick."

Richard then quickly recounted meeting Nicole.

"Damn. I leave, and you get lucky. Is her friend single?" Kevin always found a way to make everything about him.

"No. Besides, don't you have enough women to keep you busy?"

"Nope," he said proudly before continuing. "Seems feisty. She's into you?"

Doubt crept into Richard's mind for the first time. Maybe she'd used him for a free dinner. "I think so. We'll see when I call."

"And you think you can handle that?"

"What?"

"Dating a white chick," Kevin answered.

"You've done it before."

"Yeah, but you're not me."

Because talking to Kevin dashed Richard hopefulness, he called his mother, seeking advice and solace.

Shirley Knight had made it her mission to marry Richard off before he turned 30. "What church does she belong to?"

"We skipped that topic," her son fibbed. He revealed more about Nicole.

A devout Christian, Shirley Knight never missed a Baptism or funeral at her church. She was raised during the Jim Crow era in South Georgia. During those times, her religion offered a reservoir of strength. She recalled the racial slurs and indignation her father and two brothers endured. Because of it, she was very protective of her only son, who favored her almost entirely. She worried less about her daughter, Pamela, who looked more like Mrs. Knight's deceased husband but had her fiery yet genteel personality. She figured Pam, her younger child, could better fend for herself, but Richard, who was quiet like his father, needed her ever-watchful eye. She, in fact, encouraged Richard to become a lawyer to help fight injustices. Thankfully, her children grew up in a more race-neutral era. Mrs. Knight couldn't care less about the color of the partners her children married as long as they shared a foundation of faith.

She told Richard, "Make sure you ask the right questions. For your sake, I hope this girl is as special as you think."

Richard sighed.

Be careful, son. She can ruin you."

"What happened to us all being God's children?" he asked, without revealing Nicole's religious stance.

"Let's see what happens," his mom said, trying to sound more optimistic. "You've known her less than 24 hours, after all."

He got advice but still found no solace.

Chapter 2

Back home in Atlanta, Richard came to know the enticing enigma he'd met in Augusta. They immersed themselves in each other's lives over a three-month period. From exhibits at the High Museum to dinners at fine restaurants, concerts and quiet evenings in each other's apartments, they'd experienced the city and each other. He went anywhere she asked him to go, and she would go anywhere with him but church.

One evening, Kevin joined them at Fox Theatre for the latest Tyler Perry play. He brought along his latest conquest, a 20-year-old who looked like Tyra Bank's twin but struggled to contribute any meaningful dialogue. Instead, she hung onto Kevin's every word, arbitrarily nodding in agreement and smiling at him adoringly. During intermission, though, Kevin seemed more interested in Nicole than his date.

Richard grilled Kevin while they worked out at the gym early the next morning. Kevin aggressively benched pressed 290 pounds, which Richard could only dream of lifting. He spotted his friend while asking, "So, what do you think of Nicole?"

"She's chill. Most definitely hot. I'd bang her."

"Who wouldn't you sleep with?"

Kevin chuckled. "Even I have standards."

Richard waited for a serious response.

"Look," Kevin said, "You're good people. She seems like good people, but I don't think that's enough to make it work, not long term." He settled the weight on the bench and sat up.

"Once you know her better—"

"What I do know," his friend interjected, "based on what *you* told me is that Nicole's practically from a different world. She's a laidback surfer chick. You're as uptight as they come and can barely swim. From what I saw last night, she'd definitely drink circles around you. You act like the Prohibition is still going on."

"I get the point," Richard said, sounding defensive.

"Do you? Chances are she'll dump you when the novelty wears off or to please mommy and daddy if you don't dump her first."

"And why would I do that?" Richard asked, sounding defensive.

"Because you care what other people think. That, my friend, is the difference between us."

No case he'd worked on since finishing law school three years ago had proven as challenging as getting to know Nicole Eriksson. She pushed him to limits he hadn't known existed. Her beauty initially attracted him; her effervescent nature kept him wanting more.

He watched her shoulder-length, blonde hair flap in the wind as her motorcycle navigated a scenic route in the Blue Ridge Mountains. Nicole had insisted on renting Ninjas instead of watching boring July 4th fireworks. He rode behind her because she handled her bike like a pro. He, on the other hand, rode quite unsteadily.

But Richard focused on Nicole's rear more than the winding road. Letting the petite creature before him to lead the way had its privileges. He generally preferred fast yet safe cars and measured women. Nicole, Richard could tell, slowed down for no one. She pulled into a clearing, and he did the same.

"Finally!" Nicole cried as he pulled up beside her.

"You weren't that far ahead of me," he countered, settling his bike on its kickstand.

"If you say so." She grabbed him at the waist and leaned in for a kiss.

Nicole smelled of lavender. As her body brushed against his, every part of him tingled. They'd only cuddled and made out so far. Despite Nicole's carefree nature, she proceeded cautiously in the romantic arena. Their relationship had taken them to many places but not to the bedroom.

They usually hung out in her swanky downtown loft because of its proximity to Richard's job, and, quite frankly, his Lithonia apartment complex paled in comparison to the well-appointed, gated community where Nicole dwelled. They'd made out but always parted ways before going further. Sleeping next to her in the cabin's king-size bed tested Richard's resolve. Still, he found pleasure in being with Nicole although he hadn't been intimate with her yet.

Nicole backed away and then reached for the picnic basket on the back of his bike. "Damn, I'm starving," she said and handed it to him. Nicole motioned for him to follow. She chose a spot free of anthills and placed their blanket on the ground. He plopped down beside her.

"For you." She gave him one of the fruit salads she'd prepared, and a bottle of water.

While Richard prayed silently over his food, she dug into hers.

Richard knew Nicole remained unconvinced that the God he worshipped actually existed. His mother had difficulty understanding the concept, and to be honest, he did as well.

However, Richard recognized the abundant goodness Nicole possessed and wanted his mother to see it too. He decided it was time for them to meet.

Richard's mom lived in a restored one-story home not far from Auburn Avenue that he'd helped her purchase. Nicole felt honored that he wanted them to meet and drove them there in her BMW convertible. She made him turn down the radio, which blasted a pop song, before they rounded the corner. She knew his mom preferred gospel to secular music any day.

"Shit," Nicole said.

"What?" Richard asked, sounding alarmed.

"There's a run in my stockings.

"Oh," he said, relieved it was nothing more.

"You know I don't wear these things, but I figured your mother would expect it." Nicole grew slightly apprehensive as they climbed the steps to the front porch. It had been quite a while since she'd met any man's family. But this man was different, better. She'd always believed she deserved the best. Unfortunately, Nicole's past boyfriends had been takers instead of givers, but not Richard. He made a substantial living, although he didn't flaunt it. Sure, he wined and dined her as most men do during the courtship phase. Most importantly, he gave of himself.

His mother held the screen door open as they walked in. Once they stepped into the foyer, Richard introduced them.

"Nice car," his mother commented. "Like Richard's but sportier."

"It's a lease," Nicole said. "I'll probably turn it in when the new model comes out."

"I see," she glanced at Nicole's designer purse. "Care for some iced tea or lemonade?"

"Lemonade, please" Nicole answered.

"I'll get it, Ma," said Richard, heading for the kitchen.

His mother motioned Nicole to follow her into the living room. The 8 x 11 picture of Jesus and cross hanging over the doorway caught Nicole's attention momentarily. The oversized couch nearly swallowed Nicole but seemed an ideal fit for Richard's overweight mother. Dark, cherry-stained cabinetry covered the opposing wall. Nicole glanced at the numerous pictures of Richard and his older sister Pam. There weren't many of his dad, who died shortly after Richard's fifth birthday.

"They're my pride and joy," Mrs. Knight said.

"Raising them alone must've been difficult on a receptionist's salary."

"I wasn't alone, dear. I had the Lord by my side."

Nicole smiled politely.

Richard returned with the drinks.

"Sweet," Nicole commented after taking a sip of her lemonade.

"That's how we do it in the South," Mrs. Knight said.

Nicole detected a bit of disapproval in her voice but wasn't sure.

"Richard says you're from California."

"Yes, Santa Barbara" my parents just moved to Savannah. "My dad is retired too. He was a Marine sergeant. "

"And your mother?"

"A housewife."

"Richard says they're Christians, but you're not." It was part question, part statement.

"That's right."

"And they're okay with you not believing in God?"

Richard squirmed. Nicole held her ground.

"They respect my decision. Actually, I'm on the fence. There might be a God; there might not."

"Maybe coming to one of New Birth's services will help you get off the fence."

Richard cleared his throat. His eyes pleaded with his mother to stop this line of questioning.

She did, at least for now.

His mother called later. "Something ain't right about that girl," she insisted.

"You just met her."

"The girl won't step foot inside of any church, but she's dating a Sunday school teacher? Explain that."

"Aren't labels less important than intent?" Richard countered.

"From what I've seen, labels are pretty important to her. Forget converting Nicole. Can you afford her?"

Richard resented the insinuation. Sure, Nicole indulged in fine food, clothing, and accessories. She'd purchased them with her own hard-earned money. He suspected that a gold digger would gravitate toward a man who constantly bought big-ticket items. Richard had some prized possessions, like his car and Movado watch, but he had seen no indication that they influenced Nicole's attraction to him. Besides, she'd never coerced him into spending a penny.

"Ma, I've got briefs to write and cases to review. Can we continue this another time?"

"Okay," she agreed reluctantly. "In the meantime, I'll take it to the Lord in prayer."

In mid-July, the night before Richard met Nicole's mother, they had their first argument.

A pounding knock at Richard's door startled him. He peeked through the peephole and saw Nicole leaning against the door. She'd gone out with Hilary and a group of friends he'd never met.

She stumbled inside.

"I thought you were staying at Hilary's tonight," he said.

"I missed you," she slurred, pulling him onto the sofa with her.

He caught a whiff of something way stronger than a couple of martinis. "Have you been smoking?" he asked although he already knew the answer.

"It was one fucking tiny joint. What's the big deal?" Her eyelids dropped, and she yawned.

If she had taken anything other than marijuana, he didn't want to know about it. The lawyer in him knew better than to argue with an intoxicated woman, but she denied him the opportunity. Nicole fell asleep. He covered his girlfriend with a blanket and propped her head up on a pillow. She left before sunrise.

They'd already planned to catch a matinee. Richard called to see if she still felt like going. Nicole confirmed that she did and sounded convincingly sober. He arrived at her place only to discover that Nicole's mother had paid a surprise visit.

He wished he hadn't put off his weekly trip to the barbershop. He wanted her parents' first impression of him to be stellar.

Mrs. Eriksson looked youthful although she was twice her daughter's age. They shared the same stature and facial features. "Don't mind me," she said after Nicole made formal introductions.

Her husband hadn't made the trip. Richard thought of her waiting in the apartment all alone.

"Are you sure?"

"Absolutely! Nicole and I can catch up tonight and tomorrow."

Although unexpected, Mrs. Eriksson's presence helped ease some of the tension flowing between Richard and Nicole. As soon as the couple hopped into Richard's car, Nicole apologized profusely.

"My tongue isn't usually that sharp," she swore. "And I don't make a habit out of getting wasted. My attempt at unwinding obviously went a bit far."

On the ride back to her place, Nicole reiterated her regret once again. Richard accepted her apology wholeheartedly. "We all have our flaws," Richard told himself after he dropped Nicole off. He wanted, no, he needed her. Every fiber of his being felt that she needed him too.

They understood each other—no one else mattered. That philosophy propelled Richard and Nicole's relationship forward. By early August, he felt comfortable enough to invite her to Goldstein, Levy & Finch's annual benefit dinner.

Richard whispered tidbits of information to Nicole as they hobnobbed during the cocktail hour. Held in a Hyatt ballroom, the black-tie affair attracted concerned citizens from various professions as well as philanthropists. He had some key players in mind he wanted to meet and had brought along business cards in case an opportunity arose.

For now, he focused on his date. Nicole wore her hair in a bun. Pearl drop earrings drew attention to her high cheekbones. She looked more conservative yet sexier than he'd ever seen her.

Jack Kingston, an older, openly-gay colleague approached them. Richard worked in the commercial litigation division while Kingston handled estate transactions. Considering their varying areas of specialties, they hadn't collaborated on any cases. Richard, despite the 200-plus associates at the firm, tried to keep track of every lawyer and most of the support staff. He learned the basics, at least, about each employee. Kingston had never sought him out.

"Fab earrings," he told Nicole before Richard could utter a word.

"Thank you."

He extended a freckled hand and lightly shook hers. "Jack Kingston. And you are?"

"Nicole Eriksson."

"Nice to properly meet you, Nicole. I'm surprised to see you here."

She looked confused.

Jack Kingston surveyed Richard from head to toe. The inspection and his expression creeped out Richard.

"And this fine gentleman?"

"Richard Knight." They shook hands too.

Jack Kingston returned his attention to Nicole.

"How are you affiliated with the firm, Nicole?"

"My boyfriend," she said.

"Boyfriend?" He sounded as if he didn't believe her.

She pointed at Richard.

"You're here with *him*?" Kingston's mouth dropped open. "I thought I recognized you from a spot I hang out at and that perhaps we shared mutual friends."

Richard's nostrils flared. Kingston clearly had no intentions of exchanging professional niceties. Worse, Richard sensed a sexual undertone directed at his date. Either way, he wanted to leave right away. "Excuse us." He whisked Nicole away.

"What was that about?" she probed.

"Who knows?" he feigned.

Richard decided to put the episode behind him. The benefit's focus was supposed to be a local orphanage, not some bigoted fool. Richard championed any cause or organization that helped children. It escaped him how adults could neglect, abuse, or discard such precious members of society.

He and Nicole sat through dinner, dessert, speeches, and presentations. Once the ceremony concluded, he started saying his obligatory goodbyes. She hurried off to the ladies' room to check her make up.

Before they reconnected, he noticed Nicole near the ballroom entrance speaking with Stanley Goldstein. He was the most senior and respected partner. Richard wondered what they were talking about.

Goldstein saw him approaching. "Knight."

"Good evening, sir. Great event, as always. I see you've met Nicole."

"Yes, we were discussing the charitable trust."

Richard's apprehension subsided. "Ms. Eriksson has some interesting recommendations for expanding its reach."

"She's full of interesting ideas," Richard said.

Nicole blushed.

"I can tell," Goldstein commented. "Hold on to her. She's a keeper."

For Richard, Goldstein's comment had been the evening's highlight. He knew the woman in the passenger seat possessed many special qualities. Having a colleague of Goldstein's stature reinforced that they belonged together.

"I had a good time," Nicole said.

Richard agreed.

She invited him up to her loft. Once inside, she kicked off her heels and let down her hair.

Richard turned on the radio to a jazz station. Nicole poured herself a glass of wine and got some water for him. Richard joined her at the kitchen island where they sat facing each other.

He loved her. He cherished her. He wanted to have babies with her.

This moment felt destined. He'd hinted at marriage before. Nicole had appeared open to the suggestion.

She caught him staring at her. "What? Something wrong?"

"No," he answered, mustering up the courage to continue.

They had their differences.

As an agnostic, she felt God may or may not exist. As a devoted Christian, he had no doubt. She exuded a laidback, West Coast vibe. He'd grown up in the South. Their ethnicities, to outsiders, seemed the most obvious contrast. Even in a city as progressive as Atlanta, Nicole's pale skin against Richard's brown garnered curious stares, as witnessed throughout the night.

They had their similarities.

Both dressed stylishly and appreciated quality, although Richard viewed most high-end purchases as investments while Nicole shopped for pleasure. He and Nicole valued education and immersed themselves in their careers. Each came from small families. Most importantly for him, Nicole wanted children.

He'd imagined the moment he'd propose to his future wife. It always involved some grand gesture culminating with the woman saying yes and then strangers witnessing the scene and cheering for the happy couple. Others had come before Nicole. Part of him always knew that none had the mix of chemistry and morals he sought.

He looked at her. He looked deeper. He saw into her soul.

"Come back to me," Richard heard Nicole say.

He reached across the island and grabbed Nicole's hands. Richard held them tightly.

Concern covered her face. Her blue eyes grew wide.

He had no ring, no grand gesture.

Richard took in a deep breath. He resisted the urge to wait until they returned to the cabin or to the city or until he had the right words. Richard needed to profess his intentions. He needed to know if Nicole would be by his side from this day forward, for better or for worse.

He let his heart do the talking, abandoning his characteristic cautiousness. Breathlessly and simply he said, "Marry me."

Her eyes grew wider. She needed no ring, no grand gesture. She needed him.

Teaching Sunday school at New Birth Christian Church usually proved cathartic for Richard. The seven and eight-year-olds in his class habitually posed questions about the Bible and about God. Richard always answered them gladly. He relished in their sense of wonder and their accepting natures. This Sunday, however, he found it difficult to concentrate on his lesson and Reverend Peters' sermon. Thoughts of Ms. Eriksson, soon to be Mrs. Knight, consumed him, as did devising a way to reveal the engagement to his mother.

Nicole and Richard had celebrated in the bedroom, giving him another reason to glow. Afterward, she asked him to skip service. Though he found Nicole's offer tempting, he declined. Richard's mother always saved a seat for him. Only sickness could keep him from completing their ritual.

She stood beside him, their pew in a middle row near the front of the massive church. Organs, pianos, and drums played an up-tempo hymn. The congregation sang along, clapping to the beat and stomping their feet. Some sang too loud, others off key, but all with pure intentions.

Shirley Knight's wide-brimmed hat teetered on her head as she lifted her hands to praise and give glory to her Creator, as her floral moo-moo swayed. Richard wished he could bottle that energy she displayed in church and dole it out to her in doses because it unnerved him that walking up one flight of stairs made his mother huff and puff. He prayed she'd be around to see his future children grow up.

He decided to wait until after they'd eaten lunch before bringing up his October nuptials.

Richard made small talk on the way to the restaurant and through the main course. His mother had ordered banana pudding, like he suspected she would. He'd heard that this establishment served some of the best. He planned on telling her about Nicole once she dove into the sweet concoction. But, in typical fashion, she called him out well before the waiter delivered it.

"So what's with the pomp and circumstance?"

"Huh?"

"I know we didn't drive clear across town for food we could've bought around the corner." There were many eateries in the historic district near his mother's home.

His mother raised an eyebrow. "This stuff tastes half as good but costs twice as much."

He'd failed to impress her. She normally cooked after church. Her feasts full of fried, butter-laden, sugary offerings caused him to abandon his healthy eating habits weekly.

"Who you think you're fooling, Richard?"

He continued to play dumb.

"So?" She'd earned the nickname Bulls Eye after shooting a burglar. Shirley Knight's aim was equally precise when it came to spotting bullshit.

Richard wished she'd lower her voice although he didn't dare tell her that. Guests at nearby tables cast curios glances.

"Well?"

"I asked Nicole to marry me."

"My cup runneth over." She dug around in her massive purse and pulled out a pack of cigarettes.

Richard grimaced. "There's no smoking in here, Ma!"

His mother placed the menthols back in her purse. She grunted. "Wait 'til I tell your sister this."

"She'll grow on you. You'll see." Mrs. Knight analyzed the situation. "Let me get this straight. She doesn't believe in God, but she's getting married in his house."

"We haven't decided on where yet. Nicole's a good person. Just raised differently."

"I'm not calling the girl a demon. And I've seen how she makes you smile. Lord knows she's two steps above everyone else you've dated. But…"

A crease formed on his forehead. "But what?"

"That doesn't mean she's the one."

On the Monday following the proposal, Richard trotted into the towering office building that served as his firm's headquarters. Knowing he'd have Nicole forever increased his vigor. He had so much more to strive for now. Although Nicole surely could support herself, Richard wanted to be the head of their household while supporting her dreams. He had a vision for their married life. He could easily make a partner, and Nicole, eventually, would establish her nonprofit for HIV-positive women. Next, they would have children, as many as their love could produce and finances could support.

He stared at the bland, gray walls of his cubicle. The contracts on his desk demanded Richard's attention, but they'd have to wait. Richard had a more important mission. If he executed his plan well, he'd surprise Nicole with a gift to build their future upon.

"Richard, I'm not marrying myself," Nicole whined. His fiancée playfully splashed water in Richard's direction as they waded in the pool at her complex. One man swam laps to the right of them. A few other residents lounged poolside, taking advantage of the sunny yet mild weather.

"I know," he answered. "Is this a swimming lesson or an interrogation?"

"Both."

He appreciated her inclusiveness but also wanted to stick to the task at hand. Weren't women supposed to do the planning anyway?

She came closer and gazed coyly at him. "Swimming isn't how we'll spend most of our honeymoon."

He got her point.

"Do you really need my help? After all, haven't you planned this since you were a little girl?"

Two weeks since his proposal had flown by. They'd chosen rings, a cake, a venue, and a date. He wanted to participate in the experience, but the minute details bored him.

His comment ignited a spark. Nicole stepped back. "Imagining and planning aren't the same. Besides, two months might as well be two days." Veins popped in her neck. "We have to pick out food, flowers, tuxedos, dresses." Her pitch increased with every word. "Invitations, our gift registry!" she shrieked.

"Can't your maid-of-honor help with this stuff?"

"Hilary is a busy woman." She cut her eyes at him. "Bet you wish we had a wedding planner now."

No, he didn't. He viewed outside help as an unneeded

expense. With Nicole's expensive tastes, they'd come dangerously close to his spending limit. Her parents paid for the cake. He pondered why they hadn't done more for their only daughter.

"I'm here for you," he promised, "but you left one thing off the list."

He recognized the anxiousness returning. Her eyes narrowed.

"What?" She stared him down. "What?"

"Picking out a house."

Nicole dragged herself into the clinic. She barely remembered the drive in. Exhaustion had been a constant companion since she and Richard started searching for a place to call their own. They'd decided on a four-bedroom home in Buckhead. Notoriously expensive, the area of town would have been unaffordable without their combined incomes and Richard's real estate industry connections. The previous owners kept the house fairly well-maintained. The property required minor updates, such as paint to match Nicole's decorating preferences. Those could wait until she and Richard settled in, but she wanted to skip ahead to that moment.

Designed for entertaining, the home's modern, open layout appealed to the couple. She foresaw cooking in the professionally-equipped kitchen, reading on the patio at the end of a stressful day, and taking sinfully long bubble baths in the Jacuzzi. Most of all, she envisioned their kids, years down the road, playing safely in the fenced backyard. Together, she and Richard had chosen an ideal setting for creating new memories. As an added bonus, the area had an abundance of shops nearby and was only 20 minutes from their jobs. If all went well, they'd move in about a month before the wedding.

Her fiancé got involved more, but Nicole internalized the burden of making their special day unfold flawlessly. She wanted them to look back 50 years from now and still glow about how beautiful everything was. On top of planning the ceremony and all that it entailed, they had to pack and unpack two apartments' worth of belongings. Her mother and Kevin had volunteered to help. She doubted her father would lend a hand, let alone Mrs. Knight.

Nicole's soon-to-be mother-in-law had added to the pressure. Richard valued the elder woman's opinion, so both Richard and Nicole weighed her concerns carefully. At Mrs. Knight's urging, he and Nicole attended counseling on several occasions. Reverend Peters had the couple consider a bevy of pitfalls that affect marital bliss. He questioned their spending philosophies and cultural differences. He tackled the delicate area of sexual compatibility. He delved into how faith would factor into child rearing and, even more immediately, the nuptials. In the end, Richard and Nicole decided that mutual respect could and would overcome any obstacles. They resolved to find common ground with every issue that arose.

As patients funneled through the clinic, Nicole realized most of them, most women anywhere, would envy her predicament and would love to have a drop of the happiness she'd experienced lately. Nicole reprimanded herself for losing focus as she drew blood, filled out forms and gave directives. Even though she offered encouragement to her patients, she was partially absent in spirit.

Performing in a mechanical nature felt foreign to her. She and the other Horizons staff, one doctor and another nurse named Jill, had built a reputation in the area. The clinic's referral base increased steadily. Some new patients drove from distant suburbs to experience a standard of care centered upon caring.

Nicole reminded herself that despite her worries, today should be no different. Obsessing now would do no good. She pushed on.

An hour before the clinic closed, Antonia Calipari, or "Toni" as most called her, delivered syringes along with other supplies. Her UPS route normally included two weekly stops there. Her rushed schedule prevented her and Nicole from engaging in more than quick chats. They'd often meet up for drinks before Richard came along. Nicole remembered his disapproval the night she'd let loose with Hilary and some other friends, so she never mentioned their outings.

"Guess the ring makes it official," Toni observed.

Nicole admired the delicious diamond. "It does," she said fingering the pink, square solitaire.

Toni placed the boxes marked "fragile" on the counter in a quick and careful manner. Nicole couldn't help noticing Toni's broad, calloused hands. Maybe she would suggest that they go for manicures instead of martinis when they hung out again, and perhaps a trip to the mall, too, because Toni's off-duty wardrobe was as drab as her uniform. Her friend certainly lacked the fashion sense Italians were known for.

"I hear Sister Spot is having free appetizers tonight. We should stop by."

"Can't. Too tired," Nicole responded.

Toni placed the last box on the reception counter and entered data into her electronic tracker. "You're acting like an old, married lady already," she said and sped off before Nicole could respond.

The remark lingered in Nicole's mind until she decided to shrug it off. She had work to finish and a man waiting at home. Richard always took the stress away.

Shirley Knight had checked out Richard and Nicole's residence while it sat empty. She'd never seen it furnished. Nicole's mother, in contrast, had been quite involved in their transition to the place.

"Not bad," she observed. "Though I would've put the couch over there." She pointed to an area closer to a living room wall.

Her son ignored the comment. "Don't forget, rehearsal dinner is at 5:00 on Friday."

"Who ever heard of such a thing? Who does that three weeks ahead of the ceremony?"

"Her dad has a late doctor's appointment the Friday before. It was the only time he could get his arthritis medicine shot. Since the country club has other events going on, this is what we're stuck with."

His explanation ended that line of questioning.

"I do want to meet him and his wife. I hope our dresses don't clash."

He hoped they didn't clash.

"As long as you're not wearing white, everything will be fine."

"Speaking of fine, the revered told me you resigned from teaching Sunday school."

"It's temporary, Ma. We've got so much going on with our jobs and the wedding."

She frowned.

"I still make it to service, don't I?"

"Barely. What sort of lesson is that to teach your class?"

"I don't live around the corner anymore. You know how bad traffic is."

"Actually, I don't. Sunday is the best day to travel around town. You can't be bothered to wake up earlier?"

Richard answered by rolling his eyes.

"That girl is changing you," she accused.

He was her best friend, and she was his biggest fan, but he wanted his mother to leave Nicole out of the equation.

"It's me. Not her."

Mrs. Knight wrung her wrists.

"Our God is a jealous God, Richard. Don't you forget that."

"One more shot," Toni urged Nicole, who grooved to the rock music playing inside Club Synthesis. The two shared a table near the DJ booth. Nearby, men danced with men and women with women. Toni couldn't make Nicole's bachelorette party, so they'd decided to celebrate a week prior.

"Tell me about this man you can't pry yourself away from."

"Richard is wonderful," Nicole began. "It's funny." Nicole stopped to down more tequila. "I'm not the least bit nervous. Everyone tells me that's not normal, even my parents." They'd expressed a desire for her to end up with someone as straight-laced as Richard. The more her parents favored a prospect, the quicker Nicole lost interest in that person. A rebel of sorts, she leaned toward dating bad boys with bad intentions. One relationship, which proved especially tumultuous, left Nicole seriously questioning her judgment.

"I agree. How do you know he's who you belong with?"

"Because I'm not second guessing myself. Because I feel like I've always known him yet want to know so much more about him."

"Sounds dreamy," Toni commented sarcastically. She raised her glass. "Here's to you and Richard. If it doesn't last, though, know I'll be here for you."

Toni's toast struck Nicole as odd. Richard had never given her reason to doubt him. Nicole's parents, together 29 years, had always seemed content. They served as her compass.

Toni kept on topic. "Just throwing it out there."

Toni's carefree, take-me-or-leave-me-alone attitude initially made Nicole gravitate toward her more so than any other quality. Toni's demeanor reminded Nicole of a dear confidant from her past. Most others, though, chose to leave her alone without venturing past the butch exterior.

"Thank you," Nicole managed, mainly because she didn't know what else to say. The possibility of an unhappy union hadn't crept into Nicole's mind. Nicole dismissed Toni's words as drunken gibberish and took another swig of her drink. She came here to celebrate. Nothing and no one would stop her.

The tequila oozed from Nicole's pores. While not drunk, she had a decent buzz going. Richard killed that. He waited for her in the shadows of their living room.

"About time," he said.

Nicole locked the door and then switched on the overhead light. She saw him sitting on the loveseat. "I told you I was going out, didn't I?" For a moment, she thought she'd forgotten to tell him.

"Going out, not staying out until dawn."

"Like you and Kevin never partied hard."

"Not since I had a fiancé waiting on me."

She snuggled up next to him and rested her head on his shoulder. "I'm sorry, baby. Toni wanted to catch a drag show, and it ran over."

He sighed. "It's not safe out that late. And I'm not cool with you hanging out with Toni. She sounds irresponsible."

"She's harmless. You barely know her."

"Let's keep it that way."

Nicole had no intentions of arguing with Richard. They'd both feel better in the morning. They always did.

Kevin stood sideways, admiring himself in one of the formal wear shop's mirror. He and Richard both wore classic black tuxedos accentuated with pops of red, Nicole's favorite color.

The seamstress stood at Richard' side. "Okay?" she inquired. She wore a stern expression, as if she criticized her craft more than any customer could.

Kevin slapped him on the back. "Looks good to me," he answered for his friend, who nodded in agreement.

She left them to assist another customer.

Richard sat on a stool and started taking off his dress shoes.

"So you're really doing this?" Kevin asked.

Richard looked up. "Yep."

"It's obvious Nicole has a hold on you. I hope it lasts, for both of your sakes."

"Till death do us part is in the vows for a reason."

"Tell that to my ex."

"Didn't you cheat on her?"

"Minor technicality."

Richard smirked.

"We had issues despite all of our similarities," Kevin revealed. "It's just weird seeing you go from slow motion to fast forward. I like Nicole, but I hope you've actually thought this through."

"Nicole and I know politics and religion are two areas we'll probably never agree on. They're off limits."

"Great way to start out, avoiding important subjects," Kevin said, sounding more serious than usual.

"Look at us," Richard joked. "We're proof that odd couples can last."

Kevin appeared unconvinced.

Chapter 3

On a Saturday afternoon in October, a small group of Richard's and Nicole's friends and family gathered on the green at the Country Club of the South. The believer and the skeptic stood before the reverend and committed themselves to each other for better or worse. They stood at the altar promising to honor and obey, to love and to cherish each other for all the days of their lives.

"Where's your father?" Richard asked Nicole as they moved to the outdoor reception area. Mr. Eriksson had barely made eye contact with Richard while walking his daughter down the aisle or at the rehearsal dinner. Richard, who lamented his own father's absence during the joyous occasion, had hoped to bond on some level with the man.

"His joints were acting up," she said. "He went back to the hotel."

"He could've at least said bye, congratulations, anything." More than one guest had inquired about Mr. Eriksson's whereabouts.

"He didn't want to bother us with his problems. He passed the message on through my mom." His wife showed no pressing concern regarding the situation.

Doubt flickered within Richard. Perhaps he'd overreacted. He watched their mothers chatting near the bridal party table.

They looked happy, content. He resolved to focus on the festivities, not his father-in-law.

Richard wanted to whisk his wife away this very moment, but they still had guests to greet and rituals to complete. He moved toward Ethan Walsh, an associate he'd worked with on numerous projects. They often chatted while eating lunch in the break room. On his way over to Ethan, Toni approached him.

He recognized her instantly although they'd never met. She looked like he'd imagined, stocky with a low haircut and a rugged face. Her unflattering pantsuit stood out among the attire other women wore.

"So you're Richard," she said, eyeing him up and down.

"You must be Toni," he replied.

"I'm sure Nicole had her reasons for choosing you. Treat her right."

"Why wouldn't I?"

Instead of answering, she turned on her heels and headed for the buffet.

The exchange puzzled Richard and reinforced his dislike for the woman. He'd mention it to Nicole after they left Tahiti.

One week, one day, and 14 hours had passed since Nicole and Richard became husband and wife. A hint of sunlight streamed through their bedroom window. Bluebirds chirped outside. Otherwise, silence surrounded them. She gazed at the man lying beside her, trapped somewhere between sleep and consciousness.

He faced her, his breath caressing her bare shoulders. He stirred a little. She smiled.

She relished the stillness. She relished intimate moments like this before the sun rose. No patients with aches and pains for Nicole, no clients with pressing property issues or pending litigation for him.

They'd existed in a cocoon following the wedding. On this Monday morning, they'd have to emerge. Richard yawned and focused on Nicole as he awoke.

"Let's go back to Bora Bora," she whispered. The magical setting had spoiled them. Walks along the beach, leisurely lunches, breakfasts in bed, midnight strolls, and the thrill of having no pressing plans increased the peace they'd felt. The inn's staff had eagerly accommodated and anticipated the newlyweds' every need.

"Our honeymoon just ended," he whispered. "Maybe next year for our anniversary. Maybe next year, they'll be three us of celebrating." Richard gently rubbed her stomach.

"I guess it's over for now. Back to work." She pouted and procrastinated, delaying leaving his side.

At the clinic, Jill recounted what had transpired while Nicole was on vacation.

"Seems like it wasn't too crazy around here," Nicole said.

"Dr. Flannigan limited the number of walk-in patients. That helped a lot." She handed Nicole the appointment roster. "How about you pull the files, and I'll get the exam rooms ready."

"Okay."

Nicole was in the middle of pulling charts when she heard a knock up front. She hurried to see who'd come by well before opening time.

It was Toni.

"You're early."

"It's Columbus Day. Half of my stops are closed."

"Totally forgot," Nicole said.

An awkward moment passed between them and then Toni blurted out, "Did Richard mention meeting me?"

"No, why?"

"I got the feeling he didn't like me very much."

"I'm sure that's not true. You must've misunderstood him."

Toni smirked. "We'll see," she said and left without a goodbye.

Nicole wondered what had just happened and what happened at her wedding.

Steam billowed from the pasta pot, flattening Nicole's curls as she prepared dinner for Richard. Spaghetti was his favorite dish, and he enjoyed her version. It contained tons of fresh herbs and an organic sauce imported from Italy. The grass-fed beef she used also elevated the entrée.

Richard headed for the kitchen as soon as he got home. The aromas floating in the air enticed him. They'd been dining out so much that he barely recalled their last home-cooked meal. With the logistics of moving and planning their wedding no longer an issue, he looked forward to simply living as husband and wife.

Richard kissed Nicole on the cheek. It pleased him that she wanted to make him happy.

She turned toward him but didn't reciprocate his affectionate gesture. "Do you remember meeting my friend Toni?" Nicole asked.

He nodded in affirmation. Of course he did. He'd chosen to dismiss their encounter.

Nicole continued the inquisition. "Does anything stand out?"

"Other than her being rude?" he thought. "She made some weird comment about why you chose me."

"Well, Toni thinks you don't like her. She hinted that you were rude."

"If anything," Richard countered, "it was the other way around."

"Just try being nicer to her."

He grimaced and doubted Toni was worth the effort. Richard couldn't figure out if Toni was a complete dimwit or had a hidden agenda. "Honestly, I don't get why you like her."

"She's a sweetheart underneath. Give her a chance. I gave Kevin one."

Richard marveled at how she'd concealed her feelings about his best friend for so long. Her tone told him debating back and forth would do no good. "Yep," Richard thought. "The honeymoon is over."

Chapter 4

Palpable excitement filled the floors of Goldstein, Levy & Finch. Richard fidgeted in his chair and made sure the ringer on his phone hadn't been lowered. At 4:15 on this Wednesday, the senior partners would start announcing which partnership candidates made the cut. Normally, attorneys had no chance of advancing until the seventh year of service. The lead lawyer on Richard's team, Robert Smythe, had taken an interest in Richard's professional growth early on. He'd cited Richard's ability to bring in new clients, his quick wit, and business savvy as reasons why he considered Richard an asset. Smythe, who played golf with Goldstein regularly, had consistently passed along his opinions concerning Richard's potential.

Even the lawyers who had practically no tenure recognized the gravity of the pending event. The chosen would serve as examples of the right road to follow. Those overlooked would do the opposite.

Richard had studied the roster from year to year. He kept meticulous notes on those fellow associates' achievements at the firm and with various professional and community organizations. He followed their career milestones but took particular note of those who had failed to impress, some even to the point of losing their jobs.

He'd quickly recognized a pattern. Those who worked harder than expected often achieved exceptional results. Goldstein, Levy & Finch had no room for average when it came to rising within its ranks. And then there was the social element. Abrasive, entitled attitudes almost always stunted careers.

While he had confidence in his abilities, Richard had prepared himself for the possibility of disappointment. He'd memorized two short speeches to recite regardless of the outcome. He felt like an Oscar nominee being cast into the spotlight. Of course he wanted to win, but he didn't want to lose his composure. If he lost, he didn't want to appear crushed.

The review board summoned Richard into the main conference room at 4:45. By 4:50, he had his answer.

Richard and Nicole celebrated with sushi and wine. She had insisted that they dress up and mark the occasion by going out. After leaving Seaside Restaurant, they strolled around Atlantic Station, a multi-use complex that housed restaurants, a theater, retailers, and residential condos. They paused near a fountain.

"I'm sooo proud of you," Nicole said. "My husband, the partner."

She'd told him that earlier. He didn't mind hearing it again. He felt proud of himself.

They went home and celebrated again.

The thrill of Richard's promotion gradually wore off once the gravity of it set in. Now that he was a non-equity partner, a small window office replaced his gray cubicle. He held no financial stake in the business but did receive a bump in pay and added responsibility. He now oversaw major initiatives and managed employees. His hours in the office increased because he had to handle new assignments while bringing past projects to completion.

Finding balance between his professional and private life proved tricky. Initially, Nicole held dinner for him. Then, she'd sit beside him and they'd chat while he ate. Nicole eventually began preparing a plate for Richard to warm when he arrived home.

He appreciated her efforts and patience. Many evenings, though, their routine mirrored roommates who just happened to sleep in the same bed. He considered himself fortunate when he had enough energy to give Nicole the attention she deserved and craved. They were still newlyweds, and he knew he had to work at keeping his wife happy. He figured that making all the money he could to create a comfortable lifestyle for them was one means of doing that. Nicole, however, started to complain. One evening when he came home at 8:30, she said, "Another woman might accuse you of cheating, but I know my husband loves me even if he doesn't call just to say so sometimes."

That sobering remark hit Richard like a brick. He smiled uncomfortably, grabbed Nicole around the waist, and hugged her as if she was trying to escape. As he embraced her, he made a mental commitment to call, email or text her how much he truly loved her every day.

The next day, he called her at work but she couldn't talk because she was busy with patients. Still, he told the receptionist, Pita, to tell her, "The man you met at the golf course and married says he loves you." He knew she would get a kick out of that because she liked surprises, especially ones that were either funny or expensive.

Richard never got a response from Nicole, so he called her cell phone at 6:30 p.m. once he knew she would be at home. He was still at work but preparing to leave. Nicole sent the call to voicemail because she was busy shopping, her "stress reliever." She knew Richard would ask what she was doing, and she didn't want to have to tell him the truth – that she was in the mall *again*. He had tried to establish a household budget that allowed her to spend up to $500 per month on personal excursions, but Nicole had already spent almost twice that amount this month.

Once he couldn't get her by phone, Richard decided to send his wife a text message. It read: "Honey, call me. Missing you."

Nicole didn't read the text until two hours later when she turned her phoned back on after leaving the mall. She had turned it off when Richard called earlier. She responded to the text, saying, "Sorry I missed your call. Call me when you're headed home. I have to pick up something for dinner." Nicole was on her way to pick up a take-out order from Ruby Tuesday, so she felt justified in explaining why she was out and hadn't answered his call."

Shock gripped her when she read Richard's text message response, saying, "At home already. Made dinner and waiting on you."

"What do I say?" she thought. "Do I tell him I've been shopping before he sees the bags? Do I leave the bags in the trunk until next month and pretend the items were purchased then?" Taking a page from her attorney husband's playbook, she decided to mention her new purchases before the proof possibly emerged. She was okay with being a shopaholic, but she wanted no part of being a deceiver. Richard told her in defending clients that juries would more likely sympathize with crimes related to addiction of some sort but not those committed by deceivers of any kind.

"OK," she typed. "Bought a few things at the mall. Will be there in 15 minutes." Nicole hit "send" on her phone and hoped Richard wouldn't reply. He didn't.

The first things Richard noticed were the Nordstrom and Bloomingdale bags, but his attention quickly shifted to his wife, who he just wanted to keep happy. His guilt about not spending enough quality time with her allowed him to justify her spending the extra money on shopping. Furthermore, his tinge of frustration quickly dissipated when she dropped the bags, playfully tackled him to the floor and planted kisses all over his face. At that moment, neither of them cared about anything other than each other.

Richard carried Nicole to their bedroom, where rose petals were scattered over the sheets and floor. For the next 10 minutes, all they recognized were each other's touch. Richard's ringing cell phone was the only thing that interrupted their passion. He ignored it the first time, but it began ringing again moments later. He knew that whoever it was had to be important or in need of emergency assistance because the phone just kept ringing. Nicole gave him a look as if to say that it was okay to answer it. Richard took the phone off the nightstand and saw that it was one of the partners at the firm, Samuel Mayhorn.

He talked to Sam for almost two hours about a new case. Nicole eventually fell asleep waiting. She awoke the next morning feeling slighted, but she didn't mention it.

Pita saw Nicole in the parking lot as they both headed toward the clinic's employee entrance, and said, "I forgot to tell you yesterday that your husband called to say he loves you. I just got really busy and had to leave early because my son was sick."

Without turning her head in acknowledgement, Nicole said, "Thanks." A small part of her felt energized by the message. Still, she could not get over feeling rejected. A man had never left her alone, especially while making love.

No cigarette had touched Nicole's lips since middle school. That's when curiosity led her to sneak one under the bleachers. She needed nicotine today to take the edge off. No one at the clinic smoked, but she knew Toni did because the smell lingered on her clothes and on her breath although she tried to camouflage it with gum and mints.

Nicole practically pounced on Toni when she stopped by. That's when she learned that her friend actually preferred cigars but smoked regular menthol cigarettes throughout the day. They leaned against Nicole's convertible, which was parked in the lot behind the clinic.

Nicole puffed on a cigarette while Toni listened to her vent about Richard.

"Take it easy," Toni said. She pantomimed the proper smoking technique.

Nicole followed Toni's instructions. "I've taken up too much of your time," she told her friend.

"Not at all. I've been where you're at. Richard claims he's working but don't bosses set their own hours?"

"He's a partner, not an owner."

"Yeah, but he's not chained to his desk. It doesn't take a college degree to know human nature."

Nicole looked pissed, as if doubting Richard's explanations. He hadn't noticed her new outfits or the highlights in her hair.

"He might be having second thoughts."

The scowl on Nicole's face grew deeper.

"You two got together awfully fast," Toni continued.

She valued Toni's opinion and the fact that her friend might think she'd chased Richard concerned her. "I didn't drag him into our marriage," Nicole countered.

"A lot of guys flip out later. They want the woman but not the commitment."

Toni had aptly spotted losers in the past, warning Nicole of men who specialized in deception.

"Hmm," she considered the possibility.

"Maybe he's not cheating. Maybe he's hooked on drugs or something. You'll figure it out."

"Yes, I will," Nicole told herself. "Yes, I will."

That night, Nicole lounged in their king size bed, reading a fashion magazine. Outside of work and shopping she struggled to fill the void in her schedule, especially at night. Richard brought assignments home constantly, and when they were in the same room he seemed to forget her presence. Hilary's demanding schedule kept her preoccupied. Between rounds at the hospital and doting on her boyfriend, Nicole's best friend could hardly fit in anyone or anything else. They communicated mainly through short texts. Nicole missed their conversations. Meeting up seemed an impossible feat. They'd scheduled an afternoon of shopping followed by an early dinner a few weeks ago. Hilary backed out. Although disappointed, Nicole heard the exhaustion in Hilary's voice and didn't belabor the issue.

"Finally," she huffed when Richard entered.

Richard had grown accustomed to the sulking. "Hello to you, too," he said. He joined her on the bed and loosened his necktie.

She glanced at the alarm clock on the nightstand. It read 7:09. He followed her gaze.

Earlier than usual, Richard mused, but obviously still not early enough.

"How long is this going to continue?" she asked.

"I'm a partner now, honey. I've got responsibilities."

"You're a husband, too."

Richard thought he was coming home to his wife, not heading into battle. "I'm all yours on the weekend," he said.

"Don't you mean Saturday and half of Sunday? We both know you can't survive without seeing your mom, if that's where you really are."

He resented the implication. He searched her face for understanding. He found none. She sounded like a parrot reciting words someone else had fed her. Instinct led him to the culprit. "Is this you or Toni talking?"

Nicole needed a sounding board. Toni fit that bill. Nicole returned to the magazine. She resented her husband's implication that Toni possessed so much influence. After all, she was her own woman.

Her unresponsiveness sliced him to the core. Although he'd lost his appetite, Richard retreated to the kitchen. Something had to give. He didn't know what.

Nicole had never ventured near the sad East Point neighborhood where Toni lived. She passed scores of foreclosed homes, overgrown lots, and faded, peeling billboards. She questioned why anyone willingly lived within a 5-mile radius.

A wrought-iron security gate spanned the perimeter of Toni's complex. It offered Nicole some semblance of comfort. For added security, she parked under a lamppost near the entrance to Toni's unit.

"Glad you made it okay," piped Toni, who had promised a meal and a movie.

The inside of her studio apartment resembled a bachelor pad, not the dwelling of a woman nearing 30. A 42-inch, digital flat screen sat in the middle of a black entertainment center that had cubbyholes crammed with DVDs and video games. A matching coffee table sat in front of a black, leather sofa. It rested on a beige, square area rug. She had no end tables, dining room, or design savvy from what Nicole could see.

"I don't smell any food," Nicole said.

"It's on the way."

"Delivery?" Nicole scoffed.

"Yeah, I promised a meal. I never said I was cooking it. Sit, sit."

This ought to be interesting, Nicole thought. She felt a tinge of guilt because she hadn't made Richard's dinner. They had no leftovers in the fridge either.

"I've got beer, Pepsi, water," Toni called out from the kitchen.

"Water is fine."

Toni handed Nicole a glass of water and then plopped down on the opposite end of the sofa. She had a drop of her beer before putting it on the table.

"You don't have any coasters?" Nicole asked.

"Nope." She sounded exasperated. "Aren't you supposed to be relaxing?"

"You're right." Nicole put her cup on the table and her purse on the floor. "Let Richard fend for himself," she thought. She wouldn't hamper her friend's efforts. Even after confronting Richard about his "lack of consideration," Nicole had continued her wifely duties. Having someone take care of her for a change had its appeal. I shouldn't have to wait until the weekends to feel appreciated, she concluded. "So what are we watching?"

The slapstick comedy cleared Nicole's mind. The greasy, dense pizza both filled her stomach and upset it. Still, she gave Toni kudos for thoughtfulness.

"I've got the sequel, too, if you want to see it," Toni told her.

"I don't know." Nicole's stomach fluttered. "Where's your bathroom?"

Toni nodded toward the hallway. "First door on the right."

Richard answered his cell phone without taking his eyes off the proposal he'd been reviewing.

"Hello."

No one responded.

He glimpsed at the Caller ID. It displayed Nicole's name and number. Richard pressed the phone to his ear. He presumed Nicole's cell was shuffling around in her purse and it inadvertently dialed him. Then he heard the voices.

"Come on, let's go one more round."

"It's after 9:00."

"And."

The call dropped.

Richard dialed his wife's number. Her phone rang and then went straight to voicemail. He tried again. "What the hell?" Richard grabbed his keys and briefcase. He'd get her to answer one way or another.

He stood in the doorway when Nicole opened the door.

"Richard!" He'd startled her.

"Don't Richard me. Where have you been? Who have you been with?" He'd make her admit the truth if it took all night.

"At Toni's. With Toni. We ate dinner together." Nicole stepped in the doorway nudging him with her elbow to give her some space.

They stood toe-to-toe. "That must've been the longest meal in history."

"We watched a movie. Two actually."

"That's what you expect me to believe?"

"She's my friend."

"Your so-called friend has done nothing but instigate drama."

"Toni, unlike you, has been there for me lately."

That newsflash infuriated him even more than Nicole's defense of the "beady-eyed bitch." The entire situation baffled him.

"Her or me!" he screamed.

"It's late. I'm tired." She moved toward the door. Nicole bypassed dictating his circle of friends. She expected the same of her husband.

Richard blocked her entry.

"Stop! I can't..."

Nicole went limp. He caught her before she hit the ground.

Nicole awoke in an exam room. One flimsy white curtain separated her from the elderly lady beside her. Nicole tried to stand, but nausea overtook her. She recalled Richard's rapid-fire questions and accusations.

She glanced at the band on her wrist. She was in Piedmont Hospital.

The room might as well have been a time warp. A nurse eventually entered to take her blood pressure. "Glad to see you back with us," the pudgy woman said in a sing-songy way.

Nicole was in no mood for her cheer. "What's wrong with me?' she asked bluntly.

"You're anemic."

"I've never been anemic," Nicole responded. "I'm a certified nurse practitioner. I know my body."

"Then you know babies bring about changes."

Nicole felt faint again. She demanded a second opinion.

"Yep," the ER doctor confirmed. "Those tests don't lie."

She had almost eight months to prepare for motherhood.

Chapter 5

Nicole's stomach somersaulted. The acids in it rose into her throat. It was as if the baby inside her heard the doctor's announcement and decided to make its presence known right at that moment. Happenings and signs she had overlooked foretold of this moment. Her clothes fit more snugly. She dozed off while watching TV. She snapped at Richard for the tiniest transgressions. She could suddenly smell every ingredient in a meal.

"How ironic," she thought. "I deal with pregnant women almost every day and the signs eluded me."

Nicole had used protection without Richard's knowledge. As a medical professional, she'd warned patients repeatedly that birth control pills had a margin of error. She had expected to fall outside of that margin.

Nicole imagined her husband pacing about discombobulated, wondering what had transpired, and hounding the staff for updates. She hoped Richard wouldn't take it upon himself to check on her. He can wait, she told herself, and rested her head more comfortably on the pillow. Nervous, she expected an orderly to kick her out soon because some other body in crisis needed the cot.

Nicole tucked the prenatal vitamins prescription into her purse. She sought a means of cutting through the clutter clogging her brain. She considered calling her mother. Intuition stopped Nicole from doing so. Her mom would immediately slip into grandmother mode and start planning numerous ways to spoil her grandchild. Nicole had not, could not think that far ahead. And Hilary, who'd filled the confidant role often before, would slip into doctor mode. Hell, she'd probably offer to perform another examination.

She decided to try Toni.

It dawned on Nicole that Richard had her cell. She assumed that he'd turned into an amateur sleuth, riffling through her call log and messages. Surely he'd discover the innocent exchanges between her and Toni and morph them into sinister indiscretions.

Nicole peeked behind the curtain dividing the room. The elderly lady on the other side lay in a catatonic sleep. A telephone rested on a bedside table a few steps away. Nicole tiptoed toward it and lifted the receiver. She pushed "9" for an outside line and then dialed Toni's number.

Her friend picked up immediately, sounding like it was noon instead of midnight.

The jumbled words spilled out. "It's late. I know it's late, but I needed to..."

"Nicole, where are you?"

"In the hospital. Piedmont."

Distress crept into Toni's voice. "What? Why?"

"I fainted."

"You need me to come get you?"

"No, I'm just… I'm pregnant."

"Pregnant?" Toni made the connection slowly. "I see."

"Richard must be thrilled. You too, I suppose."

Nicole said nothing.

"Nicole?"

She let out an extended exhale as if thrusting out her anxieties "No one knows."

"Keep it that way."

"Huh?" The direction of their conversation threw Nicole's weary mind further off course.

"We can raise this baby together. I love you, and I'll love the baby," Toni proclaimed.

"You can't be serious.'

"More than I've ever been in my life."

Nicole's voice cracked. "But I'm married."

"You shouldn't be," Toni declared. "At least not to him."

"I can't deal with this." Nicole slammed the received down so hard that she woke the lady in the room. She gazed groggily in Nicole's direction as if she wondered what had transpired.

Nicole used a stomach virus and anemia as explanations for her continual sickness. Her coworkers urged her to stay home instead of contaminating the clinic. Richard decided to stay at home also to take care of her, insisting that she rest and eat. He kept a steady supply of store-bought chicken soup, saltines, and ginger ale within reach. He bought her magazines and made sure she took vitamins containing iron. He did everything except mention their argument.

His devotion touched her until she realized he'd been working from home.

In between naps, she replayed Toni's comment and analyzed their conversation. She wanted to know what made Toni respond like that. She wanted to know, but she didn't. She'd avoided the avalanche of calls, texts, instant messages, and emails from Toni. The relentless hounding proved unnerving. Toni had called from an unidentified number. Nicole hung up immediately after hearing her voice and turned off the cell phone. She also unplugged her laptop. She had no remedy for unplugging her thoughts, though.

Nicole recounted the interactions she'd had with Toni since knowing her. What had let to Toni's desire to evolve from friend to flame? Had their relationship, without Nicole's knowledge, veered onto that course prior to Toni professing her feelings? Had she exuded a vibe that gave Toni the wrong idea? Maybe, she thought, the notion of something more hit Toni right before she blurted out her statement. Nicole knew how the line between like and love often blurred, especially with workplace romances. She had witnessed countless co-workers lose their focus and even their jobs after crossing *that* line. Up until this point in her career, she had remained above the fray, avoiding romances and even close friendships with co-workers.

Although she told no one about the child growing inside of her, Nicole contemplated the blessings that could emerge from the pregnancy. She also contemplated negative outcomes. If I tell him, Nicole predicted, he'll use the baby as a shield, a way to take the focus off bigger issues. His passive aggressiveness irked her. Often, she'd speculated that Toni had more testosterone than Richard although she'd never disclosed that observation for fear of reinforcing Richard's angst. Who would he ban her from socializing with next? Hilary? Her mother? His desire to keep her away from Toni struck her as a manifestation of insecurity. Furthermore, his continual clinginess would only grow as her belly grew.

What did he expect, for her to dismiss Toni due to his insecurities? She'd enjoyed Toni's companionship. They'd met for lunch, hung out at the mall, discussed their favorite TV shows, and chatted on the phone. Richard most often worked through lunch or cut the allotted hour in half, making it impossible for them to eat together. The more Richard fulfilled his role as partner at the firm, the less he fulfilled his role as husband.

Even through the cyber stalking, Nicole saw that Toni cared. Her sexuality remained a non-factor before last night. Nicole, after all, had plenty of gay and bisexual acquaintances back in California. There, choosing a same-sex partner, at least among her peers, didn't have the stigma permeating the South. From the start, Nicole sensed her husband held Toni's masculinity against her.

Later that second day, Richard hinted that he might return to work the following morning. She didn't protest.

"If my patients can deal with AIDS," Nicole told herself, "I can deal with this. Besides, without him around, I can clearly sort out the situation."

He checked on her before leaving. He asked if she wanted him to pick up anything on his way home. She refused, thinking, "I don't need anything else from you."

"By the way," Richard said as he exited, "my ma says she hopes you feel better soon."

Nicole doubted that. She mustered a faint smile anyway.

"She asked if you had any special requests for Thanksgiving."

"Nope," Nicole said and ushered her husband on his way.

How about we spend it alone, Nicole had wanted to say. He'd agreed, without consulting her, to carry on the tradition of eating dinner at his mother's place. The holiday, Nicole surmised, would be far from relaxing. And that sly, sanctimonious grin of hers brought tension to every interaction. She perceived her mother-in-law's disapproval even when they were in the same room and not having a conversation.

Richard sat through a strategy meeting all the while thinking of ways to reconnect with his wife. No one warned him the first couple of months of marriage could be so rough. Communication between him and Nicole had stalled. Certainly, he hadn't bargained on Nicole's pesky friend circling his wife like a shark. The friendship, a term he used loosely, had encroached upon his marriage.

His long hours at the office benefited them both, especially Nicole, who loved to shop. Still, it concerned him that the less he was around, the less she needed him to be.

He suspected before the blowup that Nicole and Toni had spent a lot of evenings together. The clues surrounded him: extra dishes in the sink, credit card receipts showing meals for two, cigar ashes near the front stoop. He'd ignored the signs until they manifested into something concrete, something he could truly confront.

Unresolved issues lurked and created a prevalent barrier that caused Richard to tiptoe around his wife. He needed a resolution. Surely she did too, but for Richard, tending to her health issues ranked above broaching the issues he had concerning Toni.

Richard tried reaching his wife when the meeting adjourned. Her voicemail came on. He sent her a text. Hours went by without a reply. "She'll call if she needs me," he thought, and went about his day.

Nicole's breakfast revolted. She was hunched over the sink when the doorbell chimed. She quickly wiped her face and then grabbed her robe. The perpetrator had graduated to pounding on a window by the time Nicole neared the foyer.

She froze. What if it was Toni? Nicole peered through the living room mini blinds. She saw her mother outside. The panicked expression on her face caused Nicole to get nervous. She stepped outside, realizing after doing so that she had forgotten to put on her slippers.

Mrs. Eriksson rushed toward her daughter. She embraced Nicole so tightly that some of her bones cracked. "Thank goodness. You had me and your father so worried."

"Why?" Nicole asked weakly as her mother released her hold.

"We've been calling, but your phone keeps going to voicemail. Your job said they didn't expect you in all week."

"I've got a stomach virus; that's it."

Mrs. Eriksson stood back and took a look at her daughter. "You're paler than normal. Where is Richard? I thought something had happened to both of you. I imagined all sorts of terrible scenarios." Her mother watched too many crime dramas.

I bet nothing near what's actually happening crossed her mind, Nicole told herself. "He went back to work today."

"Instead of taking care of you?"

"I'm not an invalid, mother. I've seen much worse than what I'm dealing with." For the first time she noticed her mother's overnight bag.

"I suppose, but I'm here now. Let me take care of you."

Nicole let her mother do what she did best—mother her daughter. Mrs. Eriksson insisted on calling Nicole's father as soon as she got settled in the guest room. He told Nicole to take it easy. While he never succumbed to fits of hysteria as his wife did, Mr. Eriksson's concern reverberated in his voice.

Next, Mrs. Eriksson inspected Nicole's refrigerator. "What have you been eating dear?"

"Toast. Soup."

"From a can?"

Nicole nodded.

"No wonder you're not getting any better. Where's the nearest farmer's market?"

"Whole Foods is closer, but I think I should ride with you." Her mother had an uncanny way of getting lost even along the easiest routes. She'd made it to the Tennessee border once when she was trying to find Stone Mountain.

"Nonsense. You need your rest and," she concluded, "a shower."

Nicole agreed. "At least let me print out the directions for you. Better yet, I'll do that and show you how to use my GPS."

Nicole's mother completed the trip successfully and returned quicker than Nicole had anticipated.

"You haven't showered yet. Nicole, is there something else going on?"

Her daughter tried to look convincing. She wondered if parents had a cutoff when they stopped doting on and worrying about their kids. "No, my iron is just low." Mrs. Eriksson didn't dig any further for fear of her daughter completely shutting her out. Nicole watched her mother unpack the grocery bag. She'd purchased a whole chicken, celery, carrots, onions, ginger root, and a bag of oranges along with other food to make a separate meal for Richard.

"What's the lavender for?" Nicole asked.

"It'll help you relax so your body can heal faster."

"Go on," Mrs. Eriksson ordered. "I'll have some tea ready by the time you finish. And don't climb back into bed. I'll put a pillow and a blanket on the sofa. I want to wash those sheets of yours."

The steamy shower refreshed Nicole. She put on a clean pair of pajamas and styled her hair. She even put on lipgloss and earrings. She looked far from the mess her mother had initially encountered. Instead of lying down, she sat at the kitchen table and drank ginger tea while her mother prepared the soup. Nicole touched her stomach. Having her mother there had done wonders.

Mrs. Eriksson decided to take care of all the laundry. She moved about quietly while Nicole napped on the sofa. After loading the clothes she found in the hamper, Mrs. Eriksson proceeded to her daughter's bedroom. She lifted the blinds and pulled the curtains back, letting sunshine filter in. She arranged sprigs of lavender on each nightstand and removed the pillowcases and sheets from the bed. While removing the mattress cover, her foot pressed against a cool, hard object. Mrs. Eriksson discovered Nicole's phone. She picked it up and noticed that it was off. "What if Richard's trying to reach her," Mrs. Eriksson wondered. She turned it on.

The screen showed a series of missed calls. She hoped none of them were important. The phone vibrated before Mrs. Eriksson could place it on her daughter's nightstand.

"Hello?" Mrs. Eriksson said hesitantly.

The person on the other end sniffled.

"Hello?"

"Nicole?" a woman's voice inquired.

"This is her mother."

"I've been trying to reach her for days!" Toni erupted.

"Who is this?"

"Toni."

Her daughter had mentioned Toni often. "She came down with something. Nothing serious though."

"I'm not so sure," Toni said. "She hasn't been herself lately."

"Really?" Mrs. Eriksson responded. To her, Toni sounded alarmingly convincing.

"Is it okay if I come by just to check on her?"

Mrs. Eriksson saw no harm in Toni's request. Between the two of them, they could figure out if Nicole had more going on than she wanted to admit. "Of course, dear. Come by later. She's resting now."

Toni showed up around 5:15. Her arrival stunned Nicole, causing a shift in Mrs. Eriksson's demeanor. Her mother had seemed calm when they spoke around lunchtime. As the day progressed, she became visibly on edge, stealing glances at her daughter and fidgeting.

The balloons and chocolates made the ambush no easier to process.

Mrs. Eriksson told Toni to sit. She chose the love seat, which provided a frontal view of Nicole. Her mother sat next to her daughter.

"I turned my phone off for a reason." She aimed the comment at both women.

"We both support you regardless," Toni said.

Nicole considered her mom blameless but not Toni. She wanted to strangle and hug her friend, who continually displayed unwavering loyalty. With Toni, Nicole always felt protected and accepted.

With Richard, unspoken disappointment loomed around every corner. Mate or Messiah? Nicole speculated often about the role he strived to fulfill. She didn't relate to his desire for spiritual guidance but accepted and respected it. Nicole doubted his heart held no secret yearnings such as her finding religion or deciding to raise kids rather than rise within her profession.

Nicole, even as a teenager, expressed affection without limitations. She ignored the ethnic, socioeconomic, and cultural lines that others dared not cross. Dating a woman, on the other hand, was a territory she ventured into only once. That episode left a mark on her heart. Her parents considered the relationship nonsense. They convinced Nicole she'd succumbed to a whimsical bout of experimentation. They set out to pray the gay away even though Nicole hadn't labeled herself as such. She'd simply found understanding and acceptance embodied in a female. Their romantic connection proved unexpected but essential. The friend, who she and her parents never mentioned, helped Nicole through a rough patch in which she'd previously felt alone.

The front door lock turned. Nicole held her breath. Toni tensed up. Mrs. Eriksson remained oblivious.

Richard identified the car parked out front as his mother-in-law's. He now knew who owned the pickup truck.

"Good to see you, Mrs. Eriksson."

"You too, Richard. I hope you don't catch what Nicole's got."

Toni glimpsed at Nicole, who avoided making direct eye contact.

"Toni," he mustered while managing to maintain his composure.

"Richard," she responded through clenched teeth.

He placed his suitcase on the coffee table next to Toni's gifts and then kissed Nicole on the cheek. She failed to reciprocate. Her kisses lately had a chill to them, but he hadn't expected her to withdraw completely. "Feeling any better, honey?"

"Much." Richard took his wife's appearance as a sign that she did.

"I'm glad." He reached for and then caressed her hand. Sweat formed on her brow.

Toni cleared her throat.

"Someone sounds thirsty," Richard said. "Toni, why don't you join me in the kitchen? Anyone else need a drink?"

"I'll take some water," Mrs. Eriksson said.

"Honey?"

"I'm fine," Nicole said. Her body language told another story.

Richard had no intention of serving Toni. He leaned against the kitchen counter near the refrigerator, facing Toni. "Let's get one thing straight," he told her. "This is my house, and Nicole is my wife."

Toni sneered. "You silly, silly man." Her eyes burned with the heat of flaming coals.

"Isn't that what you want to be?" Richard spit back. He visually scrutinized her attire: a men's dress shirt with a white t-shirt underneath, khakis, and a pair of brown loafers.

She scoffed.

"You know nothing about our marriage," Richard continued.

"I know more than you know."

Richard lunged at her and then stopped in his tracks. He wouldn't let Toni cast him in the role of unstable husband, and she definitely wasn't worth going to jail over. "Get out, bitch!"

Chapter 6

Toni ran from the kitchen and straight to Nicole. She stood with her hands on her hips and glared defiantly. "Richard told me to leave. He doesn't want me speaking to you anymore. Is that what you want?"

Instead of responding, Nicole jumped up and turned to her husband. "You have no right!" she erupted.

Mrs. Eriksson wedged herself between them. She placed a hand on Nicole's arm, trying to ssimultaneously pull her back and console her. "Richard just wants you to get your rest."

"No!" Nicole shouted.

Richard flinched.

"Toni is staying."

"Surely she can come back another day," Mrs. Eriksson said.

"You don't get it!" Nicole screamed. "I might be in love with her."

Mrs. Eriksson's eyes darted back and forth from Nicole to Richard to Toni.

Richard clenched his teeth while Toni grinned smugly. "There's no multiple choice. I'm your husband and until death do us part. Remember?"

Tears lingered in the corners of Nicole's eyes. She started shaking. "Maybe you realized it before me." She glanced at Toni. "Maybe you both did."

Richard would've preferred chewing on a mouthful of razors to hearing his wife discard him for Toni. He looked at Toni, who had inched closer to Nicole as if claiming victory. He looked at Mrs. Eriksson, who seemed nearly as shattered as he did.

"There's something between us. I owe it to myself and to you to figure out what."

The air in the room grew heavy. Nicole had two women by her side. He had no one. He needed his mother.

Richard drove to his mother's, the only person who remained constant regardless of his missteps. He sat at her dining room table and recounted the disintegration of his relationship. Mrs. Knight sat next to him, puffing on a cigarette while he did so.

"All this was happening and you never said a word?"

"Obviously more was going on than even I was aware of."

"Humph! Lord have mercy."

Richard buried his head in his hands. "Why am I even here? I let Toni run me off."

His mother rubbed his back. "Sounds like things were heated. You shouldn't have stayed. You shouldn't have married Nicole either. "

"Here we go," Richard thought.

"Don't give me that look," Mrs. Knight instructed. "The girl's a heathen."

"How many sin-free Christians do you know, ma?"

"None, but they pray and seek forgiveness. Who's Nicole accountable to?"

"Well, I haven't given up on her yet. She's just confused."

Mrs. Knight's expression confirmed that she assumed otherwise.

Richard left work early for the second day in a row. The clouds above threatened to burst any second. He ignored the speed limit and even shot through a few lights as they turned red. One angry driver blew her horn at him. Richard dismissed her and continued to disregard the laws of the road.

His tires squealed as he turned the last corner leading onto his street. The garage door seemed to taunt him by opening slowly.

Nicole's parking spot sat empty. The sight caused Richard's heart to thump madly in his chest. He sprinted through the kitchen. "Nicole!" he shouted. "Nicole!" His footsteps echoed through the emptiness.

He reached their bedroom.

The ransacked closet revealed Nicole's haphazard exodus. Richard fell backward on the bed and stared at the ceiling. He rose an hour later. Still in shock, he called Kevin. "She's gone, man. She's gone."

Kevin reclined in an oversized leather chair in Richard's man-cave. His friend paced about, alarmingly frenzied.

"She took the coffee maker too," Kevin said. "That's low down."

"Not as cold as Toni taking her," Richard thought.

"On the flip side," Kevin said, "she kept the ring. She'll come crawling back."

The remark caused Richard to perk up.

"Let's catch the Hawks game," Kevin suggested. He turned on the TV. "How many points do you think the Cavaliers will lose by?"

Richard remained silent and fixated on his wedding band.

Kevin's walkie-talkie emitted static. "I forgot I had this on." He turned it off. "Hey, did I tell you about the gambling raid that led to a drug bust?"

"No," Richard answered, clearly not focusing on his friend's news.

"The department gets to auction off the seized property."

"I'm getting her back."

"What?"

Richard halted his pacing. "I'm not waiting for Nicole to realize her mistake. I'll make her come home."

"Legally that's kidnapping," Kevin advised.

"You've gotta help me find Toni. Can't you run a background check?"

"Not if I want to keep my job."

In a flash, Richard grabbed Kevin's gun from its holster. "I'll find Toni one way or another, and when I do, I'll kill the bitch."

Kevin viewed his friend with a mix of bewilderment and fear. "And then you'll land in jail and become some gang banger's bitch. Think about it—is Toni worth it? You'd wind up losing Nicole for sure."

"So you expect me to let her waltz off?"

"No, just find another way to fix things. Of all folks, you know premeditated murder is.."

Before he could finish, Richard acknowledged, "I know. I know."

Richard slid into the chair beside Kevin's and returned the gun to him. He laid his head back and sighed deeply. His shoulders slumped.

"Why don't you take a week off? Clear your mind."

"On such short notice?"

"What's the point in being a partner if you can't use it to your advantage once in a while? Make travel arrangements tonight and get your cases in order tomorrow. It'll do you good, man."

Chapter 7

Richard took his friend's advice despite his mother's protests. She insisted that he stay in Atlanta where she could keep tabs on him. She'd insisted they spend Thanksgiving together, especially since his sister was flying in from Chicago. Richard knew he'd sour the occasion, so he escaped to Puerto Rico.

Boarding the plane alone felt foreign. Since reciting his vows, Richard had taken for granted that Nicole would be his constant companion. He imagined other vacation travelers pitying him as the man who had no one. He decided to call Nicole from the airplane, but she sent it to voicemail, as she had every other time he called since her announcement.

Mrs. Knight and Kevin had made their viewpoints clear, scoffing at Richard's bleakness. Considering the brevity and newness of the relationship as a whole, they discarded his devastation as "overdramatic." Richard thought, "Who are they to judge?" Eons had passed since his father died, and his mother became a self-proclaimed martyr destined to stay single until they reunited in Heaven. At least she had known love although she kept herself from encountering it. Kevin fared no better. He'd treated his former wife of five years with the respect due a concubine. Richard felt that a man who held his own spouse in such low regard would hold another's no higher.

Richard called Nicole again after checking into the Westin resort. This time, he would use an unknown number to grant him clearance. As he thought, she answered the phone, but she hung up when he uttered the second syllable of her name.

The queen bed engulfed Richard without Nicole lying beside him. He desperately longed for rest. Tossing and turning greeted him instead.

He left his suite and struggled to enjoy strolling around old San Juan without Nicole's hand in his. He brushed off locals peddling handcrafted trinkets, blocked out cackling penguins, and lacked an appreciation for the abundant sunshine. Crossing oceans, venturing to other continents, flying to the moon, no distance could squelch the memories.

Compared to most guests, Richard ventured out mainly for meals and to allow housekeeping an opportunity to clean. By da,y Richard frequented a shoreside, open-air eatery that served paella cooked over a pit. The owner let diners stir the pan and pound on bongos set up in each of the main seating areas. Richard came strictly for nourishment, not for revelry.

At night, Richard redeemed a voucher for two complimentary cocktails and half-priced appetizers in the lounge. He sulked in a corner while everyone else mingled.

Endless questions bombarded his thoughts. How did Toni come to garner such power? Why did Nicole cast him off so easily? How could he encourage his wife's return?

Richard suspected Toni viewed Nicole as a mere conquest and that she despised him for undisclosed reasons. Why had she waited to pursue Nicole instead of doing so prior to their marriage?

Her actions reeked of sadism. Richard's Bible found fault in adultery, no matter the form. Her offense consumed his waking hours. In his occasional slumber, he dreamt of Nicole and how

Toni slipped in and led his wife astray. The visions, at times, would lead to cold sweats.

In his waking hours, Richard plotted a plan for severing Toni's grasp on his wife. He was going to use the same tactic she did with Nicole. He was going to charm Nicole back into his life. First, he knew he had to find out where Toni lived. The solution, although simple, had initially slipped Richard's crowded mind. When Nicole left the clinic, he would tail her. She'd never suspect such a bold, uncharacteristic move.

He arrived in Atlanta at 10:30 p.m. on Saturday. Before unpacking his bags, Richard plugged in his laptop and started researching ways to discreetly tail someone.

On Monday he left the office at 4:30 p.m., not wanting to chance an accident or Nicole leaving early and interfering with his goal. Richard parked on the opposite side of the street from Horizons. His vantage point provided an unobstructed view of the parking lot exit from which Nicole had to make a right turn.

Adrenaline kicked in when he saw her convertible. Richard merged onto the one-way street but not directly behind Nicole. Two blocks away, she plowed through a yellow light. Richard tapped the gear stick while waiting for the signal to turn green and strained to keep her car in sight.

Nicole had continued straight on. Eventually, she took the I-85 southbound ramp. Richard hung back a bit more due to the lighter traffic flow. She exited the expressway and merged onto Langford Parkway. Soon after, Nicole reached her destination.

I did it without you Kevin, Richard told himself as he pulled into the apartment complex. He stayed at the far end of the parking lot adjacent to Toni's building. He wanted to run to her but recognized that would accomplish nothing. She had, after all, rejected his calls.

The stark comparison between his neighborhood and Toni's stunned him considering how Nicole preferred posh settings. Perhaps Nicole sought a lesbian relationship to heal something within her, Richard mused. He'd guide her back to him, the person who should be the one to help her find answers.

Richard let his BMW idle as he glimpsed at Nicole going upstairs. From his vantage point, unfortunately, he saw the building that she'd entered but not the individual unit. Richard's discovery fell short. He had to be a bit stealthier. He saw a flicker coming from one window and wondered if that was the right apartment or if the occurrence may have been a coincidence. Speculating led nowhere because regardless, he could not see the actual unit number.

He contemplated waiting for nightfall and then entering the building. Maybe he'd hear conversations or see something that offered a clue. The lawyer in him ruled out that idea. The odds that Toni would arrive and notice him proved greater. Maybe he'd come to the complex tomorrow and setup surveillance ahead of Nicole's arrival.

He resolved to come by earlier and park two buildings away. He'd move about on foot and wait near the building directly opposite Toni's. From there he'd see exactly where Nicole entered. And once satisfied he'd avoided detection, run upstairs to see the apartment number.

Richard left. At home, he concentrated on nothing but narrowing down Nicole's whereabouts. He decided that coming back in the morning made more sense. Under the veil of darkness he'd draw less attention. Richard set his alarm for 5:30 in hopes of catching one of the women leaving and still reaching work on time.

The alarm proved unnecessary. Richard sprung out of bed like a commando called to action. He dressed in all black and then mentally rehearsed the pending mission as he nibbled on a granola bar. While doing so, an idea dawned on him. He'd investigate online using the information he'd gathered.

Richard accessed a paid website that his colleagues successfully use to get current addresses and so forth. In the search box he typed "Toni," "East Point," and "Willowbrook Lane." The details Richard sought were buried six pages deep. To cross-check his results, Richard replaced the nickname with "Antonia." Again, a listing for unit 219G popped up.

Calipari. That was her last name. When he typed her full name, it garnered no incriminating facts. He did learn that Toni had not furthered her education past high school. That tidbit led him to marvel even more at how she'd managed to outsmart him.

He plugged the address into MapQuest and searched for a nearby florist that sold orchids, Nicole's flower of choice. She'd remarked how they reminded her of exotic, unspoiled places. He scheduled weeklong evening deliveries.

With all his might, Richard attempted to focus on the matters waiting for him at the office. He had a pile of briefs and filings to review. In the middle of every task, he drifted to images of Nicole receiving her orchids. He assumed they'd indicate to his wife and Toni that he intended to fight for her. Richard also anticipated that she'd reach out to him in some form. He checked his personal and work voicemails. He double-checked his emails, including the spam folder. He even looked out for a letter possibly sent by postal mail. His gesture remained unacknowledged.

By Thursday, Richard had driven himself mad. Had the florist delivered the orchids to the wrong apartment or not at all? Had they placed the expensive gift on the doorstep allowing them to be stolen, ignoring his specific instructions to hand-deliver them? He knew one way to find out for sure.

Richard departed his office so quickly that he hadn't logged off his desktop or locked away files containing confidential client information. He'd go back by there on his way home and focus on unfinished tasks. Right now, though, this task's importance outweighed the others.

As he pulled into Toni's complex, Richard spotted her truck. He parked in a spot that allowed him to see her building without being seen. The florist's van arrived well before the agreed upon time. Richard held his breath, as a male, teenage driver bounded up the steps leading to the apartment. He witnessed him handing the orchids to Toni.

"That conniver had outwitted me again," Richard thought. Surely, Toni had either convinced them to bring the flowers earlier or that she was the intended recipient. Either scenario led Richard to suppose that discarding them was Toni's ultimate objective. Thinking of her dumping them in the trash, literally throwing away money, sickened him as much as her spitefulness did.

He directed his anger at the steering wheel, slamming his hand down with such force that it split his skin. He refused to let Toni win, to let her further widen the rift between him and *his* wife. Toni clearly controlled Nicole, but she couldn't be by her side every minute. Richard switched his mode of attack accordingly.

When the flowers arrived at the clinic on Friday, they caught Nicole off guard. She gave the first bouquet to a patient who needed her spirits uplifted. The second went to Jill. By the end of the next week, Nicole grew tired of dodging his calls and forcing Jill to take messages.

Toni initially predicted Richard would concede and quietly allow his wife to decide who she really wanted. His persistence amazed them both. Nicole's love for her husband hadn't disappeared although it receded. She wanted to remain amicable, but she had no intentions of trying to reconcile.

The verdict exhilarated Toni. She said Nicole deserved a clean break. The baby inside of her kept that reality from occurring even with its secret existence. She wondered if Toni caught the subliminal message in her proclamation. She wondered if Toni truly had the ability to raise Richard's child, especially if it came out looking like him.

She knew he loved her, which caused her unimaginable anxiety. She wondered if her inability to bond with their unborn child stemmed from her desire to forge a path without Richard in the equation.

Once Nicole had allowed herself to consider the prospect, she'd grown certain that she belonged with Toni. Richard had a completeness about him, but with him she felt incomplete. Instincts told her that he'd provide for her and their child in every way. Still, he wasn't Toni.

As Toni informed her repeatedly, Nicole had options. Nicole and Toni could raise the child together with Toni exerting a valiant effort to accept Richard's offspring as her own. She could also abort the fetus and upset Richard and his family, namely his God-fearing mother, if she chose to inform them. Or, she could give the child to a barren couple, all the while wondering if the child would pop up years later demanding a reunion. The adoption route would cause her parents more shame than they claimed she already brought upon them by abandoning her vows. The avenues available proved overwhelming not because there were so many, but because of the implications and gravity of each choice.

Who would she please: Richard, his family, Toni, or her parents? Nicole ultimately sought to satisfy herself instead of losing herself in the expectations of others.

Richard called again as Nicole headed home for the weekend. She kept the conversation short and to the point, reluctantly agreeing to meet for lunch on Tuesday. She'd made her decision. Everyone else would have to live with it.

Toni accompanied Nicole to the clinic, buried inconspicuously within a small cluster of one-story medical offices. The gold plaque on the entrance door read: "Ainsworth and Associates." Nicole learned that there were no associates, only a skeleton crew similar to the one at her job.

No one tried talking Nicole out of her decision. Her concentration faded in and out as a nurse outlined the procedure. She hesitated before signing the consent form. Nicole had ventured down this road as a teenager and never imagined she'd end up in such a predicament again. In her youth, Nicole could not muster facing her parents with news of an unplanned pregnancy or its termination. While Catholicism shunned using birth control, it also shunned fornication. She heard whispers of relatives and church members whose children had fallen from grace. "I'm too young to be a grandma," Mrs. Erickson joked once.

Nicole knew her parents placed her on a pedestal. She did what she had to do to avoid shaming them and herself. That ultimate decision proved no easier than the one she now made. Back then, the baby's father dumped Nicole as soon as she revealed that he'd be a dad. His proclamations of adoration fell to the wayside so quickly that his dismissal sent Nicole reeling. She confided in a female friend who became her first and only female lover. She stood by Nicole's side as Toni did today.

As difficult as the moment felt, Nicole dreaded alerting Richard and her parents even more. "I won't think any less of you if you don't tell him," Toni said. "Them not knowing might be best for us all."

"I'm done with secrets," Nicole responded.

Three weeks, five days, and 19 hours had passed since Richard learned the woman he loved had fallen in love with another woman. Waiting for her arrival proved excruciating. Nicole had insisted on the Varsity as their rendezvous point. Richard considered the choice odd, given that the historic drive-in themed eatery specialized in greasy hot dogs, burgers, and sides. As the minutes ticked by, it dawned on him that the restaurant made perfect sense. It buzzed with activity, so she'd feel safe there. The chatter also proved loud enough to keep strangers from overhearing their conversation. Most of all, the menu geared guests toward short lunches rather than long leisurely ones.

"She's trying to dump me," Richard thought, "to cast me off like some fling. I'm not going to let that happen. I'll convince her we're meant for each other."

He'd come armed with a fresh haircut, a noticeable dose of the cologne that she'd claimed made him irresistible, and with a steadfast determination no argument against them reuniting could shake him. Richard harbored no desire to assign blame. Both of their actions had led them to this moment.

Nicole showed up nearly 10 minutes late, sporting a new pair of boots that added several inches to her height and wearing a white down, sleeveless vest that she kept on despite the restaurant's warmth. The wind outside had blown wisps of her hair loose from her ponytail. Nicole's blank expression provided no hints. Dark spots under her eyes led him to believe she struggled with her consciousness.

Oh, how he missed her. "I ordered you some tea," Richard said. He slid the drink across the table.

"Thank you," she said, pulling the red and white paper cup closer to her without looking in his eyes.

He immediately noticed the absence of her wedding band, but he continued without making any mention of it. "Are you ready to order?"

She smiled politely. "We should talk."

Richard repositioned himself in the hard, metal chair. "I'm not looking for an apology, but…."

"I wasn't planning on giving one," Nicole interrupted.

Richard rubbed his temples and glanced at her with pleading eyes. "Every marriage goes through phases. Just tell me how we repair this."

"We don't."

He was taken aback by her coldness.

"I owe it to myself to explore my feelings for Toni."

Veins popped in his forehead. "You're my wife. You don't get to explore."

"What I am or about to be," she countered, "is free, and you can't cage me." She reached into her purse and retrieved what he recognized as a legal document.

He stared incredulously at the divorce papers. "We made a promise before God."

"Your God, not mine," she snapped loud enough for people from other tables to look over at them.

Those words wounded him like shrapnel, but soon he'd feel even worse. A hush fell over them as a fellow diner ventured close to their table to examine them up close, peering at them with a judgmental smirk. Nicole continued once the man moved past. "I was pregnant until a few days ago."

Richard gripped the table and stared at Nicole as if she'd just revealed her true self.

"Toni and I thought it best that I have an abortion."

His eyes bulged. He sprang to his feet and yelled, "How could *you* decide anything about something that was ours?"

Nicole slid her chair back. "You don't control my uterus!"

"*We* made a baby, not you and Toni!"

By now, they'd garnered the attention of everyone close by.

He reached over and grabbed her arm. She jerked it loose and turned on her heels.

A cashier with a Mohawk whose arms and legs were swollen masses of muscle, blocked Richard from following Nicole out the door. "Let her go," he said.

Richard flung a $100 bill at him. "Get out of my way!"

The man followed Richard as he followed Nicole, weaving past patio tables and carhops to reach the parking area. In the frenzy, Richard unknowingly passed a police officer. The cashier motioned for him to lend assistance. The officer jogged toward Richard and told him to stop. Meanwhile, Nicole kept heading for her automobile. Richard ignored the officer and kept after her, shouting, "I'm not breaking the law. This is my wife. I just want to talk to her."

He knew better than to grab or even touch her. He just kept following her because he wanted to talk about their marriage and the baby.

"I don't want to be your wife anymore," she shouted without turning around to face him. "I'm done talking too. The cashier then jostled his way in between them, allowing Nicole to get in her car and drive out the lot. The cashier stood in front of Richard, and the officer stood behind him, blocking his motion.

By now, a crowd had gathered, watching to see the next scene unfold. Some talked loudly so Richard could hear. "I bet they take his ass to jail," said one woman.

"Why you always downing the man?" said the younger man with her.

Richard stood calmly, facing the officer, who was noticeably angry. With the cashier still standing guard, the officer asked for Richard's driver's license.

He explained that it was in his car, but he was lying. He needed to get his cell phone out the car. He had left it there so his meeting with Nicole would be uninterrupted.

The officer followed Richard to his car while radioing for back up. "No need for all that," explained Richard. "I'm a lawyer. I was just trying to have lunch with my wife." Ignoring him, the officer continued talking.

Once in the car, Richard pretended to get his license out the center console near his phone. He turned his back slightly to shield the fact that he was reaching in his pocket. "Here it is," he said turning to give it to the officer. He called Kevin immediately after.

"I need you to come over to the Varsity now," he said in a low voice. "Things didn't go well with Nicole, and I got a cop standing next to me." His friend was on duty but promised to arrive soon. Meanwhile, he advised Richard to remain calm and obey the officer.

Once Kevin hung up, Richard put the phone in his suit pocket and placed his hands on the dashboard, in plain view.

"Everybody back," the officer ordered. He approached Richard's driver's side window.

"Out of the car!" the officer commanded. "Keep those hands where I can see them."

Richard gradually lifted his hands off the dashboard and stepped out of the car.

"Do you have any weapons, contraband, or needles on you?"

"No, I told you that I'm a lawyer."

The officer kept his eyes trained on Richard's hands and maintained a cautious distance, still regarding him with suspicion. "Slow and steady, place your palms on the trunk." He handcuffed Richard and then patted him down. Finally, he allowed Richard to turn around once he retrieved his wallet and cell phone. With Richard restrained, he went to his squad car to check Richard's license for warrants.

After nearly 15 minutes, the officer returned, as two other

officers were approaching the scene. Richard frantically began recounting what had ignited all the commotion, providing more details than the officer needed. He told him about Toni and the abortion. With that, the officer seemed to loosen up, listening almost sympathetically.

"You of all people should know not to approach someone who doesn't want to be bothered," he said when Richard finished. "Wife or not."

"I didn't touch her. I have plenty of witnesses here to prove it."

"All she needs to say is that she felt threatened or afraid, and she can get some judge to grant her a protective order or maybe even a warrant for your arrest."

Before Richard could continue to plead his innocence, the officer interrupted, "Man, if you love your freedom as much as her, you need to just stay away from her – at least for now."

Across the parking lot, Richard noticed Kevin driving toward them in his squad car. "My friend is here," Richard announced.

The officer turned to see Kevin emerging from his car. Kevin cast a friendly grin toward the officers without having any communication with Richard. The four men convened in a circle for nearly five minutes. Richard tried hard to hear what they were saying or determine which direction the conversation was going based on their body language. He relaxed once he saw the four men chuckling and Kevin pat the officer next to him on the back.

The officer walked up to Richard and removed the handcuffs. He never said anything to Richard as he walked back to his car with the two other officers in tow.

"How did it feel to have someone be your attorney?" Kevin asked.

Richard's head hung low as he barely mouthed, "I appreciate you showing up so fast."

"Guess Nicole hit you with a double-whammy. Believe me, I would've gone off, too. We'll talk about it later, though. I gotta head back to the precinct."

Richard nodded weakly as emotional exhaustion set in. Nicole's bombshell had whittled away at his psyche and slaughtered the prospect of a blissful future.

Her ex, Nicole supposed, had a right to his visceral reaction. She, too, bore scars, even if Richard considered her forthrightness callous. Mr. and Mrs. Erikson distanced themselves after she moved in with Toni. Nicole imagined that they and Richard held out hope for reconciliation. Sharing the abortion with Richard provided the nudge he needed to move on. Doing so caused Nicole to relive the equivalent discussion she had with her parents. She wondered if they could move on and ever again see her in the same light as before. Instead of doting, Nicole sensed distress in every interaction. She wanted to heal their relationship but didn't know how to please them without hiding her true self.

For the remainder of the day, each second seemed like an eternity. A hollow, cold sensation crept over Richard as he grappled with the complexity of his emotions. He took what seemed like an eternity to complete the simplest processes. In anticipation of missing work on Wednesday, Richard doled out assignments and collected files he needed to review, planning to do so at home. He should've stayed late, but he left at 5 p.m. on the dot.

That evening, he continued to avoid his mother's calls and Kevin's texts. Not speaking to them let Richard emotionally sort through and mentally replay the recent developments. Mrs. Knight knew of the scheduled meeting with Nicole, and Richard recognized she sought to check in for an update.

He marveled at how he'd become a character trapped in

this soap opera and reflected on where he had been less than a year ago. He wished he had magical powers and could transport himself back to the pre-Nicole era. Then, he led a lonely existence, consisting mostly of him hunkering down in his one-bedroom apartment. He'd rather return to that period when he was consumed with work, dedicated to his church, and experienced drama only through Kevin's exploits or his mother's family tales.

Richard dozed off in his leather recliner. Relentless, fragmented images of the unformed embryo his wife had snuffed out overpowered him. He tossed about, waking periodically. When daybreak came, he gave up on the possibility of rest. His muscles ached, but his heart ached more. Richard remained stoic, stuck in that chair as if secured by chains. He left it only to use the bathroom and to fix a piece of toast, the quickest and least complicated meal he could throw together.

By midday, Mrs. Knight showed up at his doorstep.

"Good heavens!" she exclaimed upon greeting her son.

He wore crumpled sweatpants and a long-sleeved Braves t-shirt that had a jelly stain on it. "What are you doing here, ma?"

He dreaded going about the difficult task of explaining that his mother's first-born grandchild had been aborted. Richard always thought that his sister would be the first to have a child because she was still dating, although not married to, her high school sweetheart. After nearly seven years, his sister was basically living with her boyfriend, Earl, but no one would admit to it, for Mrs. Knight's sake. She thought her children were physically and morally perfect, and no one dared to challenge that notion, not even her children.

She raised an eyebrow. "You didn't return my calls. Then I find out you skipped work. It doesn't take a rocket scientist to figure out things went south with Nicole."

They gazed at each other, communicating silently.

"Tell me everything," she said, softening her tone.

She followed him to the sofa where Richard revealed Nicole's merciless actions. Richard's voice shook while he unloaded his sorrows. Tears welled up in his eyes and hers.

"Come stay with me for a while," Mrs. Knight proposed.

"I don't get it," he said. "How could she do this? How could she think it was okay?"

"I don't know, son. Apparently, she's not thinking straight. Maybe that Toni character talked her into it."

"Nicole knew how much I wanted kids. She claimed she did, too." He let out a long, guttural sigh.

"Trouble don't last always," his mother whispered. "This too shall pass."

At that, Richard began weeping the way no man wants to in the presence of a woman. He forsook any pride he had and released wailing that his mother could hardly curtail with her reassurances and hugs. She held him, but she hid a transgression of her own.

Chapter 8

The holiday season brought no tidings of comfort or joy for Richard. He skipped the annual office party, and instead of buying Christmas gifts for Kevin, his mother, and his sister, he purchased various gift cards from a grocery store kiosk. They, in turn, showered him with presents aimed at lifting his morale. The gifts, however, remained in their original packages, unopened beyond the point of being unwrapped.

Richard simply wanted the season and the well-wishers to ignore his existence. He literally counted down the days from Christmas Eve to New Year's, when all the "happiness hoopla" would be over and he didn't have to pretend that he was content. His one last, prevailing social commitment was attending New Year's night church service, which he knew that his mother would not overlook or forgive his absence. At Mrs. Knight's request, even Pam was flying in to celebrate or, better yet, to help Richard recover.

Worshippers around him immersed themselves in Reverend Peters' New Year's Eve sermon regarding forgiveness as a prerequisite for reaching paradise and finding enjoyment on Earth. They uttered "amen," "hmmm," and "well." Richard, in contrast, cursed Toni and Nicole. He viewed them as the devil's pawns and yearned for their damnation.

He struggled to absorb Reverend Peters' message. His mother, who sat with the usher board, nodded in agreement with the reverend and periodically glanced Richard's way. He would politely nod, but several times, he motioned his head toward Pam, his sister, who sat in the row in front of him with Earl. For once, Richard wanted his mother to be just as concerned about his sister's life as she currently was with his. He wanted some of the attention off him, at least momentarily.

Mrs. Knight's devotion to the Lord allowed her to attest that Richard's tribulations had a purpose although currently unknown. Richard realized he lacked the conviction his mother possessed about overcoming any obstacle with faith and time. He had never faced anything similar to this, so he didn't have a point of reference to suggest that he could overcome something like abortion and divorce.

Besides Nicole, his only true love, other than his mother, had been his career. Although he dated intermittently since law school, Nicole was only his second "real" girlfriend. Richard dated the same girl, Danielle Holmes, throughout college and two years of law school, but they both admitted that the distance had put too much of a strain on their relationship. Danielle stayed in Atlanta to complete her graduate studies while Richard went to Georgetown to attend law school. Richard thought about reconnecting with her after graduation, but he decided against it when Pam told him that she had seen Danielle pregnant while shopping in Perimeter Mall. As they casually exchanged friendly glances and waves, Pam said she tried hard to see if Danielle had a wedding ring on her finger, but the shopping bags in her left hand obscured Pam's view. She wanted to make conversation, but Danielle was talking on her cell phone and navigating toward the parking lot through a crowd of people in the food court. Richard occasionally thought about her but never felt compelled or, better yet, courageous enough to go by her parents' house. He certainly would not be going by there anytime soon, especially with the news of his three-month marriage and his wife leaving him for another woman.

Reverend Peters initiated an altar call, asking that all those who needed healing of any kind to come up toward the pulpit for prayer. Fellow church members lined up in the aisles, but Richard remained seated. At that moment, he decided that he was going to officially resign his Sunday school teaching post. He felt ill-equipped to mentor and guide his former pupils in the manner they deserved. Primarily, Richard feared his sourness might taint the lessons, as it had other areas of his life.

An introvert by nature, Richard slipped further into isolation. He ate lunch in his office, barely spoke beyond conversation necessary to facilitate business, and sent associates to client conferences instead of handling them himself. Richard despised that his marital issues forced him to render public information he regarded as private. One paralegal speculated outright that the newlywed acted the opposite of blissful. Someone else noted the disappearance of Nicole's photograph from Richard's desk. He caught Mr. Smythe glimpsing his barren wedding band finger. His superior's demeanor changed afterwards.

Well-meaning coworkers spoke in hushed tones or stopped speaking all together when he drew closer. Richard caught snippets of their conversations. He had no use for pity. He also had no intention of broadcasting his split from Nicole. When Goldstein joined him in an elevator one afternoon, he unknowingly led Richard to open up about his personal affairs. He mentioned discussing HIV and AIDS-related charitable ventures with Nicole. At that point, Richard had to disclose his separation and the unavoidable, pending divorce.

Maintaining a respectful distance, Goldstein offered his sympathies without probing into the complexities that led to Richard's decision. He did, however, refer Richard to a colleague who specialized in family law. Retaining another firm would inevitably subject him to constant probing by that staff. Richard opted instead to represent himself. He assured himself that would lead to the most discreet and expeditious conclusion. Besides, he wished to rehash Nicole's betrayal as little as possible. Serving as his own counsel, despite Goldstein's implication that doing so may not result in the best outcome, provided a means of making that happen.

When he'd originally pursued a legal career, Richard fathomed the various business-related litigation avenues available for pursuit but purposefully steered clear of family law. He theorized that the deep-seated roots binding relatives caused most lawyers headaches beyond measure. That area of law comprised more than legalities. It entailed love, hate, jealousies and a spectrum of sentiments in between. In the real estate realm, especially the commercial division where Richard garnered the majority of his assignments, such reactions rarely came into play.

In preparation for the bar exam, he studied the dissolution of marriages. He forgot the basics long ago. Even in the wildest recesses of his imagination, Richard had not accounted for the possibility that he'd revisit this information. Whereas his confidence in other areas lagged, Richard remained certain he could conquer the ins and outs of handling his divorce. He spent the last few weeks squaring away the details of that undertaking and used the Fulton County Bar Association's web resources as a blueprint.

Remarkably, Nicole had filed an uncontested divorce petition and listed her affair as the primary reason their relationship dissolved. Richard saw no reason to contest. He met periodically with her attorney, Edgar Corporan, to draft their financial disclosures, marital settlement agreement, and other required documents.

The main task requiring completion, in Richard's opinion, had been arranging for Nicole to pick up her belongings. They decided on this Saturday, while Richard was attending service, for Nicole to come by. Her belongings crowded their home like tombstones. He grew tired of looking at her sofa, her dining room table, her dishes in the pantry. Most definitely, he resented her using the home as a storage unit.

To avoid them, Richard camped out in the entertainment area and two guest bedrooms, where she exiled most of his furniture after they'd moved in together. Outside home, he sought solace at either his mother's home, where she indulged him with homemade meals, or he stayed at work until late, sometimes midnight. Often, he requested that the receptionist hold his calls, and then he would lock his office door so he could partake in the restful sleep that otherwise eluded him at home.

He cringed thinking his wife and her lover were rummaging through remnants of their time together. Attorney Corporan assured him Nicole would remove only those items listed as hers. Experience had taught Richard to distrust her, so he snapped digital pictures of their home's contents and emailed a copy to himself.

Georgia law required a 30-day waiting period for divorce approvals. Due to the backlog in cases, theirs would not appear on the docket until the end of January. Richard dreaded the limbo the delay caused. He wanted to cease all reservations, to shake his disbelief that the coming year would usher in better fortune than the previous one, but he couldn't surrender to the possibility of new beginnings until his marriage officially ended.

Almost 60 days after their last meeting, Richard had to brace himself to see Nicole, but hopefully not Toni, in court for the final divorce decree. Richard and his support system, consisting of his mother and Kevin, arrived at the Fulton County Courthouse well ahead schedule because he planned on being seated when Nicole and possibly Toni strutted in the courtroom. They had all met at Mrs. Knight's home, where she cooked breakfast for everyone. The hearty meal satisfied Kevin, but Richard nibbled on a piece of bacon and a miniscule portion of scrambled eggs. He did, however, finish his chamomile tea to ease his jittery body. He also meditated silently to ease the anxiousness swelling within him.

The trio listened to contested cases in which petitioners dished dirt that should've remained buried. Still, none of the purported antics and allegations ranked close to the behavior Nicole had displayed during the disassembling of their marriage.

In their last discussion Mr. Corporan had assured Richard that the hearing would garner no unexpected motions, and that his client sought an equitable distribution of assets. Nicole, he said, indicated a willingness to severe ties by restoring each party to a pre-marital state. Reluctantly, Richard agreed to buy Nicole out and to refinance the home in order to remove her name from the loan and deed. The other option would have been selling the property and splitting the proceeds.

Richard lacked the stamina to survive another move. Staying in the residence, even factoring in the inevitable flashbacks involving his soon-to-be ex, seemed an easier alternative. Long ago, he pictured himself living in an affluent area in a real home. He refused to let her rip that dream from him, too. Without Nicole's income, he'd have to buckle down on his spending and return to the frugalness he abandoned upon meeting her.

Nicole's complacency during the negotiations struck him as less than admirable. Richard perceived his wife as a coward who struck a devastating and deliberate blow and then ran off without suffering a single consequence for her recklessness.

The same-sex couple sauntered in as if they were attending a matinee instead of a legal proceeding. Toni donned her usual crew cut, but Nicole shocked him. Her once long, blonde hair was now a fiery-red, shoulder-length bob with a bang that fell just above her eyes. From her hair to her Bohemian attire, Nicole permeated her new alternative lifestyle. The only thing that Richard recognized as the same about his wife was her steel-blue eyes. Once seated, Toni and Nicole snuggled close to each other. Nicole leaned toward Toni, who periodically whispered in her ear. His wife never glanced his way. Toni, on the contrary, glanced back and scanned the courtroom until she spotted Richard.

Toni flashed a twisted, perverse grin that showed teeth reminiscent of fangs. Her expression said, "You feeble fool."

The room grew suddenly stuffy. Richard speculated how Nicole remained oblivious to the evil emitting from her watchdog's core.

"That's who she left you for?" his mother asked. "I imagined someone…"

"Hotter," Kevin interjected.

"Uh-huh."

"Looks like Nicole's officially crossed over to lesbian land," his mother said.

Kevin chuckled.

Richard glowered at his friend and his mother. He barely recognized his wife and kicked himself for falling for her. His emotional barometer fluctuated between hatred and heartbreak even as the reality set in fully that she'd moved on.

He figured that Nicole's parents' traditional leanings conflicted drastically with their daughter's transformation. Perhaps, Richard speculated, they dealt by analyzing it as a phase. If so, he absolutely connected with the urge to rationalize. Had Nicole informed them that she aborted their baby without his knowledge? Had she taken the same rebellious tone with them that she had with him?

Each of Toni's contemptuous leers raised Richard's frustration level. She behaved as if immunity prevented Nicole from disposing of her the way she had him. Eventually, one or both women would commit treachery. He visualized that instance containing a hefty dose of deceit.

Richard had contemplated suing Toni for alienation of affection but presumed he'd lose more than the effort warranted. She possessed no viable assets from what he observed. By his calculations, Toni owed him more than she'd be able to repay even if she forked over every cent of her earnings from now until the day she retired. He pegged her as the type who'd file bankruptcy to sidestep her obligations. Most assuredly, she'd use his pursuit of justice as further ammunition against him.

The honorable Marsha Zimmerman's bailiff finally requested the parties in Knight v. Knight. Each moved to their respective places while she scanned their documents.

Richard unbuttoned his shirt collar.

"The petitioner and respondent agree on adultery as the grounds," she said, peering over her spectacles.

"Yes," both attorneys replied in unison.

Suddenly, the perception of strangers mattered to Richard. They probably assume I'm the one who cheated, he told himself.

"Property distribution has been set. Everything appears quite amicable."

She deserves less than what I'm giving her, Richard thought. He glanced at Nicole. Her smugness nearly forced his unruffled composure to fall by the wayside.

"I'll grant restoration of Mrs. Knight's maiden name."

It irked him that Nicole portrayed herself as a cooperative party who'd fallen for someone other than her spouse when actually she was a murderer of the lowest form.

"Child support is a nonissue," the judge noted.

"That's correct, thanks to my lawfully wedded wife." He hadn't intended to say that aloud.

The onlookers directed their attention his way.

"Excuse me?"

"I really just want my freedom," Nicole blurted out.

Judge Zimmerman looked confused.

"She killed my baby!" Richard exclaimed. "She told me about the abortion afterwards. There should be some sort of retribution for that."

"The law allows for a woman to do with *her* body as she sees fit."

"Even the ancient Romans took fathers' rights into consideration."

"We live in the modern age, Mr. Knight. This is not a forum for arguing constitutionality."

He inched closer to the bench; the bailiff inched closer to him.

The judge banged her gavel. "Persist, Mr. Knight, and I will hold you in contempt."

Richard retreated to his original spot.

"Back to the business at hand," Judge Zimmerman continued.

It clicked with Richard that the judge would disregard any argument he presented. He pretended to listen obediently as the proceedings concluded.

The bailiff escorted Nicole and Toni out and then allowed Richard and his party to exit. They congregated in the hallway. Richard wanted to flee the scene of his flogging, but his mother and Kevin wanted to recount the showdown.

Richard stood beside them but floated in and out of their conversation.

"Don't be all doom and gloom," Kevin quipped. "At least you got out of paying alimony."

His mother echoed the sentiment.

Their lack of tact floored him. Richard stared at them blankly while they continued.

"Can you imagine putting up with Nicole for 18 years, maybe longer?" Kevin went on. The comment underscored his friend's perception of women as disposable. Richard believed that his friend probably participated in the disposal of at least one unwanted pregnancy, and it probably never bothered him.

Richard turned to leave, assuming they'd follow. Justice may have escaped him here, but he'd find it somewhere.

Chapter 9

Finalizing the divorce left a void. With that hurdle behind him, Richard's suppressed feelings clawed their way to the surface and fought for recognition. He replayed the hearing and increasingly grew agitated by the judge's nonchalant comments. The greatest obstacle: halting the images of Toni and Nicole plotting to destroy the baby that had been growing inside her.

Exactly one week had passed since Richard and Nicole severed ties officially. He immersed himself in distracting activities: reading crime novels and watching DVDs of TV shows. Jogging had morphed from a relaxing experience to another opportunity for him to concentrate on all that ailed him. Although he spent more time in the office, remarkably, he completed less work. An untouched legal brief rested on his desk right now. He intended to complete it upon first arriving in the office four hours prior.

He formulated different scenarios, knowing full well that rehashing how they rationalized and normalized the abortion was akin to running in an endless marathon. Toni and Nicole made it clear that they considered the episode an insignificant blip.

Richard, unlike the callous women who altered the landscape of his life, found it difficult to toss aside one of God's creations. In that secret place, he retreated to where hope reigned. Richard trusted that Nicole bore some scars, even if she kept them hidden. Nicole would face the gravity of her indiscretions, he believed, when she took her last breath. Between now and then, he wished misery upon her.

Nicole told Judge Zimmerman that she wanted nothing but her freedom, but she'd already taken everything.

She left him to bear the burden of a confusing process. With Nicole's medical background, she surely understood the mechanics of abortion. He researched the procedure online. Due to varying clandestine practices, however, concrete information proved hard to acquire. Besides, he had no inkling whatsoever of which clinic Nicole chose.

The entire process perplexed Richard. He dealt in generalities, discovering methods but coming up with no information that satisfied him. Smuggled photographs showing a portion of the horrific aftermath caused him to recoil. Deciphering factual information from fanatical speculation added an unanticipated aspect to Richard's quest for understanding. He wondered if someone at the clinic tried to talk Nicole out of her decision or if money overruled decency. What happened to the embryo? Did the clinic staff literally dispose of it along with medical waste? Did anyone show it the respect due to a living being?

"Who chooses performing abortions as a career path?" Richard thought. "How did anyone possessing some semblance of spirituality reconcile the act?" He realized abortion served a slight purpose, such as in cases of rape, incest, or danger to the mother's health. However, he considered the standard of acceptance in the United States entirely too low. He knew from keeping abreast of current events that some medical facilities received government grants. It sickened Richard that politicians allocated a portion of his tax dollars toward such debauchery.

Richard remembered early one Saturday morning as he and Nicole lay in bed when a Catholic priest on a cable talk show said, "A woman's right doesn't mean she is doing the right thing by having an abortion."

Nicole started talking about how many of the women at the clinic where she works should probably have an abortion. She and Richard got into a debate that cast them at opposite ends of the spectrum on the issue. Nicole was clearly pro-choice and Richard pro-life. The only thing that ended the debate was Nicole playfully taping Richard on butt, pretending to spank him if he didn't agree with her. After a playful wrestling session, they ended up under the covers exchanging sensual groans rather than words.

She'd taken up residency with Toni, but Nicole still controlled Richard's actions to some extent. Rather than focusing on important tasks, Richard created memories that did not exist, memories that Nicole and Toni tore from the realm of possibility.

He consistently pictured the child as a carbon copy of him with a splash of Nicole mixed in. Of course, he would have been well-behaved and the envy of other parents. Junior would have possessed Richard's and Nicole's best qualities. He would have struck perfect balance between Richard's methodical, studious nature and Nicole's spontaneous streak, along with her zeal for helping the downtrodden. Whatever profession he chose to pursue, Junior would have climbed the ranks quickly, due in part to inherited intellect and determination.

Before marriage, they spoke of having at least two children and creating a stable family life. Richard speculated if some act on his part had repulsed Nicole so that she ended a life rather than continued forging one with him. Generally, Nicole had avoided discussing past boyfriends but opened up briefly on one of their initial dates. They hadn't treated her the way she deserved to be treated, Nicole told Richard. She admitted a pattern of relinquishing too much control, which resulted in staying with men who, upon retrospect, had been unworthy of the effort she exerted toward the relationships.

A guy named Benito Bryant, or "Bennie," did call once while they were out at the theater. Nicole explained how she had abruptly ended it with him three months before she met Richard. Ignoring his repeated calls and attempts for closure, she figured Bennie would've stopped calling by then. When Richard asked about why he would still be calling after so long, Nicole said, "I have no idea because he should have seen it coming. His idea of spending time together was making sure I was 'tuned up' regularly." Nicole noticed the puzzled look on Richard's face and continued, saying, "Bennie owned a foreign car repair and sales business, so that's the way he would say it. He thought that getting me a car was enough to control me and keep me happy." With a cavalier shrug, she said nothing else about him that night or ever again.

During their courtship, Richard assumed he had gotten all the pieces right. Now, Richard questioned his manhood and his intelligence. Had Nicole played him all along? Did she and Toni partake in a fling without it registering on his radar? The second-guessing and mental rehearsal mimicked madness. He was irked when he thought of each time Nicole vigorously defended Toni. Now, he regarded those moments as glaring warning signs he chose to circumvent. Nicole's guilty conscience obviously caused her to snap whenever he pointed out Toni's shortcomings. He let Nicole convince him that paranoia prompted him to find faults with Toni's actions, such as encouraging his fiancée to smoke weed and to hang out at seedy clubs. He also allowed Nicole to twist his words while ignoring the antagonizing undertone of Toni's comments. Instead of giving her the benefit of the doubt, he should have questioned why Nicole concerned herself with Toni's hurt feelings rather than siding with him.

In an attempt to get clarity on Nicole's romantic past with men or even women, Richard toyed with the idea of locating and contacting Bennie. After several days of constantly thinking about it, he searched online to locate a Benito Foreign Car Sales and Service in Hayward, California, near where Nicole had lived. He dialed the number, but hung up when he heard a woman's voice announce the name of the business. He shrunk back in his seat in shame, shaking his head in a symbolic attempt to shake off the extent to which his obsession had propelled him. "That poor guy must have gone through the same thing I am," thought Richard, "But at least he didn't have to do it with Toni involved." He doubted Nicole possessed the ability to commit to anyone, male or female. He doubted she had guilt about any of her "victims."

His thoughts fueled with memories – real and imagined – of the past, present and future, Richard felt he could now understand the heartache of parents who'd lost their child for various reasons. One night, he had a dream so vivid that it felt as if he had only ever existed in that time and space.

The luminosity enveloped Richard. It provided him with a sense of peace he hadn't felt in what seemed an eternity. Still, the calmness fell short. He needed more.

As he lay there waiting, anticipating, he sensed a shift. His heart felt a little lighter. In the distance, a steady white streak began providing further illumination. A force urged him forward. He needed to move forward, but he couldn't.

Richard saw a child in the distance. As the child drew closer, his surroundings grew clearer, revealing a brilliant landscape bursting with magnificent colors and grandeur incomparable to any earthly marvel. Wondrous waterfalls spilled over pristine mountain peaks. Even the clouds emitted radiance. Richard had glimpsed his destination, but he wanted to see more of it, especially the person moving toward him.

As he wished, the face of the child became more apparent. The small, dark, piercing eyes now staring at Richard remained fixed. They beckoned. They questioned.

The child mustered a quizzical but familiar smile, the same smile that Nicole often wore so long ago. "Junior," called Richard, but the child vanished, leaving only a light that shone brighter than the surroundings.

"No!" Richard screamed, wanting to get a closer glimpse and communicate with the child. He tried to stand. All attempts failed. He looked down and discovered a sparkling, silver chain wrapped around his ankle.

Richard tugged at the chain. A sharp, stinging sensation immediately radiated from his fingertips to his arms and his chest. Richard grasped his chest. The relentless pain intensified. Tremors traveled throughout his body.

Deflated and defeated, Richard bowed his head. Then he saw Nicole beneath him, looking up at him from the darkness. The shadows surrounding her held no comfort. It was the blackest black Richard had ever seen. Its energy held no promise.

Legions surrounded her with their faces obscured and their cries intensifying.

Nicole stood in a rocky pit that was spewing pillars and thick billows of smoke. "Save me," she called out. Nicole's smile had faded. Her features appeared haggard, ghastly. Her skin withered with the weight of it all. Richard barely recognized the physical form before him, but he recognized her spirit. That connection remained despite Nicole's attempts to sever it.

Nicole didn't have to ask twice. Richard reached below. What seemed within reach was instead an endless distance that made grabbing her hand impossible. Richard couldn't save her. He couldn't save himself. His burden was heavy.

He would memorialize Junior, but he longed to delete Nicole from his memories. Even routine tasks were becoming challenging. Whenever he was in the grocery store and had to walk past the baby aisle, Richard would purposely avoid it or refocus his attention on something else to ignore his peripheral view of pampers and baby wipes. Every night he went to bed thinking about Nicole's betrayal and the baby. Before this, his last thoughts before bed were usually about his most important tasks at work the next day. Richard couldn't foresee gains in his life, for obsession with his loss gripped him. He knew he needed to get help.

One afternoon at work, Richard pulled out his cell phone and started searching for some sort of organization or 12-step program that could offer guidance. He initially entered the keywords "men abortion counseling." To his surprise, it read, "No results found for 'men abortion counseling.'" Then he tried "pregnancy centers." This search yielded close to 200,000 results. Nearly every link involved pregnancy options for women. Sitting in a group of women held no appeal for Richard, but that seemed like his only option.

He called ten centers that offered abortion counseling. The first nine counseling groups outright told him "no men are allowed." One group facilitator explained, "These women don't want to see a man in the group. Most of them blame a man for their grief and loss, so you would be a stark remainder of their pain."

His persistence paid off when the last center reluctantly agreed Richard could attend private counseling, but not the support group. Overjoyed that he could talk to someone who might understand his pain, Richard set an appointment for the first available slot, which was the next day at 4 p.m. He would have to leave work early, but he didn't mind.

He arrived 20 minutes early to the Pregnancy Recovery Center. As expected, he was the only man there. The women who walked past glanced at him quizzically as if they needed an explanation for his presence. Richard responded with polite, wince-like smiles. Even with phones ringing and people walking past, Richard felt lonely. He had called Nicole that morning and asked her to come, but she didn't return his call. When he sent her a text message, she responded, saying, "I don't need this kind of help. Good luck."

"You're either lying or in denial," Richard wrote. To that, there was no reply. Trying again, he wrote, "Would you do it for me? I need this."

Richard stared at his phone for nearly 10 minutes before a female voice broke his fixation. A tall slender woman walked up to him and said, "You must be Richard."

"I am," was all he could say.

"I'm Sharon Murphy," she said, extending her left hand.

"You're a lefty, too," Richard said, trying to soothe his own nerves with a quip.

Richard followed Sharon into a dimly-lit room with a pink accent wall. The other walls were covered with old-fashioned floral wallpaper that was beginning to peel at the seams. Richard noticed green crayon marks near the bottom of the pink wall. There were no file cabinets, only a portable folding table sitting off to the right with brochures and manila folders with handouts. Sharon's desk looked like the only piece of nearly new or modern furniture in the room. Her faux cherry wood desk had a planner and two family photos with Sharon, her husband and two small children. Richard immediately noticed the two children's bright blue eyes and blonde hair, which reminded him of the pictures he saw of Nicole as child. He sat in the center of an olive-green loveseat across from her desk.

Wasting no time after being seated, Sharon said, "Where is *she*?"

"She isn't interested in coming."

"I think your girlfriend may be in denial."

"My wife. Well, ex-wife," Richard interrupted.

"How long has it been?"

"If you mean the abortion, it happened in early December. If you mean the end of my marriage, two weeks ago."

"This is very unusual for a man to come in a pregnancy center alone. In fact, I don't think I've ever seen a man request abortion counseling and especially so soon after the abortion. Most women wait almost six months to a year before they seek support services.

"I had two abortions, one as a teenager and then another during freshman year in college. I thought nothing about it until a few years after I had my first child. I never told my husband about the abortions because I didn't think it mattered, but one day after talking with him about having a second child, I just broke down crying. I felt guilty about the other children I didn't decide to have. He was completely understanding, but for whatever reason, I couldn't shake it. That's when I went to my first abortion support group. I discovered lots of other women like me who thought they, too, had moved on."

"So, do you ever get over it?"

"Not completely. You just learn to forgive yourself and anyone else who encouraged it." With that, she stared directly into Richard's eyes.

"Well, I didn't encourage, and in fact, I didn't know until afterward." Richard spent the next 10 minutes explaining the events of the past nine and a half months of his life, including how he met Nicole and how Toni took her away.

She handed him a spiral-bound workbook with exercises that she used with women in the support group. She told Richard that his first assignment was to write about his fears.

Before his appointment the next week, Richard decided to work ahead in his workbook. Rather than reviewing cases at night, he worked on therapy exercises. The letter assignment was nearly one-third of the way through the workbook, but it drew Richard in because he wanted to say something to his never-born child. He wrote:

> *To my first child, my son, Junior,*
>
> *First of all, I would like to say, I love you so very much, and I miss you so very much. Ever since I found out that you were in your mother's womb, I was instantly in love with you. I know that you are a handsome child with crème-colored skin and curly, brown hair. I know that you must have my almond-shaped eyes because it's my family's most dominant feature. Other than those two things, I don't know what you look like.*
>
> *There is no easy answer as to why you're not here with me. Your mother must have struggled with the stigma of having a racially-mixed child or giving birth to a child and raising it with her lover. After much questioning, thought and prayer, I'm still not really sure what she was thinking or why she didn't let me know. Maybe it was her way of getting back at me for the rejection she claims*

that she felt while we were married. I tried to make it up to her, but it was too late. She took her and you away from me. I honestly despised your mother for being so selfish. Unfortunately, the final decision would have been hers even if I had known.

I'm so sorry. I ask for your forgiveness for my part in this ordeal. You were treated like an unwanted child even though you were conceived in love and deserved the right to live. Your pending birth would've given me something to look forward to every day for the rest of my life. I visualize and fantasize often about you being here with me. I would give anything to hold you in my arms, kiss your cheeks, rub your tiny feet, and hear you cry for me.

He stopped writing abruptly because he ran out of room and the tears in his eyes blurred his vision so much that he couldn't see the paper. The next afternoon at work, he did another assignment that required him to write a letter from God to himself. After only five lines, Richard felt content and stopped writing.

Go, my son. Don't fret over yesterday's actions. Like every new morning, my love, kindness, grace, and mercy are here for you to receive day after day after day. Go forth with boldness, and do the work I've assigned for you in my kingdom. Your faithfulness will be honored and blessed.

This relieved Richard's anxiety somewhat. He went to bed that night only dreaming of his son and Nicole, but he didn't open his workbook until the next day, which was his next counseling session. Even though a full week had passed, Richard felt as if it had only been 48 hours. He couldn't wait to show Sharon how much work he had done in his workbook.

Although women stared at Richard upon his entrance, he felt more comfortable and secure today, as if he legitimately belonged to the group of grief-stricken women. What he wasn't prepared for was Sharon's response once they got into her office and began the hour-long session.

"I've got something to show you," said Richard handing her the workbook open to the letter to his son.

Sharon took the workbook and began reading the letter. Once she finished, she said, "Do you want to work with someone to get you through this or do you want me to let you do it alone as a self-help exercise?"

"What's the matter?" Richard questioned sincerely.

"You don't need my help. In fact, I don't think I'm the best person to help you. I found a men's abortion support group. There is only one chapter in the city. Here's the number."

Richard took the note and reviewed the number several times as if he was studying for a test. Maybe the numbers would explain the uncomfortable feeling he got while sitting in Sharon's office waiting for her to decide to complete their session or tell him to leave.

"It was a pleasure meeting you, Richard, and I know you'll find the right fit for yourself soon."

"Thanks, Sharon. Can I call you sometime if I need to talk?"

Handing him back his workbook, Sharon said, "Sure you can."

Somehow even with her redirecting him to a men's group,

Richard felt Sharon was sincere in her willingness to speak with him. The next day at work, Richard continued to stare at the phone number, trying to get up enough nerve to call, explain his situation and also his referral from the pregnancy center.

He sat in the same position so long that one of his feet grew numb. He adjusted his posture and plugged along, composing a contract he should've completed already. The phone number kept commanding his focus. He glanced at the wall clock and realized his department's meeting had begun 12 minutes ago. He grabbed a notepad and rushed to the conference room. The call had to wait.

He put the phone number directly into the search engine and it showed results for the Men's Abortion Group. Richard visited the website. The description promised a forum for reflection and refuge. In the forum, attendees had posted anonymous comments, all of which oozed of positivity. Over half encouraged others to attend.

The moderator, Quinn O'Reilly, held meetings each Tuesday at 7:00 p.m. on the main sales floor of his thrift shop. The store, located in a strip mall in Gwinnett, a northern county, took Richard about 45 minutes to reach. Richard slipped in right before the scheduled start. He chose a seat in the back row of aluminum folding chairs. He assumed the red-headed fellow in his mid-50s speaking to a shorter guy was O'Reilly. One attendee cast a smile his way. Richard returned it but then purposefully stared straight ahead.

The presumed leader cleared his throat. The gathering of nearly 13 men came to a hush as he walked to the front of them.

"Good evening," O'Reilly started. "Whether you've come here before or just ventured out for the first time, welcome." He glanced at Richard and another man. "I'm Quinn O'Reilly. I'll begin with the same spiel as always. Ages ago, my sister had an abortion and confided in me. I had difficulty reconciling her decision with our upbringing, as did she. The mental commotion that resulted caught us both off guard."

Richard related. Nicole's actions had infringed upon his psychological and spiritual wellbeing. Concentrating on tasks proved an increasing obstacle, and he spiraled from attending church service late to not attending at all.

"Although somewhat biologically removed, I suffered too."

Richard detected lingering pain in his voice. What chance do I have, he thought, if his heart hasn't healed?

"I harbored resentment but not as much as she," O'Reilly went on. "She committed suicide. She left me alone to sort out problems the abortion caused and issues it also exacerbated. But you are not alone. Here, we deal with issues before they deal with us. Feel free to share or simply listen. Consider this a haven and a judgment-free zone."

"I'd like to pick up where we left off," a Korean man in the second row said. He appeared to be no older than 35 and wore navy slacks, a collared, cotton shirt bearing a business logo, and cheap sneakers.

"Okay." O'Reilly sat down and the man took his place.

"I did as someone suggested and checked out TV commercials for baby products. Usually, they only feature the mom. It's as if dads have been reduced to sperm donors."

"Either that or they are marginalized to the point of becoming feminized," another man pointed out.

"That's true," the first man continued. "Our society constantly champions the metrosexual lifestyle while looking down on so-called manly men."

Richard merely observed as the men commented on how the world had become a hostile place for males who actually wanted to do the right thing. Once that discussion drew to a close, O'Reilly opened the floor for further dialogue. "Anyone have something personal to share?"

As others came forward, Richard sighed deeply. Their stories made him doubt if he could recover. Some of the men had initially attended other support groups. Some had stuck with this one for several years.

When the meeting ended, some congregated at a table stocked with assorted Krispy Kreme doughnuts, a carafe of coffee, and a pitcher of water. Others huddled in small groups. Richard made a beeline for the water and poured a cup. He stood back and then debated if he should eat something or wait until dinner.

O'Reilly joined him. Deep in thought, Richard did not notice him.

"The doughnuts don't bite," O'Reilly said.

Richard grinned and turned to face him. "Thank you," he said, "for the forum and the treats."

"Listen, some of us usually get together afterwards—"

"I've actually got plans," Richard lied.

"Okay. Well, I hope you garnered something useful, and I hope you'll return."

Richard shrugged and then grabbed a doughnut. "Maybe."

That weekend, as they did annually, Richard and Kevin attended a car show held at Phillips Arena. They always looked forward to perusing the impressive display of prototypes and the automobiles scheduled for imminent release. Electric and hybrid vehicles generally peaked Richard's interest. He predicted that the industry would soon invent reliable, striking yet affordable versions that operated without requiring constant battery recharges.

Kevin buzzed about from one sports car to the next. He gushed over exteriors and interiors. He acted as if he might eventually drive away in one of the pricier offerings although his cop's salary supported no such illusions of grandeur.

In contrast, Richard trailed behind devoid of the pep and ability to indulge in fantasy that his friend exhibited. He noted, as they maneuvered about, an array of minivans and also some station wagons. Family-friendly options bypassed his radar previously. On this occasion they jumped out at him.

"Here," Kevin said as he thrust his digital camera at Richard. "Take a picture of me for my Facebook wall." He propped a leg up on the open door of a yellow Maserati.

Richard complied. He snapped the photos haphazardly.

"Let me see." Kevin eagerly previewed the snapshots. He grimaced. "You barely got the car in the frame. Do it again." He shoved the camera back at him.

Kevin's attitude irritated Richard. He considered him consumed with torque and flash. For Richard, matters of flesh and blood rose to the forefront. He narrowed his eyes but did as Kevin commanded. Kevin previewed the photos again and then nodded in approval. They moved to an SUV loaded with hands-free Internet access and other extras.

Richard yawned.

"It's barely 11:30. You should be wide awake. Go grab a Coke."

"That's basically liquid sugar. How much longer?" he whined.

"We still have the other side of the showroom to see. What is with you?"

"What's with me?" Richard spewed. "Divorce, dead baby. That about sums it up."

Kevin looked pained, as if Richard had punched him square in the jaw. "I just thought the show would be a good distraction. Excuse me for trying. I'll hurry it along."

That evening, as he often did, Richard lounged in a chair on his patio. The sounds of small animals rustling in the treetops no longer bothered him. This was his most relaxing spot, the place that afforded him an opportunity to wind down somewhat. Richard gazed at the stars and moon above. He wished he could see the celestial plane beyond. He wondered if his son gazed down at him.

Richard reflected on how he'd lashed out at Kevin. He acknowledged that his friend offered himself as a sounding board while they worked out or hung out in general. Kevin habitually steered their conversations to more cheerful, less thought-provoking subjects, which Richard viewed as a form of dismissal. After seeing the shock on his only true friend's face, Richard equated Kevin's actions as a tactic intended to help rather than hurt. He apologized to Kevin when they parted that afternoon.

Having the debacle with Nicole affect his friendship would only allow her to steal more than she had. He actually craved to direct his anger at Nicole. Despite attempts to hide in a cocoon devoid of thoughts and remembrances, Richard kept running into situations or people who invoked images of his lost wife and child. The worse had occurred during a baby shower held for a well-known and respected colleague. Richard pooled funds with other partners to purchase a gift card. That allowed him to bypass shopping for and being surrounded by baby items. He had no plausible excuse to avoid the shower. So he attended and listened while others in the conference room regaled in the joy of the pending arrival. Before they cut the cake and opened gifts, he seized an opportunity to slip out and return to the solitude of his office. He wished he could dwell in the positivity of the present instead of the pain of the past.

His mother, like Kevin, tried her best to help Richard overcome his sorrow. Mrs. Knight said she found solace in knowing that they had one more angel in heaven. She also predicted that had he and Nicole remained married, his ex would have built upon her résumé of deceit. A brief period of misery proved better than a drawn-out one, in Mrs. Knight's opinion. While her son mourned, she wanted to maintain his physical well-being, preparing dinner and even his bath water, which he would've protested otherwise. But her love extended only so far into the depths Richard drove himself to. She suggested weeks ago that he let Reverend Peters counsel him. He had not broached the subject with the reverend; he suspected his mother had.

Richard held no desire to attend counseling at church, surrounded by members he had known the majority of his life. He preferred the anonymity of strangers. When he discussed the group he had discovered, she expressed doubt that a non-Christian avenue would suffice. He told her that regardless of differences in backgrounds, religious or otherwise, he thought listening to others who had gone through similar experiences would prove beneficial. Mrs. Knight eased off her crusade and vowed to keep praying for him.

Richard recalled the angst Mr. O'Reilly's sister experienced. In a weird way, she had aborted herself and interfered with God's divine plan. Suicide railed against the core of self-preservation. And in most religions, it rang of blasphemy. Still, Richard connected with her anguish. He realized she may have had a bevy of other difficulties but probably sought a reunion of souls, a way to reconnect with her unborn child.

A scared, inner voice urged Richard to skip the next meeting. Instead of having drawn strength from the various accounts, listening drained him. He speculated his refusal to open up initiated some of his discomfort.

He remained outside deliberating the pros and cons of returning to the men's group. Once drowsiness finally took over, Richard stopped resisting the urge to avoid the decision.

Tonight's format varied from the previous meeting. Immediately after O'Reilly spoke, men dove into tales, none of which compared to the gravity of his, in Richard's opinion. One didn't know if the baby he agreed to let his wife abort was his or her lover's. Another pressured his girlfriend into ending her pregnancy. Although they had long since broken up, the man questioned if he made the right decision. Richard remembered O'Reilly's directive concerning judging others. Despite that, he had difficulty empathizing with men whom he deemed as guilty as the women they now bashed.

Should he chronicle his despair in front of them? Richard scanned the participants. Should he risk vulnerability, the very flaw that put him in the position of needing help? Richard eased to the edge of his seat. He summoned up the courage to speak as soon as an opening arose. One man droned on and on.

Richard spoke as soon as he ended his soliloquy. "What I don't understand is why women don't have to get the father's consent."

Half of the men stared as if they had not encountered his situation.

"Has anyone else experienced this?" he asked while moving to the front.

No one responded.

"According to the law," Richard continued, "the woman you're with can hide and get rid of as many pregnancies as she wants." He launched into how Nicole did him wrong, leaving out the affair with Toni.

"That's hardcore, dude," a guy who looked too young to be a father said at the culmination of Richard's account.

Richard suspected that many of those around him sought absolution. In neither session had he heard anyone recount trying to stop an abortion.

O'Reilly cornered him after disbanding the group. "We're heading to Applebee's. Why don't you join us?"

Richard's hunger and curiosity got the best of him. He followed O'Reilly to the nearby restaurant. Six of the eleven men from the group met them there. A waitress led them to a corner table where she immediately took their drink orders and then left to fill them.

O'Reilly made quick introductions. He told Richard and another newbie that the men generally used first names or nicknames.

Richard contemplated creating an alias.

Both men introduced themselves.

"I'm curious," Richard inquired, "who has been attending the group the longest?"

Haru, the man who commented on society's view of men the week before, answered. "Actually, Richard, we don't discuss any of that outside of the meeting."

"Oh, I just thought this was a continuation. Something for guys who had more to say."

"It's a chance to wind down," O'Reilly chimed in. "My store is a safe haven where we can maintain confidentiality. Of course, if participants forge friendships and chose to hang out what they talk about is between them."

"I see."

"So what do you do for fun?" Haru asked.

"Fun?" Richard repeated the word as if it came from a foreign language.

The others stared at him, waiting for an answer.

"Mostly I chill out at home. I like to read."

"Well it helps to have hobbies that force you to leave the house," Haru said.

The waitress returned with their drinks and then took their

entree orders. When she left, someone changed the subject to sports. Richard listened but didn't actively engage in the conversation. O'Reilly glimpsed at him periodically, as if he sensed Richard's withdrawal.

The men mainly stuck to that subject as they dined. One invited the others to join his bowling league.

Richard wolfed down half of his chicken wrap. Then, before anyone else finished, Richard asked for a to-go box and his check. "Thanks for including me," he said as he closed out his bill.

O'Reilly dabbed the corners of his mouth with a napkin. "Let me walk you out."

"That's not necessary, really."

"I insist." He slid his chair back.

Richard parked near the entrance so they quickly reached his BMW.

"Tell me, what are your thoughts so far?" O'Reilly asked.

"Honestly, I'm not sure I relate to those men."

"Why?"

"I was a victim. They were perpetrators."

"Quite a big conclusion to jump to," O'Reilly countered," especially since everyone didn't speak."

"No disrespect, but that's my perception."

"None taken. Recognize, though, that this is an evolving process. Even I still find value in speaking with others and hearing their stories. No one moves at the same pace."

Richard frowned. "Maybe I was seeking a remedy that doesn't exist."

"Don't pressure yourself into recovery. I tend to focus more on dealing with than discarding pain. Regardless of how the men who attend got to the point that led them there, each has mending to do."

Richard fished his keys out of his pocket.

"To answer your earlier question, I don't track how long anyone participates. The group is ever changing and the invitation is always open. Know that some men leave but come back not just to receive support but to offer it. Sometimes an event like starting a new relationship or the birth of a child can trigger feelings. Some feel blessed and want to share that hope exists; others feel undeserving and need encouragement."

"Thank you for the clarification," Richard said. "Please, don't let me keep you."

O'Reilly patted him on the back. "You're a young fellow. Living your life to the fullest is the best way to honor your child. Good night, Richard. Hope to see you again."

Valentine's Day came and went a month ago, but O'Reilly's recent advice transported Richard back to that holiday. Richard marked it after church by grilling T-bone stakes for his mother. It was a mild afternoon, the kind that tricked Atlantans into believing winter weather had ended. He and his mother avoided the subject of romance. In the past, the holiday had amplified Mrs. Knight's insistence that her son pursue finding a special lady the way he pursued his career. This year, she kept her opinions to herself.

Richard welcomed the reprieve. Commercialized symbols of love seemed to assail him from every corner as retailers tried to squeeze as much profit as possible from the holiday. He presumed that most people fixated on the revelry of cards, jewelry and boxed chocolates rather than on commitment. For Richard, receiving such tokens had never compared to the gratification he experienced from daily expressions of affection. He replicated his father's example, which, in part, had been relayed by his mother's reminiscences. He strove to provide for his wife in the way his father had.

Rather than grand romantic gestures, Richard offered his wife stability so she wouldn't have to deal with financial stress. Sure he had a relentless, ambitious streak, but Richard pictured his success benefiting his future family. He, in turn, valued the effort Nicole exerted initially. She obviously failed to recognize how he cherished her making their new home a cozy one, and how he treasured that she prepared his breakfast and dinner. With her and his past girlfriend, Richard noted special occasions but did not wait for them to roll around to make his partners feel special. Rather than simply saying "I love you," he constantly showed how much he loved them. They never had cause to doubt his dedication or his fidelity.

Richard had been too young to interpret the intimate intricacies of his parents' marriage. His mother's reluctance to allow another man to take his dad's place served as indication that they possessed steadfast dedication for each other, the sort that would have lasted had fate not intervened. His recent personal upheaval increased his curiosity concerning his parents' relationship. He made a mental note to ask his mother how she knew his father possessed the qualities of a long-term partner.

While he cooked for his mother, the woman who would cut off an arm before abandoning him, he thought about the woman who had abandoned him. Surely she and Toni indulged in some sort of celebration. He tried blocking them out of his thoughts; they kept creeping back in. The more he thought of them, the less loving Richard felt.

Richard contemplated channeling his grief in a manner worthy of honoring his unborn son. Someone had to stand up for the fathers and the babies affected by actions such as Toni and Nicole's. Why shouldn't that someone be him?

The therapeutic aspects of the men's group had fallen short for him, but Richard took O'Reilly's suggestion seriously. It, in a roundabout way, led to his decision to challenge what he called biased laws that condoned secrecy and amorality. Transforming into a champion for reform made him feel less like a duped dunce and more like a capable advocate.

Richard delved into researching cases affecting father's rights. He utilized the firm's law library more than he ever had. In the mornings, Richard packed salads and sandwiches so he could put his full lunch hour toward reading through summations, opinions and rulings. Long after his colleagues left the building, Richard remained. The end of March snuck up on him.

His new protocol included walking to The Tavern, a tapas bar. There, he ate a light dinner and occasionally downed a cocktail. The majority of The Tavern's business came from nearby law firms. Lawyers and other legal professionals frequented the watering hole from noon to last call. He had passed by the place often although he barely noticed it. He rediscovered The Tavern when he was looking for a quick meal in an eatery not overrun with tourists or too pricey for his budget. The nonsmoking restaurant was quiet enough on weekdays that he could pull out his notepad, as he did tonight, and concentrate on strategizing.

While dissecting the information available concerning abortion rights, Richard detected numerous patterns of rationalization that left women in control. One camp believed that women should not be forced into motherhood even if they had engaged in sex for that sole purpose. Another rationalized that allowing men to weigh in on women's reproductive rights would open floodgates. They feared mentally or physically abusive men would hijack the lives of women who no longer desired relationships with them. The arguments that consistently rose to the forefront cited that women had authority over their bodies and should enjoy a constitutionally granted right to privacy.

Like most adults, Richard knew of *Roe v. Wade*, the 1973 Supreme Court decision legalizing abortion and overturning state laws requiring consent. He had no familiarity with Doe v. Bolton, a lesser known but equally important case initiated in Georgia. During that era, Georgia law allowed abortions only under strict circumstances, such as rape or foreseen injury to the mother. Also, it entailed residency requirements and approval from a panel of doctors and a special committee. On the same day that the more notable case garnered national attention, the Court also ruled against the Georgia Secretary of State. It struck down most of the limitations and allowed for the act to take place beyond the second and third trimesters.

The modern flashpoint happened in Pennsylvania in 1992. Clinics and physicians sued jointly because of the state's five stipulations that governed abortions. Richard focused solely on the spousal notification clause. It required wives to inform husbands prior to the procedure. For the first instance in ages, a viable challenge to the landmark *Roe v. Wade* emerged. After the U.S. District Court overturned all provisions, the Court of Appeals for the Third Circuit upheld Pennsylvania's right to uphold each provision except the spousal notification. The Supreme Court later concurred and refused to overturn *Roe v. Wade*.

Richard sought a way to convince those in power that fathers comprised more than minor footnotes in the decision-making process. He needed a carefully-crafted proposal to submit to interested parties. For Richard, simply requiring that a woman notify her husband of her decision would fall short of a victory.

The bartender who normally served him, a young guy covered with tattoos and piercings, removed the remnants of Richard's buffalo wings. "Ready to close out your tab?" he asked.

"Add another tea."

The bartender glanced at him sympathetically. "Looks like you could use something stronger. How about a screwdriver?"

"Sounds fitting," Richard said. The system screwed him after all. "What's in it?"

"Orange juice and vodka, extra vodka for you. I won't tell if you don't."

Richard mimicked zipping his lips.

"I'll be back in a sec."

Proofreading his proposal and sending out the same written requests repeatedly bored Richard in part due to the lack of response. Richard shifted his focus from studying cases to studying politicians. With 13 states left to target, he considered the response garnered so far paltry. Richard speculated that the public servants who, in his opinion, had not served him shied from his cause for fear of alienating constituents. He envied powerful women's rights groups. They had lobbyists pushing platforms while Richard was a one-man deal.

He had attempted to enlist interfaith counsels in his crusade but encountered staunch resistance. Religious leaders wanted to abolish abortion entirely, except when it was deemed a last resort to preserve the mother's life,. He encountered the same obstacle with pro-life advocates. That was not the futile fight Richard wanted to fight.

Richard contacted a state senator's office whose campaign had spotlighted an anti-abortion platform. The senator neither expressed any interest in Richard's cause nor exhibited enough courtesy to speak to him in person or on the phone. Richard also contacted members of the Georgia House of Representatives. Only one in his district responded. His aide told Richard to stop by at a certain time to "explore the opportunity," but then he called to cancel the appointment about two hours before they were to meet. Richard left dozens of messages with aides, who responded with form letters and emails. He attributed their unresponsiveness to the fact that it was not an election year.

The bartender plopped the screwdriver down, interrupting Richard's thoughts. "Enjoy," he said and rushed off.

Richard held the glass with both hands and peered into it like it was a crystal ball. He wondered if he'd sabotaged his efforts initially by excluding politicians in other states. Richard lifted the beverage to his mouth. He swallowed slowly, savoring the vodka coating his tongue. He licked his lips and relished this particular protocol. He pitied patrons around him who derived instantaneous pleasure from swigging beers or downing shots of tequila at lightning speeds. Richard swallowed slowly until only ice remained and then flagged down the bartender.

"Hit me again."

Chapter 10

The Tavern's lure proved difficult to resist even on his days off. It morphed from a refuge into a pacifier of sorts where he could simultaneously perform research and eat. The drinks served there took the edge off that he created by cramming a voluminous amount of research into his waking hours. He relied on the alcohol to help him sleep through the night and to help him forget his frustrations, even if they returned in the morning. Two weekends in a row, Richard tried bars near his home. Their worn, smoky interiors and watered-down drinks led Richard to appreciate his favorite haunt more. Even the cocktails he concocted on his own paled in comparison.

His favorite bartender had the night off. The female on duty proved less attentive, perhaps because the place was packed, and less forthcoming with suggestions. Richard decided to try a long island iced tea and the slider trio special.

A vixen at the other end of the bar attempted to woo him by licking her full lips and shooting him flirty gazes that screamed "buy me a drink." Richard eyed her, wondering what she expected in return. He turned his back on her and delved into the alcoholic tea rather than the atmosphere around him. It had a deceptive sweetness and a hint of some spice he had difficulty identifying. Richard drank the tea faster than he had intended. He ordered another.

When he stood up to leave, Richard's legs wobbled like licorice.

A female sitting near the entrance noticed his wobbly exit. She grabbed her cell phone and told the woman sharing the booth to watch her purse. Then, she caught up with Richard, who moved aimlessly throughout the parking lot. She tugged at the sleeve of his suit jacket. "Let me call a taxi for you," she urged. "Or maybe a friend can come get you."

"I'm not that drunk," Richard slurred. "I can make it home just fine."

She stepped back and watched him fumble with his keys. Suddenly, Richard doubled over and started puking. The woman turned her head in disgust then ran to her car. She wore a long skirt and high heels but still moved quicker than he did.

The mystery woman jumped into her hatchback and pulled up beside Richard. She opened the backseat and pushed him inside. By now, her dining companion had made it outside.

"What the heck is going on, Ladonna?"

"That guy was about to fall out." She pointed to the back seat.

"Girl, this is crazy."

"I'll be okay. Crystal is home, and he's harmless."

"It's the harmless looking ones that always get ya. Call her and then call me. Keep me on the line until you get home."

Crystal met her roommate in the driveway of their cottage near downtown Decatur. She wore a jogging suit and tennis shoes. "From stray cats to stray men, I swear!" she exclaimed.

"Just help me get him in the house."

Crystal reached into the back of the car and yanked Richard toward the driver's side door. He mumbled gibberish. She chuckled. "This is what I interrupted my aerobics class for?"

"Let's hope a Good Samaritan passes by in your time of need."

She grimaced.

Although barely, Richard stood on his own. He required assistance navigating the driveway and five steps leading to the front stoop. At one point, he tilted his head in Crystal's direction and yawned.

"Ugh! His breath! It's a major funk bomb."

"I told you he threw up."

Richard sank into the sofa. He wondered why his bed felt so soft and his eyelids felt so heavy, as if weighed down by an invisible anchor.

Crystal came from the kitchen, carrying a mug of coffee, which she handed to Ladonna.

"I brewed it extra strong, just like you ordered."

"Thanks." Ladonna eased the coffee toward Richard. "Drink this," she cajoled.

He shook his head and twitched his nose.

She repeated the attempt.

Richard slumped over. His head dangled dangerously on the arm of the sofa.

"Should we move him?" Crystal asked.

"No, let him be."

Soreness radiated throughout the back of Richard's neck. He swore a ping-pong match was occurring in his head. His eyes fluttered open. He blinked. The gold walls surrounding him shone too brightly. He squinted. Richard sat up on the sofa. Its floral pattern told him it probably belonged to a woman. He recollected, vaguely, indulging in a second long island iced tea. Richard reached for his wallet: still there but no keys. Whoever brought him to this location obviously meant no harm.

A squeaking noise emanating from the far end of the sofa captured his focus. Initially, he suspected a mouse but then recognized it as mechanical in nature. The front wheels of a plastic dump truck edged around the corner. The boy pushing it, no older than four, gazed apprehensively at Richard and froze as if afraid to cross an invisible boundary.

"Ready for your coffee now?" the woman peering at him from the kitchen entryway asked.

Thinking of drinking anything, even water, made him more nauseous. "No thank you," he answered.

"But I appreciate your hospitality." He wondered if she still carried baby weight or if she was naturally plump. She and the boy shared the same facial features: long lashes, button noses, and dimples.

"You're quite welcome."

Her soothing tone left him feeling less ashamed. "Do you have my keys?"

"Yes, I'll drop you off after I take my roommate to the MARTA station."

"No need—"

"I insist."

Crystal shuffled into the living room, wearing a blouse, dress slacks, and fuzzy slippers. Ladonna glimpsed at her choice of footwear.

"I'm almost ready," Crystal declared. Crystal's mound of braids made her head look huge atop her thin yet well-toned body.

"Crystal, this is…" She paused and glanced at Richard. "What's your name?"

"Richard."

"Well Richard, I'm Ladonna. As soon as I fill up Crystal's travel mug, and she puts on her shoes," she said sarcastically, "we can leave."

He ogled the ladies, jumping back and forth between them and the boy.

"Did you need something?" Ladonna asked.

"It's wrong," Richard proclaimed.

Crystal put her hands on her hips. Ladonna looked thoroughly confused.

"What's your malfunction?" Crystal asked.

"It's wrong," Richard continued. His voice escalated with each syllable as small wads of spit flew out of his mouth. "Two mothers can't replace one father. This country, no, this world, is going straight to hell."

"Pardon me?" Ladonna said.

"You people prancing around, corrupting kids and expecting decent folks to pretend it's okay." He stared at the boy, who promptly scurried behind the sofa. "He deserves a normal upbringing."

Crystal glowered. "You've got some nerve, especially after—"

"Crystal is my roommate and my friend," Ladonna interjected, "nothing else, and for the record, alcoholics don't make such great parents."

Richard closed his eyes.

"We're leaving in five minutes."

Richard gladly dwelled in the silence while the hatchback puttered along to the nearby transit station. Ladonna concentrated on driving. Crystal texted up a storm, and the boy played with a Spider Man action figure. Richard peered out the window, mentally teleporting himself out of the uncomfortable spot. He recognized the surroundings as a revitalized section of Decatur. The vibrant downtown area retained its charm by preserving historic buildings and fostering small businesses while carefully embracing the advent of modern retail outlets and structures.

"Let me know you made it in okay," Crystal said once they reached their destination. She cut her eyes at Richard and then rushed off.

Ladonna checked for oncoming cars before pulling off. "You can move up front."

Here we go, he thought. "I'm fine back here."

She glanced in the rearview mirror. "Want me to turn the radio on?"

"That's not necessary."

"I locked your car. Hopefully it didn't get towed."

Or broken into, he added silently. He prayed she'd focus on the stop-and-go traffic rather than his earlier tangent.

The vehicle edged up Ponce de Leon Avenue, causing Richard's anxiety to multiply. He had to rush home, shower, shave, and get dressed. He considered alerting the receptionist that he'd be in by 9:00 but suspected doing so might prompt more questions from his savior.

"Do you work by the bar?"

The boy stopped playing to listen but quickly returned to his toy.

"Yes," he answered as vaguely as possible. "If going back poses a problem, I can catch a cab."

"Nonsense, I'm headed that way."

He wondered if Ladonna happened into the bar by chance or if she worked nearby. Would she return there and blab about his antics? A more appalling possibility replaced that. Had any of his acquaintances seen him? Probably not, Richard convinced himself considering that no one else stepped in to assist him.

"I'm guessing you live alone since no one was blowing up your cell phone trying to hunt you down."

"Yeah."

The boy held up the figure and waved it around. "Superman flies high in the sky," he announced to Richard.

"Don't bother him, honey."

Richard smiled at the child, who beamed in return. "I'm

not bothered." He decided to steer the conversation. "How old is he?"

"I'm 3," he said before she could.

"Where's his dad?"

"Kabul."

"Military. That's noble."

"Negative on both counts."

Richard glanced at the boy, wondering how his father's absence affected him. "When I have kids, we'll be inseparable."

She groaned. "Clearly, he prefers distance to dedication."

Traffic eased up as their conversation stalled.

Richard breathed easier once they rounded a corner near the Tavern. He strained to see if his car looked okay as Ladonna pulled into the restaurant lot. It had no broken windows, no boot, no parking enforcement sticker.

"Your stop, sir," Ladonna said in a sing-songy voice. Her son chuckled.

"Thanks again. I really, really appreciate you looking out for me."

She smiled the warmest smile. "I've had my share of help. I'm just paying it forward."

An unidentified number flashed on Richard's Caller ID while he ran errands on Saturday. He ignored and dismissed it. Richard noticed later that the caller, Ladonna, left a voicemail. She explained that she'd jotted down his number so she could check on him. Ladonna's sunny disposition radiated on the recording. She wished him well and mentioned she'd be available to talk but neglected to leave her number. Richard pondered how Ladonna so willingly made herself available to a stranger.

She called again the next evening, and he answered. "I'm not a stalker, I swear," Ladonna said. "I just wanted to leave my number for you."

"It's nice of you to worry about me."

"Then you're not mad that I took your number down without asking for it?"

"That did catch me off guard, but you meant well."

She sighed in relief. "Good. You sound okay."

"Let's just say I'm better," Richard answered. Without thinking it through, he blurted out, "Would you like to come over?"

Upon Ladonna's arrival, most of Richard's apprehension had subsided. He presumed she'd bring her son. Ladonna addressed his absence before Richard mentioned it. "Crystal is baby-sitting even though she wasn't too keen on me coming over," she explained.

He threw his hands up in surrender. "Who can blame her considering that awful first impression I left her with. Would you like some pound cake?

"Absolutely, and some water. You cook?"

"Yeah, but I don't bake. My mother made it."

She followed him into the kitchen and gaped in awe at its amenities. "Your house could swallow mine four times over. I live in a shanty shack compared to this joint. Is it yours or do you rent too?"

"Technically it's the bank's."

"If I remember correctly, you live alone?"

"It wasn't supposed to be that way, but yeah."

"How was it supposed to be?"

"I bought this house for my ex-wife. We got divorced in January."

"Of this year?"

He nodded.

"So it's still fresh. I'm sorry. I know how messy breakups can be."

"What happened to me went beyond messy. On our wedding

day the future felt so promising. I kept our photo album. I couldn't bring myself to throw it away."

"That's understandable."

"You wanna see it?"

"Uh, sure."

Richard carried their cake slices and drinks into the living room. While Ladonna settled on the sofa, he retrieved the album from a coffee table drawer. Then he sat beside her. Ladonna munched away while he pointed out members of the wedding party and shared tidbits from that day. His divorce decree lay on the last page of the album. He showed her that as well.

"The ceremony looked lovely," she commented. "Understated but elegant. And I can see the resemblance between you and your mom more so than your sister and her."

"I should have known Toni had ulterior motives." He informed Ladonna about the cryptic comment Toni made during the reception and began detailing the deterioration of his marriage, primarily Toni's involvement with and influence over Nicole. He dwelled on her masculine appearance and rotten attitude. "I presumed the infatuation with Toni would wear off."

"Unless you're into polygamy, there's no way a marriage can work with more than two people calling the shots."

He noted that she polished off the cake quite quickly. He offered her another slice but she declined. "Nicole accused me of being a workaholic and too religious. Can you believe that? I mean, she knew I was a Christian when we met. And how else does somebody reach partner status in one of the most respected firms in Atlanta, osmosis?"

Ladonna slipped her flats off and curled up on the sofa. "I'm a believer too, primarily because my parents raised me that way. It's impossible to beat Christianity into anyone."

"I never pushed Nicole to accept my beliefs," Richard said shrilly.

"Whoa! I'm not implying that you did. I was about to say that I can't even fathom having a non-Christian roommate let alone husband. Getting along requires less effort when you both operate from the same blueprint. At any rate, I don't subscribe to this new age trend where spouses celebrate two religions. That's too much of a compromise, particularly when you throw kids into the mix."

Richard's expression grew gloomy.

"Richard?"

"Despite the affair, despite our different backgrounds, I held out hope. She trashed what we had. They both did."

"Don't beat yourself up," Ladonna said.

He told how he tried to win Nicole back. He repeated the conversation in which Nicole revealed the abortion word for word and detailed how she'd fled the scene and nearly caused his arrest.

Ladonna appeared sympathetic. "How horrible, dealing with the loss of your marriage and your baby. Surely your pastor guided you."

Richard took a long gulp of water. "Actually, I stopped going to church."

"Tell me you at least kept reading your Bible."

"Barely. Dealing with the system made matters worse." While Richard recounted the divorce proceedings and the judge's comments, Ladonna's eyelids drooped.

"Wow," she said once he completed that portion of his diatribe. Next, Richard vehemently vented his frustration over efforts to discover an avenue for changing the law.

"I'll help you with that," Ladonna said as she dozed off for good.

Richard experienced a sense of déjà vu watching Ladonna sleep. He considered waking Ladonna but ultimately decided to cover her with a blanket as she had done for him. Because he pictured Crystal growing increasingly anxious, he also decided to call her. Richard fished Ladonna's cell from her purse. The screen displayed a photo of her son grinning broadly.

It struck Richard that he'd droned on and on about himself without trying to learn a morsel of information about Ladonna. He didn't even know her son's name. He resolved to rectify that blunder.

Richard went into his bedroom to call Crystal and eventually convinced her that he hadn't harmed Ladonna. He promised to wake her roommate early so they'd make it to work on time.

Rehashing his history gutted Richard, but he mustered up the energy for a quick shower. He checked on Ladonna before retiring himself. She hadn't budged. In fact, Ladonna appeared deeper within the grips of slumber. Richard dimmed a corner floor lamp in case Ladonna awoke during the night. Her capacity for kindness flabbergasted him. He had no clue how Ladonna planned to help him but trusted she would somehow.

Chapter 11

Ladonna and Richard swapped email addresses when they parted ways, but he waited until midweek to contact her because he didn't want to scare her off with his intensity. He sent her a short email message to make sure she still wanted to assist him. They agreed to meet but earlier in the afternoon on Saturday so Ladonna would not miss her church's Easter program. Richard drank a bit of Hennessy before her arrival to ease his reservations. Letting someone else share tackling his attempts at reform had not occurred to him prior to Ladonna's suggestion. On both previous occasions when Ladonna graced him with her presence, he behaved off-kilter. Richard sought to reclaim his dignity.

Ladonna showed up armed with her laptop. "Hola," she said in her best Spanish accent.

"Good to see you," Richard responded.

"Let's sit in the dining room," Richard suggested. "The light is better in there." Once they sat at the table, he said, "Before we get started, I must apologize."

Ladonna looked bewildered. "Why?"

"For dumping all that stuff on you."

She waved him off. "It was interesting, almost like a telenovela."

"What?"

"A Spanish soap-opera. Full of drama, twists and turns."

"You speak Spanish?"

"Nowhere near fluently. I'm trying to teach myself, hence my newfound interest in Spanish TV shows."

"Ah."

"Being bilingual is essential."

She sounds smart, Richard told himself. "At any rate, I pushed self-absorption to new heights."

"No worries."

"I mean, here you are willing to help me, and I know practically nothing about you."

"Well, what do you wanna know?"

"Why'd you volunteer to help with my boring research?"

"It's second-nature to me. I'm a paralegal."

"Oh, where?"

"Denson & Sykes."

He hadn't heard of it. "They specialize in?"

"Personal injury and wrongful death mainly."

Fitting, he surmised. "I've been injured; my son suffered a wrongful death."

"They pay very little but accommodate me if Bryson gets sick, and they tailor my schedule so I don't have to drop him off at school early or pick him up late."

He wondered if she expected compensation.

"I'd hate to take you away from your son, especially since I'm not paying you."

"Unless you plan on enslaving me, I'll manage."

For the first moment since her arrival, Richard cracked a smile.

"Are you from Atlanta?"

"Almost. Hapeville. My parents still live there." She began unpacking her laptop.

"Surely Crystal can't be happy about us collaborating."

"Actually, she's cool with it."

He tried to hide his surprise. His expression gave him away.

"She's not coldhearted," Ladonna explained, "just protective."

"How did you two meet?"

"Church."

"What kind of work does she do?"

"She's a manager at a fitness center."

He had other questions but feared running her off. "So I guess we'll get started."

"Since I drifted off before, refresh my memory. You sent out a proposal, right?"

"Actually, I printed out a copy for you."

He slid the one-page document toward Ladonna, who examined it.

"It reads like a personal letter," she commented. "And it only addresses husbands, automatically excluding lesbian couples? Should they be included?"

"I only factored in heterosexuals."

"Just throwing it out there since gays can marry in some states. Suppose one has an affair or possibly after in vitro fertilization decides she doesn't want the child?"

"I'm only concerned with fathers. I'm not comfortable addressing that added element.

"Fair enough, but you still need a call to action."

"Huh?"

"Think of a sales pitch or that junk mail urging us to buy something. You have to succinctly match a want with a necessity."

He appeared puzzled.

"In other words," Ladonna continued, "make the senators feel like they'll miss out on some great deal if they don't act."

He pressed her for a specific example, which she gave.

"Let's not get bogged down by semantics. We'll tweak the proposal but developing a game plan concerns me more."

"I would think that politicians claiming to support the right to life would jump on board," Richard said.

"They have secretaries and interns who review almost all correspondence." She paused. "Listen to me. You're a lawyer. You probably know more about the process than I do."

"Honestly, I tend to focus mainly on what's useful for arguing cases instead of intricacies and interpersonal protocols of the system. Go on."

"I suppose most gatekeepers read your letter and then tossed it out. The nice ones sent some canned response."

"You mean without even mentioning it or sending it for further review?"

"Unfortunately, yes. Their bosses direct them to look for certain subject matters. Regardless of how lawmakers tout toiling for us common folk, they're, like anybody else, seeking job security and promotions. The best way to do that is championing a cause plenty of colleagues or constituents request pushed to the forefront. It's career suicide to introduce a measure no one will consider and that none of the voters deem important. But on the flip side, pioneering hot-button regulations usually leads to reelection. I doubt highly this is a hot button issue they're receiving tons of queries about."

His shoulders slumped. "Sounds formidable. Me against the government machine."

"You can do this."

"How do you suggest I proceed?"

"Streamline your strategy."

As much as he resisted admitting it, Ladonna's advice pointed out flaws in his approach. She convinced him to exert tactical effort in tracking current trends rather than solely focusing on historical rulings. They spent the remainder of their first brainstorming session searching for websites that monitored legislation, both enacted and proposed. They found a treasure trove of resources and decided that the next task would be narrowing down sites that provided succinct information regarding reproductive rights. Richard and Ladonna were in the middle of doing so when Richard's doorbell interrupted them.

"Persistent," Ladonna observed after the fourth ring.

"Excuse me," Richard said and slid his chair back from the table. He intended on shooing off the culprit. That plan fell through when he saw his mother.

"Ma, what are you doing here?"

She strained to see beyond him. "Did you forget I was leaving for the Windy City tomorrow?"

He had. He let her in.

She peered around the room.

"Did you forget this is when I meet with my research partner?"

Mrs. Knight hadn't, and he knew it. She promptly planted a kiss on his check.

"Now, is that a way to greet your ma, especially when she's bearing gifts?"

"My birthday isn't until Thursday."

"Of course I'm aware of that. I spent 27 hours waiting for you to make your entrance. You didn't expect me to leave town without seeing you, did you?" She handed over his cake and card. "Wait to open the card, but the cake won't be as fresh then. I got you a gift that keeps on giving."

Her comment heightened Richard's curiosity.

Mrs. Knight glanced around again, as if she had the power to make Ladonna materialize.

"She's in the dining room. Come on, I'll introduce you."

Richard detected a smidgen of nervousness on Ladonna's part when his mother came in. Mrs. Knight apologized for barging in.

He placed the gifts in an empty chair. Whatever uneasiness he perceived was short-lived.

"This is the woman who bakes wonderful cakes," Ladonna exclaimed.

"I do my best," Mrs. Knight said, feigning modesty. "Red velvet is his favorite, so I make that for his birthday."

"For me it's a toss-up between red velvet and carrot cake, probably because of the frosting. I'm into that real cream cheese kind, not that neon crap they sell in grocery stores."

From that point on, Ladonna and Mrs. Knight chatted as if they'd met previously. She revealed some of her baking secrets and complimented Ladonna on her attire, a purple dress trimmed with a pink ribbon.

Richard cleared his throat before their conversation hit the 15-minute mark. Knowing his mom, she'd insist they sample the cake and then offer to hang around and make dinner. He sought to regain the momentum she'd interrupted. He expected his mother to ignore the hint; however, she took it.

"Nice meeting you, dear. I'll get those recipes for you when I'm back in town."

"Sorry about that," Richard said after his mother left. "She's leaving tomorrow to visit my sister in Chicago."

"You're a Taurus." Ladonna said. "Interesting."

"Meaning?"

"Tauruses seek security. They're kind, patient, determined and reliable—characteristics that describe you. Big plans for your birthday?"

"Nope, not in the celebratory mood this year."

"Concentrate on moments of joy. That'll lift your spirits."

Richard scowled. "Easy for you to say."

"Seriously," Ladonna continued. "Strike a balance. Those who ruminate in tragedy become tragic."

He heard enough of her proselytizing. He hit the power button on his hibernating laptop. "Where'd we leave off?"

As they continued, the pair explored sites in search of succinct facts and solid, statistical data. They scanned their findings and jotted down relevant particulars.

Roughly 900 reproductive health measures had been introduced leading to the implementation of only 15 new laws during the first quarter. The majority of those laws included provisions that expanded pre-abortion waiting periods as well as pre-procedure counseling requirements. They also touched on governing clinics, restricting health plan coverage, allowing employees to refuse participation in abortions and revising sex-education curriculums.

In 49 states at least one legislative chamber had approved 120 bills. Fifty-six percent of those introduced so far sought to restrict abortion access. That represented an 18% increase from the prior year. Ladonna and Richard spotted emerging trends.

"From what we've uncovered so far," Ladonna said, "opponents of abortion have the upper hand. They're making it more difficult for women to access the procedure without rallying directly for abolishment."

"But where does that leave my cause?" Richard wondered aloud.

"Let's just keep looking." She highlighted a section of text on the screen. "It says here that three topics dominated discussion. Let's see if any of those align with requiring spousal consent."

He moved in closer to the monitor. "Nebraska's law marking gestational limits at 20 weeks passed last year. Others states, including Georgia, use it as a boilerplate but define the point when fetuses feel pain at anywhere from 18 to 22 weeks."

"I view narrower restrictions on approved exceptions for performing abortions as the more valuable part of Nebraska's law. Ultimately, you'd prefer outlawing abortions. If spousal consent pushes some women past the deadline, that will result in more procedures being declined."

"A lot of women paint the man as an abusive villain just to skirt timeframe regulations. They'll have a tougher burden of proof now."

"We'll come back to this one."

"Add finding out who sponsored the Georgia bill to our to-do list," Richard recommended.

"Moving on to the ultrasound procedure. Seven states have bills pending, and Oklahoma enacted one last year requiring ultrasounds; however, not all institute a waiting period or mandate that women must view the baby in utero."

"I think measures that avoid mandating the actual viewing of the image fall short. And a two-hour waiting period between doing so and killing the baby is ludicrous. Give me your view."

"Seeing the child might prompt some women to reconsider since ultrasounds show irrefutable proof of life."

"Nicole talked about her abortion like she'd gone in for a root canal."

"She detached herself from reality," Ladonna commented.

"Shouldn't the father have a right to see the ultrasound too?"

"Good point. We need to find out if a similar bill is in the works here or if any politicians in Georgia have strong ties with sponsors in other states. Maybe we'll find a sympathetic ear who recognizes that men are being shut out of the process." She jotted a note on their to-do list and then glanced at her wristwatch. "Oh! It's late. Gotta head home." She gathered her notebook and her computer.

Richard contemplated convincing Ladonna to stay longer. They still had one more trend to tackle. It set in that her motherly duties overrode his project. "This cake is humongous. I'll wrap some for Crystal and your son."

"Can I have a piece for my mom too? She has Bryson, and she loves red velvet."

"Sure." He wrapped up the additional slice and walked her out.

Before pulling off, Ladonna advised him again to enjoy his birthday. He doubted he could muster any semblance of happiness. In fact, he couldn't recall the last instance when he felt that emotion.

That evening, Richard promptly answered the call he'd anticipated since his mother's departure.

"Ladonna seems sweet," Mrs. Knight remarked. "And she's a Christian too. How old is she?"

"Never crossed my mind to ask. Early 30s?"

"Does she have kids?"

"One."

"I didn't see a ring."

"Because there isn't one."

"Lordy."

"And her boyfriend has no problem with you two hanging out?"

"I assume she's single. That's none of my concern." Yours neither, Richard reflected.

"How did you meet again?"

"A restaurant by the job had a grand reopening. We both showed up."

"And you felt comfortable enough to spill all your business?"

"Not initially. I let the part about trying to push a new law slip. I told her the rest later." He pondered how his mother had warned him of potential dangers allowing a stranger into his home might cause. She feared Ladonna might engage in a well-hidden agenda such as identity theft. Now, she hovered on the verge of declaring Ladonna the second coming.

"By the way, when I turned in your tithes, the reverend asked how you were doing."

"I appreciate his concern." He mustered a yawn, hoping to initiate the conclusion of their chat. "Tell Pam I said hi. Did you check the weather there?"

"Yes."

He yawned again.

"Goodnight, son."

"Goodnight, ma. Call me when you land."

The week crept along for Richard. A fog encased him. He wished to move over the birthday hump and fast-forward to Sunday. He and Ladonna reached a pivotal point in deciphering the maze of facts available on the web. He appreciated her ability to rationalize. It neutralized his reoccurring agitation. In college, she earned a criminal justice major and minor in English. As an average written communicator at best, he valued the clarity she'd bring to his overhauled proposal.

On Monday, a worrisome encounter occurred. Zach Truett, a fellow partner, brought a file inaccuracy to Richard's attention. Richard apparently overlooked required corrections, which resulted in an erroneous pleading being filed with the clerk's office. On Thursday, the staff in Richard's department presented him with the customary cake. It paled in comparison to his mom's. They also gave him a Chequers Seafood gift certificate. He steered clear of Zach even though his demeanor bore no trace of disappointment.

Kevin surprised him with tickets to Friday's Hawks versus Bulls playoff tourney. His friend waited until they arrived at Phillips Arena to divulge he'd secured box seats. Watching the players' ferocious vigor and listening to the crowd's thunderous screams drowned out some of Richard's melancholy. Kevin also treated Richard to a nightcap and dinner at a sports grille, where fans often congregated to watch game highlights and listen to commentators.

Richard indulged in a second glass of rum after Kevin dropped him off to toast the end of his birthday. He regretted that his catastrophic marriage resulted in a loss that claimed a special occasion, one he normally treated with revelry, as a casualty. As he drifted off that night, Richard pictured her. He chastised himself for lapses in coherency during which he progressed against reason. In the wee morning hours or in the stillness of a particularly uneventful night, he fell prey to foolish fancy. Such occurrences reverted Richard to when he and Nicole needed each other as much as the air around them. In those fanciful yet fleeting episodes, he inhaled her favorite honeysuckle-scented perfume and nuzzled the nape of her neck.

Richard eventually jolted back to reality when he realized that Nicole's memory bank remained devoid of the positive currency exchanged between them.

Sunday rolled around again. Ladonna arrived with an unexpected addition. Bryson clung to her side. He peered at Richard with a mix of curiosity and confusion. He carried a backpack that appeared too large for his miniature frame.

"I hope you don't mind," Ladonna said to Richard. Crystal decided to work a double shift. Bryson won't be a bother."

"Of course," Richard replied, trying his best to be courteous.

"He brought his coloring books. That'll keep him occupied." Ladonna set her son a few feet away. She instructed him to remain quiet and handed him his crayons.

"How was your birthday?" she asked while settling at the table.

"They had cake and ice cream for me at work."

"Cool."

"I went to a basketball game with my friend Kevin."

"Even better."

"My mom bought me a series of golf lessons."

"Seems like you enjoyed yourself after all!"

"Somewhat," he said following an uneasy pause. "Right before you showed up I finished going over the info on insurance restrictions."

She pulled out her notepad.

"Twenty-three state legislatures addressed the issue in a total of fifty-seven measures during the first quarter. Only six states altogether have restrictions in place that limit coverage and that includes what Utah approved recently."

"Is this one of those states?"

"Nope. South Carolina is the closest."

"Does Georgia have anything pending?"

"Unfortunately not. The focus varies. Some include government plans as well."

"Mmmm. This could turn into our best avenue, a way to piggyback consent with another measure."

"To clarify, you're suggesting we find a politician eager to support a related bill and ask him to sponsor mine, too?"

"Essentially I'm saying to prepare for the prospect. A best-case scenario would result in a stand-alone bill. Often, though, they contain at least two associated provisions."

"Without a doubt I prefer that my mine stand on its own merits."

"Definitely we'll word the proposal to highlight consent although we'll tailor it based on our research. For those who support reproductive legislation, we'll show how your idea can enhance what they recently presented or passed. For those who have no bills pending, we'll pull statistics that show a need for them."

"For my idea or one of those trends?"

Ladonna squirmed in her seat. "For stricter reproductive laws in general. At the very least the trends prove that our state needs similar regulations implemented, consent among them. Think of it as a me-me mentality. When Bryson plays with a group of kids and one has something cool that the others suppose they should have, they feel left out. Politicians, especially those in bordering districts, often collaborate."

"So we'll start with Georgia state senators?"

"Uh huh. The one you reached out to served on the federal level. He's surely bombarded with requests." She squirmed again. "Do you mind watching Bryson while I run to the restroom?"

"Go ahead."

As Richard watched Bryson concentrate on staying within the lines, he noticed Ladonna approaching. Bryson watched his mom exit the restroom, and then he returned to his coloring. "What's that you're coloring?" Ladonna asked as she re-entered the room.

Bryson lifted the book to reveal a giraffe that donned zebra stripes. Richard did a double-take and wondered if the boy knew which was which. "Have you ever been to the zoo?"

"No," Bryson replied in a nearly inaudible voice. "Have you?"

The rhythm and tone of Bryson's voice, teetering on babyish while displaying hints of a growing boy, intrigued him in an odd sort of way. "How would Junior have sounded?" Richard thought.

"Yes, and I've seen a lot of striped giraffes there." Richard told the boy.

"A lot of what live where?" Ladonna asked before sitting down.

"Striped giraffes," Richard clarified.

"I see." Ladonna opened a blank word-processing screen. "On to drafting a new proposal. We'll create a template and tailor it accordingly."

"The one I wrote may have portrayed me as desperate or overly emotional," Richard admitted.

"Between the two of us we *will* produce a document that relays your dedication to this cause without causing uneasiness for the reader. Ever written a grant proposal?"

Richard shook his head.

"Successful ones create connections on a human level. You're a broken man deprived of the joys of fatherhood seeking to protect others from such despair. Nicole's rash act dimmed a light that once shone in you. Your child could have cured cancer, developed the next great innovation, or fathered children who contributed to the world in impressive and extraordinary ways."

"Jot that down."

She did. "The finished product will touch on those points and others."

Over the course of an hour, the pair crafted a virtually new one-page proposal.

"Now," Ladonna said, "promise to set this aside until next weekend."

"Why?"

"Proofreading generally fails if it's done so soon after penning the original. No matter how tempting, try occupying yourself with other matters."

"What if I come up with a revision?"

"Place it on a separate piece of paper. Resist the urge to mull over it. We'll tackle those next week."

"Isn't Sunday Mother's Day?"

"Totally forgot." Ladonna appeared torn.

"I assume you'll want to hang out with your son and mom. How about we chat over instant messaging on Saturday? That'll allow us to update the document but be less cumbersome than speaking on the phone and typing, unless you have a headset."

"I don't."

"Then it's settled. We'll confirm when later."

Ladonna emailed a copy of the draft as agreed. Richard resisted the overwhelming urge to download the attachment because doing so would increase his desire to peek at it. While Richard went through the motions for the next couple of days, the document remained on the forefront of his mind. He occupied himself with checking in on his mom, who was still out of town, and chatting with his sister. He breezed through his spring-cleaning list. He jogged and even reviewed the list of relaxation techniques in the workbook Sharon had given him. He found listening to jazz, a hobby that had fallen by the wayside, one of the most calming recommendations on the list.

During a particularly lackluster conference call at the end of the week, Richard found ignoring the proposal extremely difficult. He muted the phone in his office and then replayed his last conversation with Ladonna. Technically, he never promised to abide by her directive. Richard opened the attachment. It contained nothing near what they composed. Instead it read, "I told you not to peek!"

He replied to the email, "Funny. When should I contact you on Saturday?" On a whim he added, "How about we meet for dinner instead?" Richard hit send. He presumed Ladonna would respond quite later, but he heard from her almost instantly.

"I don't have anyone to watch Bryson."

"Bring him along. Say 6:30?"

"Where?"

"Chequers."

"Does that joint allow children?"

"Yeah, I've seen them there."

"Okay then."

"I checked to make sure this place has a kids' menu," Ladonna told Richard once they settled in their booth.

"Let him try the awesome fries." He smiled at Bryson, who reciprocated.

"Oddly enough, he's into broccoli."

"Should we order an appetizer?"

"All I need is an entrée. Bryson doesn't eat that much." Ladonna strapped Bryson into his booster seat and then glanced around the packed eatery. "It's dim in here. Reminds me of a cigar club that only accepts old, rich guys."

Richard glanced around. Since his first visit to the restaurant, the décor felt less stuffy. He barely noticed the booths covered with reddish-brown leather and dark tapestry or polished brass accents adorning the fixtures. "Order whatever you want."

"Are you sure?"

"I have a gift card, and I also got a discount through the email club. Hope you don't think that's tacky."

"No way. I appreciate frugalness. I stretch my dollars until they scream."

Richard chuckled. "Considering all you've done for me, buying dinner for you is a mere pittance." Richard noted that she wore lipstick instead of the usual lip gloss. She also wore her hair in a bun rather than the loose curls she normally donned. The ruffled neckline of her show-stopping black dress slightly revealed her bosom.

After the waiter took their orders, Ladonna mentioned the proposal. "How do you feel about the draft?"

"Great overall template. I want to make it clear how difficult mourning is when you have no say. Not a detailed account, just a line or two. I'd expound on the topic during conversations with interested senators."

"We can squeeze that in. Before I come by again, could you make a list of the senators from yours and the nine closest districts ranked by distance? We'll add more if they don't respond."

"Tell me what to gather."

"Email addresses, phone numbers, web addresses. Use Excel," she directed. "I'm a fan of spreadsheets. The sorting function helps me stay organized. With 56 senators statewide, falling off track wouldn't be difficult."

"I'll get that done, and then we'll start reaching out to them next weekend."

Ladonna nodded.

With talk of their shared mission behind them, the conversation lulled.

Richard realized they normally spoke of his interests. He'd attempt to uncover a tad more of her history if she allowed him. "My mom enjoyed meeting you. She was shocked that you're single. After she mentioned it, I thought the same."

"By this stage, I assumed I'd be married too."

"Undoubtedly, you're one of the most sincere people I've met, ever."

"Do unto others. That's my blueprint."

"Got any sspecial plans for tomorrow?"

"Early church service and then brunch at my parents'."

"They've been together how long?"

"They grew up with each other. She moved across the street from him when they were in the seventh grade. From what I've heard, they had a sweet spot for each other early on. I came along eleven months after they married so officially thirty-four years."

"How unique."

"Both sets of grandparents stayed in the neighborhood until they died."

Bryson tapped his mom on the arm. "Mommy, can I have some water?"

She slid her glass over to him and tilted it so he could sip through the straw.

"He always seems so well-behaved."

"Overall he's a good boy, but Bryson has his moments. I had to train Crystal and my parents on how to deal with him because he cast a spell on them. He has a way of looking at you with those eyes or talking in that innocent voice of his and making you go against your better judgment. I'd say no TV, read a book. Or I'd say, no playing outside because of your allergies, and he'd convince them to override my decisions while they watched him."

Bryson displayed a mischievous grin.

"I underestimated when he'd develop the ability to strategize. I guess Montessori school is paying off. Speaking of Bryson, my dad lacks the baby-sitting gene, and my mother and Crystal have obligations the next several weekends. Are you opposed to us changing the day or time we meet?"

The prospect of seven days passing without seeing Ladonna unsettled Richard. "Bring Bryson."

"Don't feel obligated."

"He's adept at keeping himself occupied."

"Very generous of you," Ladonna commented.

"I understand you two are a package deal." He pinched off a piece of the bread and buttered it. "Service is slow."

"It's a holiday weekend." She discreetly pointed at dinners across the aisle. "They ordered before us and just got their food."

"Hmmm." He went for another piece of bread but stopped short of placing it in his mouth. "I'm curious," Richard began.

"And stop me if I'm infringing on your privacy, but what the heck is his d-a-d doing overseas?"

"He's a contractor who travels the region repairing and building infrastructures."

"No amount of dough could convince me to fly to that area let alone work there. Takes guts."

"Not as much as handling your responsibilities does. He purposely seeks out foreign companies so he can underreport his income."

"Does he at least check-in or visit when he's in town?"

Ladonna grimaced. "It's sad when my son tells me he forgot how his d-a-d looks. I show him photographs. They'll never replace the real thing. To make matters worse, I'd bet a million bucks he has siblings we know nothing of either with some naïve women over there or someone who works with him or someone he met online. Take your pick."

Richard recognized the gloomy cadence in her voice. Until now, he had no inkling he and Ladonna shared a mutual bond that incorporated hurt and betrayal. Her disclosure caused him to respect her more. He thanked the god he hadn't prayed to in awhile for allowing their paths to cross.

Ladonna and Richard revamped their game plan and decided to send out letters in increments of five. Despite meticulously crafting and proofing the initial set with Ladonna, he reviewed them again after she left their next meeting. He feared letting down Ladonna nearly as much as himself. Richard made sure that what she dictated actually appeared on each page. Then, he met each of her directives. Richard purchased heavy stock, off-white stationary. He addressed the matching envelopes by hand but printed the documents. He dropped them off at the post office where he paid extra to insure certified delivery. He mulled over delivering them in person. That concept fled his mind quickly.

Seven business days passed, and then, according to schedule, Richard contacted the senators by phone. He expected to reach none directly, and that expectation rang true. Instead, Richard dealt with the gatekeepers Ladonna had warned him about. A common theme among the responses emerged. He heard in a variety of phrases the same message: The senator is not available to pursue that line of legislation. He also discovered that the official legislative session had ended in April, adding to the difficulty of reaching lawmakers.

He recognized that they'd created a winning pitch. Still, the dawn of opportunity also ushered in a perceived loss of control. Collaborating with Ladonna nudged him forward slightly. He dwelled less on the debacle of his last attempt to change the law and more on the probability he'd gain support with this new effort.

"I supposed we'd get a nibble of interest, or at least a positive acknowledgement by now," he told Ladonna. They lounged on his patio while Bryson kicked around a ball just a few yards away. Richard suggested the change in scenery during their last meeting because confining the boy to a spot on the floor irked him.

Ladonna commented that her yard contained an abundance of weeds and anthills. Upon initially seeing the expanse outside, Richard, who had leftover pesticide and weed killer, volunteered to eliminate them for her.

Somehow, they managed to stick to normal chatter with no mention of the research that had consumed Richard for what seemed like ages. Today, they returned to the particulars of furthering his mission.

"You factored in Memorial Day?" Ladonna inquired. "No, I suppose government offices shut down. Some senators probably went on vacation."

"Politicians are people too," she reminded him, "which means they can be unorganized, busy with prior engagements, even downright lazy. Holding them to your standards will drive you mad." Ladonna grew quiet and seemingly preoccupied with scrolling through her text messages.

Richard stared into the distance, not focusing on any particular focal point. Bryson moved into his line of sight. He kicked at his foam soccer ball with all the power his little legs could muster, missing half of his attempts.

Ladonna redirected her attention to Richard, who still followed the boy's moves. "I spoke to a fellow paralegal about your situation—."

Richard jerked his head to the side. "Did you mention my name?"

"I only stated the basics."

His eyebrows furrowed and jaws clenched, waiting for Ladonna to say something encouraging to relieve him of his sudden angst.

"That's why I kept quiet," Ladonna said. "You're running through a thousand scenarios without knowing half of the facts."

Richard wanted to hear more. "Go on."

"Well, she suggested approaching our campaign like a job search and that networking might garner leads."

"Interesting."

"So I reached out to one friend in particular."

Richard wondered who else Ladonna had approached without his knowledge.

"She's an executive assistant at the Capitol."

He held his breath.

"She hinted that Senator Winston might back your legislation."

"Isn't he pro-choice?"

"From what she says, he's a neoconservative."

"I asked her to reach out to him so we wouldn't waste our energy if he's unresponsive."

"I guess it's good that we hadn't sent him anything yet."

"Yeah," Ladonna concurred. "If the senator expresses interest, he'll be reviewing our proposal without preconceived notions. Having read and dismissed it prior would have definitely created a roadblock."

Richard pointed to the third set of five proposals lying on the center of the table. "What about those? Do we still send them off?"

"Most definitely. If the senator comes on board, we'll hold off on the next set. My contact guaranteed that she'd have a response by midmonth. Composing this additional one shouldn't take long."

Bryson's ball flew through the air. Richard instinctively caught it with one hand.

"Good catch," Ladonna praised. "Not such a good aim," she mumbled under her breath. "Try kicking the ball in the other direction, Bryson."

"Bryson has no one to guide him," Richard thought, as he reflected on his own childhood. Vague but plentiful, at least Richard had memories of his father. Mrs. Knight filled in the blanks whenever Richard requested details. Intricate details, however, held less relevance than the emotions accompanying flashbacks of his father. The senior Mr. Knight projected a sense of security onto his son. Richard held him in high regard. He felt as if his father wanted to spend time with him even when work or other obligations prevented him from doing so. They would play catch sometimes after work, but for Richard, simply nuzzling next to his father on the sofa as they watched just about anything on TV was the ultimate way to connect with him. Richard equated this to a long hug.

"Let me show you how," Richard recommended. He threw the ball on the ground and then maneuvered it across the lawn with the skill of a pro until he reached Bryson.

"How'd you do that?" Bryson asked.

Richard knelt down and whispered as if sharing a time-honored secret. "The trick is to guide the ball based on where you want it to go." He demonstrated.

"Ooh," Bryson said.

"If you want the ball to go far, use the knuckle of your foot and kick hard. Like this. See? If not, kick softer and use the sides of your feet.

"You try it."

The boy did. During Richard's mini coaching session, he handled the ball much better.

Richard high-fived him. The boy's face lit up. He glimpsed at his mother, and she gave him a thumbs up.

"Keep on practicing," Richard said. He rejoined Ladonna.

She shot him an appreciative glance. "Wow! At this rate, he'll be ready for the World Cup soon."

Richard chuckled. He divided his attention between Ladonna and Bryson.

"Which sports did you play growing up?"

"Baseball, basketball, and flag football with guys in the neighborhood. Never played on an official team."

"Not in college either?"

"Money was scarce. Cheryl and I learned to forgo the extras a lot of kids take for granted."

"I led the majorette squad my senior year of high school."

"Tell me what it's like."

"Twirling a baton?"

"Raising a son alone."

She responded without skipping a beat. "Scary above all. It's tiring but the most fulfilling undertaking conceivable." Ladonna gazed at Bryson, who still concentrated on perfecting his technique. He's a tad sneaky. I think I mentioned that before."

"I still find that hard to believe."

"Here's a perfect example. I stopped buying certain snacks because he'd eat them without permission and hide the wrappers in his room. From that point, I switched to healthy options hoping Bryson would grow up appreciating real food instead of craving artificial flavors and high fructose corn syrup."

"From what I saw at dinner, your plan has worked."

"I often wish I could flash ahead to the future and see how he'll turn out. Bryson is really imaginative," Ladonna went on with a smile. "He's drawn to animals and nature. Heck, maybe he'll be a veterinarian or biologist."

"I pity parents who, unlike you, treat their kids like afterthoughts."

"My mom says I'm overprotective."

"How is that possible? That concept eludes me. Children are treasures, yet a lot of adults dote more on the material things they've acquired like houses and cars." Richard shook his head in disgust. He'd planned to teach his son the rituals of manhood. Because of Nicole, he and Junior would never share sacred moments together akin to those that kept him feeling a connection to his deceased dad. "The media reports are filled with stories of abuse and neglect. Repulsive."

"No one, I suspect, enters into parenthood with ill intentions. All actions have root causes."

"I would've made a great dad," Richard lamented.

"You will be a great dad," Ladonna corrected.

She sounded so sure. Richard hoped that at least a smidgen of her optimism and confidence would rub off on him and that her prediction would come true.

The same careful composition went into Senator Winston's proposal as to the others. Somehow it felt heavier in Richard's hand. He chided himself for dropping them off at a post office rather than an express shipping center. The monster of a line crept along at an aggravating pace. Waiting patrons exchanged desperate and disgusted glances. Richard tapped his feet uneasily against the concrete floor. He ceased doing so after realizing how loud the tapping had become. As a postal clerk closed her window and put up a "Gone to Lunch" sign, customers let out a collective groan. "Lunch this early?" one questioned. "They should open another window," someone behind him chimed in. Fat chance, Richard told himself. Ladonna offered to drop off the mail for him, but Richard declined. He should've accepted her offer. He glanced at the wall clock and debated if, based on the pace of service, he would make it to work on time. He also debated if leaving and going to a UPS or Kinko's, or even completing the task during his lunch break, might be a better option. He resolved to stay.

Once he reached work, concentrating on the tasks necessary to complete real estate transactions proved difficult. Richard fixed his mind instead on the probable outcomes of his appeal to the senator. He resisted relying on the possibility that a referral from Ladonna's associate would lead to his benefit. Richard prepared for the real risk that Winston might decline to help with his mission. He attempted to mentally prepare for the unappealing but plausible reality that he could find himself back at square one in terms of fighting for fathers' rights to consent.

He perused news and editorial articles concerning the District 9 senator in chronological order. From what Richard gathered, Winston married into money. His wife, a descendant of plantation owners who profited from slave labor, remained a central figure in her family's agricultural business. After the company sustained the fallout after the Civil War, it used Industrial Revolution innovations to reinvent itself, and eventually produced organic crops well before the current green craze. They met shortly after Winston took an executive position. Since then, he left that post although he remained on the board of directors. A seemingly mix-matched couple, commentators gradually saw the republican as a force in his own right rather than a man in the shadow of his wife's stellar reputation. Richard anticipated that the senator's three-term stature would render him less susceptible to buckle if his constituents raised concerns regarding the proposal.

During the partner's conference on Tuesday, Richard continued to drift off. He received a voicemail from Ladonna but resisted the urge to step into the hall and listen to it. Suppose the senator had contacted her or updated her friend. His palms grew sweaty. He had put an enormous amount of effort toward securing an ally in the political arena. Had that effort finally materialized into a positive outcome?

"Richard," one of his colleagues said. "Richard, did you catch that?"

He hadn't and peered at his colleague curiously.

He returned Richard's gaze with one of aggravation. "Have your documentation team gather the financials for the Bronner case. This is the second closing postponement. Mr. Bronner is anxious to finalize transfer of ownership."

"Top priority," Richard replied. In actuality, he adamantly blamed Bronner for the delay. He tasked a paralegal with contacting Bronner's secretary to collect the required paperwork only to be met with a lack of concern or urgency.

Once the conference adjourned, Richard rushed back to his office and closed the door. He pressed the speed dial button programmed for Ladonna's number on his cell. She answered just as he started to hang up.

Richard skipped the courtesy of saying hello as his question tumbled out. "You found out something?"

"Not yet. I had errands near your building, so I was checking to see if you might be free for lunch."

"Aw," he responded, sounding discouraged.

"Too late now. As far as an update, it's a waiting game."

Richard emitted a low groan. "I'll let you go then."

"Not so fast," Ladonna said. "One more thing."

Richard pressed his ear closer to the receiver.

"My son begged me to take him to the zoo, and I finally caved in. His school gave out discount tickets."

How he fit into the equation escaped Richard.

"Bryson requested your presence."

"He wants to hang out with me? Why?"

"You're responsible for his newfound interest in giraffes. He's had an overdose of estrogen because my dad has been the only consistent man in his orbit. Instinctively, he's gravitating toward you."

This revelation shocked and propelled Richard into a state of confusion. Could he meet the boy's expectations, and what were those exactly? Did Bryson seek a surrogate dad or merely a new playmate? How close should he allow himself to grow to the boy or his mother? Would Ladonna lose interest in him at the conclusion of their collaboration?

"I just figured," Ladonna continued, "that you might be free since we decided to skip working on proposals this Sunday. I'd actually prefer going on Saturday."

Richard reflected upon the proposition. Ladonna's influence, albeit gradually, allowed him to release a smidgen of the rigidity that encased him prior to their run-in at the bar. Richard abruptly ended the spiral of speculation and heeded Ladonna's previous warning concerning his tendency to over-analyze. "Count me in," he told her.

The Atlanta Zoo amazed Richard as did Ladonna's mothering skills. She led him and Bryson from one exhibit to another with determined precision based on Bryson's interests. In contrast, a bevy of other children in his age range either lead their parents or ran off and left them behind. Richard doubted they were accustomed to the amount of discipline Ladonna instilled in Bryson. She told Richard that they skimmed the zoo's web site, in particular the kids' section, to keep this initial visit from overwhelming him. Despite his youth, Bryson retained a majority of their findings. He scooted next to Richard during a snack break and sat across from his mom at the picnic table. They chatted about a lion that reminded him of a cartoon character. When everyone finished the juice and carrot sticks Ladonna packed, they resumed exploring.

Richard noticed men and some suspect women eyeing Ladonna. She wore stylish square-framed shades, faded jeans, a tank top, and tennis shoes. The sensible outfit provided comfort but also managed to accentuate her physique. Richard supposed the multitude of Ladonna's features attracted stares. People were especially drawn to theherPerhaps her unassuming confidence attracted these strangers, as it had Richard, more so than her choice of clothing. Even those who obviously had girlfriends or wives glanced her way. Their leers, above all, irritated Richard. They disregarded their partners and him. He pushed the brewing disdain into the background of his mind.

All three of them enjoyed observing the array of birds housed at the zoo. The spectrum and vividness of beak and feather colors caught even Richard off guard. While Bryson oohed and aahed, Richard contained his enthusiasm. The boy went wild when an outgoing parrot repeatedly squawked "hello." Bryson's excitement skyrocketed once they neared the wildlife enclosures. Blown-up photographs and arrows signaled the path toward each category of animal. He grabbed Richard's hand and attempted to drag him in the direction of the viewing area.

"Slow down," Ladonna commanded and he heeded her. Bryson kept clinging to Richard. His quick movements left Richard with no opportunity to react. He simply dwelled in the moment, absorbing the warmth of Bryson's tiny palm as it pressed against his.

"Giraffes are mammals," Bryson declared within steps of reaching the main attraction.

Taller kids and adults crowded around the animals, watching them chew on the crests of acacia trees.

"Find a spot where he can see everything," Ladonna recommended.

"I'll just lift him up."

"Be careful," Ladonna said as Richard gingerly placed Bryson on his shoulders. Richard barely detected the extra cargo.

"Oooh!" Bryson exclaimed. One giraffe zoned in on him. He flapped his ears and stuck his tongue out at the boy. Bryson squealed in delight, causing bystanders to chuckle and grin.

"I want to buy a t-shirt for Bryson from the gift shop," Ladonna said when they finished observing the creature. "He can walk. Otherwise he'll constantly expect you to be his personal chariot."

Richard eased Bryson from his shoulders. The trio spent the next 10 minutes viewing the assortment of shirts and souvenirs in the gift shop.

Bryson conked out less than a mile from the zoo. As much as Richard enjoyed the afternoon outing, the boy's biological dad's lackadaisicalness nagged at him. The wandering gazes that followed Ladonna throughout the zoo grounds did too. Embers of hate directed at Nicole and Toni that he thought he'd extinguished reignited. Their foolishness and selfishness wiped out the opportunity for him to share similar experiences with Junior.

He expressed his frustrations with Ladonna as she drove them back to her home, where he parked his car. She confirmed that she was oblivious to the attention she garnered.

"I can't wrap my mind around this culture of infidelity," Richard told her.

She switched lanes and then responded. "Part of the problem," she said, "is that people rely less on family and God and traditional role models and now admire figureheads they'll certainly never even meet."

Richard found Ladonna's high moral standards refreshing. "Yeah," Richard agreed, "Take Hollywood and politics for instance. Power allows celebrities and politicians to fling aside inhibitions. It turns them into pigs. We've come to tolerate their indiscretions and reward them with further recognition."

"For me, the struggle is determining the greater evil: perpetrators in relationships who cheat or predators who exchange their bodies for wealth or fame."

"My arthritic grandmother would've done cartwheels if she was around to see skanks peddling sex tapes."

Richard launched into a mini-tangent rehashing all of Nicole's indiscretions. "It's her fault I'm not 100% on top of my game," he concluded.

"As incomprehensible as we both find her actions, Nicole found an acceptable reason for her choices deep down somewhere. Her choices made sense to her, not necessarily to you or anyone else. "

Ladonna knew nothing of his past counseling attempts. The sessions minimally eased the persistent hurt plaguing Richard, but he continued to gravitate toward the source of his despair: Nicole's single-handed, life-altering choice. "So you suppose she had a valid justification?" he asked in an accusatory tone.

"It isn't for me to comprehend her motivation," Ladonna replied just as sharply. "Try considering each day a building block toward forgiveness. A little today, and little more tomorrow."

He grunted.

"Holding on to hate will halt your healing. Believe me, I've traveled down that road. Zillions have."

"And Bryson's dad. You've really reconciled his absence, his nonchalant approach to fatherhood?"

"He probably compartmentalized parts of his life, put certain aspects away in some place where he pretends all is well. I'll never know since he robbed me of the opportunity to ask the tough questions."

"So you two don't communicate at all?"

"Through paperwork mostly, filings with the court when he falls too far in arrears. What I know for sure is that I am here. In the end, Bryson is my responsibility, not my parents' or anyone else's who might enter my life. I hold no delusions that I can be a dad and a mom. I just do my best to be enough."

"My mother showed that same sort of spunk while she raised me and Pam." In his younger years Richard rarely reflected on the senior Mr. Knight's absence from his mother's point of view. Whether the result of death or disinterest, both women faced parallel problems, he surmised. "I assume she hid how hard single parenthood must've been to protect us."

"From what you've told me about her, I'm sure she leaned on her faith."

"I suppose," Richard replied, well aware of how he'd done just the opposite and turned away from God as his marriage imploded."

The car slowed as Ladonna pulled into her driveway. "Imagine all the negative energy that would be floating around in the universe if some of us didn't voluntarily let go of past hurt, guilt or shame. I resided in woe-is-me land for a spell. It's not a place you want to stay in forever."

Chapter 12

The untimely morning call came across as part of a foggy dream. When Richard's vibrating cell phone bounced from his nightstand and hit the floor, he rolled over and scooped it up. Groggy, he answered, "Hello?" Richard only caught bits of Ladonna's apologetic greeting.

"I have to go in before my normal time," she went on, "and decided to contact you now because my day is sure to get hectic. At any rate, I thought you'd want the news ASAP."

Richard sat up and pressed his back against the headboard. He braced himself for what Ladonna would say next.

"Senator Winston wants to meet with you. He's aiming for a morning time slot on Thursday or Friday."

"That soon?" Shock enveloped him along with an overwhelming tide of gratitude for Ladonna's efforts. With roughly three days' notice, he'd have to rearrange his schedule but resolved to let nothing stand between him and this opportunity. "Friday is the better choice for me. I'll make it happen. Can you come too?"

"I'll try my best. My boss might let me come in later and cut my lunch break in half until I make up the missing hours. If I can't, you know I'll be there in spirit."

"I love you, Ladonna. I couldn't have gotten this far without you."

"I love you, too," she replied instantly as if the sentiment had been bubbling on the surface waiting to emerge.

Richard's declaration sent Ladonna into a tailspin, altering the flow of her precise morning schedule. She plopped down on the side of her bathtub. She still had to apply her makeup and dress Bryson. He certainly had taken a liking to Richard. The more their research gained traction, the more their relationship did as well. While she suspected they'd eventually exchange those words, she had not anticipated hearing them so soon. Although Ladonna heard the sincerity in Richard's voice, she questioned the level of meaning.

Did he love her company, her organizational skills, or the void that she and Bryson definitely filled? How did her appeal compare to Nicole's? Ladonna viewed love and hate as the positive and negative sides of the same continuum. From what she had witnessed, Ladonna doubted anything between Richard and her could rival the intensity he displayed for his former wife. "Stop worrying, girl," she muttered to herself. Ladonna sprang to her feet and then retrieved her compact from the sink. She trusted God would lead her down the right path. For now, she had to get out the door.

She stood with Richard outside of the four-story building housing Senator Winston's headquarters. Beyond the excitement of the impending appointment, she felt additional flashes of exhilaration because they had spoken only by phone since Richard said he loved her. On those calls and today, though, he made no mention of that occurrence. She measured his movements, watching to see if he acted differently. She glimpsed no indications during the 50-minute ride over that they'd surely left the realm of friendship and entered the sphere of coupledom.

Understandably, he spoke solely of how to approach the senator. Broaching the topic of their relationship would only insert undo stress into the situation. Ladonna resolved that Richard's history required her to handle him with care. Her ability to appear calm amidst chaos, was her invaluable strong suit. She knew Richard fed off of her strength, so her focus remained on encouraging his confidence. Everything they had worked toward relied on Richard representing himself as self-assured. She straightened the collar of his dress shirt and then looked deep into his eyes. She controlled a strong urge to give him a peck on the cheek. Ladonna squeezed his hands instead and swore she felt his pulse racing. She offered a final dose of encouragement. "Be yourself. The rest will follow."

The senator moved about with an air of authority, as if he had staked out a top rung on the ladder of political power and knew exactly how to reach it. He stood to greet them, shaking both their hands. To Richard, his grip felt like it came from a sumo wrestler rather than a lanky man with graying hair whose height hovered near 6'2". Richard winced on the inside and glanced at Ladonna. She displayed no outward signs of discomfort. Richard reasoned that the enormity of the circumstance frazzled his nerves. Ladonna, as usual, remained calm. Winston offered tea, water, and coffee. Ladonna and Richard declined. "You sure?" Winston asked after everyone sat down. "My assistant found a premium blend from Guatemala."

"We're fine," Richard assured him. "Again, we appreciate you fitting us into your busy schedule and showing interest in my cause."

"I serve on a variety of committees. Of course, I've put more effort into some than others. Your cause is an issue I can raise with the Health and Human Services Committee. I let my involvement on that committee slip because of our state's banking crisis. The Banking and Finance Committee dealt with an unprecedented number of collapsed savings and loan institutions. Since I co-chaired that group, it demanded much of my focus."

Richard spotted a copy of his proposal lying on Winston's desk. The senator followed his gaze. "The vigor with which you stated your case also piqued my interest. I assume from what I read that you have no other children?"

"That's correct."

"You'll learn that I detest operating on assumptions. Solid facts and figures, that's what I've built my livelihood on."

Richard took the comment to mean that the senator had unquestionably decided to come on board. He posed a direct question to Winston instead of assuming. "So, you'll definitely help?"

"Yes," Winston confirmed.

"If I may ask," Ladonna chimed in, "what's your stance on abortion?"

"My foreign affairs post put me in direct contact with businessmen in other countries who studied the prospect of setting up commerce bases in Georgia. Those negotiations, naturally, included delving into their traditions. I discovered over and over that they placed investing in youth as a priority. Two broad themes continued to emerge: magnifying the importance of education and encouraging family planning. America, on the other hand, seems to have lost focus. How can we pump new blood into our society if we keep killing our most valuable natural resource?"

Ladonna and Richard both nodded in agreement.

The senator went on, speaking with the fervor of a leader addressing his followers. "As a nation, we rallied with the world to end Hitler's goal of eliminating the Jews. Decade after decade, we continue to pinpoint destroyers of humanity who hide under the guise of political leadership all the while sponsoring our own brand of genocide. One of my biggest fears is that our country will lose its status as a global leader. To sum it all up, I view abortion as a national tragedy but realize I'm outnumbered. Tackling an issue indirectly is often the most prudent form of attack."

Adrenaline flowed through Richard while the man spoke. He viewed taking half the day off from work well worth it. Plaques from a multitude of local and statewide civic organizations covered the walls in the senator's modest office. They confirmed Richard's perception that Winston took a genuine interest in the statewide community. He also prominently displayed pictures that provided glimpses into his life. One, set at a horse stable, showed Winston with what looked like his grandchildren. Another featured farmhands in a field of collard greens. The most striking and memorable appeared to be the oldest: a younger, jovial Winston and his bride on their wedding day.

Winston struck Richard as someone who preferred leading a laidback existence even though he possessed the means to indulge in extravagance. The fact that he chose Snellville for his residence and political hub made Winston more likeable. Situated northeast of Atlanta and far from any interstate, Snellville's official site claimed roughly 20,000 residents dwelled within the 10 square miles it encompassed. The place appealed immensely to parents eager to raise children in a close-knit society. American flags hung at every turn, and ancient oaks and pines stood guard as if protecting the area from urban sprawl.

In an impressively thorough manner, Winston laid out a road map for pursing a bill aimed at requiring spousal notification. Since the legislative session of the General Assembly, which convened in January, adjourned in April, he planned to seek cosponsors during the summer. He spoke of allies in both chambers and his confidence that they'd support Richard's endeavors. Richard asked if he'd eventually meet any of them. Winston confirmed that most likely some would want to speak with him either one on one or in small groups.

"Don't leap too far ahead of the process," he told Richard. "Consider those informal meetings where you're basically relaying your motivation. My allies, in general, will rely on my endorsement."

The senator reiterated that he knew of nothing on the books matching the verbiage Richard recommended but intended to task an intern about cross-referencing laws he could perhaps amend.

Richard left Winston's presence in exceptional spirits. That enthusiasm, however, dipped within a matter of days once Father's Day came.

Instead of basking in his recent achievement, Richard withdrew. When Ladonna called to check in with him, she detected the hollowness in his voice.

"You could use some praise music to uplift your spirits," Ladonna suggested. "My church hosts gospel concert fundraisers, and the next one is Sunday. Why don't you come? My mother has been rehearsing like crazy because she swears she's the next Mahalia Jackson."

Meeting the woman who raised such an outstanding daughter appealed to Richard, but he hadn't reached a point where going to any place of worship seemed appealing. Besides, if his own mother discovered he'd stepped foot inside another church, she'd flip out.

"Thanks for the invite, but I'm not feeling up to it."

"Did something happen since Friday? I thought you'd be ecstatic in light of how well it went with Winston."

He explained that overhearing another partner boast about

the marvelous Father's Day present he received initiated the mood swing.

"Allow me to offer a suggestion," she said, "a solution for creating the closure you need."

"I'm open. Shoot."

"I'm a firm believer in celebrating the people in my life while they're alive, but there are ways to do so after a passing. Most loved ones have memories to hold onto. Unfortunately, you don't. Some keep physical tokens. You have none. Figure out a means to mark Junior's presence that works for you."

"How? A tombstone?"

"If that's what it takes."

"A tombstone without a body. Seems eerie and such a waste."

"You could start a scholarship fund for low-income boys and name it after him."

"Funds are too tight right now to supply an adequate amount of money for that," Richard lamented. "But I like that idea."

"You could plant a tree in the backyard and put a bench by it where you can sit and reflect."

"I do plan on staying in this house." He paused as if mulling over the notion. "Then again, we've seen how well my plans work out."

"If I'm not mistaken, certain memorial parks sell plots. You do see yourself staying in Atlanta, right?"

"That much I know for sure."

"Then planting a tree or bush or patch of flowers at one of those places might work. Pick an in-town location. Since the metro area is widespread, it won't matter if you move."

"I'll consider it," Richard said. "You've opened the door to possibilities I overlooked. "You're so insightful."

She brushed off the compliment and promised to follow up with him to see if he'd come to a decision.

Richard held the utmost respect for Ladonna and welcomed the mental tune up. With each encounter, she rescued him a bit more from the rubble his life had become.

"No Bryson?" Richard asked when Ladonna arrived alone. Mrs. Knight and Kevin arrived at Oglethorpe Memorial Gardens shortly ahead of her. The location, situated within Atlanta's city limits, provided easy access for whenever Richard or Mrs. Knight wanted to visit.

"Crystal offered to watch him," Ladonna replied. "I didn't think he'd grasp the concept and didn't want him to detract from the occasion."

"Richard says he's such a good boy," Mrs. Knight chimed in. "I even baked some oatmeal cookies for him." She had prepared a light lunch to wind down the afternoon so everyone planned to meet at her house when the brief ceremony ended.

Ladonna apologized and offered to bring the cookies home with her. "I'll be sure to tell him that you baked them especially for him," added. "He'll love that." Mrs. Knight seemed satisfied, smiling proudly, as Richard then introduced Ladonna to Kevin.

All of them stood at the plot Richard chose. The facility's groundskeeper planted a Southern Red Cedar prior to the dedication. Richard discovered that cedars stood for healing, cleansing, and protection. He needed all three. The trees also marked births and deaths. The garden staff praised its ornamental structure and its drooping foliage, which provided soothing shade on scorching summer days. As a sturdy, drought-resistant variety, Richard had added peace of mind that the Southern Red would withstand the forces of nature and evolve into a glorious symbol of his unborn son's significance.

Instinctively, everyone formed a circle in front of the tree. "I'll go last," Richard said. "Would you like to start, Ladonna?"

"Today we recognize Junior, a little one who's had a big

impact. It's because of you that I met your father, and it's because of you that he's going to change so many lives. I know your light shines in Heaven." She pulled a miniature, ceramic, light brown teddy bear from her purse and placed the figurine at the tree's base.

The gesture touched Richard. He gave her a hug. "Kevin, it's your turn."

Kevin cleared his throat. "I'm sorry I'll never know you. I kept this from your dad, but I secretly looked forward to being a godfather. He spoke often of wanting to be a parent and some of his enthusiasm rubbed off on me. Watch over him, over all of us."

"Ma."

"My first grand," Mrs. Knight began, "how I looked forward to doting on you and watching you grow. My faith sustains me in the wake of your loss." She glanced at Richard. "Its power overcomes the greatest tribulations. I pray that you're with my beloved husband and that when I reunite with him, you'll be there to greet me, too. Until then, remember that grandma loves you." She inched closer to Richard. "Son, go ahead."

He let out a lengthy sigh. "Where do I begin, Junior? I learned of and lost you within a matter of moments. Know that I regret missing out on raising you. Before you even existed, and before I even met your mom, I envisioned a son. Without a doubt, you would've made me so proud. I think of you so much. I dream of you. In those dreams, I find peace. In those dreams, I find you."

Mrs. Knight requested that everyone bow their heads and then led them in the Lord's Prayer.

"Amen," they said in unison.

Richard thanked everyone for attending. "I want to finalize the plaque design," he told them and asked for his mom to join him. "It shouldn't take long, if you want to wait," Richard told his friends.

Kevin offered to let Ladonna follow him to Mrs. Knight's house since she'd never gone there before.

"Alright," Richard said. "We'll see you there."

"Let me ask you something," Kevin said as they weaved through the garden. "How can this campaign of Richard's do any good?"

Ladonna stopped short and peered at him inquiringly. "Campaign?"

"Hashing out his issues by bringing a legislator into the mix, how can Richard move on?"

Without attempting to answer Kevin's question, Ladonna said, "He's compelled to see the process through. He's passionate about keeping other men from experiencing the same hurt."

"We all know how shady politicians can be. Hell, another six months has to go by before the bill has a chance to materialize."

"Who knows what the future holds?" she countered. "I try to cheer him on so his present becomes more pleasant than his past."

"By talking about the baby constantly and calling it Junior like he knew it was a boy?"

"It's a form of coping, much better than snapping and committing a crime of passion. You've known him much longer, so I, of course, respect your opinions. I'm sure you're there for Richard in your own way. I'm just showing support and offering myself as another sounding board."

"Hmmm," Kevin responded, sounding as unsure as when he posed the initial question.

"People crave acknowledgement of their feelings and retribution when they've experienced a wrong. As a cop, you must identify on some level with your friend."

"His mother agrees with me. She refuses to say so for fear of alienating Richard."

Kevin's disclosure troubled Ladonna. Even though they avoided honestly voicing their opinions, Ladonna sensed Richard picked up on the lack of confidence emanating from his closest advisors. Kevin's comments provided her with additional insight on why Richard had turned to alcohol and away from God.

"As two people who care deeply for Richard, let's agree we both have his best interest at heart and call it a draw," Ladonna said decisively.

Alone in her car following Kevin to Mrs. Knight's house, Ladonna wondered how she and Kevin had attended the same service yet departed with drastically varying mindsets. Kevin acted as if Richard held on purposely when she knew how he struggled daily to overcome his heartache.

"He has me," Ladonna said out loud. She suspected that she had the power to save Richard if only he'd let her.

Mrs. Knight invited Ladonna back two weeks later. She expressed her disappointment that Ladonna had not brought Bryson. Ladonna explained that her parents took him to view Independence Day fireworks at Stone Mountain. She normally joined them and didn't want to totally disrupt the tradition. Mrs. Knight requested that Ladonna bring Bryson the next time she stopped by. She treated Ladonna and Richard like a couple rather than acquaintances and spoke as if she took for granted that Ladonna would be a part of their lives for years to come.

To Richard's dismay, Mrs. Knight brought out the first in a series of photo albums chronicling Pam and Richard's childhood. She regaled Ladonna with tales of his upbringing. Ladonna wondered if Richard had expressed any feelings for her to his mother or if Mrs. Knight merely treated all guests with the same warmth. In a weird sense, Ladonna felt she'd just gone through a final audition for the role of a woman worthy of being in Richard's life. He shared previously how his mom got a negative vibe from Nicole and how he regretted not taking her opinion into consideration. After all, she knew him better than anyone else. Seeing Richard and his mom interact caused Ladonna to flash ahead. She hoped that Bryson would remain close to her as he grew up.

While Richard drove her home, Ladonna reflected upon the momentum their relationship gained. She and Richard hung out more after attending the tree dedication. When they did, the air seemed lighter and Richard less burdened. They divvied up time between each other's homes, spending more time at Ladonna's place than his. Sometimes Crystal joined them. Richard played with Bryson while Ladonna cooked dinner, or he let her relax while he cooked. If they watched a movie, Richard sat shoulder to shoulder with her but fell short of snuggling. She sensed a barrier preventing him from becoming more physical. Ladonna held no expectations of grand gestures and certainly no desire to jump into bed with him. Still, she sought outward signs of his affection to validate the words he uttered weeks ago.

Richard walked Ladonna to her front door and, to her astonishment, swooped in for a kiss. He brushed her cheek tenderly. It ranked as the shortest yet sweetest kiss she ever experienced. Richard stepped back before Ladonna could contemplate her response. She merely smiled and wished him a good night. The fireworks in the sky paled in comparison to the ones she just experienced.

Chapter 13

Senator Winston called Richard to follow up as he had promised during their initial meeting. Overall, he had no status updates, but the senator provided Richard with his personal email address and cell phone number. Winston stated that he had a series of business trips planned. During those absences, which would take him away for nearly a week at a time, he would continue working on Richard's bill and wanted them to remain in contact.

Laying the groundwork for an urban, mixed-use facility demanded a great deal of Richard's attentiveness and allowed him to obsess less over Winston's progress. Richard was a project manager on what he deemed his first true high-scale partner undertaking. The complex encompassed seven acres once occupied by a defunct automobile plant. A Swedish mega-developer hired Goldstein, Levy & Finch to secure the land at auction. The firm did so successfully and now oversaw the project's next phase. With demolition of the old structure complete, Richard and another partner waded through the task of approving anchor store leases.

The firm operated under a policy of duel ownership. In doing so, no project rested on the shoulders of one attorney. That strategy came about after a substantial venture nearly fell apart when an attorney, who kept shoddy records, took ill.

His sickness resulted in decreased productivity and drastically skewed the client's timeline. Because of this, Richard paired with another newly-promoted attorney, Brad Henson.

However, Henson displayed obsessive-compulsive tendencies that grated on Richard's already frayed nerves. Henson placed documents in an order predetermined by him and corrected Richard if he veered off course. He incessantly double-checked behind himself and his coworkers. Extreme order ruled Henson's workflow. Richard thought he'd notice if someone removed a paperclip from the box on his desk. And, on occasion, Richard sensed that he'd rather operate solo. Richard diffused his stress the old-fashioned way—with a nightcap. The Hennessy, he found, let him forget Henson's eccentric tendencies and the enormity of their task at hand.

The law firm charged Richard and Henson with coordinating closings of condos situated within the mixed-use development, which added another level of responsibility and pressure. They did so with the assistance of two of the firm's in-house real estate agents. The Atlanta site was supposed to be a model, which would be replicated in other American cities and eventually in Canadian.

On a personal front, he and Ladonna proceeded cautiously with getting to know each other. Richard welcomed the downtime spent with Ladonna and Bryson. Even Crystal grew on him. He discovered that Ladonna had zero close friends besides her roommate. The demands of raising a son alone, Ladonna shared, downgraded her one friend to an acquaintance because Ladonna chose to focus on Bryson rather than to hang out. She also realized that some of the other women she associated with didn't have her best interest in mind. Richard reflected on how the birth of Ladonna's son forced her to exercise a greater deal of discretion while the death of his resulted in the same.

Richard foresaw no new entrants into his inner circle for a while. He had no strength for heartache or heart-wrenching goodbyes. Bypassing interpersonal interactions that might inevitably lead to joy allowed him to avoid pain. By the end of July, Richard had visited Junior's memorial twice since the dedication—once alone and once with his mom. Standing under the cedar grounded Richard like nothing else had. The privacy of the tree's shade dissipated Richard's fears that strangers would overhear him speaking to his son. His words flowed like an unrestrained river of sorrow, uncertainties, and hate toward Nicole.

When Mrs. Knight accompanied him, she and Richard discussed new beginnings. She spelled out her adoration of Ladonna and mentioned how they seemed equally yoked. Richard steered her away from planning out his future and making Ladonna a central figure in it. Despite his own adoration for her, seeking reform in the spousal notification arena was a higher priority to Richard than pursing a romantic endeavor. He resolved to let what he and Ladonna shared progress organically.

True to Winston's prediction, a moderate number of his colleagues contacted Richard to discuss the bill. As the senator speculated, their inquiries began trickling in early August. Most, he told Richard, desired mental breaks before delving into talks of new legislation. Some chose to chat by phone, others in person. Richard traveled wherever requested. Rendezvous points included district offices, homes, restaurants, etc. One representative, to Richard's shock, invited him to play a round of golf. During that particular outing, Richard wished he had taken advantage of the lessons his mother purchased for him.

The politicians, all of whom were male except for one, generally fell into two categories. One sector, in Richard's view, behaved as public servants content with working regular jobs during the off season. Many, Richard learned, owned small businesses, led humble lives and seemed, based on their talks, less concerned with power plays. On the surface at least, they appeared to let morals and the best interest of the public sway their policy decisions. The others seemingly parlayed their status into lucrative consulting deals or held high level positions on advisory boards. Those careers provided them with enough income to live well above the means of regular citizens and to afford second homes and lavish automobiles. Most divulged desires to hold higher public offices and how that influenced their support or lack thereof for certain issues.

Ladonna helped immensely with his preparation. Together, they dug up interesting tidbits of info so Richard could personalize his approach to each politician. Richard already had some details on file but needed to refresh his memory. In actuality, he could have prepared alone. Having her guidance instilled him with a dose of calm. Ladonna drilled him with lines he was likely to get probed with. She even called occasionally to cheer him on as he drove to meetings.

The farthest one took place in Brunswick, a southeastern town close to Jacksonville. Richard hinted at meeting virtually, but the senator insisted on seeing him. To accommodate the meetings, Richard often rearranged his work schedule. On particularly hectic days he responded to voicemails and emails regarding the Swedish project or other assignments later than desired.

Soon after Labor Day, Winston's intern delivered a draft of the bill for Richard's review. Ian, a pimply-faced college sophomore, explained that Winston wanted it to remain under wraps for now. Once he and Richard came to a consensus on its contents, he'd pass it on to a makeshift exploratory committee consisting of representatives and senators. Richard showed the draft to Ladonna immediately. Neither of them found flaws.

The bill addressed key areas Richard found crucial. It required a minimum 48-hour waiting period between meeting with a doctor and the procedure, for all women. Physicians had to present a printed ultrasound copy to all women and, upon request, to the husbands. Married women had to present notarized authorization forms signed by spouses as a minimum burden of proof prior to abortions.

Technically, the bill underwent no formal study; however, Winston and his allies followed virtually the same protocol as when their chambers were in session. His intern conducted an opinion poll prior to Winston penning the draft. In doing so, he explained, the road to creating the legal bill version and presenting it to the House and eventually the Senate would be less tedious. Richard hoped the senator's efforts during the summer and fall paid off.

Once the new session commenced, Winston's groundwork, the senator predicted, would make debate on the floor easier. He'd be well prepared for the preliminary screening in which he, the legislator who introduced the bill, had to address the Health and Human Services Committee. Legislators who favored or opposed would also have an opportunity to voice their opinions.

Richard realized the committee might go outside of the Legislature to seek opinions from doctors and lawyers. The committee maintained the means to subpoena witnesses and records. Most likely, it would seek testimony from men and women affected by abortions. Richard supposed that most, especially women, would shy away from public scrutiny.

Another level of due diligence revolved around research. The Legislature's guidelines required an analysis of the situation in Georgia and other states, primarily surrounding ones that led to reasoning for the proposed law. It additionally opened a forum for citizens who wished to voice opinions to speak at meetings. As the presiding officer, Winston planned to automatically green-light the measure, which he anticipated would garner favorable responses in the House. Within a matter of weeks, the senator's overall plan began to unravel.

A reporter from the local NBC affiliate accosted Winston as soon as he cleared airport security and headed for the baggage claim carousel. The woman quickened her step to keep up as he shot past her.

"Senator Winston!" she called out with her microphone extended in front of her. A cameraman followed closely behind her. She called out again before catching his attention.

He turned to follow the high-pitched shriek and appeared startled momentarily before gaining his composure. The senator had just commenced a series of trips to agricultural distributors located in the South and Gulf Coast regions. This last flight proved particularly bumpy, preventing him from catching a long overdue nap. He looked forward to lounging at home for the rest of the afternoon until he attended Sunday morning mass with his wife. "Yes?"

"Senator, I'm Renee Cora with WNBC."

He knew of her reputation as a dogged demander of the truth. The news station's tagline touted leading the region in investigative reporting. "Our sources indicate you've been busy in the off season preparing an anti-abortion bill." She thrust the microphone at him.

What sources? Winston wondered. He put forth extensive effort to keep the legislation under wraps in order to limit dissection from groups that surely would oppose it before he could formally present it. "I'm working on a reproductive health measure," he responded, "not an anti-abortion bill."

"We'd love to hear details," she probed.

Curious bystanders milled around them. A jokester even made funny facial gestures in the background.

"As you stated Ms. Cora, the legislation is a draft. When it comes to fruition, I'll gladly discuss the particulars."

They politely smiled at each other until Cora broke the stalemate. She directed her cameraman to stop rolling. "May I have a word with you off record?" she asked Winston. Her colleague stepped out of hearing range. She then continued. "I have a copy of the draft."

He kept his voice steady in an effort to mask his disbelief. "How is that possible?" Winston countered.

"Now we both know I can't reveal my sources," Cora said.

Winston's expression rang of cynicism.

"I've got proof if you need it."

"Go ahead," he pressed.

"Forty-eight hour waiting period. Sonogram and spousal requirements. Ring a bell?"

She had him. He knew what she'd say next.

"Grant my network an exclusive and we'll allow you ample opportunity to explain your position."

She'd offered an ultimatum in the guise of an actual choice. If Winston snubbed her she'd use the standard "refused further comment" line. Divulging details prematurely certainly proved risky.

"Contact me by Monday to confirm the details, or we'll run the story."

Winston granted an interview that ran on each of the station's four broadcasts. He neglected to inform Richard of this development. He heard about it from Mrs. Knight, a self-proclaimed news junkie who saw the interview at 11:00 the previous night. She relayed that a political insider tipped off the reporter out of fear that Winston's latest efforts might stall the women's rights movement. The senator, his mother said, debunked rumors about the bill. The biggest rumor, from what she perceived based on Cora's line of questioning, involved outlawing abortions altogether.

Richard asked his mother if the senator mentioned him. She explained that Winston conveyed how an unnamed constituent sought his help after learning of his wife's abortion. After speaking to his mother, Richard watched the interview online. As she'd stated, the senator touched upon some of the proposed bill's features. Winston's vagueness pertaining to his source assisted in dissipating some of the aggravation boiling within Richard. While he fell short of professing to know the proper protocol in this situation, he essentially considered Winston's lack of a heads up a breach in professional courtesy.

He called the senator's cell phone and left a message. Richard stated that he simply wanted to know what prompted Winston's public disclosure. After waiting more than three hours for a response, he called Winston's office and had to dial the number repeatedly since he got a busy signal. Instead of the intern's voice, an automated message greeted him.

The senator reached Richard at 9:30 the next morning. Richard asked him to hold and- then closed his office door. Winston automatically offered an apology for not responding earlier. He offered none for keeping him out of the loop in the first place. He told Richard that since the segment aired requests inundated his office and overwhelmed his intern. They decided to use the answering machine as a buffer.

Richard brought up the oversight.

"Well," the senator responded, "it totally slipped my mind. Ever since I ran into that reporter it's been a whirlwind. I had a short window for prepping for the interview, and then my intern got slammed with inquiries after it, and I had to deal with that issue."

He sounded totally sincere. "Where do you go from here?" Richard asked.

"Next," Winston replied, "I respond to the numerous other interview requests and focus on the ones that'll assist in gaining support for our cause. Then, we prep for those."

Richard thought the senator misspoke. "We?"

"Absolutely. Nothing appeals to media or the public more than human interest stories."

Richard doubted his ability and desire to display his turmoil in front of an audience. He expressed those concerns to Winston.

"I'll draw attention away from you as long as I can. Understand, though, that reporters constantly seek angles. Your identity definitely will rank highly among the info they want to uncover.

Later in the week, Richard and Ladonna met for lattes and Danishes at a French bakery by her work. He spoke to her about his misgivings.

"No sense in stressing over something that hasn't happened yet," she said. "I do agree that staying in the shadows will be difficult."

"I'm comfortable in courtrooms arguing cases," Richard said in what sounded like a musing rather than a definite statement. "I suppose I can transfer those same debating skills into interviews."

"Sure you can." She glimpsed the unspoken uncertainty he tried to hide. "Why don't you study those commentary shows on cable? All the guests banter back and forth trying to convince each other their view is the right one."

"I could brainstorm the questions they'd likely pose."

"That's a good idea too but don't overanalyze."

Richard sipped his coffee. "Or," he said pondering a new scenario, "Winston's prediction might very well be off."

"For a moment, think about all the passion you hold for this mission. Honestly, can you rely on Winston to champion it with the same zeal?"

Richard raised a brow. "Other men argued for spousal approval before. I'm hardly a pioneer."

"But we live in the present, and presently you're the one standing up and trying to grant rights to fathers. Your story holds authority. It's why I stuck around even when Crystal pegged you as a lunatic. Stop underestimating yourself."

The senator called Richard nearly two weeks after their last conversation with an update he dreaded receiving. In spite of Ladonna's pep talk, Richard resisted stepping into the role of spokesperson. The fact that none of his coworkers knew the gritty details of his breakup with Nicole made him want to continue being silent.

"Knight," Winston said, "I held the vultures off, but they're swooping in."

A knot formed in the pit of Richard's gut.

"Cora, the reporter who initially uncovered the bill, dug up your name."

"How?"

"She'd swallow a cyanide pill before disclosing that information. Members of media profess to serve by bringing news to light. In reality, that goal falls secondary to luring in viewers, which lures in advertisers. Focus on the how of handling her inquiries rather than how she discovered you."

Winston coached Richard on the ins and outs of being an interview subject. Frankly, Richard found little value in the first part of the tutoring, which involved learning how to answer the reporter. He decided prior to speaking with the senator to basically slip into the role of defendant. As a lawyer, he primarily conducted the probing but had enough experience prepping clients to draw on the skills involved in responding to questions rather than asking them. He found Winston's assessment of Cora more stimulating.

According to Winston, she used charm to disarm and hide her calculating nature. He heard through the political grapevine that the woman, who had flawless vision, wore glasses and dressed like a librarian to put her subjects at ease. Her objective with each interaction led back to extracting the more salacious sound bites.

Cora accommodated Richard from the start by arranging their sit-down on the weekend. She walked him through the process by phone: she told him where to check in, that the interview shouldn't take more than 30 minutes, and she gave him an idea about her general line of questioning. Her producer would condense the segment after reviewing raw footage. She agreed, upon request, to avoid mentioning his profession and place of employment. Against his better judgment, Richard relied on her verbal assurance. He weighed giving his boss or the firm's HR department advanced notice but decided not to.

When she greeted him in person, Cora thanked Richard again for agreeing to speak with her, as if he actually had a choice. She led him to a green room before they reached their final destination and offered bottled water, peanuts, crackers, and other light snacks.

"I recommend eating and drinking something," she stated after he declined. "It's surprising how the normally well-composed grow faint once we begin."

Cora led Richard to an unassuming room on the far side of the studio. It contained beige and blue checkered carpet, off-white walls, a pair of upholstered navy chairs facing each other, and a single yet powerful brass floor lamp. The setting contrasted sharply with the hectic scurry of activity occurring in the main newsroom.

He cloaked his uneasiness with a smile. The mix of vodka and cranberry juice he'd had prior to arriving wore off quicker than he anticipated. Maybe Cora's comments subliminally affected him or the heat from the beaming camera and lamp. Maybe the cameraman's countdown leading to inevitably uttering the intricacies only Richard's inner circle knew unnerved him. Was he actually in this spot waiting for Cora to rummage through his history and motivations?

As Cora uttered her first syllable, Richard contemplated backing out. According to Winston, resisting would prove futile and entice the reporter to do an exposé in which she skewed relevant facts.

"We're here with Richard Knight," Cora began as her facial features morphed into an ultra-poised gaze, "a central figure behind Senator Winston's proposed spousal notification bill."

Richard responded with a toothless smile.

"His desire to enact a bill containing requirements that married women receive approval from their spouses prior to seeking abortions stems from experience. Share the particulars with us, Mr. Knight."

"Essentially, my ex discovered she was pregnant during our separation and decided to abort our son, who I didn't know existed until he no longer did."

"I'm sorry for your loss," she replied in a hollow, practiced manner. "Why, though, did you leap to changing the law?"

"To prevent other men from dealing with the same damage my ex inflicted on me." He sat back in his chair and straightened his posture.

"If women possess ownership of their bodies, don't they also possess ownership of the embryos within? Why should spouses have final say?"

"Child," Richard corrected. "It took two to create the *child*. The decision to destroy it shouldn't be solitary."

"Supreme Court mandates state otherwise."

"God's law overrules man's, in my opinion. That's why his commandments, especially Thou Shalt Not Kill, have survived throughout the ages as a template for behavior. And to expound on the previous question, marriage results in one flesh, not to mention a joining of souls. Killing an innocent being created out of that spiritual bond is counterintuitive."

Cora flinched slightly, breaking her stoic stance. "So this is a religious matter for you?"

He sensed her salivating. He refused to let Cora paint him as a religious nut. It was morality, a bond that connected billions in spite of cultural variations, that served as his compass. "A moral and ethical matter. When spouses divorce each must disclose assets and split them accordingly. In essence, my wife took it upon herself to hide and then obliterate an invaluable asset that would have added to both of our lives and this world. The matter for me, Ms. Cora, stems from my desire to pay tribute to a fellow soul created in part from my being—to grant him the significance his mother robbed him of."

Nicole swooped in on her broomstick a few mornings later, ironically, on Halloween. Richard and a paralegal were huddled by his desk discussing details pertaining to the Swedish development. The recent graduate noticed her first. Richard wondered how she'd bypassed the receptionist.

"Is this my replacement? Your latest victim?" She sized up the young woman. "Watch out," she warned. "Richard isn't as innocent as he pretends to be. My girlfriend says he's unstable."

The paralegal stood off to the side, frozen.

"I was fine when we met," Richard reminded her. Veins popped in his neck.

"One minute he's all lovey-dovey, and the next he's buried in his work. Now he's trying to blame me for everything."

"My apologies," Richard said sarcastically. "I assumed we were in a marriage instead of a competition where I needed to keep score."

"This was a private matter."

"It was private alright. I don't even know what day you killed our baby. How do you expect me to mourn him properly?"

Nicole's nostrils flared. "Stop, or I'll have my lawyer sue you for libel."

"Libel only exists in written form, idiot. I haven't printed anything about you or mentioned your name."

"A quick public records search is all it takes to know who you're referring to. I told the people who matter what happened, the whole sorted mess. But I don't want the entire world in my business."

"The truth serves as an irrefutable defense to libel and *slander*. You don't get to go around killing babies and then cry foul when other people find out."

"It wasn't a fetus, and it wasn't an easy decision."

"So you say."

"My attorney says I have a case for defamation."

"So now the adulteress is concerned about her reputation? Priceless."

The paralegal piped in, "Should I call security?"

"Yes, you should," Richard answered without taking his eyes off Nicole.

The paralegal hurried out.

Richard stood dumbfounded by Nicole's distorted view of

her role in their current reality.

She glared at him as if she was conjuring up more ways to hurt him. He got to her first.

"You let Toni trot you around like some prized pony!"

"She's the only one who stood by me."

"All I ever cared about was making sure that *we* stood together. Anyway, I hope you two are happy." He glowered at the catalyst of his destruction.

"Toni and I are going to have a baby eventually," she said with a sneer. Our relationship isn't a fling or mistake."

Richard did a double take. "What?"

"You heard me."

"You and Toni are adopting? What agency would allow that?"

The security guard rushed in, interrupting them. "I'm gonna need you to leave, ma'am." He positioned himself between them as Richard stepped back.

"This way, ma'am," the guard said.

Nicole stomped to the door but turned around before exiting. "We're getting a sperm donor," she spewed.

"You bitch!" Richard shouted. "You never loved me, and now you're trying to replace our baby!"

Nicole got in one more jab before the guard finally ushered her out. "Our *baby* never existed."

After the run-in with Nicole, Richard was convinced she had what he called a "criminal mind." He discussed the incident with his mom after cooling down.

"I'm shocked she's still with that Toni chick let alone having a baby with her."

"It's like she's permanently moved to the dark side."

"Could she be bipolar?"

"That or she's in cahoots with the devil."

"Well, he's a true and volatile force in charge of many

minions," Mrs. Knight said. "The reverend preached recently on how believers and non-believers unwittingly invite evil into their lives. I saw the sin in her early on."

Following their conversation, Richard still struggled to erase his ex and her stockpile of insults from his mind. She'd loaded a gun with ammo and now complained that he'd pulled the trigger.

The tide at Goldstein, Levy & Finch shifted as knowledge of Nicole and Richard's clash and of his interview spread. The poor paralegal appeared traumatized and embarrassed when they saw each other again. None of his fellow partners or other staff spoke to him about either in an official capacity. Some whom he passed but had no necessary interaction with avoided eye contact. Some who couldn't ignore him shifted uneasily or spoke in softer tones than typical. A bold minority offered reassuring glances or brief supportive comments.

Once Cora's segment moved past the realm of the station's web site and hit newswires that printed recaps, Richard received invites from shows on standard and cable networks. Many ran in syndication. Media requests poured in from all over the country. He was flown out of town for tapings, which he tried to schedule in the evenings. Often, Richard returned on redeye flights to Atlanta. His job's vacation policy allowed associates to schedule vacation time in hour increments rather than full days. Richard chipped away at the three weeks he'd accumulated when leaving early or coming in late were not options.

Richard finally found value in sharing responsibility for planning the downtown complex with Henson. He couldn't have imagined shouldering the entire project while balancing the whirlwind media blitz that now consumed him. He preferred dealing with public broadcasting and religion-based programs. In contrast to their mainstream counterparts, which erroneously purported fair and balanced reporting, those actually provided it. The advertiser-driven shows specialized in hunting down sensational, out-of-context sound bites. That practice disappointed Richard. Ladonna continued to serve as an invaluable resource, reassuring him along the way. Winston offered insight as well and clearly suggested Richard tone down the intensity of his answers.

Richard gained momentum after subsequent appearances in major markets like LA and Dallas. He purposefully varied his arguments to strike a chord with as many viewers as he could. Richard realized from reading blog posts and message boards connected with shows he appeared on that some viewers identified with religious reasoning or morality. Others let financial implications rule their disapproval of the procedure.

Spouses dealing with the wake of their wives' actions praised him for standing firm. Winston's office fell short of handling the letters and emails of support that arrived for Richard. The senator ordered his intern to open a Twitter account to capture feedback. They helped him acclimate to the lingo and abbreviations used on the site. After they provided statistics on the staggering number of abortions performed in Georgia and the nation as a whole during the prior calendar year, many responded that the figures put the impact abortions have on society into a comprehendible perspective. Some confessed feeling stunningly uninformed or misinformed when Richard cited how much money went toward financing the procedures.

"Premiums would drop if insurance stopped covering elective abortions," one man wrote.

"Taxes, too," someone responded. "Feds support clinics and hospitals but say they don't."

A portion of replies, understandably, lacked enthusiasm for

Richard's cause. The hate-spewing from many bordered on fanaticism, of which his detractors had accused him. He picked up on a pattern of buzzwords that led him to believe organized efforts existed to halt his efforts. Richard grew used to being called a "chauvinist," "unpatriotic" and a "violator of the Constitution." He glossed over rhetoric implying his wife aborted their baby because he treated her in way that made her doubt he'd be a good father. Richard was able to withstand most of the maligning, but race-infused remarks seemed to trigger a pain that sunk almost as deep as the loss of his unborn child. One blog comment, in particular, sent him reeling. It read: "She did the right thing because having an interracial child is no good for anyone."

The senator urged Richard to lose any defensive posture and stay on the offense, albeit indirectly. He said there was an art to making a jab seem like a mere comment. Winston recommended that Richard demurely utter phrases such as "now we both know," "statistics clearly show," "do you honestly believe," and "I'm an advocate for." Richard disagreed with this spin tactic. He didn't want to become just another talking head.

Neither predicted dissenters would step outside of online forums. Pro-choice advocates picketed outside of the senator's office. Signs and placards they toted displayed messages like "Hands Off Our Wombs!" and "Whoa, Man! For Women's Rights We Will Fight!" Shortly after the protests began, someone spray painted "*Roe v. Wade*" on his black Ford Explorer in bold red letters.

News of the unrest spread quickly. Richard sensed discomfort when he spoke to his mother and Kevin about his endeavors. Both expressed worries for his safety.

"What's to stop them from doing the same to you," his mother asked.

"You've got to arm yourself," Kevin warned.

Richard doubted the culprits would rise above their cowardly deeds. He forged forward.

On the set of a popular Big Apple daytime roundtable show that appealed to females who attended from all over the country, Richard fell into a frenzied exchange. The 15-minute segment seemed never-ending. Two of the four women on the panel kept engaging him in verbal jarring as if they thought the loudest talker prevailed regardless of the validity of her argument. Richard sat in the middle of a plush sectional sofa, but nothing about the conversation felt comfortable. The level of decorum he'd grown accustomed to ruling real estate court proceedings had no bearing here.

"Most men have no clue how to raise a child," one host stated with a false air of authority. "It's really women who do all the heavy lifting. If moms went on strike, dads would run around thoroughly confused!"

The others chuckled. A wave of applause came from the studio audience, comprised mostly of housewives.

He swept the crowd and picked out less than ten males who were not tethered to a female's side. "Then why deal with men at all since they're so ill-equipped?" Richard retorted. "Why not totally cut them out of the equation and just become lesbians?"

Several of the single fellows grinned.

Even the less abrasive women shot disapproving glances. "That's ludicrous," one told him.

"So, is your assumption that men are inherently substandard parents and nurturers who must be forced into a desire for fatherhood?" Before anyone could respond, he continued, "How long do we ignore America's downward slope? It's okay for pharmaceutical companies to push pills to prevent pregnancy or terminate a pregnancy the morning after, right? It's okay for a woman to arbitrarily decide after creating a life that it would interfere too much with hers so she'd rather terminate it? Why don't women use precautions to protect these bodies they care so much about? Really, most women put more effort into picking out new shoes."

A hush fell over the audience.

The mediator of the group spoke up. "Birth control has its flaws. Countless women says that it failed them."

"My ex-wife said a lot of things all *after* her abortion. If the thought of carrying *our* child to full term repulsed her so, she shouldn't have laid down with me or she should've taken precautions. She's a nurse, after all. How babies come about shouldn't have been a great mystery to her."

The mediator cleared her throat and then looked down at a small cue card. "It's time for questions from the audience. Irene from Kansas wants to know, 'Do you really seek justice for would-be fathers or revenge toward you ex?'"

"Justice," he replied without hesitation. "But not just for dads."

A process server delivered a cease and desist letter directly to Richard's office from Nicole's attorney. Richard, however, knew that speaking truthfully protected him against her allegations and legal maneuverings.

"She has some nerve sending me a request to stop telling the truth while she has no regard for the truth," Richard explained to Kevin over the phone. "I'm tired of her trying to discredit me just so she doesn't look like the conniver she is." Her lawyer, he surmised, simply succumbed to her demands to make a quick buck. She had a gripe, not a valid case.

"Hey, this is getting serious," Kevin said in an unusually solemn tone. "Maybe you need to talk to her to find out if she needs to tell you more about how this all fell apart."

"So you're saying I could be the problem?"

"Not at all, man. I'm saying that you need to find some peace quickly before this destroys you, and maybe she, not her attorney, can provide that."

"I tried that, remember? Almost got arrested."

"Going to jail is just one kind of prison. You're in a whole different one."

Richard didn't hear the comment, focusing on his point. "I'm just getting started, and I'll need your support."

Kevin remained silent.

Without noticing his friend's quietness, Richard continued, "She'll squirm this time."

Nicole's current attempt at silencing Richard's protected speech only added more fuel to his reservoir of willpower. After ending the call, Richard tossed the letter into his shredder. Nicole, he felt, had the gall to think she'd change the course of his actions when even the threat of picketers and vandalism failed to veer him off his path. Richard comprehended that each interview served as prep for his inevitable testimony once Winston presented the bill. He thought, "I tiptoed around her long enough."

A nonpartisan political magazine located in New England but distributed worldwide wrote a piece on how Richard's plight recharged the fathers' rights debate. The writer's approach put a fresh spin on the topic. He spoke to Richard and Julia Jimenez, a well-known women's rights advocate who'd been burning bras for decades. He guided the conversation when it stalled but otherwise let them establish its course.

"Where do you draw the line, Mr. Knight? Will wives need their husband's permission to make other permanent changes to their bodies, cutting their hair, for instance?" Jimenez asked. "Will they face fines for gaining an undesirable amount of weight?"

"Your examples are so far off course we might as well be

having two different conversations."

"Then let me make myself clear," she continued. "What your wife did was a medical matter. I find your attempts at controlling someone else's body offensive."

"If your husband has any major or even minor medical procedure done, you'd like to know beforehand, right? Even if he decides to do something to his body against your judgment, at least he should have the decency to share that with you, right? Most couples discuss these kinds of things. It called R-E-S-P-E-C-T and consideration for the other person's feelings. Women want to be respected but at the same time, disrespect men – legally."

"Your wife's so-called disrespect and inconsideration is a personal matter, not a legal one. I'm not going to start a legal campaign because my husband didn't tell me about his new tattoo."

Shaking his head, Richard said, "It's didn't take both you and him to create a tattoo. A child has two people's DNA and should have two options as parents if one decides that she doesn't want to be a parent."

"But you can't force a woman to deliver a child as your parental right. It's in her body! You know what? This whole notion of you trying to control a woman's body is just distasteful."

"I find abortion distasteful. The number performed in this country represents an epic failure, not an advancement in equality."

"HIPPA, the Health Insurance Portability and Accountability Act, protects patients' medical records and other health information provided to health care providers."

"I'm well aware of HIPPA, Mrs. Jimenez. I'm also aware of your organization's song and dance. You say girls can grow up to be smart women who can do anything. Apparently, that doesn't include practicing safe sex. In one breath you tell them women are almighty. In another you encourage them to view motherhood as an inferior choice on the totem pole of options."

"Carrying a child to term is not the ideal situation for every pregnant woman."

"Instances of abuse or medical necessity don't factor into the proposed bill. While organizations such as yours devalue motherhood, I celebrate it. You claim I'm doing a disservice to women's rights. I contend that treating abortions like oil changes is much worse and that the psychological damage done trickles down to us all in some form."

"Mr. Knight, I'll grant you the nobleness of your argument. Let's deal in practicalities, though. How do you expect women to nurture children they don't want for nine months, not to mention enduring grueling labor? How is that fair?"

"I expect them to consider the blameless children who shouldn't suffer due to their mothers' self-centeredness. I expect them to tough it out for nine months so those children can enjoy a lifetime of love from their fathers or another family if possible. I expect them to be fair enough to consider that they are not the only option. Just because they don't want the child doesn't mean that no one else, namely the men who fathered the child, wants it.

"I don't want to take away a woman's rights or force her to raise an unwanted child. I merely want a father's rights and opportunity considered. And if we never get any rights or opportunities, can we at least be notified? A little respect, you know."

Chapter 14

Richard picked up one useful tidbit from Jimenez. She drilled him with a litany of mantras, so he developed one of his own: "Sanctity Over Science." He argued that ability and availability didn't equal acceptability. Not all scientific advancements advanced humanity. Many, including abortion, resulted in the opposite effect.

The slogan generated so much exposure that it placed Richard on a filmmaker's radar. Maurice Baul's documentary had an anti-abortion slant, but it sorely lacked a compelling male viewpoint. He had been in the process of casting that role when he read the magazine's piece on Richard's undertaking. Baul tried convincing Richard to fill that void and cited his endeavor as an opportunity for Richard to vent virtually unfiltered.

"Aren't you tired of reporters holding the reigns?" Maurice suggested.

Richard nodded.

He told Richard of a plan to reveal how abortions affect women. "My research shows that abortions affect women for at least five years beyond the procedure," said Maurice, sounding more personally vested in his stance but never really admitting anything overtly. "I'll expose the real reason these women are killing kids, and the world will be shocked. Everyone needs to see this."

To that, Richard somewhat recoiled, peering at Maurice as if he was a bit too radical.

"I'm gonna show pretty horrific pictures of what goes on during the produce. People will get to see how the media pushes choice but doesn't ever show what the choice costs a woman's body and psyche. It's kinda like a pharmacist giving you a prescription without including the side effects and ripping off the warning label."

"So why do you think the media never investigate what can or does go wrong?" Richard inquired. "And when anyone, like me, does expose something wrong or unfair, we're considered anti-establishment, anti-woman and on and on."

"That's not popular. Instead, they ingrain women with the idea that it's wrong to have an ounce of cellulite. Data proves the opposite. Twelve is the average clothing size for women. How many of those women do you see in anchor chairs or on TV shows, period?"

"The man has a point," Richard thought.

"A University of Florida study showed recently that nearly half of the 3 to 6-year-olds worried about being fat. How many skinny pregnant ladies have you seen?"

"None," Richard replied. The body perception angle hadn't occurred to him. He identified with the Baul's dogged determination. He cut their phone conversation short and suspected Baul would have gone on indefinitely had he not done so. His offer sounded tempting, but the analytical side of Richard refused to let him decide on the spot.

On his journey, Richard had not come across many men willing to speak openly about fathers' rights. The plight of a New Mexico resident proved an exception. He'd gone boldly where no man had gone before and placed a billboard on a major thoroughfare. The advertisement depicted an image of his unborn child and text denouncing his ex-girlfriend's actions. She, like Nicole, claimed an infringement upon her rights and sought legal counsel. He, in turn, hired an attorney to defend his right to free speech. The billboard sparked discussions of a legal nature and called into question the man's character. His ex claimed she'd suffered a miscarriage and had not aborted their child. Richard had difficulty understanding how anyone could confuse the two. He viewed her claim as a feeble ploy to downgrade the deed she actually committed. What reasonable man would willingly turn into a target for public scrutiny unless he had a basis for doing so? Though they lived thousands of miles apart and had not suffered through identical situations, Richard sympathized with and drew strength from the stranger's plight.

He viewed Baul's project as another opportunity to persuade men. "He thought, "Instead of accepting the emasculation, men could speak up through the film." Conceivably, the film would reach a broader demographic than his other appearances. Richard read trade publications to learn additional details about the filmmaker. They all spoke favorably of him and his ability to tackle taboo topics without alienating the masses. From what Richard gathered, Baul had a real investment in his artistry.

Richard envied creative types and thought such professions remained underappreciated. His mother had steered him toward choosing a practical path sure to provide financial stability. Richard always foresaw his children making their own choices even if that meant failing at a career or two prior to finding their niche. He talked to his mother about the opportunity. He sensed apprehension before his mother verbalized it. She worried such wide-scale coverage would attract more protestors and ultimately lunatics on the fringe who wished to silence him. As usual, Richard considered her trepidation, and knew it came from a valid, caring place.

When Jimenez asked Richard how far he was willing to go while they bantered, he honestly had no idea. Indeed, Richard sensed a slow change in himself and in public opinion. The forums and automated online topic alerts he monitored indicated less hostility in discussions toward men like Richard and more empathy toward them.

He ultimately saw participating in the documentary as an essential element of his evolution into a true spokesperson for the fathers' rights cause. Richard called Baul over the weekend with his answer.

"I've decided that this would be a great opportunity to further my mission." He thanked Richard profusely for agreeing to take part in the project and promised to schedule a shooting time soon.

The receptionist stopped Richard before he could ask for a copy of the weekly legal briefing, a succinct status report of firm initiatives. "They're waiting for you in conference room 7," she said.

"They?" Richard mused aloud. Would the briefing take place in the form of a meeting? Occasionally the firm announced new undertakings in such a manner.

The staunch demeanors of the ensemble waiting for him sent Richard into high alert. The hairs on his arm bristled as if they were trying to escape the scene. Henson, his co-project manager, and Ushindi Eze, a partner who specialized in corporate land acquisitions, sat at the rectangular, steel table. Only Robert Smythe stood.

Richard looked at Eze, one of a handful of African-Americans who also reached partner status. He refused to make prolonged eye contact. Henson, in contrast, gazed unremittingly as if he had front row tickets to a sold-out play.

"Richard," Smythe said in a consolatory tone, "we all know you've had it rough lately."

Is that so, Richard wondered. None of you expressed concern earlier.

"I encourage you to take full advantage of our employee assistance program."

"I tried it," Richard said. "They offered no counseling options for my needs." His comment threw Smythe off script.

"We're," he stammered, "we're grateful for the initiative you've shown during your tenure at Goldstein, Levy & Finch but..."

Here comes the 'but,'" Richard told himself.

"The senior partners feel it's best that we relieve you of your duties."

The firm handbook required that two partners facilitate disciplinary actions. He wondered why they had Henson in attendance. His overbearing coworker scrutinized his every move related to the Swedish development project. Richard assumed Henson wanted to single him out for some perceived failure in duties. From the inception of the project, Henson treated him more like a subordinate than a peer.

"Relieve?" Richard wanted Smythe to say what he meant, not what made him feel less of a coward and traitor. Smythe and Richard had crossed paths enough that he could have easily pulled his protégée to the side and given him a heads up.

"This will be your last day. Trisha is packing your belongings, and security will escort you off the premises."

The finality blindsided him. He'd never been fired. Even at the crappy fast-food job where Richard worked to gain spending money during his senior year of high school, he outperformed most of the staff. That work ethic followed him into adulthood. "Am I not entitled to a verbal warning?"

"I gave you one when we discussed the Bronner closing," Smythe responded. The procrastinating mogul lost out on the sale of prime property because he couldn't secure the closing documents. The initial buyer suffered irrevocable financial setbacks and filed bankruptcy, therefore, rendering the proposed sale null and void. A new buyer eventually emerged but purchased the property for substantially less than Bronner's asking price.

"How am I to blame for the Bronner debacle?" questioned Richard, pointing out that Bronner's prima donna tendencies were legendary.

"You let the process drag on."

"How is that my fault?" Richard asked. "Bronner's delays set his issues in motion. If he'd followed through on my requests before land values dipped, I'd be his hero."

"In retrospect, you lost focus a while ago," Smythe countered.

"All of the unpaid overtime I put in counts for nothing? My personal problems kept me from going above and beyond, but suddenly average isn't good enough?"

Richard swore he detected a gleam in Henson's eyes.

"Henson said you skipped a number of client conferences."

Flowing from his mentor's mouth, the comment seemed harsher and shook Richard's confidence. Damn, Richard thought, have I been that inept? He mentally rewound collaborating with Henson and drew a blank. "I'll need specific examples. I don't recall blowing off any crucial meetings." He returned Henson's smug stare with one of contempt. "You couldn't pull me aside man to man with your gripes?"

Henson simply shrugged his shoulders. Richard grunted in disgust and returned his gaze to Smythe.

"I'm not sure you followed the proper protocol," he said. "I'm speaking to human resources before signing anything."

"Do you want the added publicity?" Eze piped in.

In an instant, Richard realized his media appearances factored in as much as his supposed declining performance.

"Bottom line, that's it for me," he requested in order to cut short the unsavory episode.

"Your exposure shines a lens on the firm as well. It's the sort that makes associates and clients uneasy," Eze said.

"So that's it. I'm out the door?"

"Regretfully, yes," Smythe concluded.

The firm rewarded Richard's service with a month's pay. Plus, he had roughly three weeks to make the most of his medical benefits before they expired on December 31st. Richard mulled over contesting his dismissal and seeking a reinstatement. He concluded that the effort would result in wasted energy since Georgia allowed employers to fire at will. Meanwhile, he filed an unemployment claim but had yet to receive a response in over three weeks.

In between brooding over his situation, searching for a new job, and navigating the media circuit, Richard reflected on his disdain for Nicole. Although her legal threats had not come to fruition, he remained convinced that their clash and her attorney serving papers at the firm added to his superiors' notion that he had become a liability. How he detested her and now himself. Richard had to admit that in some regards he became a bigger, better liar than she was.

Over the following weeks, Richard stayed on edge in keeping his predicament a secret from everyone, including his mother. For the second time in a year, Richard had been dumped, and he didn't want anyone feeling sorry for him or saying, "I told you so." Thus, he took great measures to continue the façade.

He avoided work-related discussions. He parked his car in his garage on the days he had nowhere to go. Sometimes Richard dressed the part, carrying his briefcase or laptop, and left home. In actuality, he drove to Wi-Fi hotspots to search for work.

He planned to secure a new position prior to revealing that he had lost the old one. After all, the firm had graciously provided him with a glowing letter of recommendation. Richard perfected a cover story to use with recruiters, which included, "Goldstein, Levy & Finch trimmed its staff as a result of departmental restructuring." However, prospective employers replied to his applications with less frequency than he anticipated.

Toward the end of the year, the media shunned him and turned its attention to uplifting, cheerful topics fit for holiday consumption. His now humdrum routine compounded the vast emptiness Richard felt. In an attempt to stay motivated, he told himself over and over that his tribulations would result in triumph for Junior. Richard held on to that belief until Senator Winston announced a shattering shift in strategy.

Chapter 15

Normally, Ladonna arrived home at 5:45. Richard resisted calling her at 5:46. He wanted to tell her about the altered bill before the story hit newswires, as Winston predicted it would soon. However, he wanted to give her a chance to unwind and to prepare dinner. He decided to wait at least an hour.

Prior to them parting, Winston promised to have his intern, Ian, keep Richard abreast of developments. He also charged Richard with continuing to court media. "You personify discarded dads," Winston reiterated. "Your experience is the cornerstone for SB71."

Doubt enveloped Richard while he waited to contact Ladonna. Did he possess the wherewithal to advocate on behalf of a bill that dismissed his initial aim? Would amended terms result in his supporters labeling him a sellout? Despite his best efforts, did Winston's reach extend far enough to see their mission to fruition? Richard quelled a smidgen of his angst by setting up search engine alerts to monitor reports in reference to the bill.

Richard glanced at his wristwatch. He'd wait a bit longer before contacting Ladonna. She had less time to rest since she started taking advantage of overtime her firm offered during the holidays. She relied on the extra money to provide for Bryson's Christmas presents and to build up her emergency savings. When Richard joined her, Crystal, and the boy on New Year's to watch the televised Peach Drop, Ladonna fell asleep before her son. Richard tucked Bryson into bed.

When they got together or spoke by phone or text, Ladonna's exhaustion allowed Richard to avoid drawn-out conversations and any mention of his job. Ladonna exerting herself to provide for Bryson embodied how seriously parents should take their roles. She exhibited the sort of sacrifice his mother mentioned earlier.

Richard, in turn, questioned his role as a son. Had he ever, in depth, stopped to consider life from his mom's point of view? It occurred to him more and more that interactions with her revolved, for the most part, around his personal matters. He had no hunch if his mom held unrealized aspirations or if she bore children out of obligation rather than desire. Had his father's untimely death derailed the possibility of dreaming beyond being a housewife? Did taking care of him and Pam provide enough fulfillment?

Mrs. Knight's earlier remark insinuating that losing Junior in such an egregious manner had an upside confused Richard and, though he resisted the urge, this prompted Richard to entertain her point of view. His mother had an uncanny ability to read people and situations. Additionally, she possessed a keen sense of right and wrong that prevented her from considering the shades of grey existing in the dilemmas others faced.

Should he consider it a blessing that Junior died before he had a chance to create a connection, thereby making the loss more horrendous? How could he fathom the utter devastation, the cavalcade of emotions parents who lost children they'd cradled felt? Richard gradually comprehended the rationale behind his mother's statement. Richard thought of hearing his namesake's laughter, seeing the gleam in his eye, holding him in his arms and *then* losing him. Richard shuddered. The ebb and flow of life included death. Richard learned that lesson well before most of his peers. Firsthand knowledge still provided no shelter from the wake of unforeseen losses.

An explosion rocked Ainsworth & Associates. Reports stated that the boom sounded for blocks. A bomb shattered the windows and caused a fire in the basement at the four-story office building that housed the abortion clinic on the second floor. GBI agents arrived on the scene shortly after local police. They cordoned off the perimeter and questioned witnesses, the few that existed. The stealth assailant struck at 9:15 a.m. unnoticed. No one was seriously hurt, suffering only minor injuries from shattered glass and smoke inhalation. Speculation over various media outlets pegged the perpetrator as a disgruntled former patient or a family member of a woman who'd sought the doctor's services.

The receptionist revealed that the doctor received anonymous threats nearly a month prior, but the threats tapered off as they always did. Inevitably, reporters drew correlations between the bombing and Winston's bill. Some said pushing the measure would ignite more vigilantism and possibly lead to more deaths. Others viewed violence as a necessary means to an end.

The potential disintegration of the altered bill rattled Richard. He absolutely sought seeing the brand-new draft evade extinction. Nevertheless, Richard kicked himself for getting so wrapped up in the momentum of gathering backers that he discounted the possibility that any would back out. Squelching the qualms of supporters fearful for their safety added an additional level of anxiety. Juggling this additional undertaking with seeking a job at another law firm seemed a daunting endeavor. Would potential bosses dismiss his talent due to the media coverage his efforts brought? Would a fringe group's influence impose further limitations on the new bill's scope or stall it altogether? Would a committee member substitute important passages of text with verbiage that deviated from the bill's intended purpose?

Richard looked forward to hearing Ladonna's spin on the restructured draft, which focused on husbands rather than fathers in general. It was now officially called the Spousal Pregnancy Termination Notification Bill, or SB71. She'd assist him in plowing through the scenarios he formulated and analyze his situation from a strategic standpoint.

Ladonna listened as Richard relayed his reservations in a frenzied rush. Then, she acknowledged his apprehensions. "Stop being so hard on yourself and Winston," she said. "Who could've forecasted this outcome? Besides, you got a lot done in such a short period."

"With your help," Richard conceded.

"Because of you, the level of consciousness concerning abortion has evolved. You've given a voice to so many men and reached countless women. If you continue touching people with your story, more will seriously consider carrying their children to term instead of aborting them. More men will step up and commit to shouldering part of the burden of parenthood so those women won't feel so alone. The correlation is inevitable even though the bill is tailored for spouses. If you give up, why should anyone else fight for it?"

How much fight do I have left in me? Richard pondered. *Should I focus on this or maintaining my finances?* Thus far, he avoided dipping into his modest savings. Richard's apprehensions subsided with each soothing sentiment Ladonna uttered. "Winston did stress that it's imperative that I focus on booking appearances to drum up public support."

"Then continue to speak with confidence. Silence would be the real tragedy. And if the bill didn't pass, you'd wonder if you'd done your part."

"Thanks for the pep talk." He envied Ladonna's ability to analyze situations in a manner that put others at ease.

"Nothing to it," Ladonna said.

"Is Bryson around?"

"Yep, he asked when you were coming to help him rehearse for the play."

The play was a minor production put on by Bryson's preschool. It consisted of scenes from different fairytales. Richard agreed to help the boy perfect his character for the "Three Blind Mice" reenactment.

"That's nearly two weeks from now."

"I told him you'd come by Friday after work."

Richard felt a dash of disappointment in himself.

"Richard?"

"I'm here." He heard Bryson chattering nearby. "Put him on the line."

Richard and Bryson spoke briefly. His enthusiasm about the upcoming role made Richard chuckle. The boy instructed Richard to save room for ice cream afterwards, his way of making sure Richard remembered the treat he'd promised. Richard envied Bryson's lightheartedness, untainted by adulthood and its responsibilities. After the call, Richard felt renewed and ready to soldier on for fathers' rights.

After their separation, Richard despised Nicole for leaving him. Now, he despised himself for loving her in the first place. She kept directing her attorney to send demand letters. Her attorney now claimed that the bombing validated how Richard's crusade would ultimately put his client in danger from fanatical zealots seeking to confirm her identity. Richard responded by promptly tossing the letters in the trash. Each numbed him a bit more. He purposely avoided calling Nicole by name in public.

The best scenario for Richard involved Nicole scampering off into obscurity. She reminded him of a hard-to-catch bug that he just wanted to squash and be done with. Richard thought Nicole should consider herself lucky that he had control of his mental faculties. Anyone psychologically unstable might've retaliated in a manner that shut her up for good.

Uplifting correspondence from factions of males and females following Richard's progress fueled him. To his astonishment, Richard also captured the attention of lovelorn women who requested to date him. He let them down gently while expressing gratitude for their dedication to his mission. The hopeful letters, emails, and blog posts counterbalanced the weariness that set in while he volleyed between the media and with potential employers. Regardless of the questioner, he sensed the majority sought to trap him in a lie or to stump him.

Reporters, done with the revelry of feel-good holiday news, pounced on the controversy brewing around SB71. Richard reacted calmly without snapping at the bait they aggressively dangled in front of him.

"Movements aren't built on one piece of legislation alone," he reiterated in some form with each interrogation. He noticed a clear bias although he encountered a minute number he suspected leaned in his favor. They exhibited softer demeanors and gentler tones.

"How far are you willing to go, Knight?" one particularly approachable journalist posed.

"I see protecting and insuring the rights of fathers as bigger than the bill, bigger than me," he responded. Quite often,

Richard foresaw beyond the bill's passage to when individuals in other states would seek similar legislation. His research with Ladonna prior to meeting Winston spotted emerging trends that pointed out definite disagreement with the laws of the land. Fundamentalists, political action committees and conservatives, for example, banded together in other states to make nonessential abortions elective procedures. They limited coverage by requiring supplemental insurance policies. He brought that up when debating with one of Winston's more liberal constituents at a town hall meeting the senator arranged.

"Are you insinuating that adulterous wives looking to discard evidence of indiscretions comprise the bulk of abortion seekers?" one young woman posed.

"No," Richard retorted, "but it is unfair to force husbands to pay the associated costs. In actuality, the law lags behind the liberties married men, at least, should expect."

She scoffed.

"We've strayed, however, from the content of the bill. I'm merely seeking to implement rights husbands should already have."

Each victory in the realm of fathers' rights, from Richard's standpoint, led to the greater good. And, with each appearance, Richard attempted to calmly connect with those listening to or watching him. He emphasized how fundamentally wrong he considered the notion that a man had no say in the plight of a life he created. He'd leave the ranting to the women's rights fanatics.

"Someone has to look out for defenseless beings growing inside their mother's wombs," he rationalized. "Who better than fathers? If only the same outrage existed for their children as for other living beings. I've witnessed furious outcries for animals. Activists rail against shelters that kill strays. I've seen environmentalists chain themselves to trees to spare them from the chopping block, not to mention citizens rallying to protect natural resources from falling prey to development. Well, I say the fabric of families is endangered. SB71 won't prohibit abortions, but it will help restore balance between spouses' rights."

On the job front, Richard waded through leads. Originally, hesitant to venture past his comfort zone, he applied to positions in the real estate sector. He realized that further opportunities fell outside of his specialty and accordingly altered his approach. Richard brushed up on case laws across the disciplines that offered the most openings. The recruiters and human resources representatives he dealt with, in contrast to when he last looked for work, insisted on conducting a series of pre-interviews by phone. A fragment of them added Internet testing to the mix. They had Richard role play and respond to potential circumstances, or they quizzed him on statutes, precedents, and common rules and regulations.

Such distant interactions put him at a distinct disadvantage. He related to strangers best in person, where displaying his warmth and character required less effort. Richard decided to boost his networking efforts after reading an article that stated decision makers prefer hiring candidates whom associates recommend. Soon, thanks to LinkedIn messaging, Richard was in touch with Danielle Holmes, Richard's ex from college. She had heard a radio segment where he discussed components of the bill.

He suggested she join him for cocktails and an early dinner if she had time to spare after work. Within 10 minutes of sending the message, Richard anxiously checked his account to see if Danielle had answered. He poured a glass of Scotch and drank it while he waited. His stomach felt uneasy. Richard couldn't tell if nerves caused that or drinking before eating lunch.

The pair hadn't spoken since their long distance relationship went kaput. From her LinkedIn profile, he saw that Danielle, or "Dee" as he nicknamed her, completed her education and obtained her Master's in marketing. For the five years they dated, Danielle proved herself as a go-getter who completed any objective she set forth. Upon his departure from Georgetown and return to Atlanta, Richard never mustered the courage to contact Danielle. He figured their chance at romance ran its course and moved on to other women. None prior to Nicole compared to Danielle.

Danielle's profile showed she currently served as an advertising consultant for a marketing firm that boasted Fortune 500 clientele. Her warm demeanor drew people in as did her fierce intelligence, so Richard easily envisioned her taking command in a boardroom. She had a chill side, too, and an affinity for sports that sealed the deal for Richard when they dated. Rather than nagging him about watching games, or complaining about feeling neglected, she joined him and kicked back a few beers in the process.

Finally, Danielle replied to him after 30 minutes. She explained that because it was a school night, she had to help her girls with homework and then get them in bed. Other than that detail, she clued him in to no other personal details. They resolved to meet up one afternoon at Big Trees Trail, one of their old haunts. The setting served as an essential escape from coursework. It boasted scenic views, including a Chattahoochee River tributary and huge, granite boulders. Intimacy flowed easily within that refuge.

Exuberance entranced Richard so much so that he agreed to see Danielle on the afternoon of Bryson's play. He realized the potential scheduling conflict the next morning. The two events occurred so close together. He decided that going to the play dressed appropriately for the hike, and then going directly to the trail, would allow him to keep both obligations. He spent the next 72 hours anticipating his reunion with Dee.

Ladonna had saved a seat for Richard next to her, but he, arriving one minute before the play started, didn't want to have to step across so many people's feet to get to it. Plus, he didn't want Ladonna to ask him any personal questions. To avoid Ladonna and make sure he was on time to meet Danielle afterward, Richard left Bryson's play five minutes before it ended. Ladonna, along with Bryson, searched for him later because she saw him standing behind the back row against the wall. She noticed his rather casual outdoor attire and thought he looked unusual in an auditorium full of people wearing business or dressy attire. Only a few teenagers dressed as casually as Richard, who almost always wore a suit and tie to major events.

Nearly 20 minutes after leaving the play, Richard arrived in the gravel parking area of the nature trail. He rushed out his car, almost forgetting to close his door, and instinctively headed toward a vehicle he knew carried his first love. Setting eyes on her proved worth the excruciating wait.

"Ever the gentleman," Danielle said when he opened her car door. She'd pulled up in a Hummer with a custom body kit, which implied she'd done well for herself.

"Dee," Richard said as he leaned in for a hug. The embrace felt like coming home. He inhaled her familiar floral perfume. Her toned physique remained intact. Once they unlocked, he stepped back and analyzed her further while she unpretentiously analyzed him. She'd cut her hair, a shocking contrast to the lengthy locks he recalled. Only ladies with similar dainty features could pull off the super-short, spiky style. She beamed at him and then tugged at his shirt. He observed the absence of a wedding ring.

"Catch me up," Danielle urged.

While they weaved throughout the trail at a leisurely pace, Richard gave her the condensed version of his courtship of and marriage to Nicole.

"The Richard I knew and the one I heard on the radio definitely deserved better." Danielle sounded like she wanted to flog Nicole for her appalling behavior. He'd almost forgotten Danielle's fiercely protective tendencies.

"It wasn't all bad."

"Saying something wasn't bad isn't the same as saying it was good."

Richard nodded. "What's your stance on the whole abortion issue?"

"Humans aren't supposed to kill their young. Nobody can convince me otherwise," she stated with conviction. Danielle sped up as they traversed an incline and, pitifully, outperformed him. "You can do better than that," she teased. "Should I push you along?"

"Admittedly I've slacked in the exercise department. I'm not that feeble though."

"Prove it," she dared and sped up. Danielle's laughter reverberated throughout the virtually isolated clearing they'd reached. "Our bench is still here," she cried out and pulled him toward it. "Let's sit. You look like you need the rest."

"Ha, ha." Her presence thrilled him. Even so, Richard suppressed his urge to gush.

Danielle plopped down close to him. "You're staring," she pointed out.

"The hair is throwing me off."

"Dabbling with that mop I used to wear took too long."

"You must be busy," Richard said. "How many girls do you have?"

"Just the one set of twins. They're 6."

"And their dad?"

"We divorced going on four years now."

"He must be an idiot for letting you go."

"He's a great dad but not a long-term partner. We eventually fell out of love, out of lust, and into a rut like roommates ready for their lease to expire. Neither of us saw any sense in dragging out the inevitable. Besides, not many men can live up to the standard you set, Mr. Knight."

Richard glossed over the compliment. His blush said it all.

Dreams bombarded Richard. Nightmares involved mobs wielding pitchforks and threatening to hang him due to his radical ideology. They dragged him through the city streets and up the Capitol steps. Happier dreams repeatedly involved Danielle. The pair spoke often following their hike. She lived in Sandy Springs, not too far from Buckhead. Danielle's ex-husband, she revealed during a chat, resided in Atlanta. He and his family actively participated in the twins' upbringing. Danielle invited Richard to tag along when she picked up the twins from her parent's home in Alpharetta a couple of weeks after they reconnected. She mentioned that her dad especially expressed interest in seeing him. Richard agreed and welcomed the chance to see Mr. and Mrs. Hamilton, whom he lost contact with after the breakup. Richard fleetingly entertained reaching out to them shortly afterwards but determined it best to severe all ties. He by no means forgot their kindness nonetheless or how her dad called him "Son."

"Regardless of who I'm dating," Danielle said on the ride over, "they compare him to you."

"Are you exclusive with someone?" Richard asked. Danielle neglected to mention her love life past the divorce. And when she invited him over to her house, Richard spotted no evidence of a boyfriend.

Danielle clarified that her boyfriend served in the Air Force and was stationed in Japan.

"You're trying the long distance route again?" he questioned.

"Against my better judgment, yes."

Danielle offered no additional details about her beau. Richard considered the fellow a fool for not snagging her.

The Hamiltons greeted Richard without the awkwardness he feared might creep into the reunion. It touched Richard that they thought of him over the years as well. Seeing them interact with the twins offered Richard a glimpse of the joy Mrs. Knight missed out on. The Hamiltons clearly adored their granddaughters. The twins were well-behaved, energetic, and inherited their mother's charisma. Before Danielle ushered him and the girls out the door, her parents confirmed his open invitation. The visit ended too soon for Richard. Danielle, like Ladonna, possessed a knack for alleviating his insecurities and reassuring him. Perhaps that's why he felt comfortable sharing his job loss with Danielle early on in. Richard could have opened up to Ladonna, who left a voicemail for him days after he attended Bryson's play, but he found it easier to steer clear of her rather than to continue pretending that he had a job. He imagined she'd display the same disappointed stare his mother had if he told her the truth. Like with his mother, he never wanted to disappoint Ladonna, especially after she had done so much to ensure his success otherwise.

Richard sat alone one night, drinking scotch and watching the passing cars' shadows reflect on the walls. The alcohol dulled the sting of rejections. Richard wondered how applicants who lacked the ability to compose compelling arguments on the fly coped with the barrage of questions thrown at them. Experience equipped him with the know-how to handle interrogations. Regardless, the routine wore on him.

Recruiters spouted jargon, which irked Richard to no end. He supposed that they dealt with such an influx of applicants that they lost sight of how to relate to real people rather than qualifications neatly arranged on a page. "Team player" and "atmosphere of collaboration" grated his nerves the most. Richard pondered how he allowed Henson to scam him and inevitably orchestrate his downfall. During a prior conversation, Richard explained to Danielle how his co-project manager duped him.

"One-man shows have little room for supporting roles," she expressed. "It's shameful how grown folks would rather advance by badmouthing others."

Richard also told Danielle how he'd wrestled with his resume and created multiple versions to see if a particular adaptation attracted extra interest. Danielle offered to critique them and advised he should brand himself. "Really lockdown how you differ from other applicants," she advised.

He considered the approach. All lawyers, he thought, are salesmen of some sort. I've got to sell myself to these employers.

"Take a break, then regroup," she ordered.

Richard groaned. He compiled a job search to-do list and barely tackled one-third of it.

"No kidding," Danielle warned. "Finding a job is as stressful, if not more, than working is."

"Okay," he conceded, as if he had the ability to defy her.

Stomping the media circuit kept Richard preoccupied, and Ladonna accepted that fact. She had supported and accommodated him on every step of his journey. Still, his demeanor struck her as off-kilter. Communications from him ceased since her last message, which she left over a week prior. Richard acted distant when he joined her at Bryson's school and practically inhaled his ice cream before running off. She had no intentions of overstepping her bounds even though their status surpassed mere friendship months ago. Neither officially labeled it as something more but that proved irrelevant in her opinion.

"Richard has never gone this long without contacting me," Ladonna told Crystal. They sat watching an episode of "America's Funniest Videos" with Bryson close by.

Her son perked up. "Richard is coming?"

"No," his mom said. "Watch the show." Ladonna turned her attention back to Crystal and whispered so Bryson couldn't hear. "I'm not overreacting, am I?"

"He is a big boy," Crystal countered.

Ladonna propped her feet up on the sofa and tried to enjoy the slapstick high jinks on TV. Crystal and Bryson laughed hysterically. Meanwhile, Ladonna's imagination gripped her. Had Richard fallen ill? Had he slipped into a melancholy mood and overindulged in alcohol again? Had home invaders taken him hostage? Ladonna shook her head. Stop being silly, she told herself. If anyone knows what's going on with Richard, his mom would. "Call her," she thought.

Chapter 16

"I'm sorry to reach you so late," Ladonna began. She rarely contacted Richard's mom without his involvement or knowledge, and those instances typically revolved around receiving culinary advice and recipes.

"It's barely 9:00," Mrs. Knight replied. "And it's never too late for you. Is something wrong, dear? You sound wiped out."

"Richard has been so preoccupied lately. He recently stopped responding to my calls, my emails. I know relatives who withdraw as a defense against pressure or anxiety. I couldn't rest without confirming he's fine."

"Nothing comes to mind. Oh, wait," she said. "Richard complained about an interview when we spoke last week."

He's crammed a lot of appearances into his schedule, Ladonna thought. *He's probably exhausted.* "Any particular reason why?"

"Richard said they really grilled him. They sent him from department to department speaking to managers. That forced him to reschedule another interview, which of course didn't sit well with the other recruiter."

"Recruiter?"

"Maybe that's the wrong term. Human resources rep?"

"He's leaving Goldstein, Levy & Finch?"

"Uh..."

Ladonna bit down on her lip. "Forgive me if I placed you in an uncomfortable position, Mrs. Knight."

"Richard lost his job in December, honey," she blurted out.

"Oh," Ladonna said, quite astonished. She rarely found herself at a loss for words.

"He told me he was going to tell you," Mrs. Knight said. "I thought you knew."

"And I thought I knew him," Ladonna said to herself.

Recognizing the uncomfortable silence, Mrs. Knight added, "He only broke down and told me after I showed up looking for him at his office, and they told me first. And they didn't outright say it either. They just said, 'He's no longer here.'"

After that conversation, Ladonna told Crystal what she learned.

"Some shady mess is going on," Crystal counseled. "Richard should've at least given you a card to commemorate your first Valentine's Day. Damn." She emitted a series of grunts. "Now you find out he's been lying about work, too? Double damn."

Without a word, Ladonna left to sulk in solitude and let Crystal return to the tube. "I've intruded on her evening enough," Ladonna thought as she headed to the bathroom.

The bathroom bore the brunt of Ladonna's frustration. She scrubbed and sanitized already sanitized fixtures to eradicate phantom grime and germs. She plunged the sink and tub and then snaked a wire down both drains to scrape them free of sludge. She mopped the floor, wiped down the walls, but couldn't cleanse the uneasiness Mrs. Knight's disclosure brought on.

Surely Mrs. Knight would alert her son that Ladonna called. She expected Richard to conjure up excuses disguised as explanations, none of which she'd fall for, rather than fessing up to the blatant disrespect he showed her. He essentially wrote her off, and she'd gladly return the favor. Ladonna deemed herself immune to the spineless groveling and double-talk males engaged in. By no means could Richard persuade her the secrecy resulted from a misunderstanding or oversight. "Oversight my ass," Ladonna said. She cursed when angry. No, she cursed when furious. She stopped cleaning the baseboards to consider another scenario: Richard might continue ignoring her. "I don't give a damn what he does," she said.

Ladonna then rearranged the linen closet's contents. She moved partially full containers of beauty supplies to the front of shelves. She faced all labels forward. She convinced herself she'd created order out of disorder. That sliver of control prevented her from exploding.

When Crystal walked up, she startled Ladonna. "Are you doing demolition in here?"

Ladonna smirked. Crystal disregarded her roommate's snippy retort.

"Send him and his bags packing," Crystal vehemently urged. "Focus on someone who'll focus on you."

Ladonna checked the clock every few hours, praying for dawn to break. Once the clock on her nightstand read 5:47 a.m., she sat up rather than lie there staring in the dark. While gazing out at the window next to her bed, Ladonna studied the situation from Richard's standpoint. "Only crazies flip out without a trigger," she thought as she sorted through the logic. She attributed Richard's drastic behavioral change to the strain of his unemployment. The structure of male DNA prompted them to be protective providers. Despite having no dependents, Richard likely felt inferior since he faced an uncertain livelihood. Mrs. Knight revealed no specifics as to why the job loss occurred. The root cause mattered less than the effect for Ladonna. She viewed Richard as the type of candidate who outshined other applicants. If he'd confided in her, she would've asked one of the attorneys in her office to write a stellar reference. After ruminating for hours, Ladonna decided that Richard's refusal to seek help would not prevent her from offering it.

"The farmer's market near here has a better selection than my usual spot," Danielle exclaimed. She stood in Richard's kitchen chopping an assortment of yellow, orange, and red bell peppers. "I'm definitely swinging by there again."

Richard grabbed one of the raw slices and chomped on it. "I can't get over you making tortillas from scratch."

"It's not that complicated."

"You're my guest, Dee. It's weird for you to put in so much effort."

Danielle chuckled. "Are you kidding? You did everything else. I'm practically on vacation over here." She nodded toward the blender on the counter. "Margaritas and fajitas, I'm imagining myself poolside on the Mexican Riviera." She tossed the peppers and some onion slices in olive oil and then set them on a preheated, stovetop grill.

Richard retrieved guacamole, sour cream, and crumbled cojita cheese from the fridge. He laid the spread out on the dining room table. "Does your ex keep the girls every weekend?" he asked upon returning to the kitchen.

"Yeah, but normally not on Fridays. He's taking them to the circus tonight. Danielle flipped the vegetables then shut off the grill. "He put me on notice that he wants alternating weeks eventually. They're too young for that now in my opinion. They need stability instead of shuffling back and forth."

"That's reasonable." Richard retrieved plates from the cabinets and chilled glasses from the freezer. Then, he finished setting the table. Once Danielle concluded saying grace, Richard dug in to the spread. She poured herself a drink. After taking a tiny sip, Danielle cleared her throat and put her glass down.

"Too cold?"

She shook her head from side to side. "That's a monster concoction. The tequila is smooth but potent. I'll definitely need to pace myself. No seconds for me."

"It won't go to waste," Richard responded. He moved the pitcher closer to glass.

"So you're not a lightweight anymore," Danielle teased.

He raised his glass and took a long sip. "Nope," he responded as if the question required an answer.

They indulged in the hearty meal and reminisced about college. Meanwhile, a figure from his present prepared to make an entrance.

"Breath," Ladonna coaxed herself while parking in Richard's driveway. Ladonna's kindness overrode her disappointment. She set out to track down job leads for Richard the morning after speaking to Richard's mom. For the remainder of the week, she told everyone at the office to alert her of openings. She reached out to associates at other firms in the building and members of the paralegal organizations she belonged to.

Mr. Wreyford, a lawyer at her job, tipped off Ladonna on a construction law firm seeking new talent. He and the hiring manager ran in the same professional circles. Ladonna's colleague asked for background info on Richard. Ladonna supplied him with a verbal recommendation and insight on Richard's responsibilities at Goldstein, Levy & Finch. Her diligence paid off. Wreyford gave her an application to forward to Richard, who in turn, needed to supply a cover letter and resume along with it. Ladonna headed over to Richard's after dropping Bryson of at his grandparents.

Richard's garage doors had tinted windows that shielded the interior. Ladonna assumed he was home. If he didn't answer, she'd slip the envelope containing the application and a letter behind his storm door. If he answered, Ladonna resolved to relay the information without coaxing Richard to reveal the logic behind his virtual exit. Ladonna forecasted that Richard's behavior to come would reveal his true intentions. She was too busy to chase a man. She'd willingly write off their friendship and the prospect of it flourishing further if he offered no indication of appreciating it.

"Ladonna?" Richard said, clearly caught off guard. His chilly reception revealed that she ranked low on his list of concerns, if at all. He appeared shocked that Ladonna had the chutzpah to show up unannounced in light of his obvious dismissal of her. Richard stepped aside. "Come in. It's cold."

Ladonna struggled to detect warmth in the gesture. She took the offer as pretense rather than real courtesy. She detected whiffs of charred vegetables. He's in the middle of cooking, Ladonna thought. She resisted readily composing an excuse for his shell-shocked stare. She resisted feeling guilty for interrupting him. His inconsiderateness led to her visit in the first place. Ladonna operated on autopilot and stepped inside.

The foyer held greater warmth than what she felt flowing from Richard. "I'm here to deliver this lead," Ladonna reminded herself. "I won't enable him though. I won't share a meal with him, not tonight. If he asks me to stay awhile, I won't. I'll listen to what he says, and then I'm gone."

The man before her offered no inkling of an apology. She followed him from the foyer into the living room. Before she dove into the purpose of her visit, the sound of a chair scraping against the wood floor caught her attention. Ladonna realized they weren't alone.

The woman in the dining room doorway held no resemblance to the pictures she'd seen of Richard's sister, Pam.

"Danielle, this is Ladonna. Ladonna, Danielle."

Noticeably, neither understood the other's connection to Richard. Danielle gazed at him inquisitively.

"Ladonna helped with the bill research."

"So I'm reduced to a researcher," Ladonna thought after he failed to elaborate.

"Oh," Danielle replied. "Cool." She beamed at Ladonna. "Nice to meet you."

"Can't say the same," Ladonna wanted to say. "Looks like I've intruded on your evening," Ladonna stated snidely. She stared squarely at Richard. "Your mom told me about your job situation. Here's info on something that might interest you." She placed the envelope on the coffee table and turned to leave.

"Stay and join us," Danielle offered.

"Stay," Richard echoed.

His hollow words contained not a smidgen of authenticity. She'd go on a hunger strike before subjecting herself to a meal with them. If only she possessed the capability to teleport from that house within milliseconds.

Ladonna straightened her posture, held her head high, and strutted hastily to her hatchback. She blocked out Richard's voice. "Richard severed all communication with me," Ladonna reflected. "Now he wants us to break bread together? Correction: she extended the invitation, not he." Ladonna slid behind the wheel and pushed her puttering automobile to take flight. She drove far enough down the winding street to shield her car from Richard's view, determined not to let him or that woman witness her distress. She sensed Danielle's visual critique. That perturbed her. Richard's blasé attitude did, too. Ladonna broke into tearful convulsions, pounding her palm against the steering wheel. One blow landed with such force that she mistakenly blew the horn. It scared her, but not enough to stop crying.

After dealing with Bryson's dad, Ladonna realized that she can't change someone who wanted to remain stagnant. In the wake of their split, she learned that disappointment and discouragement proved difficult to shake but not impossible. After their relationship disintegrated, she retained her optimism instead of crawling into a shell of resentment toward him or all men. Feeling sorry for herself then or now would amount to copping out.

"No more," Ladonna decided while driving just below the speed limit on the interstate. She formed a pact with herself. She'd focus on a man's actions rather than future potential. Richard's behavior absolutely indicated he placed less importance on their "friendship" than she did. Ladonna silently chastised herself. How could she, who usually displayed a knack for reading others' intentions, have journeyed off base to this degree?

She dreaded telling Crystal what transpired, namely because Crystal predicted Richard's issues ran deep. Otherwise, her roommate had speculated on the outset of meeting him, why did he drink himself into oblivion? Did Crystal possess an innate ability to spot trouble she lacked? Had Bryson and Richard's adoration for each other blinded her? Now, Ladonna doubted if Richard cared for the boy at all. She'd become Richard's comrade, counselor, and colleague of sorts. She frequently rearranged her schedule to accommodate him and his needs and spoon-fed him healthy doses of encouragement along the way. Richard spun tales of wounding betrayal with the eloquence of Shakespeare, causing Ladonna to express genuine empathy and activating her nurturing disposition. At present, however, she viewed him as the crafty antagonist who delivered a destructive blow without hesitation.

The forewarning her skeptical mother gave rang out in Ladonna's memory. Mrs. Payton expressed dissatisfaction with the unbalanced state of affairs between her daughter and the man she knew of strictly from Ladonna's accounts and interview clips. "When a fellow wants you, he lets you know," her mom said. "Attraction is not a guessing game."

Trying to overcome the pessimism Richard ignited gave Ladonna a migraine. One simple call, email, or text from Richard would have saved her from worrying about his wellbeing. The current experience reiterated the need for Ladonna to tune into what she required to lead a fulfilled life. Focusing on herself fully meant creating the most ideal situation all around for her and Bryson. She was tired of entanglements with men lacking authenticity and consideration for others. Ladonna's faith, family, and friends reiterated then and now that she deserved an uncompromising love. She gambled on Richard and came up short, but she refused to let that debacle define her. After all, she did have another man on standby.

Richard assured Danielle that Ladonna normally exhibited a sunnier disposition. She implied that Ladonna's curt reaction hinted at more existing between them than Richard let on. He dismissed it, saying, "It's nothing, really."

The winter wore on with unusually frigid temperatures sweeping the region. A snowstorm, the worst in a decade, paralyzed the city for four days. Richard kept pushing onward toward his ambitions. He resolved that the weather would not stall his progress in searching for work, spreading awareness of the necessity of spousal notification, or learning more about Danielle.

He called the firm he learned of from Ladonna, who he hadn't spoken to since she dropped off the information. He tried calling her afterward out of gratitude and concern, but she neither answered nor returned the call.

And, although he regretted detaching himself from Ladonna in such and abrupt manner, he accepted their split as an inevitable outcome. He couldn't fit in Ladonna with Danielle, and his other endeavors. Something or someone had to give.

Hanging out with Danielle served as a tension reliever. She never talked about work or the proposed legislation. They just hung out, going to garage sales to seek discarded treasures on the weekends that the twins spent with their father. Or, they met for brunch or to catch a movie on cable. Essentially, Danielle and Richard rediscovered each other. She impressed him as much in adulthood as she had when they met during her campaign for freshman homecoming queen. Votes for Danielle outnumbered the runner-up by far. Her gravitational pull prompted students to bask in her presence. Surely smarter and sexier coeds roamed the campus, but Danielle's down-to-earth demeanor made her more approachable.

Richard told Kevin about Danielle when they met for a round of golf. Richard cancelled the outing twice before they met up this time. Kevin, who threatened to disown him, demanded to know why his unemployed friend had gone essentially missing in action.

"Ladonna has no problem with you and Danielle chilling out?" Kevin asked after hearing Richard's glowing accounts of Danielle.

"We're not an item," Richard told him. "I don't need her permission."

"Could've fooled me."

Although Richard tried to expound on his feelings for Danielle, Kevin declared emphatically, "No woman was *that* special."

Richard disagreed but knew arguing with Kevin would have aggravated him further. Danielle's presence affected Richard with a sort of effervescence that invigorated him when his energy dipped. He skipped coffee when she was around. Danielle consistently provided a boost of adrenaline that kept him from crashing. She also provided sensible advice. Danielle operated on a plane of decency outside of the realm of Nicole's foolishness.

When his ex and Toni left a hateful tirade of insults on his voicemail regarding their opinion of him and the senate bill, Danielle rightly suggested how to diffuse the situation.

"Ignore their tests. Reacting only persuades them that your buttons are worth pushing," Danielle advised. "Take the pleasure out of their taunting."

Richard didn't tell Danielle that he had already retaliated with a message of his own and was contemplating leaving a second. He did tell her how Nicole trampled over his trusting nature and left him with a smothering air of suspicion. She had some nerve to tag team him with Toni. Richard considered Nicole and Toni vultures of vulnerabilities that resurfaced to pick at his scars whenever they started to heal. Their callousness continued to shock his conscience.

"Why do I stupidly search for *any* indication of remorse from those two, Dee?"

"Do you still love Nicole?"

"Not at all."

"You're sure about that?" Danielle probed.

He wanted Nicole to cease all communication, including those filtered through her attorney.

"I'd rather tie a raw T-bone around my neck and jump into shark-infested waters than into any sort of affiliation with Nicole," Richard proclaimed.

Hindsight revealed volumes. Failing to establish a solid friendship with Nicole prior to jumping into their courtship attributed to the collapse of their marriage. Richard suggested that he and Danielle both let romanticism and lust wipe out logic when choosing partners. Danielle shared that she intended on marrying again and planned on the union lasting until one of them croaked. "I want to do it right this time. That means till death."

Richard took the opportunity to be frank with Danielle. "Well, do you consider your boyfriend the right guy?"

"He may be right for now, but who knows," said Danielle with a flirtatious grin.

Richard had his doubts but kept them to himself. Oddly enough, she mentioned him rarely. Even on Valentine's weekend when they picked up the twins, she hadn't expressed missing him. He wanted to ask if she loved the nameless figure. The constant omissions caused Richard to see him as a fictional character rather than flesh and blood competition.

Unlike Nicole, Danielle continuously had his wellbeing in mind. She tore into Richard after learning he stopped attending church. "The devil accepts all invitations," she cautioned.

Richard pondered her comment. Could he be embroiled in a spiritual tug-of-war? Had the dire events occurring resulted from his dwindling faith? Did some ominous force view him as an effortless target? The moment he let go of his religion, he tightened his reliance upon Nicole. Then when she cut him loose, he couldn't fully release the anger she invoked.

"I haven't given up on God, and I pray He hasn't given up on me. I just put that on pause when I got married."

Shaking her head in disappointment, Danielle said, "Why don't you come to church with me this Sunday? It'll probably do you more good than you know."

"Can we try Bible study first?"

"To make sure you don't change your mind, I'll be here at 6 on Wednesday to pick you up."

"I'm all yours," said Richard in such a way that she could apply it to church or their burgeoning relationship.

The Bible study teacher delved into scriptures about letting go of idols. Richard later wondered if worshipping an idea instead of a physical entity qualified as idolatry. Fatherhood as a concept had certainly enraptured him.

Richard never returned to Bible study with Danielle, but he periodically communed with God in prayer prior to falling asleep. He didn't kneel as he typically had in the pre-Nicole years; he simply lay in bed communicating through his thoughts. Of course, Richard requested employment. He requested resolve to continue promoting the new bill. He also requested passage by legislatures, but he secretly held out that a miracle would prompt the Assembly to do a U-turn and reinstate the bill's original provisions. Another concealed wish involved Danielle. He pictured her falling for him again and severing ties with her absentee boyfriend.

Chapter 17

Ladonna's referral paid off. Richard, based on the note accompanying the application she left, believed Zeigler & Associates to be a law firm. He realized upon further research that the construction/architectural business merely maintained in-house legal counsel. He applied and completed the standard pre-employment procedures: filling out forms and meeting with decision-makers. Ultimately, the firm extended a fair offer that he accepted gladly.

On the outset, Richard perceived a laidback feel at Zeigler & Associates. Employees referred to the firm as Z&A and greeted each other by first or nicknames. Most occupied decked-out cubicles instead of offices. Z&A promoted work-life balance, which included opportunities to bid for flexible schedules. The flex schedules did include a core period during which superiors expected employees in the office or on construction sites. Top brass took special circumstances into consideration; however, they typically expected employees to adjust if required to accomplish goals.

Z&A shunned the stuffy atmosphere Goldstein, Levy & Finch sanctioned. Here, casual clothing ruled for the most part. A siesta of sorts occurred when workers congregated for complimentary beverages and snacks during the day. The short, mandatory break rejuvenated everyone. Richard graciously declined repeated requests for him to join the softball team since he generally kept his private and professional dealings separate. At any rate, Richard had a load of procedures to master. His daily agenda, between acclimating to Z&A and stomping for SB71 held no room for leisure activities.

He tried reaching Ladonna to share what transpired. His emails went unanswered. Her phone emitted a fast, busy signal, and then an automated message stated the recipient was unavailable.

"Should I go check on her?" Richard asked Danielle after repeated attempts to reach Ladonna.

"She seemed like a capable gal to me. Maybe she just doesn't want to talk to you. She seemed pissed off when I met her."

"Maybe she's just busy," Richard supposed, totally unaware that his actions propelled Ladonna into Vincent Simmons' waiting arms.

Bryson giggled at the sight of his mom and abandoned the toy train his grandmother bought for his birthday last month. He found Ladonna's expressions hilarious.

She reclined while Vincent, on the loveseat also, massaged one of her feet. "You're supposed to put out fires, not ignite them," Ladonna uttered breathlessly. She half expected a bunch of grapes to materialize and for him to start feeding them to her.

He smiled that sly smile of his.

Her gut told her that Vincent was using his fabulous foot massages as a means to get her to break her 90-day no sex rule. Ladonna had already waited longer than that since her last sexual encounter. She hadn't been with anyone since her son's dad, right after Bryson turned one. While she adapted to diaper changes, feedings at all hours, and the stress of motherhood in general, he held on to his freedom. Bryson's dad, who lived apart from them, promised eventual matrimony. He failed to carry through. He popped in for visits when he saw fit and dropped off the radar when he should've been available at least by phone.

She collected enough circumstantial evidence to convict him in court but ignored glaring infidelity indicators. Instead of taking the reins herself, Ladonna regretted that she allowed him to decide what he wanted, which obviously wasn't a family. She equally lamented that she catered to the cheater even though he offered so little of himself in return. When he withdrew from their lives officially and accepted employment oversees, Ladonna mourned his departure for Bryson's sake, believing a half-decent dad was better than none at all. She prayed for a worthy and God-fearing partner to fill the void. No man since then or before Richard came close to delivering until Vincent materialized or, to be exact, she gave him a chance.

At 6'4", Vincent ranked as the tallest man she ever dated. In the kindness and generosity categories, he easily outshone his predecessors. They met what felt like eons ago. The crew from Fire Station 42 attended a "Super Show and Tell" at Bryson's daycare as a favor to the owner, Florence Barros. The retired principal had no children of her own, but she acted like a mother hen to all the children.

The monthly event featured one community member, business, or group that volunteered to teach the kids under the guise of having fun. Vincent's crew went over basic safety tips and then let the kids climb aboard the fire engine. Each received a red hat and miniature truck as parting gifts. When Ladonna arrived to pick up Bryson for a doctor's appointment, Ms. Barros introduced her to the men without singling out anyone.

Ms. Barros pounced on Ladonna when she dropped Bryson off the following week. Vincent, apparently completely smitten with Ladonna, had left his phone number for her.

"Why?" Ladonna inquired.

"He swears he got a good vibe from you. Obviously he's interested in getting to know you better."

"We barely spoke."

"A look often sparks attraction," Ms. Barros declared. "A look leads to…"

"I'm flattered, but I'm not calling him."

"His chief tells me he's a respectable gentleman."

Ladonna nervously tapped her heel against the floor.

"Just take the number." Ms. Barros shoved the slip of paper inside of Ladonna's palm.

She took it knowing she'd discard it.

Ms. Barros learned of Ladonna's inaction and periodically repeated a standard reminder.

"Vincent said he's still waiting."

His gesture elevated Ladonna's ego and concurrently set off alarms. Vincent belonged on the cover of GQ. In a city where women drastically outnumbered their male counterparts, he could take his pick. Ladonna mustered multiple excuses to ignore his advances. Vincent's job was too dangerous and demanding. He planned to conquer her and then move on to the next conquest. Bryson deserved her undivided attention, not a competition with a man whose attentiveness would surely pale as the thrill of the chase wore off. She spilled her concerns to Crystal.

Crystal chided Ladonna. She criticized the reasoning used to avoid Vincent. "You're the youngest old maid I know," Crystal concluded.

Ladonna left the discussion with an unchanged assessment.

The events around Ladonna unfolded like poetic justice: she shunned Vincent, and later, Richard shunned her.

After the Richard debacle, Ladonna went over her list of non-negotiable characteristics in a romantic partner. He needed to be an ambitious, church-going, family-oriented, educated man. He needed to embrace Bryson rather than just tolerate him. She resolved to move on past men who required more coddling than Bryson did, and men who were still haunted by their past lovers.

Ladonna apologized to Vincent for dismissing his advances. "I'd understand if you don't want to be bothered. I had a lot going on," she said.

He assured Ladonna the reason behind her reversal held no significance. "We're straight. I just keep pinching myself to make sure I'm not hallucinating."

The truth embarrassed Ladonna. She reached out to Vincent anticipating a brief fling at most, a self-esteem boost at best. She'd find a defect and, instead of lingering in fruitless limbo, dispose of him before he disposed of her.

Vincent emphasized a desire to trek the globe on their first date. "Any lady of mine needs to experience other countries too." He had a lot of animated gestures and moved his torso a lot when speaking.

"Any lady of yours?"

He swatted the air as if erasing his previous comment. "That sounded a bit possessive. I'm just saying my partner must have the travel bug."

"Have you been to any exotic lands?"

"Nope. Spain is on my wish list. No one in my circle cares to venture that far."

"Coordinating group trips isn't easy. I went on a family cruise. We stopped in Cozumel," he said. "Beyond that, I've only been on domestic excursions."

Vincent rented a condo downtown by the fire station that served his purposes for now. His immediate family resided primarily in the Midwest. They visited during the summer and at Christmas. Some older cousins, whom he saw occasionally, lived in the area. He had no kids, but he said he planned on having half a dozen if he found a willing and compassionate woman.

"That's a lot!" Ladonna cried. She cringed at the visual of popping out multiple miniature versions of him and her.

"I'm fine with stepchildren."

Her heart rate fluttered.

"I'm interested in adoption as well," he added.

"Awesome," said Ladonna apprehensively, looking him directly in the eye for signs of deception. "Too perfect," she thought. "This guy either has no major flaws or knows how to hide them."

"Hands on, that's how my parents raised me. That's the example I intend to follow. I'm glad I grew up before computers and video games and CrackBerries came along and turned kids into virtual zombies. Technology shouldn't replace old-fashioned rearing. Investing in children builds their character and their confidence."

"We're on the same wavelength. Half the kids on my block stay cooped up in the house. I've seen some at Bryson's daycare with cell phones. Ridiculous."

He asked about Bryson. She described her son.

Without warning, his opinion mattered. She awaited his calls, the sight of him, and his touch. She made herself beautiful for him. Insignificant happenings gained significance. A budding pimple caused anxiety. She learned, however, that men of character placed greater value on inner than outer beauty. Still, before every encounter, Ladonna would ask Crystal, "How do I look?"

Ladonna had almost worn herself out reassuring Richard, aiding him, pining for him. Vincent, however, revived her. With him, she rediscovered equilibrium. Vincent's schedule consisted of 24-hour shifts twice a week with the availability of occasional overtime. He contacted her to say hi in the midst of those spells. Even if only with a brief email, he replied to all messages. Their conversations ranged many topics and kept confirming their many similarities.

Their bond blossomed rapidly in part because Vincent expressed himself freely and on a wider range of subjects than her last string of boyfriends. His openness led to hers. "I've seen people howling with grief because tragedy ended any opportunity to share feelings they'd held inside," he lamented after a grueling recovery mission that yielded only one survivor. "My job forces me to appreciate the people who appreciate me."

Outside of public service, Vincent operated a home-based sole-proprietorship. He prepared taxes for individuals, and payroll and billing for small businesses. Vincent explained that he attended college intent on graduating with an accounting degree and then passing the CPA exam. Crunching numbers partially fulfilled him. The yearning to make a lasting impact on society overrode his original career aspirations. He applied to the fire academy right after completing his undergraduate studies.

She speculated if he expected his spouse to forgo professional aspirations while he pursued his. Someone, after all, had to care for his proposed brood. She was also bursting for dirt on his last girlfriend. Why had a fine specimen stayed on the market so long? Ladonna held in those ponderings partly so she could avoid revealing her own history.

Ladonna aimed to loosen up and let down her guard. She pushed aside the hazards of Vincent's profession. She reminded herself that danger lurked in many places, like on expressways. Fear of injury from an automobile accident hadn't hampered her ability to operate a vehicle. Fear wouldn't thwart this budding relationship either.

They powered on learning more about each other and even double-dated with Crystal and a guy she met at a gas station. His overall aura paled in comparison to Vincent's. As the roommates dissected the outing back at home, Crystal ultimately declared Ladonna landed the "better catch."

Vincent's unconventional work hours allowed him to see Ladonna quite often. His presence proved supportive. He prepared dinner for her and Crystal and completed minor repairs they'd rather not bother their landlord with. Vincent attempted to entertain Bryson with kiddie puzzles, toy cars and stories about his boyhood. Bryson reacted to him with less gusto than he put forth with Richard. Even though he didn't shun her new beau, the noticeable detachment frustrated Ladonna. She reasoned Bryson was aloof because he didn't get to know Vincent well. From what she observed Vincent either felt the same or hadn't noticed the disconnect.

Nonetheless, Vincent had won over the other person in Ladonna's household. Even Crystal melted in his presence. She morphed into an unrecognizable damsel who awaited his visits nearly as much as Ladonna. Crystal commented on how Vincent's uniform caressed his toned physique. He was muscular but not freakishly so. Ladonna experienced a close-up taste of his deliciousness during a series of salsa lessons he surprised her with. He purchased them shortly after she mentioned her interest in the Spanish language and culture.

"I see myself owning a legal outsourcing agency," Ladonna shared on that same occasion. Hispanic populations are multiplying. I've seen an increased need for translators and paralegals who communicate beyond English. Did you know that Mexicans, Spaniards, and Portuguese speak varying dialects?"

She had trouble recollecting the last instance a mate gave such a thoughtful, spontaneous gift. Best of all, Vincent joined her at the classes. For her birthday in late March, he gave her a Rosetta Stone. Ladonna was thrilled.

"You can't buy me," she teased.

"Didn't think so," Vincent responded, "but update me if your policy changes."

He spontaneously spouted funny lines, and she found his humor refreshing. With Vincent, the mood remained light.

They frequented a salsa club to gain extra practice. During the day, it operated as a lunch joint, which is how Vincent became aware of it. In the evening, Havana Club switched to an adult-only spot. It served appetizers and alcohol to nourish and hydrate salsa enthusiasts. The staff constantly greeted Vincent with reverence. They basked in his attentiveness. He chatted with them and, when they persisted, told work-related tales. He also told everybody but the DJ how Ladonna wanted to be bilingual. Waiters and bartenders and the owners, all native speakers, drilled Ladonna on her vocabulary and pronunciation. She equally enjoyed the ambiance and the dancing.

Her body, which last participated in dancing of such a strenuous sort in middle school, resisted the flurry of physicality at the start. Not since those long ago ballet courses had she swayed, turned, dipped, and twirled so energetically. Ballet ceased as a result of education budget cuts. Her parent's budget couldn't sustain the cost of private instruction. As an adult, Ladonna habitually rejected indulging in non-necessities. She instead channeled her miniscule discretionary funds toward providing for Bryson.

From her neck to the soles of her feet, Ladonna ached. She put on a gracious grin when in actuality she wanted to stop in mid-stride and kick off her heels. She entertained wearing sneakers. Those, she concluded, would counteract the sexiness she strived to convey. The discomfort subsided as the sessions continued and she learned additional routines. Soon, Ladonna noticed her pants fitting looser. Irksome baby weight began to drop off. Her midsection shrunk and appeared slightly toned. Her emerging, improved physique led her to having more confidence and to focusing more on the lessons.

Their instructor advised upon meeting them that they had to submit to the movements and each other. Anything less let them and the dance down. Ladonna ultimately embraced his methodology. Dancing together in the studio deepened the intimacy between Ladonna and Vincent, the sexual tension between them building and releasing with each step. Ladonna relished the tender strength Vincent exuded while leading her through the pulsating, melodic rhythms.

Ladonna glanced at her carefree son. She chided herself for assuming so but suspected their future involved Vincent. Still, her son had yet to develop a fondness for the firefighter. He maintained an unsettling soft spot for Richard and had asked her to call him. She blocked the request with lies veiled as excuses that cast Richard in a better light than he deserved. Richard left a lame, generic voicemail way back when thanking her for the lead but glossing over everything else. She wished him no ill but concurrently refused to feed into his delusions. He recently began contacting her again. Ladonna promptly deleted his emails. Luckily, she had lost her old phone and no longer had to deal with his calls. She thought she could get by using the phone at work until Vincent insisted she use his spare.

"You don't have a landline," he said, "and what if there's an emergency, and Crystal isn't here? What if your car conks out?"

He presented valid points. She conceded.

Bryson, thankfully, mentioned Richard only when Vincent wasn't around. She explained in four-year-old terms that Richard probably would not visit or call because he was so busy. He quizzed her periodically regarding Richard's whereabouts. He didn't associate the fireman's presence with the lawyer's absence.

Bryson's confusion compounded the offensiveness of Richard's deeds. While he lacked the vocabulary to articulate it, Ladonna's motherly intuition recognized the unprecedented betrayal altered Bryson's being. Her son wanted everyone to be his friend and Richard's baseless vanishing act destroyed some of her son's accepting nature and his innocence. At least Bryson's trifling father abandoned him before they formed a bond and before clear memories set in. If only she had averted this crisis with a preemptive strike and called a cab for Richard when he stumbled past her.

Vincent ceased stroking her foot. She pouted.

"Let's blow this town," he said.

Ladonna sat up. The suggestion seemed too sudden and too enticing. "I can't just leave without giving notice."

"I'm not referring to the next ten seconds."

"When?"

"Spring break. Does that sound okay?"

"Crystal would've agreed in a flash," Ladonna thought. Ms. Barros and the fire chief maintained glowing opinions of Vincent. The referrals made Vincent seem like less of a threat. Otherwise, Ladonna wouldn't have considered crossing state lines with him just yet. There was the issue of Bryson.

Vincent's voice broke Ladonna's deliberating.

"If you're worried about sleeping arrangements," he said, "we can book adjoining suites or one with double beds."

"There's no guarantee my parents will watch Bryson that long," Ladonna mused. In retrospect she thought they'd oblige her. Hell, they'd probably pack her bags and offer a ride to the airport. Mrs. Payton remarked that the pair would produce stunning babies. The typically skeptical Mr. Payton remarked that Vincent struck him as a stand-up type of fellow.

"I'm leaning toward a short getaway, not a sabbatical. At any rate, you could bring him along."

The prospect hadn't occurred to her. Maybe escaping the city with Bryson in tow would shrink the divide between him and Vincent. Maybe doing so would foster forging a new beginning.

Vincent inched toward Ladonna and took hold of her hands. He alternated between planting sublime kisses on them and whispering words intended to ease her qualms. "I'm thinking Miami…near South Beach…You could brush up on your Español…"

She made the decision yet let him keep pleading his case.

Chapter 18

For approximately two weeks, the senator's intern kept Richard on standby and updated him on the status of SB71. The forthcoming vote would reveal if Richard and the senator's efforts had been in vain. Winston intended, regardless of the aftermath, to hold a press conference and to issue a press release. He personally contacted Richard to confirm his attendance.

"It's only fitting for us to stand side-by-side," he said. "Try to arrive by 4:30. That'll allow ample opportunity for the conference to air on nightly newscasts."

Filibustering regarding other measures delayed the resolution of SB71. Agonizing over the final tally wore on Richard. Despite Winston's assurances, he realized the uncertainty of a favorable vote. Richard tried channeling his anxiety into locking down the responsibilities of his new position. That task, in conjunction with worrying while the House plowed through its docket, left him immensely drained.

Kevin complained that Richard kept spacing out when he stopped by. "I drove clear across town to have you practically ignore me?" he asked.

Danielle blasted Richard for falling asleep during a phone conversation. "Am I that boring?" she questioned.

In those instances when he remained alert, Richard swore his nerves were performing a gymnastics routine. No amount of confiding in his mother or focusing on other subjects calmed them. A potent concoction of rum and coke proved a suitable remedy.

On particularly hectic days, he strolled to a wine bar near the office and downed a serving or two of Riesling. It took the edge off without rendering him useless. He kept a supply of mints at his desk to mask his breath since the company handbook prohibited alcohol consumption during shifts. No one at his job mentioned his current or past media appearances. Richard supposed that his boss, Mr. Engle, knew of them prior to hiring him but considered them of no professional bearing.

On the second Friday in May, the Georgia House voted for the Spousal Pregnancy Termination Notification Bill.

"We no longer have to concern ourselves with political wrangling or the prospect of my colleagues voicing opposition at the last minute or insisting we add superfluous clauses," Winston virtually sang over the phone.

"Doesn't the governor have to sign off?" Richard asked.

"I've locked in his endorsement."

"I appreciate your investment in this drawn-out process," Richard said.

Richard left work at 3:30 instead of 5:00. He assumed Mr. Engle, a self-proclaimed hippie, wouldn't sweat the early departure. He left for a jobsite anyway, and bothering him seemed counterproductive. Moreover, Richard planned to arrive early the next morning. Richard envied the carefree manner in which his boss operated. Mr. Engle stated during their first encounter that he shunned the taskmaster mentality and trusted his personnel to police themselves and each other. "If someone's slacking, it'll come to light without me micromanaging," he said.

Finding an empty spot in the packed parking garage, clearing a security checkpoint, and navigating bystanders in the crowded lobby caused Richard to arrive precariously close to airtime. The senator's press secretary ushered him into a media room, where Winston waited. He said hello to Richard and then returned to his note cards.

Richard followed the secretary's lead.

He thrust a small bottle of water at Richard. "Take a sip. We don't want you croaking. "Maintain a neutral stance, a steady gaze outward, and refrain from any facial gestures other than a slight smile while the senator speaks."

Winston's press secretary gave Richard a visual once-over. He picked a piece of lint from his suit jacket. Then he directed Richard to a spot off-camera. "Remember the sound-bite rule," he reiterated. "Keep your comments short." He pointed to a chair at the end of the first row. "Sit there after your remarks."

Richard took in the directives and the setting. A sea of empty chairs sat in front of the podium. Each had a slip of paper on the backrest that designated the correlating news outlet. He had not anticipated coverage by any news-talk radio broadcasters. He assuredly had not anticipated the number of magazine and newspaper reporters scheduled to attend. Some, Richard noticed, worked in Augusta, Macon and other adjacent municipalities. His gaze landed in the center of the front row. That seat's sign read "CNN." Richard took a deep breath.

"Send them in," the press secretary ordered Ian. The intern complied. A stampede of reporters entered and began seeking their respective spots.

With everyone in place, the press secretary welcomed the reporters. "We're live in 90 seconds," he announced soon afterwards. "Senator Winston and Mr. Knight will each make a brief statement. Then, the senator will permit a few questions."

All chatter ceased. The senator stood front and center. "Welcome. Thank you for joining me to mark a momentous juncture in Georgia history. Senate Bill 71 signifies the culmination of an extensive collaborative effort that crossed political lines. With its passage…"

Richard zoned in and out. Standing before the press corps caused more anxiety than doing ten interviews at once. Their stares suggested they sat poised to pounce on the senator with a barrage of queries. The cameras' glares and the heat they emitted made Richard's collar seem stifling. He wanted to loosen it. Trepidation that the demanding press secretary might reprimand him kept Richard still.

He thought of Bryson and how little boys and girls brought happiness into the world by their mere existence. He hoped the bill would prompt women, namely wives, to reconsider terminating a pregnancy.

"At this juncture," Winston said, "Mr. Richard Knight will offer remarks." He moved to the side and nodded toward Richard, who came forward.

"I represent many men. We all owe a debt to Senator Winston. We all applaud the perseverance he and his constituents showed. The birth of SB71 protects the rights of husbands statewide and will, hopefully, grant them reprieve from tragedies such as the one I endured."

Richard marked the occasion by visiting Junior's memorial, which he did periodically, but this instance held special importance. The cedar had grown significantly. Spring foliage had begun to emerge. Richard sought a renewal as well. He sat there watching the sun sink into the horizon and communing with his son without saying a word.

Danielle, Kevin, and his mother all congratulated Richard on his victory. The latter two, he speculated, did so begrudgingly. He recognized that they obviously desired the best for him and believed he believed the legislation would solve a plethora of his woes. His statement to the press indicated acceptance. Factually, he considered notification a mere step in the father's rights campaign.

Dissenters continued to rally against SB71 and women's health organizations urged women to snub the pending law. Some clinics vowed to disregard it as well. The prospect that the mayhem might force a recall loomed over Richard even in light of Winston's reassurances. Portions of a controversial immigration bill passed earlier faced blockage by an appellate court. Richard fretted that SB71 might encounter a similar fate. He relayed his concern to Danielle that the bill had not gone far enough and that it might be repealed.

"The bottom line," Danielle commented, "is that women own their bodies and the babies in them. I don't see mainstream pro-choice opinions evolving either."

While on break one morning, Richard checked the search engine alerts he set to track publicity surrounding SB71. Nearly a week had gone by. Richard predicted the bill's passage would lead to an instantaneous and spectacularly euphoric state. Instead, he felt flashes of agony and relief intertwined with joy and uncertainty. Since Nicole dropped the details of her deed, or perhaps prior, Richard had been sucked into a vortex of sorts. He grew so accustomed to encountering conflicts that, subconsciously or not, the prospect of serenity frightened him. The affair, the divorce, the death of Junior, the backstabbing betrayal by Henson and subsequent unemployment, the collapse of the consent bill — each event forced him to retain a defensive stance. If he alleged the worst had passed and presumed gleeful contentment lay within his grasp, Richard feared he'd put himself at a detriment when the next adversarial blow struck.

No one understood his journey quite like Ladonna. She anchored him. Ladonna, in retrospect, had discreetly yet ferociously protected him from reservations that could've sunk SB71 before it set sail. It surprised Richard that she hadn't reached out to him.

Commencement of the legislative session and the resolution of controversial regulations including SB71 dominated the otherwise humdrum news cycle. A photo of the senator and Richard appeared in the *Atlanta Journal.* Unless Ladonna practically sequestered herself, she had to know what occurred. Even his sister heard of the decision from a Chicago broadcast before their mother informed her. She called earlier to congratulate him, but he ended the conversation by congratulating her on the fact that Pam's boyfriend finally proposed.

Richard speculated if Ladonna's contact told her that Zeigler & Associates hired him. He owed Ladonna for helping him on both fronts. "I'll swing by her job at lunchtime," Richard said to himself.

The receptionist beamed at Richard and buzzed him in while she answered an incoming call. He met the young woman and some paralegals in Ladonna's office before. Ladonna's cubicle sat empty. No files or effects lay on the desk indicating her imminent return. A vase of multicolored roses graced one corner. "Did I miss her birthday?" Richard pondered. Then he realized he had no idea when it was.

Richard speculated that Ladonna and a group of coworkers went out to eat. The coworkers he knew were away from their cubicles too. No other conclusion proved reasonable since the receptionist would have stopped him if Ladonna was off.

He reached for a pen and a small yellow notepad to jot a quick note. The screensaver on her PC flashed pictures of Bryson. Richard stopped to view them. Following a brief series of shots showing the boy striking silly poses, a photo of Ladonna and a lanky guy covered the monitor. The pair relaxed on a beach towel close to a tropical shore. "Huh," he mumbled and placed the pen and paper down without leaving a message.

He decided to ask the receptionist to have Ladonna contact him. Upon exiting, Richard found an abandoned receptionist station. He glanced at his wristwatch. This manhunt cost him half of his lunch break. He'd worry about reaching Ladonna later.

Back at his office, Richard sat staring aimlessly out the window at the passersby, mainly the women. He attributed his distraction to Pam's announcement. She and her beau had no date or location set. Richard generally remained detached from his sister's private matters. Pam flaunted her seniority over him and, in Richard's opinion, erroneously dubbed herself the wiser sibling. Their mother chided Pam, reminding her, "Mama didn't raise any loose children, and God don't accept that kind of stuff either." Living with a man without a ring or no imminent nuptials on the horizon was a no-no.

Pam claimed, "We don't need a piece of paper or a label to define us." Richard suspected otherwise. His sister's desire to wed had been well-documented in their adolescence, from conversations with Mrs. Knight to scrapbooks containing ceremony ideas. Richard pondered if her boyfriend's proposal stemmed from an ultimatum.

He pushed Pam out of his brain. Richard still had a great deal of construction procedural and compliance material to absorb, not to mention complex lingo. His fingers cramped due to all the notes he jotted down and typed. Mr. Engle assigned him to the Construction Support Division. The division mainly dealt with ensuring deadlines remained on track and diffusing disputes that arose among superiors, laborers, contractors, suppliers, etc. In short, Richard served as second-tier project manager tasked with insuring participants adhered to compliance and contractual obligations.

Resolving issues before they escalated saved time and secured profits for all involved. Currently, Richard shadowed other lawyers. He'd soon venture out to sites solo and build his own caseload as the firm initiated new projects. In retrospect, however, Richard enjoyed the fieldwork aspect more than the confinement of Goldstein, Levy & Finch's indoor powwows. He welcomed the departure from the duties that prior position entailed. He would've been content climbing the partnership ladder there, perhaps too content. Richard's new role built on prior experience while offering him a means to expand his skill-set. As an added bonus, it paid a wage comparable to the other firm.

Until Richard got fired, failure on a professional level was an unfamiliar concept to him. Countless rejections from potential employers placed Richard in a powerless state, unable to showcase his talent. He tried shifts in strategy such as rewording his resume and lowering his desired salary range. The unsolicited yet totally essential referral Ladonna extended provided an advantage over other applicants. Richard locked his computer, grabbed his cell, and sought out an empty meeting room.

The call caught Ladonna off guard. Her palms grew clammy. She refused to hash out anything with Richard in earshot of her peers.

Richard relayed that he stopped by earlier. "So um," he was saying, "I left messages. Did you get them?"

"I lost my phone," she fibbed. Ladonna knew full well he left a voicemail before that occurrence. She replaced Vincent's loaner with a new cellphone since then and could've easily contacted Richard via email.

"Oh, I thought not hearing back from you was unusual."

The irony humored Ladonna. She suppressed a snicker. "I called to thank you for the lead and again after landing the job."

She feigned enthusiasm. "Good for you."

"I wanted to make sure you realized how grateful I am."

"I'm sure you'll do well there. I should get going though."

"Uh, wait. I was hoping to stop by your house around 6:00 to see you and Bryson."

The request blindsided her. If she granted it, Ladonna risked reversing her efforts at getting Bryson to detox from the allure Richard held. Then again, did that much actually ride on her decision? At his young age, she reasoned, Bryson should better be able to recover from the impact if Richard entered their realm and then vanished. He would encounter a bevy of uplifting experiences as he aged that would cleanse him of the disappointment. If Richard took an active interest in Bryson, the result would justify integrating him back into her son's life. But how could *she* accept Richard in any capacity? Ladonna conceded Bryson's best interest should override her preferences and biases. "Um, okay. I won't be there, but he will. I'll let Crystal know. "

"You cost me $5," Crystal said after letting Richard in.

"Some greeting," he said.

Her gaze pierced him. Her folded arms and scowl shocked him. "Apparently I'm missing something."

"I bet Ladonna you wouldn't show."

He responded with an oblivious expression.

"Never mind. Bryson is in his room."

Richard snuck up on Bryson, who was dressed in his superhero pajamas and playing with his train set. He knelt beside him. The boy gasped and threw his arms around Richard's neck, almost knocking him over.

"Easy there." Richard steadied himself. He lifted Bryson and tickled him. The act sent the boy into hysterical giggling fits. "You've gotten big."

"I'm 4 now!" Bryson exclaimed.

"That explains it. You must be even better at kicking that soccer ball then."

"Wanna play?"

"It's dark outside, buddy. One day soon, though."

Bryson insisted on showing Richard each of his new toys. Crystal interrupted them. "It's 7:00. Gotta get him to bed."

To Richard, it seemed like only a matter of minutes had gone by.

"Aah!" Bryson whined.

She moved in front of his bed. "You know the drill. Bring your butt on."

Bryson stomped over to her.

"Any idea when his mom will make it in?"

"Not a clue."

"Care if I stick around a bit longer?"

Crystal glanced at Bryson, who eagerly awaited her response.

"I'll read him a bedtime story," Richard volunteered.

"That's fine. Once he conks out, you'll have to leave."

Richard nodded in agreement. Crystal left them alone.

Bryson pulled a book out of his toy chest and handed it to Richard. Then he crawled into bed.

"Felix the Cat," Richard said. "Cool." The book's cover showcased a cat wearing an enormous grin, sunglasses, and high-top sneakers. Richard recollected Mrs. Knight reading him mostly parables from the Bible and Sesame Street tales. Bryson struggled to stay awake as Richard read slowly and with dramatic flair. The theatrics engrossed Bryson. Sleep overcame him before the story concluded.

Richard watched him sleep. Bryson snored heavily, which surprised Richard. He observed the boy until Crystal tiptoed in and tapped his shoulder. She motioned toward the door.

Richard quietly put the book back in the chest and followed her into the hall.

"No use in waiting around," she said. "Why don't you come back when he's awake? Check with Ladonna to see when they'll both be here."

Richard looked like he was pondering another option. Crystal stared back like he shouldn't be.

"Alright," he said with reluctance oozing from every syllable and sauntered out. He may have missed Ladonna tonight, but he wouldn't miss her tomorrow.

Richard realized too late that he still had no regular contact number for Ladonna. He considered 10 a.m. early enough to catch her at home. Her hatchback sat in the driveway. So did another vehicle: a white Acura RSX. "Someone has company," Richard thought and assumed that someone was Crystal. For a split-second, he contemplated leaving. He decided to stay so he could put an end to the phone tag. Yesterday, Ladonna sounded a tad miffed that he called her at work. He needed to get her new number. He forgot to request it and to thank her for assisting with SB71. With his mission clear, Richard headed up the walkway through Ladonna's yard.

"Can I help you?" asked the man who towered over Richard and spoke without opening the storm door.

"Good morning, is Ladonna home?"

"And you are?"

"Richard."

"Hold on." Vincent turned and shouted, "Babe! There's a Richard here to see you."

It clicked. Richard realized he'd just met Ladonna's beau. "Explains why she's been too busy to get back to me," he thought, while subconsciously assessing his competition.

"Let him in," she shouted back.

Vincent locked the door behind them and told Richard to have a seat.

Bryson bounded into the living room before Richard sat down and headed straight for him. "Richard!" he squealed and hugged one of his legs.

Vincent curiously observed the display of fondness.

Ladonna entered the scene wearing one earring and putting the other on. Her gaze darted back and forth between the two men.

Richard immediately pinpointed her slimmer physique.

"I wasn't expecting you," she said. "Vincent, this is Richard. Richard, Vincent." After the men nodded toward each other, Ladonna focused on Vincent, adding, "We worked on a legal project together."

"Excuse me for dropping by unannounced."

She glanced at Vincent again.

"I realized I didn't get an updated number for you. I also neglected to thank you for helping with the bill. It's official now, you know."

"I heard, and you're welcome."

Bryson tugged at Richard's jeans. "You came to play with me?"

"No, honey," his mom interjected.

"Actually, I promised Bryson I'd run some soccer moves by him. Let him spend the day with me."

Ladonna froze and glanced at Vincent again. After regaining her composure, she said, "Bryson just started taking allergy meds. I don't want him outside for long periods."

"Not an issue. We'll check out one of those indoor spots with the inflatable bouncy thingies."

"We were on our way out," Vincent piped in.

Retracting the offer occurred to Richard. As Bryson frowned and clung to Richard, his mother caved in. "You'll need his booster seat."

Ladonna evaded locking eyes with Vincent. A dumbfounded gawk plastered his face. He clearly expected and deserved an explanation. So did she.

Chapter 19

"Must've been one hell of a project." Vincent almost roared after Richard's BMW pulled off from the curb.

Ladonna hadn't heard him utter profanity prior to this occurrence.

"You let him baby-sit, and I know how protective you are," Vincent exclaimed.

She attributed his raised voice to trying to speak over the neighbor's lawnmower. "We spent months together researching info on a bill that Richard introduced."

Vincent folded his arms, waiting for her to say more.

"Remember that new law that's all over the news, the one requiring spousal notification for abortions?"

"Yeah."

"Richard coauthored that legislation," Ladonna said. "I helped him make connections with key people and strategize until he got to this point. We would spend long hours working, and of course, I had to bring Bryson with me sometimes. Me and Richard would take turns entertaining him until he fell asleep."

Sensing that Vincent wanted to know more, she added, "Of course, it was platonic, all business." As she spoke, Ladonna felt as if she was convincing herself more than she was Vincent. She still held a flame for Richard, and seeing him reminded her of that even though he seemed to have aged a bit. She noticed fine lines forming on his face that weren't present before.

"Now that you mention it, I vaguely recall an interview of his."

"Then you will agree granting him an afternoon with Bryson is a small sacrifice considering all he's gone through."

Vincent's arms fell from his chest to his pockets, where he buried his hands.

"He's more trustworthy than most when it comes to my son. And you witnessed firsthand how much Bryson wanted to go."

"I saw. We were supposed to spend the day at my condo, though," Vincent griped. "The three of us."

Vincent clearly took their relationship and connecting with Bryson seriously. As they closed in on the three-month mark, Ladonna mulled over her emotional readiness. Should she drag out completely giving herself to him? She glimpsed from Vincent, in fleeting moments, a yearning to fulfill a carnal longing. She recognized it in his gaze, his touch, his seductive tone. Ladonna dreaded physical intimacy nearly as much as she desired it. Despite her best efforts, once sex begins, Ladonna completely succumbs to sensual pleasures and looses all common sense.

Her blunt mother advised her once, "Most men love you when they're making love to you, but it's how they handle themselves outside the bedroom that matters most." Vincent had handled himself with poise and grace until Richard entered the scene.

"I'll make it up somehow," Ladonna swore without knowing how.

Vincent's whole body tensed. "How come this guy just popped up, though? You know all of my female associates."

"It's complicated."

"Un-complicate it."

No one sought clarification on the nature of their association more than Ladonna. With his reappearance, Richard evoked an undercurrent of suspicion on Vincent's part. Ladonna, by no means, had forgotten or forgiven Richard's aloofness. She intended to broach his behavior when an opportunity arose. She marveled at Richard's aptitude to circumvent his obvious slight. She presumed he'd offer a sanitized version of how events went down. For her sake and Bryson's, Ladonna intended on snapping Richard back to reality and setting clear boundaries. Richard, otherwise, would treat her as a proverbial doormat.

"We lost touch with each other," Ladonna said. "Therefore, I had no reason to mention him." She put her hands on Vincent's waist. "You know all the people who are important to me." She drew him in for a kiss, not caring who spied them.

He said no more.

The mayhem at Jumpin' Johnny's left Richard reevaluating his choice. He swooped up Bryson to prevent an older, rambunctious boy who ran by from sending him reeling. Bumping, thumping, and sliding noises bounced off the walls as the children explored bulky, oversized structures. They entertained themselves in rubber cages decked out with all sorts of contraptions. In one, a pair of boys boxed with gigantic gloves and helmets. Another, in the form of a castle, boasted dual slides that were perfect for racing. Yet another contained a mock rock-climbing wall.

Richard scanned the room for an area suitable for the preschooler. "Let's hang out over there," he said and pointed to a set of inflatable slides, jumps, and obstacle courses designated for smaller kids. They headed to a rainbow-colored cage filled with plastic balls. One side of it had wide, winding slides. The opposite side had an easily navigable ladder leading to an observation booth overlooking the facility. A couple of boys and one girl were already inside.

Although Jumpin' Johnny's allowed adults to interact with children inside the structures, most opted to indulge in the free high-speed, wireless Internet and computer stations in the lounge. And, to Richard's dismay, they barely looked over at the play areas. Trained staff members patrolled the floor to ward off safety violations. Richard trusted no one but himself to watch over Ladonna's precious baby.

"Take off your shoes," he directed Bryson.

"My socks too?"

"No."

"Take off your shoes," Bryson said while pointing at Richard's almost new sneakers, which he may have only worn one other time.

Richard had no intention of joining the boy inside the actual inflatable. "I'm not the one who's going to be playing."

Bryson stood his ground.

That adorable mug made Richard give in.

Bryson waited for Richard to remove his sneakers before removing his own.

Richard encouraged Bryson to play with the other children. He seemed slow to warm up to them. Once Richard initiated a game of dodge ball with Bryson, the others wanted to join in. Richard eventually eased himself out of the action and sat in corner of the cage. He became the group's chaperone and watched as Bryson enjoyed the slide and other features. When they tired of that inflatable structure, he led them all to another one with an obstacle course.

"I'm thirsty," Bryson said after another 20 minutes went by.

Richard guided him to the concession stand and bought him a juice box. He planned to take Bryson out to eat after leaving Jumpin' Johnny's. Ladonna instructed him that Bryson napped around 1 p.m., so she'd pick him up around 3.

"Hope you're having fun," Richard said.

Bryson nodded his head up and down.

"Tell me about your mommy's new friend, Vincent."

"He's a fireman, and he let me go in his truck."

Richard stopped short of asking how long Ladonna knew Vincent when he realized the boy had no real concept of time.

"Do you and your mom see him a lot?"

"Yep."

"Does he take you guys out to fun spots like this?"

"Nope, but he gives me piggy-back rides." Bryson took a gulp from his drink. "He promised to buy me a bike," Bryson stated excitedly.

"What happened to your tricycle?"

"That's for little kids," he proclaimed and gazed at Richard as if he should've known better. Then Bryson began scoping out the room for his next adventure.

Richard blurted out the question that piqued his curiosity more than any other. "Seems like your mom really likes Vincent."

Bryson slid out of his seat. "She kisses him a lot." Bryson mimicked the smooches and sent himself into a fit of giggles.

From his antics, Richard surmised the pair exchanged mere pecks. Bryson's disclosure, for some reason, threw Richard off-kilter. He considered Ladonna someone who shied away from public displays of affection. On the flip side, maybe his suppositions lacked rationality. Ladonna was reserved but not a total prude. Bryson served as proof of that. "Why should I care at all?" Richard asked himself. Before he could answer his own question, Bryson grabbed his arm and tugged him back to the play area.

"I'll wait in the car," Ladonna told Vincent. She hoped the gesture would reassure Vincent that Richard posed no competition and diffuse the awkwardness Richard's impromptu appearance caused.

"Alright."

"Tell him I said thank you," she said as Vincent closed his car door.

Pulling Richard aside earlier and confronting him would have resulted in more uneasiness for Vincent, so Ladonna planned to contact Richard once she and Vincent parted. Prior to this, she and Vincent had practiced frankness and full-disclosure. He didn't cringe if she grabbed his mail from the postman. He expressed no qualms at leaving his emails visible or taking calls in front of her. Unlike past boyfriends, she never sensed he slithered about heaping lies upon lies. Ladonna anticipated they'd keep on that same path.

"I'm here to pick up Bryson," Vincent announced.

Through a crack in his blinds, Richard saw Vincent's car but presumed Ladonna would come to the door. He couldn't tell from his vantage point if she was in the passenger's seat. "I'm not comfortable just handing him over to someone I don't know," thought Richard as he opened the door.

"I'm here to pickup Bryson."

"Where's Ladonna?"

"She's outside, and she asked me to get him. You can confirm that fact if you think it'll score you brownie points." Vincent puffed out his chest like a gorilla ready to defend its troop.

Richard thought this joker had some nerve trying to strong-arm him. He wanted to have a real conversation with Ladonna, but Vincent seemed dead set on preventing that. "Wait here," he told Vincent and closed the door in his face.

Upon his return, Richard handed him Bryson's car seat and

a stuffed Mexican jumping bean he bought the boy. He patted Bryson on the head and told him he'd see him soon.

"Do *we* owe you anything?"

Richard furrowed his brows.

"For food, games or babysitting," Vincent expounded.

"No, *Ladonna* doesn't. I'll call her later."

"I'm sure you will," Vincent grumbled.

"Let her know he skipped his nap," Richard said as Vincent lifted Bryson onto his shoulder and marched off.

Bryson regaled his mom and Vincent with a detailed description of the revelry he and Richard shared. "I swam in a bunch of balls, and I climbed on a wall."

"You climbed on a wall!" Ladonna exclaimed. "Even I can't do that."

Vincent gripped the steering wheel with one hand and rested the other on Ladonna's thigh. "How about I put your bike together when we get back, and then I can show you how to ride it?" he offered.

Ladonna glanced at Vincent, who remained focused on the road. "He's had an eventful afternoon already. You'll wear him out."

"He'd be fine if he'd had his nap," Vincent mumbled.

"Since we can't time travel, it is what it is, and I don't want him falling asleep too early."

Vincent removed his hand from Ladonna's thigh and put it on the gearshift even though he wasn't changing gears.

"Ah, ma!" Bryson wailed.

"You need a helmet."

"Can we go to the toy store?" Bryson asked.

"Maybe next Saturday. I bet Vincent can help you pick out something cool. For the rest of this weekend, mommy wants to chill out at home with her two favorite fellas."

Vincent glimpsed at her and smiled. Ladonna released an internal sigh of relief.

Undeterred by Vincent's brooding, Richard attempted to reach Ladonna that evening. His top priority was thanking her for letting him hang out with Bryson. Subsequently, he sought to catch up and fish for more info on Vincent. He particularly pondered how they met.

Vincent answered her cellphone before the second ring completed.

"May I speak to Ladonna," Richard asked, sure the firefighter recognized his voice.

"She's busy," Vincent answered gruffly.

Richard doubted that. He pictured Vincent standing guard over her phone, ready to block any contact with him. "Will you let her know I called?"

"Uh-huh." Vincent immediately disconnected.

The sudden dial tone coupled with Vincent's tone led Richard to believe the firefighter would rather run into a blaze without his uniform than relay the message.

Vincent's blatant gall set a new record for Richard. Never in his life had he formed such disdain for another human being so quickly. Richard sulked in his man cave. He downed some scotch on the rocks and then poured himself another, and then another. He wondered what Danielle was up to. They hadn't spoken since Tuesday and that was through texting. He knew she had her girls this weekend. He estimated they'd be in bed by now. He decided to call Danielle. At least he wouldn't have to contend with some pit bull of a boyfriend screening her calls.

She sounded exhausted.

"What's up?" Richard slurred.

"Who's this?"

"Richard."

"Oh. I'm just lying down. I took the twins clothes shopping and swear we hit all the malls in the metro. They're sprouting like beanstalks. They definitely get their height from their dad."

"I don't envy you."

Danielle yawned an extended yawn.

Even in her drowsy state, Danielle's voice lulled him. He fought an extreme urge to see if she'd let him come over. In actuality, he was tired too. Although Richard only had Bryson for a short while, the responsibility of insuring his safety and that his needs were met proved taxing. Richard respected single parents who handled that responsibility on a daily basis. "I was busy with Bryson," he said.

"Have I met him?"

"No, he's Ladonna's son."

"So you hung out with him and her."

"Just Bryson. We went to Jumpin' Johnny's."

"Huh. I didn't know you and Ladonna were tight that way."

"What way?"

"Not long ago you complained that you couldn't get ahold of her. Now she trusts you to watch her 3-year-old?"

"He's 4 now."

"Three, four, not a huge difference."

"I spent months getting to know them both. Our situation isn't too uncommon. We lost contact, but we're reconnecting, kind of like you and me."

Danielle didn't respond. He wondered if she drifted off.

"I'll let you get some shut eye," he told her.

After visiting his mother, Richard spent Sunday checking his email, which he'd neglected lately. He also checked his Twitter account, which he'd considered closing after interview requests diminished. An unexpected pattern presented itself. Instead of inquiries from media, he received the bulk of correspondence mainly from political action committees, religious organizations, and right-to-life groups. He attributed the growing interest to the governor officially signing off on SB71.

Their requests generally fell into either of two categories. Some invited Richard to speak to audiences on a personal level, recounting his experiences from the perspective of a father-to-be. Others requested his expertise regarding the act of seeking policy change. The latter seemed interested in his research methods, factors that led to determining the proposed bill's elements, and how Richard broached politicians for backing. Almost every inquiry, regardless of the source, included an offer of payment or at least compensation for travel and meals.

Richard found it ironic that strangers held him in such high esteem when, in actuality, Ladonna deserved more credit than he did. He knew she could use the extra funds this revenue stream offered. Ladonna's employer bought back the value of unused vacation hours and sick days. So, Ladonna explained to him before, she adhered to a meticulous schedule to maximize her earning potential by taking off from work only when necessary. Richard speculated if she'd consider joining him on the consulting gigs. He decided to chance calling her again even if it meant dealing with Vincent. To his delight, Ladonna answered.

"Are you free to talk?"

"Yeah," Ladonna replied. "I'm just folding laundry."

"Bryson had a blast."

"I heard."

"Thank you for letting him go with me."

"Thank you for offering. He definitely missed you."

"Maybe I can take him to a soccer game next weekend."

"Hmmm. I not sure that's a good idea."

"You just said he missed me. And I missed him too."

"That's it? You have nothing else to add?"

"Your boyfriend seems intense. Is he the reason you're hesitating?"

"You're the reason I'm hesitating, Richard. You and you alone."

"Hold up. You've lost me."

"Allow me to break it down for you," Ladonna said. "I got tired of running behind you and don't want my son to suffer if you disappear again."

"Disappear?" Her forcefulness boggled him.

"Yes. How do I know I can count on you to show up when it matters? Bryson moped around for days because you slipped in and out of his play. You bailed before we went for ice cream." She barely took a breath.

He hadn't realized it was such a major deal.

"That leads me to the calls and the emails. I thought something had happened to you. I was so concerned that I contacted your mother."

"I assumed we both understood," Richard shot back just as angrily. "I thought we established how important securing the bill was to me."

"Of all the people on the planet, I understood that. Hell, you didn't think I was busy too, especially when I was helping with your research?"

"When I did try reaching you, I couldn't."

"That was well afterwards."

"I don't remember us going that long without talking."

"Do you remember lying about your job? There's no excuse for how you handled things."

"Wow," Richard said. He heard the hurt in her voice. "For whatever I did or didn't do, I'm sorry."

"I hope so," she said after a lengthy pause.

"Give me a chance to make it up to Bryson and you."

"I'll think about it. I gotta go."

"My gut says Vincent isn't right for her," Richard shared with Danielle while she focused intensely on her computer screen. She asked for his feedback on a sales pitch she intended on presenting at a regional tradeshow in a few days. A promotion, she explained to Richard, hinged on her success there. The twins sat in the kitchen completing their homework while Danielle and Richard took over the dining room. Danielle had mock posters and a PowerPoint draft completed so far. Based on Richard's reaction and pointers from some colleagues, she'd shore up her strategy.

Unable to hide her annoyance over yet another interruption, Danielle closed the slideshow. "Ladonna deserves to reach that conclusion on her own, if for no other reason than to preserve your friendship."

Richard clenched his jaws.

"Have the two of you ever hooked up?"

Richard scoffed. "Nah. It just irks me how Vincent prances around like he's in charge. I mean, he's been in the picture for what, a minute?"

Danielle put her laptop on hibernate mode.

"Who's he to dictate who she talks to? I know he's the reason she's been distant."

"Granted," interrupted Danielle, "I've formed opinions of him and Ladonna from your perspective, so I'm biased. But even I can admit that Vincent has a point if what you suspect is correct."

Richard rolled his eyes. "Seriously?" He wanted to simultaneously dismiss her words and kiss the mouth they came from. Her lip gloss shone a tantalizing deep red cherry shade.

"Consider his position. He's forming a bond, or attempting to, with a woman *and* her son. Then her male friend strolls into the equation. You're two stubborn bulls clashing, competing for their attention. As Ladonna's friend, you owe it to her to back off."

"She was my friend before she was his girlfriend."

Danielle patted his shoulder.

Richard felt a spark.

"As your friend, I'm duty bound to say that bestows no special privileges."

"Ladonna deserves better."

"If I heard you speaking about my boyfriend that way, I'd definitely draw the line. I might even end our friendship."

"Yeah, your boyfriend."

"Glenn's discharge is coming up soon."

Hearing Danielle utter his name made the mystery man real. Unsure of his next move, Richard remained silent.

"If this world were full of fairytales and rainbows, I wouldn't be divorced. We deserve what we choose." She finished off her statement by leaning over and kissing Richard sensually and reassuringly on the lips. Once he tasted the cherry flavor of her lip-gloss, he began kissing her more deeply and pulling her toward him. The sound of the twins' giggles from across the room was the only thing to break his momentary trance. Danielle seductively licked his bottom lip before pulling away and turning to face her girls.

The spark he felt suddenly faded.

"Soon, I'll be out-putting you," Kevin predicted. He and Richard stood on the green of a public golf course. Kevin had one more opportunity to master the current hole.

"Keep dreaming, pal," Richard said. For the last six holes, he intertwined giving Kevin pointers with listening to him relay intriguing accounts of his latest conquest. Kevin met a widow in her 40s whose wealthy husband left her a substantial fortune. Richard couldn't resist bringing up the age difference to Kevin, who had a well-documented proclivity for younger ladies. In this instance, Kevin bluntly stated, the widow's willingness to lavish goodies upon him boosted her appeal.

"The best part," Kevin said, "is the more I tell her not to buy me stuff the more she insists." He held up his wrist to display a silver, designer, chain link watch.

"Use that reverse psychology to get us into a private golf club. I'm sure she has connections," Richard said.

"I'm not saying she's the one. She is the one for right now."

On holes seven, eight, and nine Richard updated Kevin on his new job and new plans to push spousal notification legislation. Then, the topic somehow switched to Ladonna and her beau. The conversation, or confrontation rather, between Richard and Ladonna still had him feeling perturbed.

"In short," Richard concluded, "Vincent is a cocky son of a bitch."

"Predictable. We cops generally consider firefighters pretentious pricks. They hide out in firehouses waiting for action while we patrol the streets."

Kevin's assessment caused a mischievous leer on Richard's face.

"Thought you dismissed that chick, though," Kevin went on.

"How'd you get that impression?"

"Uh, I dunno," he said condescendingly. "Could be because you stopped mentioning her. I figured your deal was strictly platonic."

"And it is."

"Does the guy abuse her? Treat her like an indentured servant? Oppress Ladonna in some way?"

"It's far from that deep," Richard said. He glanced at the golfers ahead of them to see if they'd progressed. The longer they took, the longer his game lasted since he and Kevin couldn't advance ahead of them. "Just a hunch concerning his character."

"We should hit up the clubs Friday and Saturday. You need some action to ease you over that post-divorce hump."

"Thanks for the concern, but I'm set."

"Porn doesn't count," Kevin quipped.

"See, now you're tripping."

"What I am is an officer of the law, trained in reading body language and dialogue analysis. Convince yourself otherwise, but I'd bet a nut you're hot for Ladonna." He started grinding his body slowly and then made one last humping gesture while moaning.

Richard feigned a gag. "I should be used to your gross visuals. Somehow you continually disgust me."

"A man who is getting laid could care less about a woman some other man is laying unless…"

"Unless?"

"He wants to bang her himself."

Richard grimaced. "I'm into Danielle."

"I've let some good women slip through the cracks. Don't follow my lead."

Chapter 20

Richard missed hearing Danielle's voice but, besides checking in on Tuesday, refrained from contacting her. He kept that call brief because she was engrossed in her regular duties and preparing for the upcoming tradeshow. He wished her good luck even though she had perfected a top-notch presentation. Danielle's comment about her relationship revealed she took it more seriously than he'd thought.

Devoid of Danielle's company since Glenn's arrival, Richard allocated additional time to researching the consulting and speaking gigs that cluttered his inbox. His employer supplied all associates access to an online legal database containing links to articles, sample documents, and a repository of rulings. Richard skimmed the database searching for resources to use to validate the verbiage of offers. The terms in some suffered from ambiguity.

For example, a number of organizations referred to "compensation" as a check. A number of others meant it as an all-inclusive term encompassing lodging and transportation. Those tilting toward conservative or religious ends of the spectrum implemented clauses prohibiting the use of, according to their standards, distasteful or offensive vocabulary. A fragment of the requests extended invitations to events minus contractual particulars. Richard essentially set out to determine industry standards and to compose a list of stipulations he required as well as a template contract to use where no contract existed.

Tackling these details inevitably prompted thoughts of Ladonna. The contentious content of their last exchange left Richard unable to relay this new revenue stream or to move the discussion beyond his deficiencies. He hoped she'd call. He also hesitated to push for contact.

"I'll get her some flowers," Richard said to himself. He located a florist close to her job. The owner, an elderly gentleman who spouted botanical facts, enthusiastically relayed recommendations. The proprietor sold him on a "Spring Revival" bouquet. Its massive, multicolored assortment put the roses he saw on Ladonna's desk, which Richard now assumed came from Vincent, to shame. The card accompanying it simply read, "Sorry." As he squared away the order, Richard decided to deliver the bountiful blossoms in person to circumvent an exorbitant delivery fee. Richard figured there was a fifty-percent chance he'd run into Vincent. He'd risk that prospect.

Realistically, they couldn't snub each other forever if Ladonna restored Richard to the level of friendship the two once relished. Presenting the peace offering in person lent to indicating his sincere regret. It had to mend the divide between them. Richard couldn't withstand the brunt of another icy interaction with Ladonna.

He contemplated calling to see if Ladonna arrived home. He settled on popping by. In the least desirable scenario, Richard determined the best alternative would be leaving the daffodils on her stoop. He presumed, based on the distance from the stoop to the street, that passersby would barely notice the bouquet. And, he presumed if Ladonna was there, she would let him hang around if only for a bit.

The empty parking spot indicated Ladonna's absence. Regardless, Richard rang the doorbell.

"Three visits in less than two weeks," Crystal bellowed. "I've gotta play the lottery."

"Buy me a ticket while you're at it, "Richard retorted in the sweetest manner he could muster. He needed an ally with full access to Ladonna. He'd won Crystal over once and planned on doing so again.

"Apparently those aren't for me."

"I counted on both of you enjoying them." Richard held out the vase.

Crystal took it and then buried her nose in them.

"Can I say hello to Bryson before I jet?" Richard asked.

Crystal came up for air. "Bryson!" she yelled. "Bryson!" she yelled again when he failed to materialize.

Bryson stomped to the door. His scowl disintegrated when he spotted Richard.

"Why are you moping?" Richard asked.

Crystal provided the cause. "He's mad because I wouldn't take him outside. I led back-to-back aerobics classes today due to a no-show with one of our instructors. I'm beat."

Richard cast sympathetic looks in each of their directions.

"How about I take him outside?"

The boy nearly jumped for joy.

"He could ride his bike."

Now, Bryson's enthusiasm dissipated.

"My bike's not ready," he said.

Richard glanced at Crystal and then back at the boy.

"He means it isn't put together," she clarified.

"We can correct that," Richard said.

"We?"

"Me."

"He doesn't even have a helmet."

"We'll stay in the driveway. Do you have tools?"

"A basic wrench and pliers and some screwdrivers. And a hammer. I'm not sure what else is in the toolbox."

"Let me check it out," Richard said. "It's worth a shot, right?"

Bryson bombarded his mom and Vincent, ready to spill his recent accomplishment. "I rode with training wheels!"

"Rode what, honey?" Ladonna asked.

"My bike."

Vincent looked toward Crystal. So did Ladonna.

"Screwing in a light bulb is the closest you've come to being handy," said Ladonna. "What gives?"

"Richard swung by," Crystal explained.

The air in the living room grew thick.

"Break it down for me," Vincent implored. "You let Richard put together the bike that I bought for Bryson, that I said I was going to put together?"

She reacted with a blank stare.

"Priceless," he said.

"Last I checked, it wasn't a federal offense to make a child happy," Crystal finally piped up.

"I'm sure he's ecstatic."

"Tar and feather Crystal, why don't ya?" Ladonna said in an effort to eliminate traces of tension. "She meant no harm."

"Is Crystal in trouble?" Bryson chimed in.

"No," his mom said.

"Is Richard?"

"No, baby. Nobody's in trouble. How about you go pick out your school clothes?"

Once Bryson exited, Vincent clarified his stance. It's her *research partner* I have the issue with," he told Crystal. "Why'd he stop by?"

The daffodils prompted a discussion Ladonna tried avoiding and ruined the hope of her lying back and relaxing with Vincent. They supported Vincent's supposition that Richard held ulterior, detrimental motives. She attempted to explain the nature of her last interaction with Richard to Vincent. She attempted to correlate it with the bouquet. Her boyfriend continued to create controversy where none existed. She hoped to categorically quell his insecurity. The two of them, after all, couldn't thrive in a bubble in which no one else entered.

Vincent left early. She didn't try to stop him. Prior to retiring for the night, Ladonna's thoughts bounced back and forth between the two men. Richard generated the only spats she and Vincent had. Half of the cells in Ladonna's brain screamed, "Danger ahead!!!" The others tuned into the Christian notion of forgiveness. She decided to sleep on it.

Ladonna sent Richard a short text as soon as she awoke. It read, "Thanks for the flowers. Apology accepted."

"Trying to liquor me up?" Danielle precariously waved her champagne flute in Richard's direction. A drop splashed above the rim and splattered onto her bedroom balcony. "And you splurged on the good stuff."

"I," he said, "am merely celebrating your accomplishment. Only the best for the best." He plucked a chocolate-covered strawberry from the platter on the table in front of the chaise they shared. Richard dipped it into the bowl of whipped cream next to it. He held the fruit close to Danielle's mouth. She bit off the entire flesh, leaving only the stem behind. Then, she licked the lingering cream from her lips.

He admired her career aspirations and considered them one more area of compatibility. Danielle's mental prowess made her sexier. Even in her seemingly inebriated state, she maintained an elevated caliber of clarity and conversational cohesiveness. When the shock of his divorce wore off, Richard began dreading dipping back into the dating pool. He loved relationships but not the awkward intermission from the point of meeting to deciding if the woman proved a suitable mate. Danielle's reentry into his world created an outlet in which he wouldn't need to participate in such rigmarole.

"I'll make you a mimosa for breakfast."

"Cool. When should I arrive?"

She reached for one of his hands and intertwined her fingers with his. "Who says you have to leave?"

Richard's palpitating heart threatened to poke through his rib cage. Had he read too much into the remark?

Danielle told him not to be gentle. He followed her command.

Richard pried himself from Danielle shortly after brunch. She insisted he join her and the twins at Six Flags the following Saturday. He viewed the suggestion as a shift in status. Richard and Danielle generally hung out sans the kids, or, when they were present, he had limited interaction with them. In all likelihood, her girls would become his step kids. It made sense for Danielle to gradually integrate him into their routine. He anticipated both relationships blossoming.

Shortly before sunset, Richard went by his mom's to cut her grass. She was away at worship service but returned prior to him leaving. She reached to embrace him.

"I'm all sweaty, ma," he said.

Mrs. Knight ignored his protest. "Jesus said, come as you are, and so does your ma." She hugged him tightly. "I changed your diapers in case you forgot. Nothing could compete with that funk."

"Ha ha."

She poured him some lemonade and then they sat in the den. Mrs. Knight caught her son up on happenings among her circle of friends and at church.

"Honestly, son, I worry about you not attending church at least once in a while."

"I doubt if God tallies how many services his followers show up for."

"The devil is busy as Him."

"No one can take your soul unless you offer it. If I were participating in séances or fooling with Ouija boards, then you'd have cause for concern."

She deviated from the topic temporarily. Richard knew it would resurface on another occasion.

He filled her in on his reconciliation with Ladonna. Richard purposely avoided mentioning Ladonna when he last saw his mom. Since he was unsure of the course their friendship might veer, Richard refrained from giving Mrs. Knight false hope.

"I wanted to reach out to her but didn't know if that'd be right," Mrs. Knight commented. "After I let it slip about your job, I was afraid to make more of a mess."

"Ladonna was mad at me, not you."

"She's a keeper. Now I know why you're glowing. I knew you two would wind up together."

"Whoa, ma. You have the wrong idea."

"If you say so."

"Really. She has a boyfriend."

"That's a wrinkle I didn't see coming."

He recounted their run-in. "As much as the dude makes my skin crawl, I suppose I have to deal with him to keep the peace. Otherwise, Ladonna won't let me near her or Bryson."

"This Vincent fella might be a short-term distraction. Hang in there."

"I'm in love with Danielle," he declared.

"She dumped her boyfriend for you? I'm confused. I thought they'd been together for a while."

"They had. I wanted to make sure Danielle felt the same before I made a public announcement."

"I don't know, son."

Richard speculated that her hesitation stemmed from not seeing him and Danielle interact as mature adults. Maybe she still viewed Danielle as his college crush.

"How did you know dad was the one?" he asked.

She blushed. "We had a connection greater than lust: the kind laid out in the Bible. Sure, everything new sparkles. Mates are no different. It's when the shine fades that most couples buckle." The glint that surfaced when she spoke of Mr. Knight lit her eyes. "Your dad was a looker. The more I fell for him, truly fell, the less his looks or how much money he didn't have mattered. I knew I'd stick by his side through any hardship and never doubted he'd do the same for me." Mrs. Knight grew silent as if stuck in the reminiscences. Far beyond general health and happiness, and a good education, my greatest wish, your father's too, was that you and Pam found mates to grow old with."

"I can see Dee and me reaching that point," Richard told her.

"Don't get me wrong," Mrs. Knight said. "I'm fond of Danielle. With you and Ladonna, though, everything seemed to click. Maybe you should pray for guidance in making the right choice."

Richard respectfully listened to his mother, but he had already made his decision.

"Bummer. This sucks!" Danielle announced loud enough for the group bowling next to her and Richard to overhear. His score on the monitor remained a measly fraction of hers.

He barely nicked pins while she racked up strikes and spares. Frames ended quickly due to his paltry performance.

She held her fingers in front of the hand fan while waiting for her ball to return. "We should've put this on hold when Kevin and his girlfriend cancelled. Or," Danielle added, "we should've turned around and picked up the girls from my parents' and let them tag along."

"Kevin's chief called him in unexpectedly and, my dear Ladonna, fighting crime trumps bowling. I was looking forward to meeting his girlfriend too, but I suspect she didn't want to hang out with strangers. We can leave early since you've beat me to a pulp. So what do you want to do?" Richard winked and gave a twisted smile, hoping she would get the hint for more of what they had intimately shared.

"Start with getting my name right."

"Huh?"

"You said, 'my dear Ladonna.'"

"I apologize if I did."

"You did."

"I'm on edge I assume. I haven't heard from her since she sent that text. I'm anxious to book lecturing gigs, and she's full of great ideas and contacts."

"She's not the only one full of something," Danielle muttered.

"Speak up. I didn't catch that."

Danielle shut the scoreboard off. "We're obviously done here."

Chapter 21

"You're ditching me for Ladonna," Kevin said when Richard abruptly announced his pending departure. Kevin's girlfriend, Marcie, arranged for the men to tour Perimeter Pines, a golf club that boasted a 17,000-square-foot clubhouse, topnotch tennis and racquetball courts, an Olympic size pool, and a restaurant serving healthy gourmet cuisine. The family and friends membership was $500 per month, but the membership committee had to first approve the application. Marcie had contacts on the committee, which essentially green-lighted Kevin and Richard.

Although they had agreed to meet at the precinct and then to head over to the golf club together, Ladonna contacted Richard via text while he was waiting for Kevin to finish filling out a report. Ladonna inquired if Richard wanted to swing by to talk. The last message from her, sent approximately two weeks prior, simply thanked him for the flowers. Richard jumped at the opportunity.

"I better go meet with her now because, at any point, Vincent could easily bully her into backing out," Richard said. "She would've probably reached out sooner if it weren't for him."

"I pimped myself out to Marcie to make this happen," Kevin said.

"And I emphatically commend your efforts." Richard reached for his keys. "You can handle the tour on your own. Anyway, we did a virtual tour on the Web site, so I consider this a minor formality. If you're cool with the facilities, I'm cool too."

Kevin waved Richard off. "Leave already."

Bryson bounced on Richard's lap. His presence buffered the unavoidable uneasiness his mom and Richard felt. The adults commenced the customary greetings and moved onto cordial conversation.

"Catch me up," Richard requested. "Fill me in on what's been happening with you."

Ladonna mentioned studying Spanish. "I'm searching for a social group with bilingual members. I found a few. They're too advanced. The software I use is great, but hearing the language in person will undoubtedly help me pick up on nuances."

"I remember you mentioned becoming bilingual. Which program do you use?"

"Rosetta Stone."

"Top notch. Government agencies train employees using that."

"Vincent bought it for me."

Richard smiled politely.

Ladonna told him about the dance lessons.

Aloud he said, "A guy voluntarily learning salsa. That's unusual."

"Vincent isn't the usual guy," she retorted.

"Indeed," Richard said as he mustered another smile.

She remained stoic.

"You've got a busy slate." He hesitated before adding, "I hate to impose; however, I have a proposition. It's a project you might find interesting."

He predicted she'd prompt him for details. Instead, Ladonna

said, "Part of me thinks you're coming around again because you need an assistant."

His stomach turned.

"I had a stressful, hectic vortex swirling around me. I closed myself off in an effort to shield you from it. Once the craziness died down, I tapped into how much I missed you and Bryson."

Ladonna looked like she was formulating her response but said nothing, prompting Richard to continue.

"Tell me what'll take to be back in your good graces, and I'll do it."

"Just be truthful with me," she said. "Tell me about this new project."

He detected less defensiveness in her tone. Richard explained how the spousal notification bill spurred speaking and consulting opportunities.

"After the bill was approved, I would get at least 20 calls and e-mails per day requesting that I speak to or advise some type of group or even individuals."

"Why wouldn't they hire a professional consultant or a firm?"

"SB71 represented the latest in a miniscule amount of successful reproductive legislation efforts. Since an ordinary citizen spearheaded it, I suppose these groups feel more comfortable reaching out to me."

Ladonna seemed receptive.

"Disparaged dads all over the country have approached me. There are collective rumblings from men who want to set in motion similar bills. Nonprofits and political action committees are seeking to do the same. Both want to hear how I, how we, went about the process. You commented yourself on how I was a pioneer in Georgia. What I know, and mostly no one else does, is that you deserve as much credit as I do."

"I suppose. How do you foresee this collaboration unfolding?"

"For the consulting, an initial video chat with the individuals or organizations to gauge their expectations and to determine how far their efforts have progressed. Then, I foresee us filling in the holes and pointing them in the right direction. I'm developing a checklist of sorts that'll be customizable. I'll solicit your help with that, of course. The last phases would entail reviewing their print deliverables, coaching them on approaching legislators and supporters, and navigating media."

"And the speaking gigs, how would I fit in?"

"Who better to review my speeches and to steer me on the best paths for each presentation? I plan to rely on note cards slightly but not to the point where I sound stilted. I need to transfer my expertise while maintaining approachability. Absolutely I don't want to sound like a preachy, lawyer presenting an argument."

"Give me your email address."

He answered with a perplexed expression.

"I deleted it," Ladonna said before he quizzed her further. "And I didn't have it memorized."

Richard couldn't deny he caused Ladonna immense hurt, and that realization hurt him.

"I'm not able to guarantee a yes on the spot," she said.

"I understand if you need to run it by Vincent."

"We're not conjoined. Sure, I'll discuss it with him. I make my own decisions, though. I'll get back to you."

"Your consideration is more than I deserve," Richard said and hoped she believed him.

Later on, her roommate returned from the gym. Ladonna conveyed to Crystal the quasi-reconciliation with Richard.

"Stress, the king of excuses. Problem is it pops up over and over again." Crystal snickered. "The measure of a man, your mom once told me, is his ability to handle hardships instead of letting them handle him. Do you really think it's smart to welcome Richard back so easily?"

"Clearly, I'll establish boundaries. He's hardly harmful or a lost cause though. However, he and I arrived at this juncture; it's resulted in a ton of introspection. We all set the standards we'll accept in our lives. Pretty much, I'm stronger than before I meet him."

"Mm-hmm. The new you seems no different than the old you, a softy. Letting Richard infiltrate your life is as silly as when fools hunt tornadoes and then act surprised when shit starts flying through the air."

"You're equating me to a fool?"

"Are you in a league of your own? Yes. A fool? No.

"You're misunderstanding the situation. He has that Danielle chick. I've got Vincent."

"We'll see."

The puppy adoption sponsored by a pet superstore displayed cages housing dogs, cats, and an assortment of other forgotten creatures, which all sat under tents. Despite the canopy shielding patrons from the sun, Richard suffered from immense thirst. He purchased a second bottle of water from the onsite vendor. Danielle's daughters had been bugging her for a dog. She caved in but subliminally attempted to coax them into choosing a poodle or some other petite breed. The adults hung back in a less populated area while the twins hopped from cage to cage checking out their choices.

Danielle tracked her kids from afar. "Their father is set on getting them a pet to promote responsibility. I say it's just an added responsibility for me."

Richard stood transfixed with his gaze set on a cobra. He didn't respond to Danielle's remark.

She repositioned herself and stood in front of him. "Thinking of picking out a snake?" she asked.

"Thinking of how it reminds me of Vincent and how Ladonna deserves to know he's not so nice. Honestly, who brazenly attacks a stranger and issues a cryptic warning?"

"He apparently.'

"She literally propped me up when I lacked the strength to stand."

"What do you expect as the outcome?"

"I worry about the impact he'll have on Bryson."

Danielle drew in a deep breath. "Set aside these predictions of doom and gloom for everyone's sakes."

Richard scoffed.

"Vincent strikes me as a man in love."

Seconds skipped by while Danielle awaited a retort. Following the lull, Danielle continued, "While we're on the subject of men in love, I've got a development to share. My boyfriend proposed."

As if bright light had impaired his vision, Richard squinted while he processed the announcement. He considered Danielle more than a one-night stand and pictured them together again intimately. Neither spoke of her boyfriend. Omitting him abided by the blueprint they established early on.

"Did you accept his proposal?"

"Yes, after much deliberation."

"I didn't know it was that serious," he replied. "I suppose congratulations are in order."

Danielle convinced herself at the outset that Richard had yet to register the news. Why, otherwise, would he congratulate her? They left the adoption site sans a dog and then checked out other pet stores. Richard had ample opportunities to speak about the engagement while the girls explored their options. Instead, Richard made small talk. He put forth no passionate plea for her to reconsider. He offered no counterpoints to persuade her to choose him over Glenn.

From the moment they slept together, Danielle questioned if she viewed Richard as a safe fling, someone who provided attention her absentee boyfriend couldn't. She also questioned if Richard viewed her as a placeholder for the woman who eluded his grasp. He hadn't made another move after they celebrated her promotion.

Richard denied romantic intentions concerning Ladonna with the same fervor he displayed when bashing Vincent. It weighed on Danielle that he showed no oomph at the prospect of losing her but basically went ballistic defending Ladonna from an invented threat. His relentless regurgitation of Vincent's defects felt akin to pricks from radioactive thorns. Danielle stuck to her primary policy relating to matters of the heart: "Let men chase after you, not vice versa." Danielle had a limited span in which to arrange her nuptials to a giving, selfless man. Pondering her position in a love triangle definitely detracted from that undertaking. Even so, as Richard said his goodbyes, Danielle felt an undeniable tug. In that moment, Danielle knew she'd re-evaluate Glenn's proposal if Richard swiftly swooped in and confessed his devotion.

Danielle's proclamation doused Richard with a dose of reality. It stymied his prolonged delusion that they would have a viable future. It didn't, however, sting in the same vain as Nicole's declaration that she'd fallen for Toni. In any case, Danielle's decision made protesting futile in Richard's mind. He would permit her happiness with Glenn without his interference and instead focus on his personal and professional flaws that would hamper his further success. Drinking was excluded from this self-imposed intervention, though.

For the remainder of the day, Richard concentrated on mapping out strategies to jumpstart his freelance ventures. He inevitably returned to Danielle's comments regarding his latent feelings for Ladonna fueling his insistence on safeguarding her from Vincent.

Ladonna left a message stating she intended to assist him and that Friday nights or Saturday afternoons worked best for her schedule. They agreed to meet at his place on Saturday afternoon. When she entered his dining room and pulled out her spiral notebook, a sense of déjà vu hit Richard as did the realization of how their circumstances changed since they researched spousal notification.

Prior to delving into the schematics of collaborating, Ladonna inquired about Richard's job transition. Richard excitedly spilled details of the company's culture. Then, Richard outlined his duties within the Construction Support Division.

"Surely you'll make your mark there," Ladonna said once he finished. Compared to when he saw her last, the prickly cadence in Ladonna's voice had dissipated.

"I'm forever indebted to you," Richard said.

Ladonna looked uneasy, as if unworthy of the praise.

"For real," Richard went on. "You were there for me from the moment we met. Know that I accept full responsibility from the lapse in our friendship. I've done some introspection. My goal is to be someone you can lean on, not someone who's always leaning on you."

"The beauty of history is that while it shapes us, we maintain the power to shape it."

"Touché." Reshaping his personal relationships, his professional path, and his take on civic duty sometimes left him feeling trapped in a whirlwind. Richard hit the escape button on his laptop and opened a spreadsheet consisting of three columns. "I've divided the prospects into categories: purely political, non-profit, and individual requests. Each has contract templates associated with it. I need your keen eye to proof them."

"Email the drafts to me."

"Will do."

"Shouldn't I have one too though?"

Composing a contract for Ladonna hadn't occurred to him. Richard credited Vincent with implementing that mandate. "I'll draw up terms for you too."

"Great."

"I'll probably donate my services to some of the smaller charities. Studying the tax implications is on my list of priorities."

"Vincent will know if that type of donation constitutes a write off. I'll check with him."

"Isn't he a firefighter? Is he a tax preparer also?"

"An accountant."

"I'd hate to bother him," Richard said. "I'll find the answer online."

"Nonsense, I'll ask him tonight."

"How did you and Vincent meet?" he blurted out.

"The owner of Bryson's daycare tried setting us up for the longest. Eventually I took her advice." Ladonna cleared her throat. "I was mulling over approaches for crafting proposals similar to what we presented to Winston. I think tapping into current events will make the requests more compelling."

He noted her attempt to subtly steer their conversation back to business. Richard decided to shelve further mention of Vincent for the time being. Voicing his distrust right now, Richard conceded, would only put a damper on the good vibes flowing back and forth. "You've got a keen ability to tie together details most people, including me, overlook."

"Two facts that popped up in Internet news coverage are stuck in my head.'

"Shoot."

"Well, there's been a rash of babies disposed off in trash cans. A segment of them were delivered early, whether from natural causes or induced labor. The crux of it is that if these same moms had gotten abortions, they wouldn't face criminal charges. I suspect those discarded babies garner attention due to sensationalism. Abortion, in contrast, has become main stream."

"Why would anyone do such a thing? Safe harbor laws allow women to deliver in hospitals and then turn the babies over to social services."

"Why would anyone want an abortion? Desperation, ignorance, selfishness? I discovered that the majority of states prosecute drivers who kill pregnant women and charge them for the deaths of mother and child. How in that sense are fetuses categorized as living beings and accidents akin to murder while abortion isn't classified as killing?"

"Therefore," Richard chimed in, "we can argue inconsistencies in the law and illogical ideologies."

"Exactly. I understand we're technically crusading for rights of fathers rather than seeking to stamp out abortions, but I think spotlighting these and similar issues will strike a chord with the socially conscious."

"I agree."

"I'll count on you to keep me on track and to insure I put a fresh spin on each project."

"From those interviews you did, I'd say you're well-equipped."

"The monetary factor," I suppose, "rattles me somewhat. I'm afraid of letting any of my clients down."

"Exploring uncharted territory generally stirs reservations. I'm up for the challenge if you are."

Richard sat glued to his computer composing Ladonna's contract. His limbs began to numb at one point. He stood, stretched, and then returned to the task at hand. Upon completion, he viewed the finished product. It was chock full of features designed to sell Ladonna on attending his on-site meetings. She expressed surprise that Richard wanted her to accompany him. He hadn't explicitly mentioned that tidbit. Nevertheless, Richard thought he'd implied her attendance.

"Forgive my lack of clarity," he asked of Ladonna before she left. "Review what I put together and let me know if it's acceptable. If you remain uncertain about the traveling, please express any concerns. Agreeing isn't a deal breaker. I'll work around whatever stipulations you insist upon."

The provisions Richard laid out included covering Ladonna's travel expenses on top of her being paid per project. Rather than breaking down financial compensation based on an hourly rate, he devised a task-driven percentage system. The more involved the venture, the more he'd charge the client, and the more Ladonna would earn. Richard settled on twenty-percent as a fair entitlement. Additionally, he addressed care for Bryson. Richard included a $25 per day allotment, which he'd spring for out of his profits, to cover expenses Crystal or Ladonna's parents might incur when they watched Bryson. He realized that they currently did so free of charge. The bonus, Richard surmised, would allay Ladonna's inevitable misgivings over increasing the frequency of requesting their services.

He concentrated on trying to spot errors in the document until fatigue forced him to step away for a while. He then opted to call Pam to see if she'd set a wedding date. She hadn't. All during their brief chat, Richard kept wondering if he'd covered each pertinent area in Ladonna's contract. With any luck, Ladonna would accept his terms before he retired for the evening so he'd rest instead of tossing and turning.

"Relaxing with you and the munchkin, that's the highlight of my week. This side project will cut into that. I thought you'd be using Skype, not meeting with Richard every Saturday," said Vincent. Together, he and Ladonna sat in his home office and combed through the text of Richard's proposal. Bryson napped in Vincent's spare room.

"Me too, to begin with," said Ladonna

"I certainly didn't expect he'd have you jetting from gig to gig with him."

"His plan makes sense, though."

"Why can't he come to your house?"

"Bryson is a distraction."

"Then I'll watch him," suggested Vincent.

Ladonna gazed at him suggestively, saying, "For the record, you are too." She touched his beyond-washboard-abdomen and mentally compared it to the mid-section pouch she spied on Richard yesterday. Her first thought then was that Danielle must be feeding him well.

"It's a profitable endeavor for me," said Ladonna. "Plus, jobs are hard to come by lately, especially those offering any flexibility."

"I'd float you a loan if something came up. In fact, I'd give you the money, but I realize you're too proud to accept a free and clear bailout."

"Your generosity is one of many reasons I love you."

His gaze pierced her. Ladonna's blood pressure raced.

"What?" she asked.

"You love me. I suspected so. I hoped so. To hear you say it…"

Vincent's kiss filled in the blanks.

Chapter 22

Predictably, Mrs. Knight delved into the status of her son's involvement with Danielle when she spoke to him.

Bypassing an urge to fudge how Danielle essentially cast him off, Richard spilled the latest developments.

"Guess you won't be seeing her much anymore."

Richard detected underlying glee as if she said "I told you so" without actually saying it. He wished he'd kept his proclamations of love to himself. He already dealt with ridicule from his best friend.

"This isn't the end. We'll still hang out," Richard said. "Maybe not as much."

"In what universe do you think her husband is gonna want you hanging around?" his mom asked.

Richard's last call to Danielle went straight to voicemail. Since Danielle rarely stayed out late when she had the girls, he presumed that she fell asleep after the twins went to bed. It never occurred to him that she might have evaded his call until now.

He didn't respond.

"It's probably for the best," Mrs. Knight said.

"I do have plenty to keep me occupied," Richard said. He was done with discussing Danielle. He brought up the requests he received to pen op-ed pieces in magazines and newspapers in addition to the consulting and speaking gigs. While he updated her, Richard scratched his forearm so furiously that red blotches formed.

"Need some lotion, son?"

"Actually, do you have any Benadryl? I've slathered myself with lotion and even cocoa butter and Vaseline, but these itching spells keep creeping up."

"Could be something you're eating," she said. "Go grab some cortisone cream out of the medicine cabinet."

Richard followed her directive and applied the ointment.

"Keep it," she said once he finished.

He tucked it into his pocket.

"I've thought a lot about your predicament, trying to sort out who you should spend your life with, wondering if you'd meet a worthy woman."

"Not again," Richard thought.

"That whole fiasco with Nicole wounded you. That's why I think you thought I wanted Danielle for you. Love requires work, son. People who realize that find so much happiness in their relationships that they don't look for it everywhere else. Nicole jumped shipped because, let's face it, she was selfish. Selfishness falls to the wayside when you're in love."

Richard felt flush around his collar.

"Convincing yourself you fell for Danielle was like reaching for a security blanket you'd outgrown instead of finding a replacement that fit better."

Mrs. Knight's summation had at least a morsel of merit and Richard knew it.

"That leads me to Ladonna, seeing as she agreed to help out with your freelancing, I'd say there's still a chance to win her back."

"She has a boyfriend."

"Isn't she worth the work? Stop running your mouth to everyone else about Ladonna's new man and tell her how you really feel."

Mrs. Knight's suggestion galvanized Richard. He pledged to put promises made to Ladonna into action, especially since she unequivocally stated reservations concerning allowing him back into her realm. This bolder, more straightforward version of Ladonna clearly refused to let him or anyone else take her for granted. Richard devised a plan to further ingratiate himself. First, Richard needed to broaden their interactions. Even if he professed his intentions until he lost his voice, Ladonna rightly required proof of the improved Richard. He intended to illustrate through doing rather than telling that he valued her and that she could count on him. Engaging solely in business, he realized, would trap them in a counterproductive pattern. He sought an activity that rang of fun and had nothing to do with his upcoming projects. He spent an entire afternoon conjuring up excuses to get Ladonna alone. He needed no Vincent looming nearby or Crystal chirping snide remark in the background.

Richard called Mrs. Knight after his brainstorming stalled.

"Since you asked, I'm positive it *would* help if the woman saw a less uptight version of you. You're always so serious, so focused on business. I know what took your happy away. It's time to get it back."

"I need Ladonna to let her guard down without me being so obvious."

"The annual carnival is after service next Sunday. Her son would like it, I'm sure."

"Totally forgot. Smart idea." Bryson tagging along would lend to the casualness of their interaction. Besides, Richard wanted to see the boy.

"I could catch up with Ladonna. You could catch up with the church members who keep asking me to tell you hello."

Richard missed his fellow brethren as well. Such a neutral setting seemed ideal. "I'll mention it and get back with you," Richard told his mom.

He immediately sent a text to Ladonna informing her of the upcoming event. She replied that she had numerous plans and that she couldn't commit to fitting that in. Richard responded that she could skip their meeting if that'd cause less strain on her schedule.

"Aren't you trying to finish that editorial?"

A regional weekly, "The Gulf Gazette," approached him to pen a counter argument in its upcoming edition. Since the paper hit the press on Thursday, he had a submittal deadline of Tuesday.

"Perfecting that is my main priority. We can correspond through email though," Richard suggested. He added that Mrs. Knight wanted to see her and specifically requested Ladonna's presence.

"In that case," Ladonna replied, "count me in."

Moments after concluding the conversation, a worrisome thought occurred to Richard: Ladonna showing up with the fireman glued to her side. He prepared himself for that scenario. Richard refused to let Vincent bait or bully him. The second phase of his plan required maintaining his composure.

Ladonna told Vincent the basics about the carnival: when and where it took place. She left out the reason she chose to go. She pictured her beau freaking out if he learned Richard belonged to the host church. At any rate, Vincent's shift at the firehouse prevented him from accompanying her. Ladonna equated her omissions to performing a public service. She considered it imperative that Vincent focus on his duties rather than dissecting Richard's intentions.

Prior to letting it slip that she loved Vincent, Ladonna craved his displays of affection. A switch flipped afterwards. Ladonna feared that Vincent, although he hadn't said so, leaped to assuming she'd graduate from making out to making love in a flash. He handled her as if he had something to prove. His once fanciful kisses grew forceful. His hugs hinged on possessive.

Ladonna left Richard's reemergence out of the story when consulting her mom. Maybe, as her mom suggested, Ladonna let fear of the unknown undermine an otherwise healthy, budding relationship. Mrs. Payton indicated her daughter was experiencing a "fight or flight" scenario. "Perhaps," her mom said, "you're apprehensive because Vincent has all the qualities on your checklist."

Other love interests fell short of Ladonna's demands. Of course Ladonna eventually moved on. She couldn't understand the connection between the crucial character traits she refused to compromise on and her apprehension.

Mrs. Payton spelled out her theory. "With Vincent you have more to lose. That realization, oddly enough, can be paralyzing."

Ladonna took in her mom's sage guidance. The couple dated for less than five months; however, Vincent impressed Ladonna and her parents in a manner that effortlessly surpassed previous partners. An inexplicable instinct, surprisingly enough, kept Ladonna from fully expressing herself with the fireman. Ladonna thought Vincent's agitation in turn threw her off-kilter. She questioned if finding such an ideal match meant she'd found Mr. Right.

In comparison to Richard, Vincent operated at warp speed. He displayed his desires in plain view whereas Richard's emerged at an excruciatingly sluggish pace. Ladonna blamed herself for previously misreading Richard's intent. Thinking he would accelerate their interactions from friendship to romance so rapidly had been a foolish notion. The brief kiss he bestowed upon her nearly a year ago was a sincere kiss, not necessarily a romantic one, she surmised. Obviously, he had to overcome the damage Nicole dispensed before delving in too deep with another female. Ladonna sighed at the thought. Danielle achieved what she failed. She broke through Richard's protective barrier. "If Richard wanted her, fine," Ladonna thought, "but he should've been a man and said so."

Ladonna looked forward to the carnival and knew Bryson would have a blast. She decided to tell him about their destination during the ride over. Revealing it sooner would jumpstart a barrage of questions and incessant nagging. Knowing her son, he'd surely spill the details of his fun afternoon to her mom, Crystal or Vincent or all three. She intended on filling Vincent in before Bryson did. Ladonna speculated that Danielle most likely would be there. Ladonna, for now at least, needed distractions from the conflicting combo of sentiments swirling about in regards to her boyfriend.

Richard neglected to establish a spot to meet up with Ladonna. He stood near the carnival entrance by a stand where the treasurer collected money and handed out tickets. A few yards away, in the field adjacent to the fellowship hall, games of chance were lined in rows. Despite forecasts threatening rain and mainly overcast skies, blotches of blue and warming rays of sun peaked through scattered clouds.

Mrs. Knight flitted about along with other auxiliary committee members. People, as she predicted, stopped to chat with Richard. He attempted to concentrate on their comments and to push aside anxiety concerning how his outing with Ladonna might unfold. He found unexpected comfort in revelations that so many followed the progress of SB71 and prayed for him during his quest.

He excused himself from one conversation to use the restroom. He spotted Bryson and Ladonna in the ticket line as he exited and returned outside. She noticed him approaching.

"Hey. We were looking for you."

Richard scanned the perimeter: no Vincent. He gave Ladonna a quick hug. Then, he gave Bryson a high-five. "I got tickets covered," he told Ladonna and practically pulled her out of the line. When he touched her arm, Richard detected an electrical current flowing between them.

"Oh, okay," she said.

He thought she sounded surprised.

"Nice set up," she commented as they approached the center of activity.

"Yeah, it's an annual event. Fortunately, a lot of members have businesses connections. They volunteer with the setup and donate a portion if not all of their supplies and profits. Most of the proceeds benefit our missionary society."

"Cool."

An elderly man holding a sizeable corndog sauntered by.

"I want a hotdog," Bryson said.

"Maybe later. Let's see what else there is before we decide."

"Not many healthy options, I'm afraid," Richard commented.

Sugar and grease wafted through the air.

"A smidgen of indulgence won't hurt him."

Bryson grab each of them by the hand. He swung his arms as they proceeded.

"Can we start with snow cones?" Richard asked. "I'm thirsty."

"Mine is sooo good," Ladonna said after the vendor filled their order. She bit another chunk out of her grape-flavored treat. "Try it." She held the cone out to Richard.

He shook his head, indicating that he didn't want any. Richard and Bryson both opted for multi-flavored cones. "Mine is good too. Want some?"

She didn't.

He took several bites before continuing. "There aren't any real rides. I think Bryson might enjoy the funhouse or the inflatable slide."

"We can check those out," Ladonna said.

The trio headed toward the games. Along the way, church members said quick hellos or acknowledged Richard with smiles. Some stopped to chat briefly. In those instances, he introduced them to Ladonna.

"A dunking booth," Ladonna squealed. "I've only seen those on TV."

Richard pictured her forcing him to sit in the hot seat. If so, he predicted Ladonna would hit the target and send him to a watery fate. He steered them toward a strongman contraption. It consisted of an oversized mallet. Anyone who struck the adjacent strength indicator with enough force to send it into the red zone won a prize.

"Let's see who's stronger," he told Bryson.

"Let's see," the boy echoed.

"Something tells me your mom might win."

Bryson chuckled, "Nooo!"

"Huh," Ladonna responded.

They joined the short line.

"Lady goes first," Richard said when their turn arrived.

Ladonna made a valiant effort. Her target barely reached the halfway mark. "That thing is rigged."

Bryson's attempt fared worse.

"Great try," Richard told him.

"You try," he urged Richard.

Richard missed the prime target too but hit higher than Bryson and Ladonna had.

"Oooh," the boy said, amazed nonetheless at Richard's prowess.

"I didn't win either, buddy."

They ventured on until a familiar voice stopped them in their tracks.

Mrs. Knight hugged Ladonna. No, she nearly smothered Ladonna. The length of their embrace made Richard jealous. His mother then pinched Bryson's cheeks. He contorted his face. The adults all laughed.

"I missed seeing you," she said.

"Likewise," Ladonna responded.

Mrs. Knight mentioned the upcoming pie-eating contest. "I want you to meet Sister Inez. Her specialty is pecan praline pie. I told her how you're into baking."

"Sure, if Richard agrees to watch Bryson." She looked in his direction.

"Don't keep her too long," Richard said as he picked up the boy.

"I'll have her back before the sack race."

The women left, arms intertwined.

Mrs. Knight looked over her shoulder and winked at her son. Richard realized in that moment his ally had a mission of her own. He considered phase one of his plan to complete.

Ladonna let Richard know as soon as she stepped inside of his home on Saturday that she read his column. "Kudos. Quite insightful even for me."

"Gracias."

"Denada."

They moved to their usual spot in his dining room.

"Before we delve into our agenda, I wanted to thank you for inviting us to the carnival. Everyone was so pleasant. I see why your mom loves her New Birth family."

"I'd almost forgotten how welcoming they are myself. Reconnecting felt good."

Ladonna cast a puzzled stare. "Wait, you still haven't returned to church?"

"I went to Bible study at Dee's church. Danielle," he clarified to clear up Ladonna's obvious confusion.

"That's a start, I suppose. Must be a special lady. Even your mom couldn't get you near a sanctuary."

"I haven't been back. I'm considering attending evening service with mom next Sunday."

"I find relying on my faith easier than questioning it. Sitting in a sanctuary grounds me. And there's something about fellowship that's also uplifting."

"Danielle made a similar comment."

"Was she at the carnival?"

"I didn't invite her."

"I thought you two were an item."

"In college." Richard explained that Glen recently proposed to Danielle.

Ladonna looked wary.

Richard saw an opportunity to initiate phase two of his plan: verbalizing his disdain for the fireman.

"Since you broached the subject, I have to say your boyfriend strikes me as wound too tight."

"You met him once."

"Twice. At your house then again at mine, where he made some cryptic comments."

"For the record, he's no fan of yours either. I learned to sidestep your egos. You two should learn to do the same."

The days melded into a repetitive blur. Ladonna and Richard hit a stride of synchronicity, bouncing ideas off each other and cranking out deliverables. Preparing for subsequent projects propelled them closer to each other until only trace evidence of their divide existed. They mainly worked remotely since he had activities planned for the two upcoming weekends. One consisted of consulting a man in Houma, Louisiana who had a similar experience. The other took place in Chicago, where a group of religious leaders requested he address them. Prior to that event, Ladonna shocked him by suggesting they meet at her house. "I think we get more done when we're face-to-face," she said.

He disagreed but didn't object.

"Furthermore," she continued, "I should help you prep for your speech. Although I read it, I need to see and hear you run through it."

Ladonna had invited Richard to her place only once since he dropped off the flowers. On that occasion, she expressed her appreciation for the gift while cautioning him against popping up unannounced. He heeded her warning.

Richard scheduled all engagements on Saturdays. He figured that arranging them for late mornings at the earliest allotted enough of a buffer from flight delays. He had yet to convince Ladonna to accompany him. Nevertheless, Richard valued her input.

He looked forward to the change of scenery for their upcoming meeting and hoped to hang out with Bryson as a bonus. Ladonna resisted bringing the boy around although Richard told her repeatedly that he posed no distraction on his part.

"This situation is just weird," Kevin told Richard, who forced him to come along to the mall. "If you insist on buying Danielle a wedding present, get a gift card and be done with it."

To Richard, doing so signified that she had meant much less to him than she did. He wanted to buy her something useful that she actually wanted. The men went to Macy's and perused Danielle's registry to see what items remained. Richard chose a 20-quart cast iron Dutch oven.

With that task completed, Richard filled Kevin in on his somewhat stymied efforts at wooing Ladonna.

"Stealing another man's woman," Kevin said, "requires more than badmouthing him. The tricky part is showing her why you're right for her. Come correct and Ladonna will choose you over Vincent."

Richard contacted Ladonna via Skype while he traveled to fill her in on both of his trips. He also chatted with Bryson. His mom, who tagged along to Chicago, commandeered the laptop and talked to Ladonna longer than he had. Richard presumed Mrs. Knight hitched a ride so they could drop by Pam's place. While that was a secondary goal, she seemed keen on supporting his efforts. Her enthusiasm flabbergasted Richard in light of her opposition to SB71. He wondered if Ladonna said anything at the carnival that influenced her perception.

Richard relished in the concept that one person could affect change. Mrs. Knight taught him and his sister that lesson. She regaled them with recollections of visionaries who dared question the status quo. She spoke of Martin Luther King Jr. and freedom riders and other fighters of injustice, some of whom history deliberately overlooked. She proudly proclaimed how their dad participated in marches. She told them that he joined forces with a union once when he worked in a warehouse. Unified, he and other laborers forced the owners to implement safety measures.

The reason his mom supported him mattered less at this point than the fact that she stood by him. Having her with him, as well as talking to Ladonna, broke the monotony of cramming facts and talking points.

Richard avoided booking anything for the weekend after they returned from Illinois so he and Ladonna could fine-tune his approach. He confessed to her that he froze for an instant while delivering his speech.

"Understandable. The first of everything is usually the hardest."

"You're right."

"Do you think this whole experience made you a better lawyer? I mean, shaping the law instead of just practicing it?"

"Definitely."

"When I run my own firm one day, I'll be able to pick cases that resonate with me on a personal level. How are your Spanish studies going?"

She caught him up on her progress. Ladonna hadn't found a bilingual group to join. Still, based on her studies, she'd advanced to an intermediate level. She told him previously about her entrepreneurial dreams and how broadening her language skills played a role.

"Years from now, your agency can supply me with bilingual job candidates. And I can connect you with lawyers who need your service.'

"Ahhh. Being our own bosses. That's my idea of freedom."

Richard nodded in agreement.

"I envy how Vincent has his accounting to fall back on.'

If he believed in magic, Richard would cast a spell to make Vincent disappear. He admittedly bordered on obsession when it came to conjuring up a method to coax Ladonna from Vincent's clutches.

Richard absorbed Kevin's suggestions and sought to implement them. He accepted Dee's disassociation with him. Of course, he missed her; he also understood her actions stemmed from a logical need to forge ahead with a clean slate. She did send an email thanking him for the Dutch oven. He responded that he wished her well and would forever consider her a friend. Beyond that communication, Richard set out to let Danielle have her space. He assumed she and Glenn had departed on their honeymoon by now. He couldn't imagine Glenn returning to Japan right after the ceremony rather than basking in Danielle's presence awhile longer.

"I wish you'd reconsider traveling with me," Richard blurted out. He hadn't meant to verbalize the thought. "Who knows how long I'll be in the limelight?" he asked before she could object. "The opportunity to travel for free doesn't come around often."

"But it's business, not pleasure."

"It would be pleasurable if you were with me."

They stared at each other, neither daring to utter the obvious.

"There's bound to be something in each stop worth checking out," Richard continued.

"I don't know," Ladonna stammered.

"Just say you won't rule out the possibility," Richard pleaded.

Mentioning Richard in Vincent's presence promptly provoked palpable tension. Ladonna, as a result, kept details of their collaboration from Vincent. They last spoke of Richard when she returned from the carnival. Her boyfriend's reaction to her going without mentioning it to him deflated the uplifting mood the festivities had triggered. Ladonna downplayed her omission while Vincent, in so many words, viewed her slight as a tear in the fabric of their relationship. "I," he haughtily proclaimed, "never would have done that to you."

The more Ladonna mulled over traveling with Richard, the more she found herself drawn to the idea. She let Vincent in on prospect when he picked her up for a date.

"Geez," Vincent said when Ladonna raised the issue of accompanying Richard. "This dude has some nerve."

"Going to the carnival really seemed to upset you, so before I definitely decided on this, I wanted to talk it over with you."

"Correction. I got upset because you told me after the fact.

That's backwards and jacked up. From Bryson's account, it was damn near a family reunion."

"It's Mrs. Knight's church too, and she's harmless. The more people love my son, the happier he'll be. "I'm trying to respect your feelings. That's why I'm weighing the possibility with you, but I agree with Richard. When else will I get to travel on someone else's dime?"

The flight to Seattle encountered turbulence. The plane cut through strong wind currents as they flew westward. Richard stole glances, or so he thought, at her. Ladonna looked stiff. Her posture reminded him of a mannequin.

"Would it help if I sat near the window?" Richard asked.

"It would."

They switched seats.

"I've flown less than five times," Ladonna said apologetically. "I've never experienced this sort of choppiness."

"Air traffic control wouldn't clear us for liftoff if it wasn't safe."

She still appeared anxious.

"It'll be alright."

They hit a bump. A piece of carry-on luggage banged against the overhead compartment across from them.

Ladonna jumped in her seat. Richard patted Ladonna's knee. She relaxed somewhat.

Richard peered out past the Boeing's wing as if willing the turbulence to tame itself. He stole another glance at Ladonna, who looked more at ease. He regretted that their inaugural joint trip started with such a tumultuous beginning. Richard counted on the deliberate distractions he had in store to provide Ladonna with magnificent memories of the Emerald City and of him.

Chapter 23

Ladonna called Vincent as soon as she and Richard checked into the Moore Hotel. Richard chose this hotel due to its locale and ambiance. Situated in downtown Seattle, Washington, the Moore was close to public transportation and tourist attractions. He ranked each as essential for the itinerary he arranged.

The hotel boasted restored marble floors, redwood doors, and the original molding dating back to 1907 when it was built. The lobby and the 120 guest suites displayed a mix of old-world charm and contemporary chic. Their room had two queen beds and a tiny dinette. It lacked air conditioning but, as did all rooms with private baths, had a decorative claw foot tub equipped with a shower.

Richard determined he had a short span in which to leave a lasting, positive, game-changing impression on Ladonna. Fear of overreacting in terms of making an impact on Ladonna fell to the wayside. Richard supposed Vincent held him in contempt for encroaching on his time with Ladonna. He predicted the fireman would, as a result, exert his best efforts toward convincing his girlfriend to reconsider her choice. If roles were reversed, Richard would resist the prospect his woman journeying from state to state with another man.

Primed for eavesdropping, Richard unpacked quietly. Ladonna ended up leaving a voicemail alerting her boyfriend of their arrival and how she'd try reaching him later. Ladonna then called her parents. She requested that her mother put Bryson on the line. "Do what grandma and granddad tell you." She paused. "No, not tomorrow. The day after."

"Can I say hello?" Richard asked.

She gave him her cell phone.

"Hi, bud."

"Yeah, it's Richard. Yeah, I'm with your mom. We're on the other side of the country. Far from Atlanta. I just wanted to say hi." Richard glanced at Ladonna. "I might be able to come see you."

Ladonna motioned for him to return the phone. "He'll keep you on the line forever if you don't cut him off," she whispered.

"Here's your mom again."

"Mommy loves you. Give the phone to grandma." She waited. "I'll call again tomorrow night." Ladonna hung up. "Bryson is starting to learn about geography and time in school. He apparently has trouble grasping these concepts."

"We need to tackle that immediately if you expect Harvard to accept Bryson," Richard joked. "Chill out. He'll grasp them sooner or later."

"I know. I know."

"Hope you're cool with the one room," Richard said. Truthfully, he wondered if she'd disclosed the specifics of their lodging to Vincent.

"It's fine that you're frugal."

The remark stung. Richard interpreted it as an unconscious comparison to Vincent, who splurged on dance lessons, software, and surely other stuff. By the end of their jaunt, however, Richard intended to demonstrate his knack for executing grand gestures. He issued a disclaimer. "The real deal is that my contracts include allotments covering double occupancy. I incorporated those in hopes of you eventually agreeing to join me."

"Oh, thoughtful." Ladonna unzipped her suitcase. She pulled out a pair of matronly flannel pajamas.

Referring to the two-piece plaid set, Richard, almost chuckling quipped, "So did Vincent get those for you just for the trip?"

Ladonna smirked without answering.

Before she removed any additional belongings, Richard interjected, "Then tell me if you're cool with strolling over to Pike Place Market. It's five minutes from here. I figured we could also buy some snacks and groceries for a quick breakfast tomorrow.

Richard's client requested a 10:00 a.m. consultation at his home located near downtown. Seattle's notorious traffic made Richard antsy, as did the many conventions and other events occurring over the weekend. Both reinforced his objective of leaving early.

"Makes sense. We can rest up tonight and won't have to rush in the morning. I read about Pike Place online. Give me a minute to freshen up." She grabbed her mouthwash and headed for the restroom.

A light mist fell upon Ladonna and Richard as they strolled along Western Avenue, lined with mixed-use developments, residential condos and shopping centers. "Good thing you suggested I pack a windbreaker," Ladonna said. The nine-acre market was a municipality in its own right. Seemingly, it housed every conceivable consumer necessity and an array of specialty goods. Fishmongers slapped their catches against crushed ice. Rows upon rows of rainbow-colored produce lay in neatly-arranged heaps. Pike Place was filled with booths displaying artisan cheese and wine, gallery-quality art, and other treasures. The market was lively and stimulating.

"I could spend hours in here and blow my budget, but I'll contain myself," Ladonna exclaimed.

Richard sniffed the air. "I hope the food tastes half as good as it smells."

"Pike is huge. We'll starve trying to see the whole place."

"Let's try something neither of us has eaten before," Richard suggested with sincere excitement. "We'll settle on the first one we find."

"So no pizza for you even if it has unusual toppings, right?"

"And no chicken sandwich for you," Richard retorted.

They ventured past a section of kiosks. "Falafel," Ladonna said. "That's out of the ordinary." They browsed a menu posted on Falafel King's exterior wall. It featured dishes made with chickpeas and fava beans, which neither of them had ever tasted. Ladonna asked the cashier for recommendations before she and Richard ordered.

"Did you confirm our appointment?" Ladonna asked while they waited.

"Nope. I will, though."

"Well, I'm glad we're seeing him in the morning. Leaves us open for more sightseeing."

"Any particular places you're determined to see?"

"The Space Needle, of course."

"Me too!"

"And we must try the fresh seafood. I hear they import a bunch from Alaska."

"I'm sure we can accomplish that."

"What about you?"

"I figured we could hop a ferry across Elliott Bay tomorrow after the meeting instead of heading straight to the hotel and then grab lunch."

"Sure."

"Great because I already bought the tickets."

"Ummm." She seemed stunned by his foresight. "Subtract the price of mine from my pay."

"It's on me."

"I insist."

"No, it's only fair since I signed us up without asking you beforehand." The tickets cost a total of $30. Luckily, the dock was in walking distance of the Moore, eliminating the need for a return cab. Despite factoring in expenses when negotiating pay, Richard still searched for money-savers. Curtailing expenditures meant more revenue.

He saw the jaunt to Bainbridge Island as an absolute bargain. Travelers' reviews consistently described the scenic ride as very romantic. Richard banked on it and his charisma to awe Ladonna.

Ladonna conceded. "Then I'm buying lunch."

Smooth jazz pouring from the alarm clock woke Ladonna and Richard.

"I thought I was dreaming," Ladonna said. "Then I smelled the ocean air and knew I wasn't in Georgia any longer." She brewed a serving of instant coffee that the hotel provided. "Want some?"

"Instant isn't the same as regular."

"I agree. It's ironic. I'm in the coffee mecca and haven't had a decent cup yet."

"We can buy some on the way out."

"Nah. I'll manage."

They discussed itinerary details while munching on fruit and toast. After bathing, each donned casual attire appropriate enough for business yet comfortable enough for their outing. Ladonna swapped out the dress she planned on wearing for a shirt and pants.

"You're sure these flats are fine?" Ladonna double-checked.

"Yep. Save your heels and fancy clothes for tonight."

Her curiosity heightened. "I thought we were heading to the Space Needle tonight."

"We are. Afterwards, we'll have a nice dinner."

Their meeting, although productive, ran long. Richard and Ladonna conversed about it as they headed toward the dock.

"That was intense," Ladonna commented.

"Minus the infidelity, his ordeal paralleled mine. I'm aware of the roadblocks he'll face."

"But you're finding it easier to deal with it, right? You've reached a level of acceptance."

"Disbelief still sneaks up on me." He peered out the window then turned to Ladonna. "Before we go any further, I've got to set a ground rule."

Ladonna contorted her face like a child preparing for a scolding.

"Leave the business talk behind after our work is done. We can chat about everything for a bit then we should switch into tourist mode. Otherwise, we won't fully unwind. Don't get me wrong. I immensely enjoy our conversations." She smiled that comforting smile of hers. "I concur."

Richard held the cab door open as Ladonna exited. Then he paid the driver. "Easy," he told her when Ladonna ascended the vessel's stairs. "It's slippery."

They stood in front of the upper deck railing, eager to draw in the surrounding natural wonders. They stood so close that Richard had easy access to her lips. Occasionally when he felt alone, he imagined Ladonna and Vincent in intimate situations. With her to himself, Richard focused on heeding Kevin's advice. He fought the instinct to bash his rival.

"We caught a nice run," Richard said. "From what I read, the ferry is normally packed."

He and Ladonna took in Puget Sound, Mount Rainier, Mount Baker, and the Olympic Mountains.

"I feel like an ant compared to them," she said.

"Give me your camera. I'll snap a picture of you."

Ladonna positioned herself with a mountain range as a backdrop.

After disembarking, Richard stopped a teenager about to hop on a scooter. He appeared to be familiar with the island. Richard asked him for lunch spot suggestions. He named a number of favorites and directed Richard on how to find them. Ladonna proposed checking out the eateries located in the town center. She and Richard hurried up the hill leading to Winslow.

They picked an open-air café. There, they shared an over-sized basket of steamed crab claws complemented with grilled white corn on the cob and freakishly fluffy biscuits. Ladonna insisted that they stroll about the commerce district to burn off a portion of the gluttony they'd indulged in.

"I feel like a blimp," she quipped.

"Blimps must be beautiful," Richard responded.

"Stop it. You're only saying so 'cause you're my friend."

"I said so because it's true."

Back at the Moore, jetlag overcame the pair. Ladonna knocked out earlier than Richard. He lay on his side and watched her. She snored, but even her snores sounded lovely. Eventually, he dozed off as well. When he woke up, she was watching him.

He yawned. "Did I oversleep?"

"Nah, it's just past 5:30." She'd opened a window and then obviously hopped back into bed. "I'll go shower since you're up." Ladonna slipped on her slippers and reached for her robe. "I was afraid I'd disturb you."

"FYI, I'm a hard sleeper."

"Duly noted, Mr. Knight. I'll be quick."

"No rush."

Richard sauntered to the closet and checked his slacks and his shirt for wrinkles. Neither required ironing. A muffled, vibrating noise emanating from near the beds drew his attention. He traced it to Ladonna's purse.

Temptation nudged Richard over a boundary he otherwise dare not cross. Richard reached for Ladonna's cell phone. He held the contraband. A swift review of the call log revealed Vincent's number. Without pause, he deleted the number.

The shower nozzle squeaked as Ladonna moved it to the off position, signaling her imminent return.

Richard scrolled to her voicemail. He found no recent messages. He scrolled to her text messages. He found one from the firefighter. It mentioned missing Ladonna, loving her, and for Ladonna to call him at 9:00 p.m. "Sorry, pal," Richard said. He pressed the delete button. A warning appeared asking if he wanted to complete the action. Richard selected "yes." That maneuver erased any trace of Vincent's latest attempt at contact. Curiosity led Richard to scroll through the outgoing history. It showed no outbound calls following the one to her parents.

The bathroom doorknob turned.

Richard scrambled to toss the phone into Ladonna's purse in the exact spot he found it. His feat left him fully confident, at last, of his ability to loosen Vincent's vice grip.

Ladonna and Richard navigated the route from the Moore to the monorail station in silence as they weaved through throngs of pedestrians. Ladonna commented on how the terminal and trains appeared hi-tech in comparison to those back home. And at the entrance to the Space Needle, she marveled at its size.

"Wow," she said. "Photos don't do this place justice." She asked Richard to snap one of her in front of the landmark.

The elevator ascended 520 feet in under 50 seconds. On the observation deck, they viewed parasails, cruise ships, and seaplanes.

Richard pointed out Safeco Field. "Skiing, sailing, and major league teams, I understand why sports fanatics flock to this city."

As Ladonna explored, he feigned interest in trivia facts she read out and tried to cloak his anxiousness.

"Ready to go inside?" Richard inquired shortly after sunset.

They took the elevator down and stopped 100 feet from the ground.

"Good evening," the host said. Welcome to SkyLine level. Names?"

"Richard Knight. And this is my guest, Ladonna Hudson."

"Follow me," the host said. "You'll be enjoying your meal in the Lake Union Room."

"It's empty in this joint," Ladonna said, scanning the area. Multiple tables occupied the Lake Union Room. No one sat at them. "Where is everyone else?"

"We have another couple dining in the Peugeot Sound Room," the host answered. He pointed to his left. "Behind that retractable wall. My name is Allen. I will be at your service tonight."

He offered Ladonna a dark dinner napkin instead of the white one on the table. "We wouldn't want lint landing on your dress," he said. "Can I pour either of you some Starbucks coffee or Tazo tea? All entrees include your choice. Or, if you prefer, I can place an order at the bar."

"Do you serve champagne by the glass?" Richard asked.

"Certainly."

Richard glanced at Ladonna. "I'll have whatever the lady prefers."

"May I have a glass of water for now?" Ladonna asked. "Light ice, please."

"Two glasses of water then?" Allen confirmed.

"Yes," Richard replied.

"I'm confused," Ladonna said when their server moved out of earshot.

"I figured we'd benefit from the seclusion of private dining. How better to celebrate our collaboration and to spend our last night in Seattle? Do you want to deal with yapping tourists at every turn?"

Ladonna looked at the polished wood paneling. Rectangular windowpanes with unobtrusive frames let in twinkling cityscape lights. Tropical bouquets bursting with bright orange, green, and pink hues graced the middle of each table. As a centerpiece, candles in jars provided subtle illumination.

Richard went on, "The room completes a 360 degree rotation every full hour."

"The expense though."

"A law school colleague has connections. He got me a deal."

"If I'd known the perks of hanging out with you, I would've agreed to travel earlier," she joked nervously.

"As corny as I might come across, I was elated when you did agree."

"Elated?"

"Over the moon. Ecstatic. The dictionary falls short of an adequate description."

Ladonna raised a brow. He tried reading her.

Allen returned with the water. "Which of our scrumptious soups or salads would you care to begin with?"

"Allen," Ladonna said. "I haven't browsed the menu. I'd prefer soup though. Which is your favorite?"

"Gazpacho. I generally pair it with poultry. Considering you're fond of seafood, I'd steer you toward the Seattle Clam and Corn Chowder. It's loaded with local clams, potatoes and velvety cream. The chowder is delicate and won't interfere with the flavor of a salmon, scallop, or shrimp dish."

"Sold."

She and Allen focused on Richard.

"Ditto for me."

Allen hurried off.

"You told him I like fish?" Ladonna inquired.

"The restaurant made me fill out a preference survey."

"High class. Thank you." She paused. "Bryson would have flipped over this view."

"The height wouldn't frighten him?"

"Uh-uh."

"Speaking of Bryson, any chance I can see him soon?"

"Swing by Tuesday right after work if you're free."

"Will do."

Their vantage point revealed phenomenal architectural details that go unnoticed in the daylight. They touched upon light topics, enjoyed the haven, and Allen attending to their needs. The meal and Ladonna's presence nourished Richard. As the restaurant slowly revolved, a revelation overcame him: he yearned for more of Ladonna than he'd admitted. He yearned to make her his wife.

En route to Seattle Tacoma Airport, Richard and Ladonna took a detour. He lured her to a specialty coffee shop.

"Our flight leaves at 1:00," Ladonna said. "Is it really necessary to check out so soon?" she asked before they left the Moore.

He convinced her that was necessary because Mocha Java is popular and would be crowded, and the traffic was likely heavy.

"How did you find this shop?" she asked him.

"One of those sites where users rate businesses."

Upon arriving at Mocha Java, Richard requested the manager on duty. Mrs. Guinn, along with other owners, maintained the family business. They set up exclusive, fair trade co-ops with growers in South America and Africa. As a result, the brew masters offered unique, specialty blends unavailable to competitors.

She greeted them like relatives coming home from a long journey. "I have everything set up," she told Richard.

"It's too much," Ladonna insisted.

Lines in Richard's forehead creased.

"The ferry ride, the Space Needle, now customized coffee."

Richard leaned forward. "It's far from too much. It's not enough."

Ladonna exhaled.

"Ladonna, you're a lot like my mom. Sacrificing for you is second nature whether it's for your son or for your friends. You tend to think of others first. I simply tried to create situations where someone catered to you for a change."

He stirred his coffee. "Just know there's no one else in the universe I'd rather share these experiences with."

"I couldn't see myself doing this with anyone else either."

"Promise that when you return to the real world and encounter bumps or frustrations, you'll reminisce about our experiences here. Promise that you'll remember how special you are and how much I appreciate you."

She reached for one of his hands and squeezed it. "I will."

They touched down at Hartsfield-Jackson right on schedule. The plan was for Richard to drop Ladonna off at her house. Instead, Vincent waited for the duo at the arrivals. Except for not holding a sign, to Richard he looked like a limo driver anxiously awaiting a high-profile fare. After spotting her, Vincent immediately scooped Ladonna off her feet with a bear-like hug. He then patted her on the butt and glanced over at Richard. She stammered his name and appeared dazed. "Vincent? What are you doing here?"

"Picking up my honey," he responded as if the question was silly. Vincent planted a kiss on her stoic lips.

"Why?"

He flinched. "Because I missed you. What other reason would there be?"

"I'm just shocked. I thought you were on duty today."

"The chief let me off early." He grabbed her bag. "Richard," he grunted in acknowledgement.

"Vincent," he mumbled in return. Richard fantasized that he hauled off and shoved Vincent's teeth down his throat.

"Now," Vincent said, "You don't have to inconvenience Richard."

"Helping out Ladonna couldn't be any further from an inconvenience. He gazed at her. "I owe this woman a debt I can't repay." He fixed his gaze on Vincent. "That won't stop me from trying."

Ladonna tugged on Vincent's sleeve. "We should get going. Thank you, Richard, for everything."

He watched them disappear into the maze of travelers. Richard believed Ladonna would avoid relaying the extent of all they'd shared. He reflected on the awe she expressed during the ferry ride, the delight she found in the gourmet meal, the childish twinkle that lit her eyes as she and Ms. Guinn produced signature blends. Richard accepted Vincent's right to whisk off Ladonna because he knew full well no distance held the capacity to erase the memories he helped create.

Chapter 24

Richard dropped by on Tuesday bearing a gift. The oversized plastic bag had a bright orange ribbon that kept the top closed. Ladonna let him in and eyed the package suspiciously.

"Relax. It's for Bryson."

"What do you say?" Ladonna asked her son.

"Thank you, Richard," he said in a sing-songy voice. "Can I open it?"

Richard looked to Ladonna.

"Go ahead," she said and then sat on the loveseat while Richard and the boy settled on the sofa.

"Ooh!" the boy said once he unwrapped the present. "What is it?"

"A globe."

His expression unmistakably indicated that the item didn't register in his vocabulary.

"More like a round map," Richard explained. "Do you guys have maps at school?"

"Yeah," Bryson said. "And we live in Georgia."

"That's right." He glanced at Ladonna. "Is it okay if I put it on the table? I wouldn't want to scratch it."

"Be my guest. It's not an heirloom or anything."

"Since globes are round and come on stands—" Richard

placed a finger on the metal stand. "you can turn them." He demonstrated.

"Cool!"

He showed Bryson the United States, and then Georgia.

"Mommy, can I take my globe to show-and-tell?"

"We'll need to check with Ms. Barros, but I think she'll be fine with that."

"The large graphics and print appealed to me. I figured," Richard said, "this would last Bryson throughout elementary school and give him a clearer understanding of where you are when we travel."

"Excellent idea. Wish I would've thought of it." Ladonna watched her enraptured son. "You handle him so well. Were you around a lot of younger kids growing up?"

"Barely."

"Hmmm."

"He's not hard to handle. Quite the opposite. A testament to his upbringing rather than any skills I possess." He grew silent. "Sometimes I fear someone will come along and convince you to cut me out of his life. Out of yours, too."

"You ditched us, not the other way around. Stick to your word and you won't have any worries."

Richard heard the hidden message: I've forgiven you, but I won't twice.

He felt compelled to reiterate his intentions. "Kismet or karma. We crossed paths for a purpose, and I'm so grateful. Never question my commitment to Bryson and to you."

Ladonna and Richard's collaboration rolled on. They touched down in Maine and Tennessee on consecutive weekends. Upon reaching the second destination, Richard's body ached. He had a grueling week at the firm caused by groundbreakings on numerous job sites. Overseeing his professional responsibilities combined with constant travel wore him out. He hid the weariness as best as possible when in the presence of peers. He especially attempted to pep up around Ladonna.

In Fort Kent, a town bordering Canada, they went ice skating at an outdoor rink. Richard possessed a modicum of experience over her. His fearlessness in regards to tumbling gave Richard an edge. She leaned on him to maintain her balance. Richard grasped Ladonna's hips gently as she swayed dangerously, threatening to force both onto the hard surface below. Later during that trip, Ladonna lamented that lacking a passport prevented them from crossing into New Brunswick for a day tour.

"I procrastinated and even picked up an application at the post office but never filled it out."

"We can come back," Richard blurted out.

Ladonna simply said, "Maybe."

Richard assumed Ladonna knew he meant a leisurely jaunt outside the realm of professional tasks. He envisioned them with Bryson, a perfect family unit, exploring America's northern neighbor. Neither expounded on the logistics.

Blues and barbeque beckoned them in Memphis. When they stopped by the concierge desk for restaurant and club recommendations, the young lady providing assistance mistook Richard and Ladonna as married. Neither corrected her.

He continued to scope out her cell phone log and pounced on another opportunity to erase a message from the fireman. Ladonna conducted brief communications with Vincent, from what Richard could tell. Of course, Richard fell short of keeping Ladonna from contacting her boyfriend. Deleting all of Vincent's texts and calls would have raised flags. Richard, nevertheless, considered any victory integral in terms of securing his conquest. Richard savored the pretend existence he created with Ladonna. He had an inkling that she also appreciated their mini-escapes from reality.

Mrs. Knight grew worried. Richard was supposed to join her for dinner. He'd cancelled on her the two prior nights. She let those cancellations slide. Since his flight from Maine got delayed, Richard had to bow out of dinner on Sunday. On Monday, he said so many assignments awaited his attention that he had to work late. He assured her he'd make it on Tuesday. Mrs. Knight expected her son to arrive by 6:00 at the latest. She kept calling him for 30 minutes to no avail. She called Kevin. She called Ladonna.

His friends provided no leads on his whereabouts. Ladonna assured her he'd probably lost track of time or lost cell phone reception. She told Mrs. Knight to contact her if she needed anything further. Kevin said the same. He offered to have a squad car patrolling the area stop by Richard's home.

"Thanks, but I'll keep trying."

Richard awoke in a cold sweat, unaware of his surroundings. It dawned on him that he'd fallen asleep at the desk in his home office. Richard's entire frame shook in a jittery fashion similar to a drug fiend.

"Ugh." Immense hunger pains emanated from his stomach yet the notion of digesting food nauseated him. He realized his phone was ringing and dug it out of his briefcase.

"Finally!" Mrs. Knight exclaimed. I was about to drive over there."

"Ma," Richard muttered groggily. "You sound bad, honey."

Richard moaned. His knees knocked together. "I feel bad."

"Hold on, honey. Mama's coming."

Mrs. Knight took one look at her pale son and then made an executive decision. Richard required medical attention, not mothering. She whisked him off to Piedmont Hospital and contacted Ladonna once they arrived. She told Mrs. Knight she'd try to get there soon.

Shortly prior to 8:30, Ladonna rushed into the emergency room. She found Mrs. Knight sitting next to Richard, who slept upright.

"I tried getting here earlier," she said apologetically. "How's he doing?" She glanced at Richard.

"Better. The shakes have gone." She touched his forehead. "No signs of fever. Did he mention feeling ill to you?"

"Not at all."

Mrs. Knight wrung her hands. "I should've taken him to Grady even though his insurance card lists Piedmont."

"Service there is worse. Between being bogged down by indigents and trauma victims, who knows when a doctor would see Richard."

A resident nudged Richard to wake him. "Mr. Knight," he said. "I'm Dr. Cowell. Come with me."

Richard blinked. "Ladonna?" She was the last person he wanted to see him in this state.

"Follow me," Dr. Cowell instructed.

Inside the exam room, Richard sat on a gurney. "Do you need me to disrobe?"

"Remain dressed." The doctor placed his stethoscope on Richard's chest. "Take deep breaths in and out for me."

Richard did as instructed.

"Sounds normal." Dr. Cowell flipped through sheets on a clipboard. "Tell me your symptoms Mr. Knight."

Richard relayed them.

"Your mother filled in part of our intake questionnaire. Help me fill in the blanks. Smoker?"

"No."

"Drinker?"

"Sometimes to relax. I can go weeks without drinking."

"Drugs?"

"No."

"Unprotected sex?"

"No."

"Any change in bowels?"

"No."

"What about your daily routine."

Richard relayed how his consulting led to additional pressure and how he'd experienced exhaustion. "I do a lot of walking on the weekends. I used to jog regularly, but then some personal issues took a toll and exercising fell to the wayside."

"Your busy schedule could attribute to your weariness," the doctor said, "but it's probably not the underlying factor. Have you traveled to any third-world regions?"

"No."

Dr. Cowell wrapped a blood pressure monitor around Richard's wrist. "Breath normally." The doctor jotted down his findings on Richard's chart. "Well within range."

"Your mother wrote that your father died of a heart attack. When was your last physical?"

"December. My physician found no irregularities."

"Have you experienced other episodes in the last nine months?"

"No."

"Other than tonight, how has your appetite been?"

"Regular. I've never skipped meals because I wasn't hungry. Believe it or not, I eat better when I'm on the road. My friend Ladonna keeps me on track. Otherwise, I put off eating until I'm starving. I've developed a tendency to grab what's available or what I can cook quickly rather than what's nutritious. I started taking vitamins under a month ago."

"Allow me to take some blood. I need to run a test to confirm my suspicion."

"Sure."

"I'm leaning toward hypoglycemia. Low blood sugar in layman's terms."

Dr. Cowell requested that Richard sign a consent form. Then, he grabbed a vial and a needle from the supply cabinet.

"Prepare for a pinch."

Ladonna knew Vincent would balk at her assessment of him. So, she kept the opinion to herself. She went to his condo as soon as she left work. Ladonna and Vincent had planned to catch a movie last night. Richard's medical scare sidetracked that plan.

Ladonna reached for her keys and purse once again. Vincent kept coaxing her into staying longer. He even snatched her keychain and hid it in his palm, knowing full well she couldn't break his grasp.

"Not fair," Ladonna said.

She decided to stay a bit longer. He asked her to come back with her son and spend the night. Ladonna refused, citing Bryson as the primary hindrance.

"Bring him along," Vincent implored.

"He has a routine. You know that."

"But he stays at his grandparents' just fine."

"That's different. They've got a room set up for him and everything."

He pouted.

"I feel like a booty call. No matter how late you stay, you manage to slip out." He sighed. "What about Friday night? He doesn't have school the next day."

"Uh," Ladonna stammered, "I have a major conference this Saturday."

Vincent grimaced. "And?"

"And, I agreed to attend it with Richard."

"He's still going?"

Dr. Cowell recommended that Richard call out sick today and that he shun stressful situations for a while in light of his hypoglycemia. Richard refused to follow those orders. He agreed, however, to stop skipping meals and to eat smaller, well-balanced meals throughout the day.

"Why can't he handle that on his own?"

The group invited Richard as a roundtable panelist for the mental health and wellness portion of their conference.

"It's an awesome opportunity for him and me. Basically, it's a captive audience of influential business owners and decision makers. A mix-and-mingle session will follow the conference. Networking is part of why I'm eager to go. I'm sure plenty of them could benefit from my bilingual employment agency when it materializes."

Vincent disregarded her attempt at logic. "The whole reason I approved when you brought up traveling with him was your guarantee to save at least one weekend for us."

Ladonna considered the term "approved" off base. It implied she sought his permission. "Technically," Ladonna said, "I'm not traveling."

His tone escalated. "Are you blind?"

"Vincent, be realistic."

"He's clearly taking advantage of your kindness."

"I'm done arguing about Richard. For the record, I volunteered to go."

"Volunteered?" Vincent scoffed. "Just so you know, I'm done with Richard inserting himself into *our* relationship."

"I should go. Give me my keys."

"Uh uh. Not until we settle this."

"Are you serious?"

"Him or me. Choose."

"Maybe we need a break."

"I don't do breaks."

She went with her gut. "Then we're through."

"You prefer that chump?" Vincent hissed.

"I didn't say that," she retorted. "Give me my keys."

Because Ladonna theorized that her mother and Crystal would resort to armchair psychology, she kept the breakup to herself.

Speaking in front of such an influential group of men, and their equally influential female counterparts, petrified Richard. He linked his apprehension to the proximity of his audience. Some attendees at the 100 Black Men conference flew in from out-of-town. Most had deep roots within the metro Atlanta area. He would, in all likelihood, encounter them at other events as his prominence grew within the legal community. Richard's performance as a panel member could open doors to an upper echelon of professionals. Members of this esteemed group held the power to shape policies, to grant funding, and to provide recommendations that insured promotions.

Richard expected Ladonna to bow out of this event. Overwhelming gratitude swept over him when she mentioned helping him craft responses to potential questions and actually tagging along. She offered to pick him up.

"I'm not incapacitated," Richard told her. "I've been driving."

He supposed his mom, fearful that he'd overexert himself, suggested that Ladonna do so. Mrs. Knight denied enlisting Ladonna's assistance. Richard sipped on a cocktail and pushed past the fatigue that still plagued him. He tweaked talking points in the privacy of his home. He knew Ladonna would breakdown the good, the bad, and the ugly of his performance once he finished. Faltering in front of her would embarrass him to a greater degree than faltering before the prestigious crowd.

Ladonna looked on the *100 Black Men of Atlanta's* website to see who'd attend the conference. She developed a partial target list within the organization to seek out and connect with, if circumstances allowed. Vincent's ultimatum hijacked her thoughts. He exemplified masculinity and proved on countless occasions that she could count on him. Early on, she foresaw her son benefiting from observing his work ethic, kindness, consideration, and other first-rate qualities. In her opinion, the dating pool was flooded with freeloaders and mamma's boys suffering from a deficiency of strong male role models. With Vincent, she'd happened upon a treasure, but Bryson and Vincent failed to gel. Their inability to bond created a crack in Ladonna's ability to submit to Vincent for the long term. Richard's reemergence further complicated issues. He fostered a spark in Bryson no other man managed.

Knowing he had Ladonna's support, Richard avoided making missteps in front of those at the 100 Black Men gathering. Ladonna rushed to his side once the panel disbanded.

"All those trial runs paid off," she said.

"Guess so."

"Prepared to hobnob?"

"Certainly."

They moved among the crowd together, making connections. The only connection that truly mattered to him was with Ladonna. She understood him better than he understood himself. While feeling unworthy of her affection, he hungered for it.

After a drawn-out chat with an advertising executive, he pulled Ladonna aside. "Can we speak privately?"

"Something wrong?" she asked discretely.

"No, but this can't wait."

The walk from the conference area to a smaller, vacant meeting room felt like forever. Richard nearly psyched himself out. He closed the door behind them and locked it. Then, he drew the shades.

"Must be important enough for you to leave the function," Ladonna said.

"I can't concentrate on what's going on out there."

"Why?"

Subjecting himself to rejection was unavoidable in the quest to stake his claim. Richard stood so close to Ladonna that her breath caressed his face. "How can you act like nothing is going on when something is?" he asked.

Ladonna's breathing grew shallow. "Could you be specific?"

Intuition coaxed Richard to react nonverbally. Using his index finger, Richard lifted her chin. He leaned into Ladonna until his lips hovered over hers. Richard braced himself for rejection.

Ladonna leaned into him. Their lips locked. Approaching footsteps prompted them to release and step away from each other.

Once the footsteps faded, Richard asked, "Specific enough?"

On the ride to her house, Ladonna disclosed that she and Vincent parted ways. "Losing you must suck," Richard told Ladonna. He held her hand as they continued on.

Richard, eager for details, assumed he contributed to disassembling their relationship. She supplied no specifics. Richard wondered if they'd slept together. He knew posing that question would instantaneously ruin the mood. More to the point, he'd come off as pompous and uncouth. He'd let his inquisitiveness remain unquenched unless Ladonna broached the topic.

Chapter 25

Uplifted and energized, Richard strolled into Zeigler & Associates a changed man. Whether Ladonna's acceptance or adhering to the doctor's dietary directives initiated the exuberance mattered not. Coworkers perceived Richard's upswing and commented on it over the next few days.

Once Richard and Ladonna dropped the veil of mere friendship, they saw each other constantly and even attended church with Mrs. Knight. "Should we add you to the lease?" Crystal quipped one evening.

Richard especially took pleasure in performing what Ladonna referred to as thankless, mundane tasks such as taking Bryson outside to play, picking him up from school, or reading him bedtime stories.

"I'm definitely going to miss him when we leave for Houston," Richard told Ladonna as they prepared for an upcoming video chat. "How do you manage to stop from falling to pieces?'

"Competent caregivers. Without Crystal or my mom and dad, I'd be a wreck for sure."

On Thursday, Ladonna joined Richard for lunch at a sushi bar. Ladonna stopped eating her sashimi to rub her temples. "You know Vincent thought you wanted me the whole time. I kept discounting his suspicions over and over. Now that we're together, that must've been hard to handle. That's not an easy situation to deal with. I know from experience. When I rejected him, he probably assumed I'd been cheating."

"Frankly, he's a coward. He skulked around knowing you'd be at the conference."

"Needless to say, my mom is eager to meet you. My dad, too."

Richard grinned proudly. At that moment, he didn't want to discuss anyone else but them.

By 2:00, queasiness set in. Richard called Ladonna to alert her that he would skip hanging out later.

"Could be the sushi messing with you."

"We each ordered it, and you're fine."

She offered to come to his house. He talked her out of that idea.

"I'd feel horrible if you caught whatever this is and passed it on to Bryson."

"Take it easy then. I'll check on you later."

Richard plowed on. He went to a construction site and tried his best to focus on blueprint modifications the lead architect suggested. Nausea plagued him. As soon as their discussion ended, Richard ran to a Porta-Potty.

He fully expected to vomit. He didn't expect to vomit blood.

"How can we rely on this diagnosis?" Mrs. Knight asked Dr. Olson. "The last doctor said my son's sugar was low. Today you're claiming liver disease."

"Medicine, despite popular perceptions, is not an exact science. The symptoms of both illnesses mimic each other. Luckily for your son, the liver has the ability to regenerate itself." Dr. Olson turned to his patient and stared at him sternly. "Dr. Cowell did order you to set up an appointment which you failed to do. The previous doctor didn't spot this; however, he followed the proper protocol."

Dr. Olson, in Richard's opinion, exuded an air of experience Dr. Cowell lacked. He looked considerably older than Dr. Cowell, by twenty years at least. "Richard seemed fine until recently," Mrs. Knight said. "Now you're saying he has to stay overnight?"

Richard regretted allowing his mom and Ladonna in his hospital room while he received the test results. Their reactions increased his anxiety. He needed to process the doctor's information without added distractions.

"Observation tonight and over the coming weeks is crucial. It's clear now that the sporadic itching, extreme tiredness, and fluid retention in the abdomen were symptoms. Many other conditions can cause those. Odds are, understandably, that he ignored symptoms. Approximately half of the people who have liver disease don't show any symptoms. Mr. Knight presented none of the noticeable indicators such as yellowing of the eyes and skin, mental confusion, discolored urine or bowel movements.'

"I don't understand what triggered this," Ladonna said. Mrs. Knight echoed the sentiment.

"Liver damage occurs due to a variety of risk factors. For Mr. Knight it was alcohol."

The women glanced at each other. Judgment swirled in their eyes. Richard developed a disease of his own creation.

"I was pretty much a recreational drinker prior to Nicole killing our baby." Richard clarified for the doctor, "My ex-wife had an abortion while we were married."

"I see. Could be that you suffered from post-abortion stress syndrome. Trauma victims often rely on alcohol to numb reactions. Contrary to popular belief, it's a depressant and rarely results in the desired effect."

"I'm not a binge drinker or an alcoholic," Richard uttered defiantly.

"The quantity your liver ascertains as toxic might hardly register in someone else's system. I should note that alcohol is a poison. Any amount can produce damage. Therefore, the quantity one can consume safely varies."

Ladonna interjected. "What about those studies touting wine's health benefits, especially the red variety?"

"Even those tend to trigger genetic predispositions in drinkers who consume them responsibly. Men metabolize alcohol more efficiently as a general rule."

Dr. Olson prescribed a regimen of meds to assist in reversing the damage. Mrs. Knight and Ladonna listened intensely as he told Richard the dosing requirements. "Refer to your prescription pamphlets if questions arise."

"Will do," Richard said.

"The most crucial step is for Mr. Knight to cease consumption. The body cannot distinguish among wine or whiskey or beer."

"Lastly, I can't emphasize enough the necessity of scheduling a follow-up appointment."

"We'll make sure he does," Mrs. Knight assured the doctor.

Mrs. Knight and Ladonna watched Richard like a hawk following his discharge. Mrs. Knight picked him up from the hospital. She spent the majority of the morning and afternoon at his house. Ladonna came over after retrieving Bryson from school.

"Are you mad?" she asked Richard.

He left his laptop on the coffee table with his company email server in plain view.

"Seems someone threw the doctor's orders out the window."

"You're sick?" Bryson asked him.

"I wasn't feeling too well, but I'll be fine, buddy." Richard closed the computer and unplugged it. He glanced at his girlfriend. "There. I'm all yours. Yours too," he said to Bryson.

"We can't stay long. He has a field trip to the science museum. I volunteered to chaperone. Gotta get up extra early."

"My mom made a casserole. Take some."

"Okay."

They ventured into the kitchen.

"Sit," Richard urged. "I'll fix it for you."

"You should be chilling out instead of checking emails and doing who knows what else."

"I was online for a short while. Lying in bed bored me."

"Can I have a cookie?" Bryson asked.

"Yes," Ladonna said. She grabbed two from the cake platter on the table. She put them on a napkin and then slid the treats in front of him.

"My mother made those while I *rested*," Richard said.

"Will you take Monday off as well?"

"Nope. Dr. Olson cleared me. He did say I should be prepared in case another episode occurs—basically head to the restroom if I feel nauseous and let him know if I experience more bleeding. He reassured me that a spot or two presented no need for alarm."

"Dr. Olson also said no alcohol whatsoever. Curbing your intake isn't an option."

Her tone indicated an underlying accusation: she suspected he'd been less than forthcoming concerning his consumption. Richard prayed his predicament hadn't planted hesitation in regards to their relationship.

"That's a non-issue. I'm not guzzling beer or rum or champagne. Certainly, I'm not reliant on them. Have you ever smelled the stench of liquor on my breath?"

"No, but—."

"Check my cupboards. Check every inch of this place. I don't have any hidden stashes. Really, I can go without another ounce of alcohol. I can't go without you."

Richard spent the next two weeks demonstrating to his mother and to Ladonna his ability to function at a somewhat normal capacity. Mrs. Knight tagged along to his follow-up appointment where she probed Dr. Olson more so than the patient. One of the medical shows she had watched mentioned milk thistle as a treatment for liver inflammation. Mrs. Knight, in turn, mentioned the natural remedy to the doctor.

"It's safe, but bear in mind studies show mixed reviews of its effectiveness."

Ladonna tried talking him out of the trip to Texas. At Ladonna's prompting, they postponed work on other projects. Those didn't require traveling. He refused to allow his health hiccup to impede further on the fathers' rights initiatives of his clients.

"I'm ready to re-immerse myself into that mission," Richard explained. "And, I'm ready to start spoiling you again instead of the other way around."

The Hudsons requested that Ladonna bring Richard by when she dropped off Bryson before departing for Houston. They seemed sincere enough while welcoming Richard into their modest abode. He noted that the open floor plan kept it from appearing dated. Ladonna remarked that she grew up there. Her parents converted her old room into a space for Bryson.

Richard saw the Hudsons in photos. Ladonna obviously inherited her father's facial features and her mother's frame. He'd never seen photos of Bryson's dad or his family, but the boy clearly took after his maternal grandparents. He sat wedged between them on the sofa.

"Our grandson raves about you," Mrs. Hudson said.

Her husband glanced at Richard, almost sheepishly. Richard detected an undertone of suspicion.

"In light of recent events," she continued, "we had to meet the man who's been spending so much time with him and our daughter."

Richard was curious if they'd readily accept him into their tight-knit circle in the wake of Vincent's seemingly random exit. Ladonna shared that beforehand her parents held the fireman in high regard. As a result, Ladonna feared the fallout of announcing their break up. She said they saw Vincent as a gentleman. He wondered additionally if she made either of the Hudsons privy to the ups and downs of their involvement, including his recent hospitalization.

The flow of conversation so far indicated that Mrs. Hudson ruled the roost. She asked general information about his career and his upbringing. As much as Richard intended on ingratiating himself with the Hudsons, Ladonna unintentionally sidetracked him from that undertaking.

She sat on the settee by his side. Periodically, Ladonna glimpsed at him reassuringly. He concentrated on the curvature of her wrist, the daintiness of her fingers, and the natural beauty of her unpolished nails.

"We should head out to the airport," Ladonna interjected.

"Not so fast," Richard said.

Everyone, even Bryson, honed in.

Richard's gaze darted back and forth from Ladonna to her parents. "I'm so fond of Bryson and his mom. Rest assured that I've got their best interests at the forefront. She's a special lady; he's a special boy."

Ladonna's cheeks reddened.

"Forgive my bluntness," Mr. Hudson said, "actions count more than proclamations to us."

His wife nodded in concurrence.

Richard seized the opening. "Yes, sir." Richard felt like he was standing on a cliff with no guardrail. He choreographed his next step, unbeknownst to Ladonna, yet that preparation evaded him. "Visions of my future include Ladonna and Bryson without fail. I'd be forever grateful if you granted me permission to wed your daughter."

His announcement stunned them all.

"She's grown," Mrs. Hudson said. "The decision is hers."

Everyone stared at Ladonna.

"Ultimately," Mr. Hudson chimed in, "her happiness outweighs our opinions."

"Married or not," Mrs. Hudson continued, "we'll keep tabs on her and Bryson. She'll always be our little girl."

"Ma."

"A proper proposal requires a ring," her mom said.

With trembling hands, Richard reached for Bryson's duffel bag. It lay at the foot of the settee. He retrieved a jewelry box from inside. Then, he kneeled in front of Ladonna and opened it. An oval solitaire diamond graced a gold band dotted with smaller, stunningly clear stones.

He asked her to marry him. Without hesitation, she accepted. As tears rolled down her face, she grabbed her son to give him a reassuring hug.

"Mommy, Richard will be my daddy?"

"Yes, if you'll have me," responded Richard. With that, Bryson abruptly turned to hug the only place he could reach on Richard's body – his knees. Richard swooped down and picked him up, saying, "I guess we'll be a family now."

"What about me, guys?" questioned Ladonna, whose mascara almost covered her cheeks.

Richard used his other hand to reach over and pull Ladonna in the circle of two. Providing the only indication that she was pleased, Mrs. Hudson started taking pictures of the three of them with her phone.

Concourse C's seating area felt like a private hideaway for the newly-engaged couple. They found a free corner and blocked out the buzz of activity surrounding them.

"If you'd prefer a different setting or style, we can arrange that."

"Nonsense," Ladonna exclaimed. "This will stay glued to my finger from this day forward."

Richard let out a sigh of relief. "Cool because my mom helped pick it out. She'll be elated that it fits and that you like it."

"I'll thank her in person when we return."

"Knowing my mom, she'll try to pull off a double wedding with Pam and me."

Ladonna chuckled. "They haven't set a date yet so that might pan out."

"Nah. I'm not sharing the spotlight."

They locked lips.

"Mr. Knight, when do you plan on making an honest woman out of me?"

"Let's aim for a year from now so we can get our affairs in order. That entails clearing my work calendar and completing my medical regimen. I intend on actively participating in planning our wedding."

"Good to hear."

"I steadfastly believe in paying cash for large expenditures, which means buckling down on a budget and opening a savings account specifically for our special day."

"I don't need fancy frills, just a scrumptious cake or cupcakes. I read in Martha Stewart's magazine that higher-end bakeries offer those as an option."

"I'd prefer an intimate ceremony with close friends and relatives."

"No objections here." Richard realized from his first go at marriage that filling an expensive venue with friends and acquaintances was a waste of money and detraction from the ceremony's sanctity. As he and Ladonna exchanged vows, Richard intended to see close friends and relatives who understood and supported their journey.

"Okay, we've established we're not going broke. We should save enough to linger in Spain for a week minimum."

"Yes," he said, returning her gaze, "I remembered your ultimate honeymoon destination."

"I mentioned voyaging to Barcelona ions ago."

"I'm confident you'll speak Spanish fluently enough to translate by then," Richard said assuredly.

"I hope so."

"You will. Remember when we kissed on your porch that evening you met my mom?' he asked.

"You hurried off afterwards."

Richard ran the back of his hand along her cheek slowly, tenderly. "I was foolish and afraid," he confessed. "I wish I wouldn't have waited to admit that I loved you."

"Slap me, pinch me, shake me," Ladonna said after their flight touched down. "I keep rubbing my ring to make sure it's not a figment of my imagination."

They cuddled in one of the suite's double beds. Ladonna gave no indication of desiring to cross that line. Experiencing the ultimate intimacy with her enticed him. However, Richard opted to avoid raising the prospect. And, honestly, the apprehension he'd experienced in relation to meeting the Hudsons and extending his proposal wore him out. He hesitated to attempt such a physically-draining act at less than full capacity.

He rose before her and ordered breakfast through room service. They nibbled on each other more than the food. After consuming enough bacon and eggs to satisfy their appetites, the couple snuggled under the covers.

"Can't we stay here indefinitely?" Richard asked.

"Regrettably not. Work awaits."

Going on 24 hours after meeting the Hudsons, he remained on a psychedelic high. Throughout his speech in front of a counter-abortion coalition, Richard stole glances at his fiancé. While joy at the thought of spending the rest of his life with Ladonna filled his mind, his body suffered an alternate ill feeling. His heart fluttered so rapidly that he grew flushed at times, so he relied on his outline more than usual.

When they retired for the night, he hit her with another proposal. "Move in with me."

"Living together never pans out for me. I'm trying not to jinx this."

"Impossible. I'll convince you otherwise."

Back in Atlanta, they announced the engagement to their cohorts separately.

"I deserve some sort of consultation fee," Kevin told Richard.

"You're that full of yourself?"

"Face it, my advice was priceless."

"My mom gave as much as you did. She's content on knowing I'm content."

Kevin burst into a grin.

"Instead of payment, would you settle on being my best man?"

"Without a doubt."

Crystal reacted to the recent development less graciously.

"I'm so happy for you," Crystal spouted sarcastically.

"Excuse me for sharing the news with my best friend."

"You're entertaining this idea for real?"

Ladonna rolled her eyes and roared, "Yes!"

"Vincent exited the picture not so long ago. Taking a break from serious dating wouldn't hurt."

"Richard isn't Vincent."

"Like it or not, I'm less trusting than you. Although you've contracted amnesia, I recall the dude who ignored your calls."

"Richard isn't holding a shotgun to my head." She recounted how Richard apologized profusely for his actions. "These past months convinced me he's sincere. Besides, we've all got a year to absorb all these changes. You might not trust him, but trust me."

"Your mother posted the pictures of you three online. I guess it was the day he proposed. You looked a mess."

"I was crying and my makeup ran. I have to tell her to take those pictures down."

"It's too late. Vincent saw them and commented. He wrote: 'Glad you finally found someone to love you.'"

"That's low. Shoot, I wouldn't be surprised if Richard's ex somehow sees those pictures and writes something crazy too. I know my mama means well, but I'm going to tell her to take them down."

"Why would you be embarrassed by your love?" Crystal said quizzically.

"Not embarrassed at all. I just know Richard doesn't need any more stress right now. I'm a little worried about his health."

Chapter 26

"The meek voice on the other end of the receiver inquired, "May I speak with Richard Knight?"

"Repeat that, please." He walked yards out from the construction site hustle and bustle.

"May I speak with Richard Knight?"

He attempted to place the older, meek woman's voice. "Richard Knight speaking."

"Hello, Richard. It's Mrs. Eriksson."

"Mrs. Eriksson?" The reason for the contact escaped him. No one associated with Nicole, Toni's harassment excluded, reached out to him since the separation. Trepidation washed over Richard despite his ex mother-in-law's kind approach.

"I wrestled with contacting you, dear. My husband and I feel it's only right."

Richard pressed his cell phone against his ear. "How can I help you?"

"Nicole passed on."

"Huh…How?" he asked incredulously.

"A robbery." Her grief vibrated in each syllable.

"Please accept my condolences and pass them on to Mr. Eriksson." He craved details. But alleviating her discomfort overrode his inquisitiveness.

"Thank you, dear. Our apologies for the brief notice. The service is at Saint Pius Cathedral the day after tomorrow at 2 o'clock."

The scene grew silent and invisible. Everything faded—the grind of bulldozers, the clank of metal beams, the red clay swirling in gusts of wind and the gruff orders passed back and forth.

Richard didn't remember the drive from his job site to the precinct. He did recall requesting that Kevin dig up the details of Nicole's death. Kevin greeted him with a manly hug.

"Shocker, huh?"

Richard cleared his throat. "Yeah."

"I reviewed the video footage. It's grainy at best."

"There's a tape?"

"I'm jumping ahead of myself." Kevin filled in the blanks, adding, "A group of suspected gang bangers ambushed Nicole last week at an ATM machine while she was depositing funds from the clinic. Do you want specifics?"

"Everything."

"When they asked for the money, your ex threw the money satchel at the thugs. She resisted, though, when they reached for her purse. She ran to her car and hit the gas. They shot through the roof of her convertible. A bullet lodged in her brain."

"Defiant to the end," Richard murmured.

"Junior would be how old?" Richard imagined. Thoughts of his unborn child resurfaced with greater intensity than usual. Richard snuck off to Junior's memorial one afternoon after he left a construction site. He filled Junior in on his grandma and his aunt. He told Junior about the changes in his relationship with Ladonna. If only he could access a do-over button that eliminated meeting Nicole and also let him meet Ladonna earlier. He also mentioned Bryson. "He's a good kid, but he'll never replace you," Richard said.

"You're not obligated to go," Mrs. Knight told her son when they spoke later in the evening.

"I realize that. I practically promised Mrs. Eriksson I'd attend. She's always been kind to me. I owe her that much."

"Nicole's murder has been the lead story on every newscast because the police are still looking for the robbers. They're even offering a reward. The news showed the video from the bank camera, but you can't really see the guys' faces. Can't be easy for her parents if they're watching it. Where's the service?"

"Saint Pius."

"Looks like she'll end up in a church after all."

"She loved all people as much as any devout…," interjected Richard, his voice trailing off in disbelief of his own remarks. "Except for…"

Ignoring his comment, she questioned him further. "And the burial?"

"She opted for cremation, according to the obituary."

That night, Richard lay in bed replaying the incidents of Nicole's murder as if he was a prosecutor trying the case. He could hardly think straight, much less sleep. At some point, his body surrendered to a death-like sleep.

He seemed to have awakened, immediately feeling the presence of ancestors waiting to welcome him. The tsunami of tension throughout his being had now halted. Still, the pleasure of peace eluded him. Was this Heaven, his salvation? He expected to connect with the One he'd never met but so desperately desired to meet. He lingered in solitude, though, unable to see the Promised Land.

Richard again tugged at the sliver chain around his ankle that kept him immobile and triggered tremors and a sharp, stinging sensation in his chest when he moved. Seeking help or answers, he looked above him but only saw a sheath of white space. The only contrast from the hazy light that enveloped him was the darkness beneath, from where Nicole peered up at him.

"Why?" Richard screamed. He peered down, cursing the fetter as he tugged at it. It grew heavier with each wrenching tug.

A guttural stirring within Richard prompted him to acknowledge Nicole. By doing so, he'd cleanse himself of the festering stench of blame that chained him on Earth and Heaven.

Richard spoke into the abyss. "I forgive you, Nicole."

Immediately, the shackles binding Richard suddenly unfastened. Realizing his mobility, he stood in place, eyes beckoning hope. At first, the light blinded Richard. Focusing on the slight form before him, he saw what appeared to be celestial perfection. His son. His beloved Junior stood before him.

Junior's smile reflected the happiness Nicole's heart held initially, which captivated strangers, Richard included. He had his father's eyes, black and piercing. Those eyes now stared at Richard. They beckoned. They questioned.

"Junior!" Richard cried.

The innocent creation of warring parents possessed the best attributes of both of them. Even so, he wasn't enough, not for his mother then or for his father now.

"Junior!"

His son stayed silent. He gazed lovingly at his father, then his image dissipated gradually. The child vanished completely, as did his radiance.

Richard reached out to the son he had never known. He needed him. He prayed for his reappearance.

"Daddy!" Junior's delicate voice summoned. Richard's son leaped off a glorious, golden perch. Junior, upon reaching him, grabbed his father's hand. He guided him onward and upward into the light.

Outside of the cathedral, Richard searched for Nicole's parents. He saw a physician and a nurse from the clinic. He spotted other people he assumed were relatives and a sea of women with unclear sexual orientation. He felt like an anomaly. He swore some in the crowd mumbled about his attendance. He swore others stared at him.

Richard pivoted abruptly after he felt a ferocious pounding on his shoulder.

"What in the hell are you doing here?"

He stared down Toni as she did the same to him.

"Lower your voice," Richard said.

She wore a salivating leer. "Nicole was done with you," she announced loudly.

Richard's muscles tightened, most notably in his chest.

"And you made her out to be a monster," Toni kept on. "The nerve of you showing up."

"Nicole's mother invited me."

Toni cut her eyes and scoffed.

He thought, "Her hatefulness has no place at such a solemn event. Regardless of Nicole's opinions of me or religion, the people who came to mourn her deserve a peaceful opportunity to process Nicole's passing." To Richard, Toni's jabs confirmed that she fell short of the basest human decency. He refused to succumb to her bullying or to allow her to paint him as a devilish creature who destroyed lives. She owned that title.

"I'm staying," he told her and headed inside before Toni could respond. Surely she'd show respect for the sanctuary and leave her sinister tendencies at the door.

Richard waited in the vestibule until the funeral procession began. Then he slipped into a back row in the main cathedral. Nicole's mother and father appeared battered. They made eye contact with Richard as they moved up front.

The Erikssons and Toni sat on opposite ends of the front row. Richard sensed the divide spanned more than simple proximity. He listened as a childhood friend reminisced, and Nicole's boss delivered the eulogy. The woman they conjured up images of sounded nothing like the vicious Nicole who disrupted his life.

Toni wept quietly. An older, black woman sitting beside her handed Toni a tissue. Death stole Nicole from Toni, as Toni had from him. It accomplished what Richard's numerous pleas to his ex hadn't – pried the women apart. The notion that Toni would experience, in solitary moments after the shock wore off, a realization that she'd lost Nicole forever elated Richard.

As Richard began his stealthy exit after the final remarks and before the family could even leave, he felt a slight hand touch the center of his back. He turned to reconcile the gesture, literally praying that it wasn't Toni. To his surprise, Mrs. Eriksson stood before him in a poised but defeated posture. She spoke slowly and clearly, only loud enough for Richard to hear. "She had Rh disease. She knew she could probably never have a healthy child with you, so she destroyed everything you two had together. She wanted another woman to give you what she never could."

Richard listened more intently to every word that Mrs. Eriksson spoke than any sermon, lecture or testimony he had ever heard. She explained how Nicole had learned of the condition during pregnancy and how she even had Richard's blood tested to see if it would conflict. At that moment, Richard recalled the afternoon he went to visit her at work and Nicole said, "Let me test you to see if your blood is as pure as your heart."

Mrs. Eriksson must have broken any promise she had made to her daughter about sharing this information. She obviously felt it was time that Richard had some peace. After less than two minutes of sharing, she grabbed Richard's right hand and then abruptly walked off to join her awaiting husband, who smiled in consolation.

Rather than instantly scour the Internet on his phone or tablet to learn more about Nicole's condition, he instead waited to share the news with Ladonna.

Ladonna immediately inquired about the funeral. Richard detailed the specifics of the service, leaving Toni's lashing out for the end.

"I'm sure that was grief talking."

"I'm sure it wasn't." He winced.

"Another headache?"

"A tiny one." Instead of spending another moment on Toni, he decided to discuss Mrs. Eriksson's news to him. Richard sobbed like a child as he tried to explain a medical condition and decision he knew nothing about. Ladonna groaned when she saw how this new revelation was affecting him.

For the first time, Ladonna felt pity for Nicole, but still, she resented her for how she handled the situation. "She could have told him in a note or something," she thought, afraid to shovel any more pressure on Richard. She planned to keep her "real" thoughts to herself for now and simply remain supportive while they both learn more about Rh disease. What more, however, was how this would affect Richard's campaign for paternal notification.

Richard shared funeral details with his mother and Kevin. Nicole lacked faith, according to his mother, who believed God could have performed something miraculous if she had only believed in Him. She lacked courage, according to Kevin, who surmised that his friend would have been there for her and any type of child that would have been born to the couple. Richard's only thought until now was that he lacked a child. He had never considered Nicole's circumstances – physical, mental or emotional.

He remembered learning more about the journey of Norma McCorvey, or "Jane Roe" of *Roe v. Wade*, who had become a Christian and pro-life advocate after that monumental Supreme Court decision. Norma had never had an abortion. She says she wouldn't have gotten one, which originally made her the perfect plaintiff for abortion rights. After she got involved in the abortion rights movement personally, even working in an abortion clinic, she says she witnessed the despair of many of the women who chose to have an abortion.

Richard had combed the Bible and legal annals to prove that what Nicole had done was immoral, insensitive and unfair, especially to men. He understood that some women who had abortions made selfish decisions, such as wanting to postpone child bearing or thinking a child would disrupt their education or career. He saw himself as a victim of a selfish woman, but he had come to realize there are many sufferers in the abortion decision, including the women themselves who don't always feel proud or as if they have options in making this decision. Richard learned that it is rarely an easy decision, no matter the motive. Caught up in his own grief and pain, he never sought to question Nicole's.

Ladonna and Richard stood in the aisle of Party City. She thought it would be fun for him and Mrs. Knight to tag along as Bryson chose a costume. At this point, her son and his mom had ventured further down the aisle and were the only ones actively involved in the process.

"The real deals happen right before Halloween. That's why I wait. Want to go trick-or-treating with us next Saturday?"

Richard stared blankly at his surroundings, completely unaffected by the decorations, holiday displays, and his companions.

Ladonna rubbed Richard's back. She repeated the question.

"Sure," he answered. "But don't expect me to dress up."

"Gotcha."

"It's normal to experience melancholy," Ladonna assured her fiancé following another lull in the conversation.

"I'm not sad to say the least."

"If your appetite is any indication, that's not true. Or I'm suddenly a lousy cook."

"Quite the opposite," Richard declared. He didn't want to offend her, so he turned to look her in the eyes as he spoke. Ladonna's acquaintance had redirected Richard's focus and helped him manage self-destructive tendencies. He needed her by his side, especially now.

"Something has been bugging you lately. You keep zoning out."

Did Ladonna recognize a reality he refused to face? Had learning of Nicole's disease and death opened hidden chambers of unresolved emotions? Richard blamed his lack of concentration on major work projects that were occupying his thoughts.

"How are you going to juggle those responsibilities with your freelancing?" Ladonna asked.

"I'll manage."

"If you think it's hectic now, wait until we add planning our wedding to the list of priorities."

Ladonna mentioned how she facilitated their last couple of conference calls and how he chimed in occasionally.

"You had the agenda under control."

"I'm supposed to be the sidekick, not the leader. Your clients pay for one-on-one interaction with you."

"I'll step it up," Richard pledged.

"Try the opposite approach," Ladonna suggested. "Try stepping it down. While I admire your determination and dedication to all that you do, you're not Superman."

After his recent work review, he started having more responsibilities, mostly overseeing employees at sites. Ordinarily, his superiors' increased trust and confidence in him would thrill him. However, now the additional assignments made him feel in turmoil. Richard frequently found mental rest difficult to obtain. The firm, the freelancing, and his fiancée occupied his waking thoughts and his dreams.

"Something has got to give," Ladonna said. The easiest area of adjustment, from what I've observed, is the freelancing."

They had a trip to Reno scheduled on Friday. The following week they'd remain in town for Halloween.

"As you gain exposure, it seems more people want a piece of you. I think it'll be beneficial if you accept fewer clients, or at least schedule the projects to allow for some breathing room. No one would fault you."

Over the next couple of weeks, Richard sincerely weighed Ladonna's observations but didn't adjust his schedule. Before Nicole died, he was motivated by his feelings of victimhood; he saw himself and men like him as underdogs. Now, he simply didn't know how to stop or if he should. Should he, like Norma McCovey, do an about-face but still maintain his core belief in notification? Should he simply abandon the effort altogether? For now, he would just keep going until the answers became clearer.

Richard didn't expect Ladonna to be at his house when he arrived from the office. He welcomed her company, though. She greeted him at the door, took his briefcase, and plopped a wet kiss on his lips.

"Welcome home, Mr. Knight."

He gave her a once-over. A floral scent surrounded her. She wore an apron with a slightly longer dress underneath. He detected a dab of flour on her cheek. He wiped it off.

"Don't take this the wrong way, but what are you doing here?"

"Helping you take the edge off."

Richard raised a brow.

"Tonight, I'll feed your every desire."

"Intriguing." Richard sniffed the air. "What's cooking?"

She led him into the kitchen. "For you, Mr. Knight, I'm preparing a rack of lamb with red potatoes and lemon sage sauce."

"Delectable."

"The lamb isn't quite ready, though."

Richard frowned.

"Never fret. I have a main course I hope you'll find satisfying in the meantime."

The comment threw him off.

"Other than the meat?"

Ladonna placed a finger on her lips. "Shush."

She took off her apron and laid it on a counter. She grabbed his arm and pulled him out of the kitchen toward the bedroom. Richard's temperature spiked. Was the oven making him hot or Ladonna? What did she have in mind? He jumped to a barrage of conclusions during the swift trek and struggled to keep his main hope at bay. The couple, after all, glossed over the topic of sex. Was Ladonna ready to leap into that realm?

Candles and the fading sunlight of dusk lit the room. The bedspread was turned down.

"I considered tossing rose petals everywhere. Thought you'd find them girly."

She could've covered the bed with twigs and it would've been wonderful to Richard. Ladonna led him to the edge of the bed, where they kissed again. Richard began unbuttoning his shirt.

"Let me."

She finished for him and then slipped the shirt off his shoulders. Richard stared at Ladonna, still unsure of how far she cared to go. He decided to inquire instead of possibly making a fool out of himself.

"Where are we going with this?" he asked.

"Wherever you lead me."

Richard convinced Ladonna to return the next night.

"I agreed to let Crystal borrow my car on Saturday and to let her pick out the bridesmaid's dress in exchange for baby-sitting."

"Small price to pay."

"I can't stay over again, though."

He took silverware out of a drawer and then retrieved a pair of plates. They planned to eat leftovers while watching a movie. "Probably for the best. You wore me out."

She tugged on his necktie, pulling him toward her. "Huh, I wore you out?"

His fiancée's image pixilated. Richard winced. A supersonic boom exploded between his temples.

Ladonna released the tie instantaneously. "Oops, I didn't mean to pull so hard."

The plates crashed to the floor, shattering on impact.

The left side of his face seized. He fought to string together a sentence. "I…I. One, nine…"

Ladonna snatched Richard's cell phone from the kitchen table.

Ladonna posted herself in front of room number 482, waiting for a physician, a nurse, or anyone able to provide particulars on Richard's condition. The single morsel of information she possessed came from the fact that the hospital transferred him to Piedmont's Stroke Center. They had arrived nearly 25 minutes ago and spent half of the time in the emergency room.

She returned to the nurse's station. "Excuse me," she said to the same nurse who assisted her earlier. "I need an update on Richard Knight."

"Sorry, I can't release information."

"Of course you can," Ladonna pleaded.

"I'm afraid not without authorization on file."

"But I rode over in the ambulance with him. I provided his insurance card."

The nurse looked like a gentle grandma. She guarded Richard's medical records like a seasoned sergeant. "Only relatives bound by blood or marriage."

"Pretend I'm his sister if you have to." Ladonna inhaled and then exhaled sharply.

"I sympathize, but I have to adhere to regulations."

"Is Dr. Olson on duty? He can vouch for me."

"He won't break protocol either, ma'am."

"Please! I waited outside of his room, but no one came out."

The nurse relaxed her stoic posture. "Let me check for you."

Ladonna followed her back to Richard's room. The nurse entered quietly and closed the door behind her.

"Damn," Ladonna thought. "How could I forget to call Mrs. Knight?" She dialed Richard's mom. The answering machine came on. Ladonna tried again. "Pick up. Pick up." She got the machine again. Ladonna left a message. "Mrs. Knight, it's Ladonna. Richard's in the hospital. Piedmont. Room number 482. Details are sketchy so I don't want to alarm you. I'll leave his cell on."

Ladonna pressed her back against a wall. Talking to the machine instead of his mom left her uneasy. Should she alert Kevin too? Yes, Ladonna decided. She retrieved his number from Richard's call log. He picked up immediately. Ladonna gave him the same spiel. She also relayed her inability to reach Mrs. Knight.

"Odds are she's at church. I can have a patrol unit swing by the sanctuary."

A second called beeped in.

"Maybe this is her."

"If she's home, I can pick her up."

"Hold on." Ladonna clicked over. She felt instant relief upon hearing Mrs. Knight's voice.

"I just got out of the tub. Any update?" she asked.

"No, and they won't talk to me."

"I should be there soon."

"Kevin is nearby. He'll bring you."

"Okay, let one of us know if anything changes."

Ladonna clicked over to Kevin and told him she spoke to Mrs. Knight.

"Good. I'm on my way."

Just as Ladonna hung up, the doorknob to Richard's room turned. The nurse exited. She glanced at Ladonna sympathetically. A male physician exited behind her. He halted while the nurse continued on.

"Ms. Hudson I'm the attending neurologist, Dr. Veronesi."

"What's going on? Did Richard have a stroke?"

"Yes, he suffered what we classify as an ischemic or hemorrhagic stroke."

"But he's so young."

"Disorders tend to strike all age ranges."

"How is he?" Fright permeated the inquiry.

"He's conscious and communicating although that ability is impaired. Basically, Mr. Knight understands us better than we understand him. We've discussed his condition, viable options."

"So you know he's under treatment for liver disease?"

"Yes, I reviewed his charts."

"Honestly, I'm flabbergasted. And I'm not clear how and why that happened."

“In layman’s terms, a rouge clot reached his brain. Enlarged liver tissue likely contributed since that organ assists in clotting and can affect blood pressure.”

“No one warned us of this possibility.”

“On the surface, he possesses a variety of risk factors: race, stress, alcohol intake. Even remaining in a seated position for prolonged periods, especially at high altitudes often provokes abnormalities.”

“Tell me how we proceed. What’s the proposed treatment?”

“I conducted two CT scans of Mr. Knight’s brain. As anticipated, they detected bleeding. Also, I administered anti-clotting agents and analyzed his blood work. The second scan indicates that the bleeding on his brain has increased significantly.”

“Then give him a different drug.”

“I’ve consulted a neurosurgeon. He concurred that surgery is the next step.”

“That’s radical. You see no other options?”

“Surgery offers the best prognosis. Removing a miniscule section of his skull will relieve the pressure.”

These facts boggled her mind. How could Richard comprehend them? “Richard agreed to this?”

“Mr. Knight did, and he’s asking for you.”

Chapter 27

The chaplain's presence visibly startled Ladonna more so than her fiancé's feebleness. He stepped back from Richard's bedside to let Ladonna slide into that spot. Richard's right arm dangled over the edge of the bed railing. She held on to his hand.

"Your mom will be here soon. Kevin too." Afraid to actually make eye contact, she gave the chaplain a fleeting glimpse. "You've got to stop scaring us like this," Ladonna said.

Richard grinned faintly and then motioned for her to lean forward.

"It's okay," Dr. Veronesi said. "Here, allow me." He lowered the railing.

"I love you," Ladonna whispered.

"M. Mar. Marry me now," he whispered.

"When I said no frills, I didn't anticipate to this extent."

He attempted to squeeze her hand. His grasp barely registered.

The chaplain piped up. "I'm Reverend Albritton." He inched closer. "Mr. Knight summoned me to officiate."

Ladonna looked at her fiancé. "You should be focusing on getting well, nothing else."

"He wishes to provide for you and your son."

"Richard will be recuperating soon I'm sure," Ladonna said.

"As his wife," the doctor said, "you'll attain authority over Mr. Knight's medical care should complications arise."

"Complications?" Circumstances dictated that she grasp the state of affairs completely.

"No need for alarm, although surgeries and even rehab always carry risks."

She turned to the reverend. "Would it be legal?" Ladonna asked. "Don't you need to see our license?"

"I'll let your word and Mr. Knight's, since he's an officer of the court, serve as proof for now. We can address the paperwork verification tomorrow."

Richard pledged his allegiance to her and Bryson often since they reunited. This selfless act cemented his sincerity.

Ladonna covered Richard's hand with kisses. "Once you're in tiptop shape, we're gonna repeat this properly. Should we wait for the gang?"

Dr. Veronesi cleared his throat. "Pardon the interruption. "We have a diminutive window available before he's off to prep."

With Ladonna's help, Richard propped himself up.

"I'll perform a truncated version," Reverend Albritton said. "Doctor, can we bother you to serve as a witness?"

Dr. Veronesi agreed.

"Join hands," Reverend Albritton instructed the couple.

"We're gathered here tonight for the union of Richard Knight and Ladonna Hudson. Mr. Knight, do you take Ms. Hudson as your lawfully wedded wife?"

"I do." His response rang of conviction.

"Ms. Hudson, do you take Mr. Knight as your lawfully wedded husband?"

"I do."

The chaplain pronounced them man and wife.

Ladonna kissed Richard gingerly on the lips. He struggled to manage a peck on hers. She cradled her husband in her arms.

Dr. Veronesi moved over to the monitors and noted Richard's chart. Then he pressed the call button attached to the bed.

"Nurse's station," a male voice answered.

"This is Dr. Veronesi in room number 482. Page neurosurgery to get ready for patient arrival, and summon a transport nurse," he directed.

Kevin and Mrs. Knight rushed in. They stared at Richard, still secure in Ladonna's arms.

"Oh, honey," Mrs. Knight cried out.

"Ma," Richard replied feebly.

Seeing his mom alleviated a portion of the destructive anxiety plaguing Richard. Her arrival, as much as he adored his new wife, trumped Ladonna's. Even she couldn't surpass Mrs. Knight's brand of motherly soothing.

Richard got the gist of his prognosis. Dr. Veronesi presented the operation as the only viable option. He had to trust the assessment mainly because the medication pumped into his veins fell short of its prescribed duty.

Mrs. Knight swooped in and planted a kiss on Richard's forehead.

Kevin stood at the foot of Richard's bed. He patted one of his friend's legs. "Despite my teasing, I consider you the stronger one. You're like a brother. Just know I'll help out with whatever you need when you leave here."

"Me, me and La, Ladonna."

"He's trying to say we got married minutes ago. We tried to postpone it. Under the circumstances..."

"No explanation required," Mrs. Knight said.

"Long overdue," Kevin added. He set his gaze on Richard. "Bachelor party is on me."

"We'll plan another ceremony once he's up and about."

Mrs. Knight smiled at her daughter-in-law. "Glad you're officially in the family." She kissed Richard's forehead again.

"Jesus, he's sweaty!" She patted his cheeks. "He's burning up." She now noticed all the medical staff and the chaplain. "How sick is my son?"

Dr. Veronesi pulled her and Kevin aside, where he summarized Richard's condition and subsequent prognosis.

"You're prying open his brain?"

"The procedure is less invasive than it appears and quite necessary to preserve intact cells."

Mrs. Knight looked skeptical.

"Victims of trauma from gunshots, falls, and other accidents go through this type of operation routinely."

Kevin laid a hand on Mrs. Knight's shoulder. "He's right. I see miraculous recoveries all the time in my profession."

"I suppose."

"The scope of your son's injuries isn't insurmountable," Dr. Veronesi stated authoritatively. "I'll ring an orderly to escort you to the waiting area."

"May I offer a short prayer?" the chaplain asked.

A reverberating jolt pierced Richard's chest.

His vitals went haywire, setting off a series of beeps on the electronic equipment.

The doctor dashed to his patient's side.

"His pressure is spiking," the nurse called out.

"He's crashing," Dr. Veronesi responded.

The doctor shouted orders. For Richard they meshed into undecipherable gibberish.

Ladonna stumbled backward. Mrs. Knight gasped. Kevin shuddered.

Richard convulsed. He teetered on the brink of either of two enticing scenarios. The urge to join all those he cared for tugged at him. In one direction his mother, Ladonna, Bryson, and Kevin waited; in the other Junior, his father and his grandparents. Fighting required more exertion than he could muster.

The rustling of the staff surrounded Richard. Gut-wrenching wails cut through the murkiness. They muted as Richard's body decided for him.

Ladonna alerted Senator Winston of Richard's death. She felt her husband would've expected her to contact the man he admired. He urged her to issue a statement, which his public relations rep distributed to local media. It read:

> *With immense sorrow, I announce the passing of Richard Knight: beloved son, friend, and crusader. A lawyer by trade, Richard aspired to attain meaning out of loss and to galvanize other men who endured similar situations. Richard exposed biases against husbands and men in terms of parental rights. Often misunderstood and misquoted, he humanized the unborn. Ironically, some hated him because he cared too much. Death silenced Richard Knight. It won't silence the army of those he motivated.*

Richard's demise made national headlines after CNN's Atlanta division acquired the story from an affiliate.

Outpourings of condolences reached the Knights, mainly filtered via the senator's office. While individuals and groups Richard worked with as an attorney and as an advocate sent sentiments, an awe-inspiring number arrived from strangers.

Winston and Ladonna granted the network a brief interview before Richard's public memorial, which she and Mrs. Knight held at Junior's plot in Oglethorpe Gardens. They'd end the service by scattering Richard's ashes at the Southern Red Cedar's base.

The CNN anchor maintained a respectful tone although he posed hard-hitting questions. "A majority of women found fault with Mr. Knight's stance," he stated.

"Actually," Winston corrected him, "he had female supporters also."

Ladonna added, "Richard didn't try to strip women of their rights. And I think in the end, he probably gained more understanding of a woman's mindset, but he simply wanted respect for a man's."

Rubbing her portly midsection, Ladonna felt queasy and restless. Her morning sickness, she assured herself, would subside once she had some mint tea. The routine each day began with a prayer, usually asking God to keep her strong without the presence of her husband. Afterward, she sat silently at the kitchen counter with a cup of tea until Bryson awoke. Her phone's chiming finally broke her stupor.

"Hey, turn on the television to channel 7," instructed Kevin. To that, Ladonna slowly moved to the coffee table for the remote control.

"Up at 6:30," the news anchor, Sara Townsend, declared, "we'll find out why a new community health center is being dedicated to the memory of a man that many women hated."

"What's this about, Kevin?"

"Just keep watching and call me back if you need to talk."

After too many useless advertisements, the news came back on in time for Ladonna to raise her slightly swollen feet on the sofa and prop her back with an oversized pillow.

"Several months have passed since the death of the controversial pro-life attorney Richard Knight, said Sara, looking as serious as possible, "but it seems his memory will live on, courtesy of the Hammond Community Health Center's board. Reporter Dayle Scott spoke to the board chair from his home in Rome, Georgia."

"So, why are you dedicating this new facility to Richard Knight's memory?" questioned the reporter.

Visibly disturbed at the reporter's presence in front of his home, Ronald Warhop, spoke few words, which seemed to slip through his clinched teeth and puckered lips. "It will be called the Richard Knight Community Center in honor of a man we can all respect and his former wife who chose to make a difficult decision."

"A difficult decision," repeated Scott. "Wasn't Knight's stance that the decision would be less difficult if men were involved in the decision-making?"

"Are you here because of one person's decision or was more than one person involved?"

"What does that have to do with anything?"

Ronald opened the door to his gray Audi coupe, plopped in the driver's seat and quickly slammed the door before backing out his driveway. Scott turned to the camera, saying, "Sara, we'll try to have more on this story at noon."

Ladonna clicked the red power button on the remote. She needed silence to weigh in on all that she had just heard. "Difficult decision," she murmured. Had Nicole's parents spoken to the press about Nicole's medical condition? Did Toni try to vindicate her lover's name? Would her husband seem more like an insensitive monster?

She called Mrs. Knight, who instinctively detected her angst. Before Ladonna could discuss or explain anything, she merely said, "Rest. Rest his case."

www.ingramcontent.com/pod-product-compliance
Lightning Source LLC
Chambersburg PA
CBHW020322180626
46812CB00001B/17

9780988733275